DAWN APOCALYPSE
RISING

DAWN APOCALYPSE RISING

Book 1 of The Windows of Heaven
A novel series by K.G. Powderly Jr.

DEDICATION

For my departed wife Dianne, who now dances before the Once and Future King. These books are a tribute to your patience, encouragement and caring.

For Shannyn, Wes, and Laurelin Mae – no father could be more proud of his children and grandchild.

For Rob and Jim, without whose belief in the fundamental worth of this project – a belief put to deeds by their time and creative effort on my behalf – I would have canned it and moved on. The Lord reward you both kindly and generously.

For Katarina, whose friendship I will always treasure.

Thanks also to Martin, that great lurking Sasquatch, who oversees web site and other essentials from a distance, where he always appears as a photographic blur in the background.

For the Promised Seed – the suffering servant, wonderful counselor, mighty God, and the Once and Future King who waits to welcome us with those who are willing at Time's End…

Acknowledgements

Chapter epigraphs appear from the following books with thanks and respect:

- All Bible quotations not from the *King James Version* **(KJV)** or *Revised Standard Version* **(RSV)** come from any of the following versions and will be identified accordingly:
  - *New International Version* **(NIV)** © 1973 by New York Bible Society International
  - *New American Standard Bible* **(NASB)** © 1960, 1962, 1963, 1968, 1971, 1972, 1973, 1975 and 1977 by The Lockman Foundation, La Habra, Ca.
  - *New King James Version* **(NKJV)** © 1982 by Thomas Nelson, Inc.
- *Webster's 9th New Collegiate Dictionary*
- **Flavius Josephus,** *Antiquities Of The Jews* (circa 80-90 AD)
- **E.W. Bullinger,** *The Witness of the Stars* (1893)
- **Bill Cooper,** *After the Flood,* © 1995 New Wine Press, England
- *Ethiopic Enoch (1 Enoch),* translated by Richard Laurence, LL.D in *The Book of Enoch the Prophet,* Kegan, Paul, Trench & Co. (1883)
- *Slavonic Enoch (2 Enoch),* translated by W.R. Morphill, M.A.
- *The Complete Dead Sea Scrolls in English,* translated by Geza Vermes, © 1998, Penguin Books
- **S.L.A. Marshall,** *World War I,* © 1964 by America Heritage
- *The Modern Past: Batteries of Babylon,* ©1996 Lumir G. Janku in *Anomalies and Enigmas Forum Library* at *enigmas.org/aef/library.shtml*
- **Donald E. Chittick,** *The Puzzle of Ancient Man – Advanced Technology in Past Civilizations?* © 1998 by Creation Compass

TABLE OF CONTENTS

The thing that hath been, it is that which shall be; and that which is done is that which shall be done: and there is no new thing under the sun.

— *Ecclesiastes* 1:9 (KJV)

POLAR MOORS

NORTH
LUMEKKOR

Met'U-Say'El

Wurmwood

Bab'Tubaala
(Tubaal-qayin's Gate)

Kharif Aedenu
(Mountains of Aedon)

Yawam
Tsafuni

Kharis Ardisu
(Mts. of Ardū)

BALIMAR

AEDEN

Sarutaj

Paru Ainu
Kharmul Land
(Mts. of Terror)

S
A
T
Y
U
R
A
T
I

SETI

KHAVILAKKI

AKH'UZAN

THE
HAUNTED
LANDS

SOUTH

Ayar Adi-In

Erdu

Telemnuk

LUMEKKOR

Kushtahar

Ayarak

Safaanim Surupag

South Sky
Lord Fortress

Iglat-
Meldur

NEAR KUSH

Uggu-stavaar

The Pillars
of Uggu

Straits of Kush

Firth
Dracan

E-Tanna

Regati

Central

Bab'Kusha

Sea

FAR

I-Ra

Aqqu

Burunatu Fleet Anchorage
(Lumekkor)

KUSH

Sea of Gebur

Geburat

El M'E

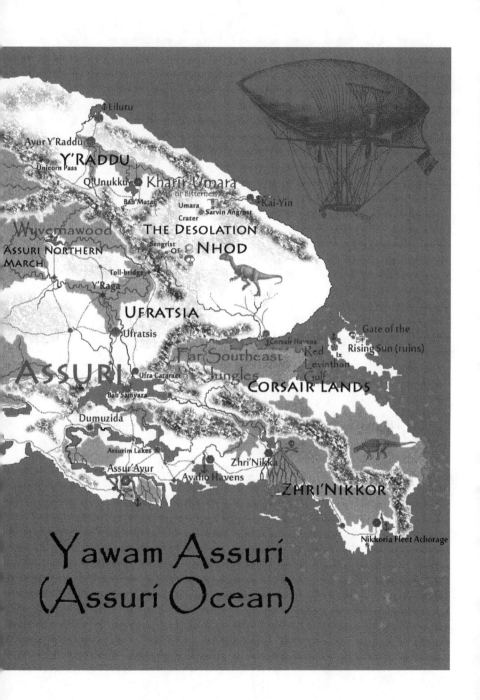

Lilutu

Ayur Y'Raddu

Y'RADDU

Unicorn Pass

Q'Unukku   Kharu Umara

Bab'Mataq   Mts of Bitterness

Umara   Kai-Yin

Crater   Sarvin Angmat

Wyvernawood   THE DESOLATION

ASSURI NORTHERN   Sengrist   OF   NHOD

MARCH

Toll-bridge

Y'Raga

UFRATSIA

Ufratsis

Gate of the

Corsair Havens   Rising Sun (ruins)

Far Southeast   Red   Ix

ASSURI   Jungles   Levinthan

Ufra Cataract   Gulf

Bab'Samyaza   CORSAIR LANDS

Dumuzida

Assurim Lakes   Zhri'Nikka

Assur'Ayur   Ayafio Havens   ZHRI'NIKKOR

Nikkoria Fleet Achorage

Yawam Assuri

(Assuri Ocean)

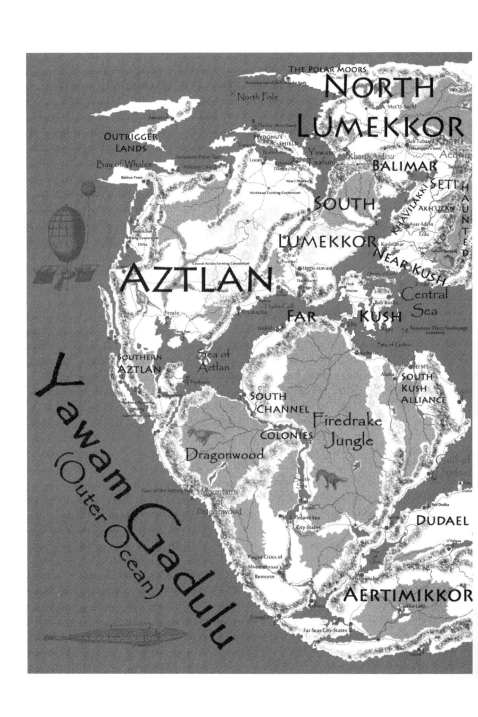

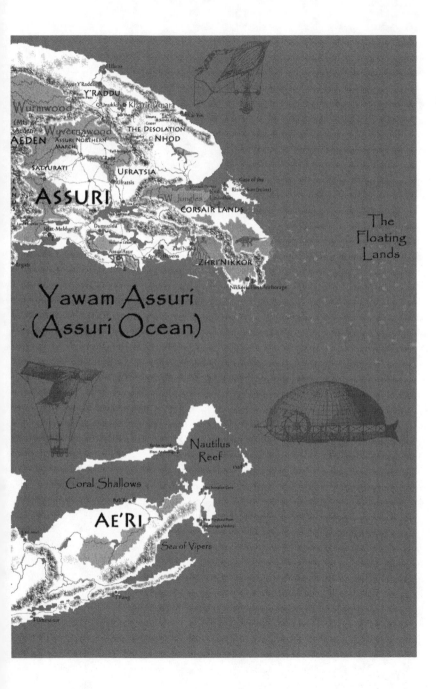

After many of the soldiers had been seized in its mouth, and many more crushed by the folds of its tail, its hide being too thick for javelins and darts, the dragon was at last attacked by military engines and crushed by repeated blows from heavy stones.

—Livy
(A Roman historian, describing a dragon attack on
the army of Regulus in Africa)

And Enoch lived an hundred and sixty and five years, and begat Mathusala. And Enoch was well-pleasing to God after his begetting Mathusala, two hundred years, and he begot sons and daughters. And all the days of Enoch were three hundred and sixty and five years. And Enoch was well-pleasing to God, and was not found, because God translated him.

—Genesis 5:21-24 (LXX, circa 250 BC)

Lamech lived one hundred and eighty-two years, and had a son. And he called his name Noah, saying, "This one will comfort us concerning our work and the toil of our hands, because of the ground which the LORD has cursed."

—Genesis 5:28-29 (NKJV)

PROLOGUE

People could only sense the Shadow, not see it. Daybreak proved that much.

Inside the monastery, incense smoke danced over Q'Enukki's head like ghosts carrying silent petitions that seeped into the ten heavens through the thatched roof of the stone hall. Outside the east window, the sun over the mountains seemed odd, disconnected, as if it shone on some other world, in some other valley that existed only as a picture.

The young men gazed at him, as if afraid to remove their eyes for just a second, lest he vanish.

I will vanish. Q'Enukki had known for some time that his sons had reason to grieve. With their mother long dead, he had wanted this time for them alone, but the extended clan had nosed itself in as always.

The hearth fire died before Q'Enukki spoke. "How were you finally able to send the others away?"

The voice of his firstborn, Muhet'Usalaq, cut the incense haze like a sword. "They camp in the lower valley, and will go no farther. They 'fear the Watchers will think their zeal small,'" he mimicked the mewling speech of one of his uncles, revealing premature frown lines in his mahogany face that Q'Enukki blamed himself for putting there.

He reacts against all the childhood pampering from his mother and her sisters. Q'Enukki remembered—still unsure whether to laugh or cry. As a father, he had put a stop to it whenever he could. As a seer, he had been away from home far more than he would have liked. Many of the people camped below were from his wife's side of the family. *All that burden on the boy from just a name. If only there had been another way.*

Muhet'Usalaq. The contraction meant, *"His death shall bring it."*

Q'Enukki smiled grimly and realized that there had been no other way. "See that their clan chiefs get copies of the scrolls," he said.

"All of them?" Muhet'Usalaq furrowed his dark brows.

Q'Enukki had written three hundred and sixty-six scrolls of law, prophecy, and science—some during his famous (and to many, infamous) voyage into the heavens. Others he had authored in mystic seclusion within sight of the Sacred Tree in Aeden's Orchard, where E'Yahavah A'Nu's Great Curse on the cosmos had become a physical pain in Q'Enukki's bones.

"In Aeden I aged over a century in three months, and could father no children afterward," he whispered. His son would catch his meaning. That Q'Enukki had returned alive from there at all had established him as the "Great Seer" even in the minds of those who bitterly resented the idea. He added, "As for the texts, that press-printer contraption your brothers invented is fastest and best. Do not fret over scribal tradition. Ignore those clay tablet purists too. Send copies to all the world's tribal chieftains."

"It will be done, My Father. I meant no disrespect."

Even Muheti uses the Formal Voice with me all the time now. Q'Enukki sighed, and laid a hand on his son's shoulder. "I know this is unsettling. Do yet one more thing for me…" He whispered into the young man's ear, "Whenever possible, think of the good times and laugh."

"We will."

"Oh, and this is very important…" Q'Enukki gazed into Muheti's deep blue eyes that seemed to cover his soul like tossing waves over the dark abyss. "In warning the world, do not burden the children in my name, as the priests would. Heaven's Comfort comes of your line — the A'Nu *Ahqui* — rest, not coercion. You will do this for me?"

Muhet'Usalaq's eyes questioned, but his head nodded.

Q'Enukki turned again to face his other sons. "Very well, everything seems in order. I suppose it is time."

A voice among the young men trembled, "For the Sky Watchers?"

Q'Enukki nodded.

His sons exchanged glances filled with objections none dared voice. He could almost hear their worry like maggots eating away at their sense of perspective, leaving a rancid waste of silent panic. They felt, as well as he did, the awful presence that hovered in the hilly forest, unseen, waiting. *They fear what they do not understand. Dread colors it darkly. Yet fear is appropriate — considering...*

He smiled for them. "Do not be afraid. Good is still good, and evil cannot hide its true nature forever. I must go now. We shall meet again. Where I go, someday you shall each follow. Our reunion will be joyful."

He rose from the circle of his sons and left the hall, passing through the courtyard, and out the stone fortress-monastery's timber gate.

The terrible presence grew more palpable with each step along the hilly forest path. Swirling fire-fly points of light danced around his head, as the earth itself hummed with a strange deep rhythm. The twisty lights seemed to wither the very fabric of existence around him until Q'Enukki felt dark things watching him from just behind that fluttering veil. The dark things wanted to tear through with fiery claws, and snatch him off the trail. Others guarded his way, invisible, protecting the fabric from penetration. The guarding ones were greater than the clawing things on the other side.

The sky chariot sat in a hillside clearing a little north of the villa. A fishing-boat-sized horizontal teardrop of smooth reflective metal, it rested on living wheels of swirling light within swirling light that seemed to press inward toward some kind of center, odd dents in the same fabric of reality that the dark things hid behind. The dents pressed inward no matter which angle Q'Enukki tried to view them from — as if at right angles away from everything humanly knowable.

Shining Watchers sat forward, enclosed in a transparent bubble arc that stretched across the wide front of the liquid-silver object, above the swirly-light dents in space. They peered out at him with what seemed a sad kindness; their bodies covered with dark calculating eyes that he suspected might evaluate a single man, or an entire world, with an absolute impartiality given them by the Three Aspects of E'Yahavah.

Q'Enukki approached an opening that appeared in the fluid-metal-glass surface of the thing. A quicksilver bulge grew beneath it, not-quite-hardening into steps. Only then did he turn for a last look back at the fortress that bore his name, now almost completely concealed by forest.

The sky went black before he could spot the ramparts, as if a celestial gryphon had passed its webbed wing in front of the sun.

From far below, an unnaturally cold breeze carried the distant wails of those camped in the valley. Q'Enukki heard other voices too, hushed and closer, from the foliage where the trail opened into the clearing. His sons had not been able to resist the temptation to follow. He had no way to protect them now, neither to help them understand.

The Watchers viewed the cowering brothers with what seemed a tolerant silence. Behind them, the normally green valley of Akh'Uzan lay in murky shadows from the untimely dark that was neither cloud, nor solar eclipse. An endless black sheet simply rippled across the sky.

A tall, man-like Watcher guided Q'Enukki up the waterfall ramp, into a cabin of sorts. The thick liquid-metal surface of the enclosure healed itself to perfect smoothness behind them, sealing them inside a flattened bubble that was transparent on either side. The luminous being blinked huge dark eyes at him filled with warmth, and a veiled power that Q'Enukki could feel deep in his chest whenever they gazed at him—even from behind. He sometimes heard strange words in his head when those eyes turned his way.

The Watcher motioned Q'Enukki into a reclining seat by one of the transparent sections of the bubble. It would have offered a magnificent view outside if not for the darkness. The chair gently grew several pairs of silvery restraint tendrils from its arms that wound their way about his body into a loose harness. The caress of the seat somehow removed his apprehension. He was among friends, after all—friends he trusted.

The Watcher spoke. "Welcome back, Son of Atum."

"Thank you for waiting, Samuille. I trust I was not too long?"

The Watcher smiled. *"It is the appointed time."* This time the Being spoke only with his eyes, inserting words directly into Q'Enukki's mind.

"Yes, I suppose it is. My sons will be alright, I trust?"

"They will remember only a moment of darkness, then the flash of our departure. For the rest, you have trained them well."

Q'Enukki recalled his first experiences with the Watchers and their mind-speech. It had taken some time for him to realize that they could not actually read his thoughts — only project their own words into his mind.

From the time of the Beginning, there had been tales of their comings and goings among the children of Man, but these had always been rare errands of great import to special seers among the Zaqenar elders. That either the Watchers or elders should see him in that group at the relatively young age of three-hundred and sixty-five years still surprised Q'Enukki. Especially since his first experience with a Watcher had not been with a holy one, but with the Fallen.

Those manipulators had been happy to let him believe they could see his very thoughts, when really they had just cleverly suggested ideas to him to mold his perceptions into predictable patterns — all because their captain, Uzaaz'El, had wanted something from him. Q'Enukki still marveled at the darkening of such powerful beings to the point where they thought that he — a man — had any authority to intercede for them! What were they thinking?

Weirder still, they had thought he would do so even after he had caught them in their lies. It was as if they could not even see the problem!

How different from Uzaaz'El this Samuille was. Uzaaz'El had always overpowered Q'Enukki's senses by his presence — with a stifling hunger from a calculating, amplified personality that always seemed to want something and somehow had a child-like need for his approval. Bald, high-browed head sheathed in pale glow, with dark white-less eyes of serene arrogance, the self-styled Watcher "Upholder" spoke just a bit too much in his musical voice about his benevolent plans for humanity to be believable.

Samuille projected a different sort of calm—a genuine willingness to subdue his power rather than a barely restrained necessity that he do so for some hidden motive. Q'Enukki felt he could speak freely with Samuille without fearing the perversion of his words into something monstrous.

That is the crux of all this, is it not – something monstrous?

The question angered him, even now.

"Why do we need all this?" Q'Enukki said, motioning at the surrounding sky chariot as though it were a useless extravagance. "The last time we merely traveled in a flash of light. Simple, dignified, no machinery—I assume this is some sort of machine. It looks as though it could be one."

The vehicle itself made a noise below their feet—some escaping gas that sounded like... *it could not be laughter!* The restraint tendrils around Q'Enukki's middle gave a sudden yank that forced his breath out.

"You need air and materiality must be maintained this time," the Watcher said. "You must be patient until the time of your quickening. We have errands on the way that require you to be in your present state a little longer. Most of our journey will be in the lower five heavens. We will only be fully translated to the higher ones after our final stop."

Something rumbled below, as if the world itself was vomiting out something it could no longer stomach.

Or someone.

Normal daylight flooded in through the bubble's view-ports, as Q'Enukki's body pressed deep into his seat by some crushing invisible force. He could turn his head just enough to watch the ground fall away beneath him. The mountains around Akh'Uzan shrank to wrinkles on a greenish brown patch of land that soon retracted into a contoured blob north of a dark ocean. The hazy gold that was merely the *Face of the First Heaven* faded to white, and then to ever darkening shades of blue, until it too fell off below. The First Heaven's ebony night engulfed the chariot, filled with stars so clear and crisp that he felt he truly saw them for the first time.

What Q'Enukki had long ago deduced to be the 'planet' Earth shrank to a jeweled curve that receded ever rearward. The pressing sensation dwindled then stopped. He felt himself float within the restraints of his harness and laughed. *Could Samuille be wrong? Has my quickening come?*

No. The neck pain from hunching over his scrolls still bothered him.

"Why do I float like a feather on air?"

Samuille's eyes said, *"Do you not recognize your own predictions on planetary attraction now that you have become a heavenly body?"*

Theory had not prepared Q'Enukki for experience. His decades of noting positions of fixed and wandering stars, first with inferior pictographs then in the joy of manipulating numbers, had accurately produced a working model of cosmic attraction and motion. Yet it all seemed trivial now.

"I was right. Celestial bodies have their own attracting power; a curve of the three dimensions stretched over the contours of the Fourth Heaven. The Chains of Pleiades—leash of the Planetary Wanderers—or for the simple; that force which makes things fall down instead of up."

Samuille nodded. *"It is given to you to know such secrets, which after the first World-end, shall be lost to the children of men until the approach of the second. Much greater things will you also be shown. For as you have been a messenger upon the face of this Earth, so you shall be on another—though it not be until you have traversed these binding forces to emerge again from their grip near the end of time."*

cockatrice \ [Middle English] \ *cocatrix ichneumon* [Middle Latin]: a legendary serpent that is hatched by a reptile from a cock's egg and that has a deadly glance

— *Webster's 9th New Collegiate Dictionary*

1

COCKATRICE

The tracks showed two big dragons, spade-backed spike-tails, according to the harvesters. The workers made frantic hand signs against the evil spirits that haunted such monsters, and other kinds more bloodthirsty, all too near.

A'Nu-Ahki reined his mount, stroking the scaly rim of the unicorn's bony collar-shield to soothe it after their charge at the ram's horn alarm. The threshing floor around him was a trampled mud bog. Migrant workers began to knot about the mounted men, jabbering of ruined work and lost pay.

The broad five-toed prints showed a casual gait for the forest cover, southwest. A'Nu-Ahki knew that spikers grazed mostly in the western grasslands, beyond the jungle. That didn't mean they couldn't use the woods to good advantage. He pushed an irritating shock of black hair that had fallen over his eyes back into his bronze helmet, and signaled his scouts to fan out.

Not good country for mounted tracking, he thought, as he shot a wistful glance over his shoulder at the big river. The twist of his neck only freed the clump of hair to fall back into his eyes.

North, on the far bank, past the mashed-in wheat fields and palm tree rimmed waterfront, the city of Salaam-Surupag reclined like a queen by a garden fountain. A'Nu-Ahki could almost see her motion him home to the stepped pyramids that flickered in the sunlight. The red-gold domes mocked him with their call from a token attempt at a job for which he already knew he had no instinct. He turned to the jungle, and lowered his lance into its riding notch behind the semi-reptilian unicorn's broad collar of scale-covered bone. Only then did he gouge his hair back under his head armor.

After a muttered invocation for the *Hunt,* he signaled his remaining men forward, line abreast, with mounts spaced at ten cubit intervals. They entered the forest on either side of the trampled undergrowth. *Procedurally correct – as if that'll make any difference when the time comes.*

Greenish-gray shadows swallowed A'Nu-Ahki, as he led his hunting party past the last wurm-repellent smoke pot. He checked his flank guards on either side only to see them absorbed by the thickening jungle.

The size and weight of the spike-tails left clearly marked trails. These soon vanished to all but skilled eyes, as if the dragons had fled through some magic gateway hidden in the green. It still amazed A'Nu-Ahki how such huge seemingly slow-witted monsters could erase their passage. He knew it was not sorcery – at least none from the beasts themselves. Spikers habitually reared up and hopped diagonally over thorn patches or other obstacles to elude trackers and predators.

Consequently, A'Nu-Ahki never followed the main spoor, but assigned that to one of his trackers. "Somebody who actually knows what he's doing out here," he muttered to himself.

The jungle stifled sound in balmy mists heavy with mold and nearby swamp gas. The unicorns slowed wherever they had to either hop over or stuff their toothy beaks with thicker ground cover. Mostly they ate.

The urge to shout always came with the constricting green. A'Nu-Ahki resisted it. Even a tapping code could scare spiky into a rampage. He remembered getting sick the first time he had seen a man impaled on one of those stake-ended tails. Nor could he dismount to cut his way through. It had become far too dangerous since the strange migrations started about twenty years ago — not because of spikers, but for other lurkers in the green gloom with more demanding hungers.

A'Nu-Ahki's mind began to wander. *Other lurkers...*

He shook himself. *"Nu, a drifting mind is a good way to get killed out here,"* his father had told him all too often.

Wood clinked against metal off to A'Nu-Ahki's left, through the trees, followed by a violent rustle in the ferns. *Swoosh-thud!* Metal cracked, as unseen body armor caved against the bludgeon of a hidden spiked tail.

Nu's dreams burned with the accusing eyes of wives and children from fallen subordinates. It was hard not to wonder just how many of them had originally requested duty in his band because they wanted to be led by the prophesied Comforter of heavenly A'Nu. *Some comfort I am!*

He tugged at his lance, only to tangle the tip in some hanging vines.

An invisible juggernaut smacked the small of his back, knocking away both his wind and his perch on the unicorn's saddle. A'Nu-Ahki flew, rag-doll, into some ferns, where he lost his helmet and bashed his head on a giant tree root. Swimming eyes only half-saw the shadow-creatures mount his unicorn in bird-like hops, while the world faded in and out around him.

They moved from the trees in black-green blurs, elusive chameleon ghost-furies that became fully visible only for split seconds whenever they paused or changed direction. The cockatrice matriarch, perched atop the saddle of the thrashing unicorn, summoned more of her army from the undergrowth with a demonic screech.

Nu willed himself to scramble away, but his body could not budge against his frozen diaphragm. Panic distantly forced his fading mind to resign itself to death, until he blacked out.

Shallow gasps. He was gone only a few seconds. When light returned, he saw the phantom basilisks swarm over his mount, their throaty squawks like the mocking taunts of evil children. Darkness came and went several times through the sickening rips of hide and his unicorn's dying squeal, as the cockatrici disemboweled it with scimitar toe claws.

Nu tried to prop himself onto his elbow to get more air, but the effort only made his world spin faster and the dark spells last longer.

The thorny jungle re-focused. One of the wurm-pack muckled its jaws onto the base of the unicorn's whipping tail, only to be slapped by it through the dense foliage. The reckless cockatrice crumpled with a broken neck against a giant tree trunk, skin colors faded to gray in death. The remaining pack fell to their grisly feast as Nu blacked out again...

When the jungle reappeared, A'Nu-Ahki's gorge rose. Fiery needles jabbed his spastic diaphragm. Shaken brambles and stringy red shreds flew upward from nearby. Croaking taunts from cruel children tortured the air; sounds which slowly clarified into the calls of the cockatrice matriarch.

The beast on the unicorn's haunch paused from her lightning jabs. Blood and mangled flesh dripped from a needle-toothed grin that seemed to float free with enchanted bird-of-prey eyes against a greenish backdrop. She looked up and cocked her neck back and forth, as if to range in a new victim.

A'Nu-Ahki fought to focus until he could make out the matriarch's size and shape—about that of a grown man crouched over. He knew it could not have missed him even in the ferns. If not by sight, terror scent alone gave him away. Yet the cockatrice must not have found him worth leaving her meaty perch to pursue. Instead, she jolted her head back to devour the still-twitching unicorn.

No intelligence, no malice – only animal hunger, Nu realized.

Time slowed to a hyper-conscious mélange; the moment of clarity just before death.

He groped to pull the ferns over him, hardly able to squeak in the breath to keep from passing out again. A new thought assailed his airless panic. The wurm pack should have pounced on his helpless body! *If these are servants of the Great Basilisk, they should leave the unicorn and attack me! I'm the prophesied Comforter from A'Nu!*

The big doubt.

"The big lie!" he thought he heard some scuffling boys shout at him through the rattling bushes.

His neck lost strength until his head flopped back hard into the root. The blackness returned, full of noise, as flesh ripped and bones snapped amid the laughter of the jeering boys.

The diabolical children gaggled and screeched with the wurm pack, lashing out at him from the void. *"They spare you because their master knows you will spread the seed of your own doubt to others!"*

"You carry Basilisk seed!" barked their leader, who had eyes like the cockatrice matriarch. *"You are not A'Nu's Comfort! How can A'Nu – the vastness of E'Yahavah-in-the-heavens – comfort us through the likes of you? You are spared because you are dragon seed – wurm kin!"*

In the turbulent darkness, old memories and evil rumors gushed out like hot blood from an open wound, disjointed, but all too familiar.

A putrid twilight grew in A'Nu-Ahki eyes, a faded shadow realm where the frenzied wurms and the brutal children all became one. The boy with the cockatrice eyes hovered over him, while the others barked and scraped around him in a devouring circle.

"You know what they say about your mother!" howled the vulture-eyed boy.

A'Nu-Ahki had somehow been here before. Soon it grew clearer. He had lunged at his tormentor and missed – long ago. During his moment of imbalance, the cockatrice-boy had swept in and tripped him up. Nu had landed with a humiliating thump on his back, the wind knocked out of him. The ring of boys laughed in wild guttural croaks at his clumsiness.

"Bhat-Aenusa, daughter of Bara'Ki'El, from Clan Aenusi – Princess of the Balimar apostates. Whore princess of the snake-eyed Watchers!"

The boy with the wurm matriarch's eyes now had the leering face of Nu's cousin, Uruk. The ferns had become the green belt-way around Salaam-Surupag Boy's Academy.

"I bet she was Uzaaz'El's personal favorite."

A'Nu-Ahki's respiration grew to a shallow pant. He tried again to push himself free of the paralysis.

"She couldn't resist him, could she? He just took her over and she did things for him like a harem puppet. And she loved it, didn't she?"

Gibber-laughter came from the academy boys, who all had needle-toothed mouths and fire-hungry eyes.

"Not much of a titan, are you, Nu?" Uruk laughed with the others. *"The Nae-fillim are not all so big. Some are degenerate little things with two heads, or stupid ape-like beasts with one eye. They say that many even look normal and walk unknown among us."*

A'Nu-Ahki wanted to scream, to leap up from the ground and take Uruk by the throat and throttle the life out of him. But the airless panic would not release him.

Uruk kicked him in the side to prolong the effect. For a flashing instant Nu saw the talon of a cockatrice slashing by. *"The 'normal' ones always give themselves away, though. They can't hide their true appetites forever. How long before yours pop out, eh Nu?"* The tormentor knelt on A'Nu-Ahki's chest and made obscene hand gestures over his face.

Uruk's features melted into those of the wurm matriarch, smiling teeth splattered with fresh blood and unicorn entrails. A great curved gutting claw twitched expectantly against Nu's chest as her bird-like foot pressed onto his stomach, which constricted his diaphragm yet again.

The snuffing cockatrice head lowered to where a quick peck would have torn out A'Nu-Ahki's throat. Her neck muscles coiled to strike, but instead she became Uruk again—same eyes, same grin, only a human voice.

For Nu it was like being in two places at once, as if he watched everything from outside his body—panic and a place beyond panic.

"Your father almost divorced her when she wound up pregnant with you, old boy," Uruk said. *"All that stuff about Lumekki having a prophecy over his firstborn son was just to cover for your mother after you were born, and they saw you looked halfway normal. Of course, it's only halfway..."*

White light shimmered through the trees overhead. Other voices approached from beyond the circling pack-wurm-boys, as if carried down from above the rain-forest.

A flicker of uncertainty seemed to touch Uruk's eyes. He barked something unintelligible to his minions, and rose from his victim's chest. As if angry at the interruption, he kicked A'Nu-Ahki's side again, just as breath seemed ready to return fully. Then he and the jabber-wurm school-boys scuffled off into the green twilight and left Nu huddled in fetal position, gasping, bloody, and marinated in tears of humiliation.

I couldn't fight! I didn't fight! I tried to fight, but I was too slow. I'm always too slow! Always too late...

The Light drew nearer until A'Nu-Ahki heard a man's voice from its center. At first, it seemed like one of his hunters searching, but as it grew clearer, it began to sound more like his father.

"Yes, it is true I once doubted your mother," Lumekki admitted to the Light, and to his son — long ago.

"How could you?" Nu heard the voice of his younger self shout with a boy's indignation.

"I'm much ashamed of it now."

"You should be!" A'Nu-Ahki still regretted the outburst two hundred and fifty-odd years later.

The Light dimmed to a saddened gray.

Lumekki's voice carried through the trees. *"Your Grandfather Bara'Ki'El sent her away to protect her from the sons of the gods. It probably got him killed. His was the last clan in Balimar that followed the Archon. Your mother must have conceived you on our wedding night. I went off to war at Zhri'Nikkor, and did not see her again for many months. When I returned and found her heavy with child, I dwelt on how her sister had played in Ardis Temple against Bara'Ki'El's wishes. My suspicious nature got the best of me."*

Nu willed for his younger self to soften, to try to understand. Yet he was as helpless to change history as he was to make his arms and legs carry him away from the cockatrice pack.

"I had dreams," his father's voice said, *"horrible nightmares."*

"What dreams?" demanded the shadow of Nu's outraged youth. *"Were they a seer's vision? Did you know something?"*

The Light darkened more. A'Nu-Ahki feared it would go out, leaving him alone; exposed to the cockatrice-boys, who could not be far.

"No," his father said. *"I would see your mother wake up in cold sweats, screaming. She would hold her belly in torment…"*

"So she goes into labor — that's supposed to hurt!"

"Not labor, son. In the dream she would shriek that it was clawing its way out from the inside!"

The Light continued to fade until A'Nu-Ahki saw Uruk with the cockatrice pack circling him hungrily amid the trees.

The voice of Lumekki withered with the Light, pleading to the boy A'Nu-Ahki still sometimes felt like he was. *"The child was birthed in blood from the womb of a dead woman. Each time I had that nightmare I saw the infant emerge from her body, aglow with a sickly sheen, its moldy gray head, and black white-less eyes devoid of humanity."*

"Is that how you see me — diseased and unhuman?"

"No, son! It was Dragon-talk! I took my fears to my father, just as you have now taken yours to me. He dropped everything and made pilgrimage

to *Paru'Ainu, and found wisdom on my behalf. The Messenger of E'Yahavah appeared to him, and reassured him about you!"*

"How can I know?" Nu wept with the boy he once was.

The Light lingered in his father's oath. *"On the day of your birth, I received the seer's gift of our ancestors. I knew that you would grow up to be the Comforter from E'Yahavah A'Nu. I swear this to you by the Divine Name! Don't be afraid!"*

Yet A'Nu-Ahki was afraid — both the boy and the man.

The forest darkened somewhat as the searching voices moved off. The wurms began to poke their heads out again from the foliage. Some of the smaller ones pounced onto the unicorn carcass, fighting for scraps left by the feeding frenzy of the larger ones. Into their midst stepped the Matriarch, her demon-rooster head turned with a baleful eye straight at A'Nu-Ahki.

"Don't desert me to them!" Nu pleaded toward the fading Light. "I have no seer's gift, and no idea how to be this 'Comforter' they say I am!"

The cockatrice Matriarch croaked at him and narrowed her eyes while her toe hooks thumped the bloody ground with anticipation. Once more she transformed herself into Uruk — and Nu saw for the first time an effeminate insecurity hiding behind his older cousin's witty smirk and charmed eyes. If Uruk were simply a thug, Nu could have dismissed him. There was something more. Uruk was not just bigger and stronger — he was smarter, more cunning, and a natural leader. Nu had never been able to compete with him in anything as a child.

Why then does he feel the need to tear me down? What do I have that he wants? The Prophecy? He flat out rejects it! Why would he want that? A father? His died before he was born...

Uruk stepped closer. Nu saw a cockatrice toe-claw click from his cousin's sandal in the departing light.

"So what does my being A'Nu's Comforter mean if it all ends for me here and now?" Nu demanded of the forest.

The Light halted its withdrawal.

Uruk again hesitated and lost the initiative.

Air flooded into A'Nu-Ahki's lungs. A golden shaft of sunshine shot obliquely down into the glade.

The leader of the wurm pack stopped in mid-stride when the fiery beam touched the ground in front of Nu.

"This is not over!" Uruk's specter said, before dissolving into cockatrice form again for the last time.

Nu pulled himself to sitting position against the giant tree root, and caught his breath. The pack followed their matriarch off into the trees. The noise of many armed men approached, and the wurms were heavy and unwilling to clash with them from having just fed.

"What am I?" A'Nu-Ahki asked the shaft of light.

No answer came but the rustle of leaves.

"A nother unicorn!" Muhet'Usalaq shouted. His reddish-brown hands jerked in the air. "That makes five in less than so many years! Have you any idea how much it costs to hatch and train a quasi-dragon? We are fortunate your tracker took the spiker's tail by its base and avoided serious injury. He got himself clear of the area too, only he managed to retrieve his mount! Now, that took bush savvy!"

Wall tapestries fluttered in the breeze through the windows of the red clay palace, as if animated by the ire of A'Nu-Ahki's grandfather. Gold-white skies smiled outside like shiny brass madness on the forest and river.

"I am sorry, my Father," Nu said, using the Formal Voice, eyes down. "I will pay double for the lost mount."

"You will do nothing of the sort, though the Ten Heavens know you should! I suppose this is your way of squirming out of the Hunt again."

A cloud passed in front of the sun outside.

Nu's eyes came up like swords. "The Hunt? Quasi-dragons? Why is it we call unicorns that, anyway? Does a prefix change what they are? Do the priests and elders think no one notices the word game just because it's taboo for the Dragon-slayer Order to use dragons to fight other dragons? You have many grandsons. Why do you, as Salaam-Surupag's Prime Zaqen, take such personal interest in the exploits of one lackluster hunt-captain?"

Muhet'Usalaq did not blink. "Stop pretending to be so juvenile, Nu. You are heir and almost a junior zaqen. You may be the Comforter from E'Yahavah A'Nu, but that does not shelter you from basic responsibilities. The Archon gave your father's prophecy only tentative confirmation. So the people say, 'wait and see,' while they dismiss 'Comforter prophecies' as being too vague to really mean anything. That puts the larger burden of proof on us! Have you no sense of pride for your place among our people?"

"Pride! Is that all this is to you? Haven't you heard what's been going on out in the bush lately? Used to be we'd have to pick fights with reclusive crop-stompers just to keep up our training. Now all wurm-kin swarms through this place. It gets worse every season. I've made report after report! Where are they going and why? The Haunted Lands? Nobody seems to know or care! It's just track them, kill them, pray the invocation and the exorcism after each kill, and don't ask any questions!"

Muhet'Usalaq said, "I read your reports. It's your field-work that..."

Nu cut him off. "I know I'm no real huntsman! I don't claim to be, but I'm not stupid, either. I'm nearly three hundred years old. Don't you think it's time you stopped treating me like a 'tween?" The reddish-tan skin on the back of his hands beaded with cold sweat, as he noticed a look on his grandfather's face that he had never seen before—an expression he did not quite know how to deal with; *Amusement?*

"You are right, Nu, I need to stop doing that—well, I am going to try to stop doing it quite so much, at least."

Did Pahpi just admit he's wrong?

The Old Man raised his finger, and started to pace the chamber. "Though you reek with deficiency in practical matters—even sacred ones like the Hunt—you do excel in scholarship, medicine, astronomy, and knowledge of the Prophecies. Your punishment is to accompany me to Sa-utar as my aide for the upcoming council. I need a man who is unafraid to strip the mold that eats at the foundation stones of our civilization, and who knows the difference between mold and stone. Too many of the Zaqenar do not. They cannot be trusted because of it."

Nu arched a single brow. "I'm being punished with a promotion?"

Muhet'Usalaq glowered. "Do not let it go to your head. It is only to shelter your father's prophecy from further ridicule around here."

"Oh, of course it is. I would never imply otherwise! But I have no seer's gift, only a scholar's eye..." Recollection of his cockatrice encounter hit Nu as he spoke. *I was protected from them, not by them!*

"No matter—I had no gift until E'Yahavah took my father from the world. Your father had none until the day you were born.

E'Yahavah El-N'Lil will give you yours when it suits him. Get your affairs in order, and feel free to bring your lovely wife — although this will be strictly business."

A'Nu-Ahki thanked him, but declined on bringing his spouse. "We have daughters in courtship. The other families are good folks, but some of them are about as skilled at supervising 'tween-agers as I am at leading the Hunt. If Emzara stays, she can watch things."

"No matter, just be ready quickly. We leave the day after Rest Day." Muhet'Usalaq flipped the back of a gnarly brown hand at him in dismissal.

Nu paused. He almost told him of the vision during the cockatrice incident, but decided against it. It was probably just his head wound anyway, and there was no sense picking any fights with Uruk should he find out about it. Age had mellowed Nu's cousin some — but not much.

A'Nu-Ahki still bore a euphoric grin of disbelief when he returned to his wharf-mansion. His wife met him in the inner court gardens.

Emzara said, "What is it, Nu? You look like sky chariots came for you." Her gold eyes danced like fire as she joined him in the flower beds.

"Almost! Pahpi's promoted me to an advisory position. That's zaqen territory. This after I finally stood up to him and spoke my mind."

She stopped walking, hand on her hip, and cocked her body in a way he always found inviting. "I hope you didn't speak all of it."

He laughed and kissed her smooth mahogany forehead. "I wasn't banished, was I? He's never liked the way I handle myself in the bush."

"People fight the Basilisk in different ways. The worst dragons don't have scales and teeth. He's wise enough to know that."

"I guess I never thought I'd hear him admit it, that's all. Even so, he's more than happy to let me wonder at his real motives."

Emzara bit her lower lip and took his hand, while her eyes sparkled up at his playfully. "You can't take away all the Old Man's fun, can you?"

"The Ten Heavens forbid."

They strolled into the foyer, arm-in-arm.

Their two-storied house faced its landward side in baked red-orange brick, while teak wood levels stretched on gigantic pilings out into the wide river in back. A half-wall of brick curled around a fireplace, partly enclosing the landward side of the breezeway greeting chamber on the inside, which blocked much of the river view. Nu and his wife came in behind the hearth, and turned at the half-wall toward the library.

That was where they heard noises.

A shuffle and some stifled girlish giggling came from behind the waist-high room divider.

Emzara stopped short and detached herself from Nu to lean over the barrier to investigate.

"What do you think you are doing behind there?" she said to the unseen culprits.

Up jumped four 'tween-agers—Nu's unmarried daughters with the boys who would be their husbands in about six more years—if Nu let them live that long.

A'Nu-Ahki was in too good a mood to be instantly cross, but the youngsters' mussed up hair and loosened clothing forced him to put on a sober face that grew darker as the implications came home.

He addressed the young men first. "You two, go. I'll call for you when it's alright to come back."

The boys, one a young soldier fresh in from the War Academy, and probably all the more hot-blooded because of it, scrambled around the wall and out the garden door. The two girls still fidgeted with their clothes and tried to smooth their hair.

"Uranna, Tylurnis, talk."

Uranna said, "That's just it. We were talking is all."

A'Nu-Ahki's eyes must have flared, for the two girls took a step back from the hearth-wall. For a split second, he felt like he was still catching his breath near the pack of flesh-gorging cockatrici. The impression pricked him, and vanished, leaving something dark to throb in his spirit.

He paused and wondered what had just happened.

"Talking needs no hair or garment adjustments," their mother said.

Tylurnis said, just a bit too quickly, "We slid along the wall as we sat. It messed our clothes and hair. We should have picked a better place for courtship visit. It must have given the wrong idea. It won't happen again."

The girls were twin images of Emzara at an earlier age; golden eyes, red-streaked sienna hair like bronzed halos of fire around polished earthen-toned faces. Nu tried not to play favorites with his children, but the twins made it hard. Sometimes there was no resisting their identical dimpled grins.

Both now smiled perfect rows of pearl teeth up at him with a forced tightness that somehow revealed grinning skulls not far beneath the flesh of their faces — twin skulls set in wreaths of livid bronze flame.

Nu shook himself free of the image. "Well enough, 'Nissa. Both of you, off to your evening chores now."

The twins fluttered away, their clothes like flapping wings on a pair of raptors shooed from a soldier's corpse. *Flaming Watchers, what a weird day!* Nu heard their giggles trail off into the house's vastness, and shivered.

His wife turned to him, eyes of soft fire. "Nu, was that really wise?"

"What? It could have been as they said."

"Could have, but I doubt it!"

"Come on, Emza, they're young. They have poor judgment at times. None of the older girls turned out badly, and they each had their share of wisdom lapses while learning the social graces."

"Hiding?"

He shrugged. "It wouldn't have been hiding if we'd have come in through the river door, they'd have been in plain sight."

Doubt seemed to cloud Emzara's eyes. Then she shrugged and smiled up at him. "Well, done is done."

A'Nu-Ahki laughed. "I suppose it's a good thing you're getting so suspicious in your old age, since I have to leave right after Rest Day with Pahpi for Sa-utar. I could be gone several weeks."

"Old age!" She socked his arm and grinned. "Weeks?"

He told her about the council, and Muhet'Usalaq's distrust of the Zaqenar. As he spoke, her eyes narrowed.

"Nu, be careful," she said when he finished.

"Why? It's just an Upper Family council. It's not like I've never been to one before — just not up front as an adviser."

Her eyes pleaded. "I grew up there, Love. The Archon's city is not a Seer Clan freehold like Salaam-Surupag, despite Archon

Iyared's fondness for his vanished son. In Sa-utar a council is never just a council and nobody is ever really who they seem."

But for what degree of zeal they had formerly shown for virtue, they now shewed by their actions a double degree of wickedness, whereby they made God to be their enemy; for many angels of God accompanied with women, and begat sons that proved unjust, and despisers of all that was good, on account of the confidence they had in their own strength, for the tradition is that these men did what resembled the acts of those whom the Grecians call giants.

—Flavius Josephus
Antiquities of the Jews 3:1
(Circa 95 AD)

2
ENVOY

The Obelisks of Fire and Water at Sa-utar stood like twin sentries of bronze, brick, and stone, helpless against the mob's violence. They watched over a garden, until recently a fraction of mystic Aeden's beauty, which now lay trampled under thousands of angry feet. The monoliths warned of the two World-ends in raised hieroglyphs with meanings devalued more by each passing generation. The rioters only noticed to avoid crushing against them.

On a fortification wall overlooking the ravaged flowerbeds, three men watched the soldiers clear a path through the mob for an ambassadorial caravan. The youngest, A'Nu-Ahki son of Lumekki, tried to peer down into the strange self-propelled chariot that carried the dignitaries. The vehicle's reflective glass windows blocked his view.

"That will be Avarnon-Set's group," said the eldest, Muhet'Usalaq of Salaam-Surupag. He and A'Nu-Ahki had arrived late last night.

The third man—Muhet'Usalaq's brother, Urugim—lived in a tree palace just outside Sa-utar. He leaned against the parapet with his face half turned from the ruckus, as if disinterested. His thick woolly hair, like a million tiny salt and pepper springs, pressed against the stone. However, Nu saw that he always kept one eye trained on the caravan.

Muhet'Usalaq continued, "Our delegation returned from Ayar Adi'In with news that the Khavilak Sacred Mercantile has formally joined Lumekkor's Alliance. The Archon will hear them and this envoy from Bab'Tubila next. Oh, and the rioters demand we join too—unconditionally."

Nu asked, "Why then do they block the way of the Nae-fil consul?"

Urugim said, "They want a look at the Beast. Rumors say he has the head of a wolven-hound."

"That would insult wolven-hounds everywhere," Muhet'Usalaq said. "He is just misshapen like most of his ilk."

"I think it more than a mere deformity—at least by accounts I have heard from those who have actually seen him. They say his eyes have no whites in them at all, just solid hate-filled obsidian—except that they glow coldly in the dark like some preternatural predator's. The shape of his head seems to shift in subtle ways the longer you look at him, according to some. They say at times it is more wolfishly long at the snout, at others more ape-like, and then merely like a hairy disfigured man—all at a single encounter."

Muhet'Usalaq snorted. "People make too much of him. The truly disturbing thing is that Adiyuri rides with him. It is a rare honor having a candidate for Archon-in-Waiting as your personal escort. If that were not bad enough, the priesthood also wants Iyared to join."

A'Nu-Ahki slapped his palm against the parapet. "How can they? I know there are sympathizers, but to completely sell out?"

"They either do not see it that way, or imagine they can still turn things around through further appeasement," the Elder almost spat, his brown face crinkled in what seemed an almost physical pain.

"So now our own priests also serve the fallen Watchers!"

"Oh, not in word," Urugim said. "They have been careful about that! But in substance, they copy Uzaaz'El's undermining of Iyared's foreign and domestic policies. The Alliance has patrons in every Family tier; all claiming to be 'personally opposed to foreign Temple vices,' while they promote Erdu's anti-dogmas and stifling economic regulations to open up our cities to those same vices and the debt that inevitably follows them. They dress it in cleverly redefined words from Atum-Ra's Rite to make it palatable to our elders, but 'down' is the new 'up,' and 'cold' is now 'hot,' all the same."

Nu grimaced. "And if I called them dragon-tongues I'd have every little old lady in Seti whining about what a hatemonger I am."

"Something like that."

"They're making us look like fools, you know. That they do it so easily bothers me!"

"Half of Seti wants change! You think we made it easy for them?"

Nu glared. "In some ways, yes!"

"What?" Urugim looked to Muhet'Usalaq. When his brother kept silent, Urugim's eyes fell.

Nu explained, "We tend to lecture the younger generations in stuffy High Archaic without giving them compelling reasons to care if what we say is even true. No, don't tell me about threats of Divine wrath and World-end – even the words we use to describe those things have become cliché and unreal to them! We talk down to them rather than reason with them. We hardly even understand their dialect when they live in our very own homes!"

"Is it so wrong that they should learn the Language as it was given?"

"It's not about that! Alliance-sympathizing sages actually study Younger-speech. They've convinced academy 'tweens that they care and we don't! Theaters gush with misleading heart-wrenching dramas with themes that systematically suggest the ugliest possible assumptions about the teachings of the Seers. By the time we react, we look weak and phony!"

Urugim shouted, "Are you blaming us for their apostasy?"

"Of course not! I'm saying that telling people what to think without adequately equipping them with reasoning skills never ends well."

"Pah! You are not even a First Tier zaqen yet, A'Nu-Ahki! Do you think anyone wants to reason anymore? You have no idea how hard it is to kill this thousand-headed hydra worming through every civilized institution, eating at the foundations! Talk to me when you have been at it for five hundred more years!"

Muhet'Usalaq laughed — something that grated Nu's nerves — and put an arm around the shoulders of both men. "Peace, Uru. The youngster is right. We too often confirm the enemy's propaganda by how we respond to opposition. They bait us, and we jump for it. We've spiritualized everything, and retreated from academics, the arts, and the practical sciences."

"There aren't enough of us left to cover every gap! They shunned our scholars centuries ago! The Academy is the worst viper nest of all!"

Muhet'Usalaq said, "The Sacred Academy of today is a prostituted institution — I think Nu would agree..."

A'Nu-Ahki vigorously nodded.

"I think what the boy is saying is that many of us, in our desperation, have deserted an appreciation of learning itself — not on purpose, but because opposition has too often come from sages who systematically use the tools of reason to violate reason. Our father would have never done this. What is now 'Low Archaic' used to be the Younger-speech of his day. Though we have fought well on other fronts, we have been complacent here, Uru. Whoever controls the Academy shapes the future. I fear we will pay for it soon in young blood. I may not live to such a ripe old age."

The other two glared at Salaam-Surupag's Prime Zaqen; A'Nu-Ahki shocked that his grandfather understood his position so well.

Muhet'Usalaq — *His death shall bring it.*

"It was a mistake for Iyared to send Adiyuri to that foreign council," Muhet'Usalaq said, breaking the uncomfortable silence.

"I wondered about that," Urugim replied, who no longer seemed to have a problem with criticizing elders. "Did the priests badger him?"

"Could be. He certainly asked no counsel of me. Maybe he thought 'Old Grease Slick' would be less offensive to the titans."

A'Nu-Ahki smirked. "Is 'Old Grease Slick' a name the Great Seer would have approved for his own brother?"

Muhet'Usalaq said, "Who do you think first called him that?"

Nu smiled. "So what of the foreign council?"

"Oh, is that not obvious?" Urugim answered. "They condoned Gununi's black alchemy with Uzaaz'El's fertility rites, as, get this…" He pantomimed flatulence, and even flipped his kilt up a little in the back with his hand for emphasis, "…'a progressive step toward achieving the Promised Seed!' Even Adiyuri was a bit repulsed by it all, though considering the rest of his report that is not saying much…"

A'Nu-Ahki knew things had gotten bad, but this sounded like the crumbling of the last bastion of the Archon's moral authority.

Urugim went on, "Erdu's scholars have redefined the Seers' tablets into smarmy platitudes to sell back to the Archonic Orthodox for decades. How is it that our own leaders forget that the reason they named their city 'Erdu' in the first place was to identify it in their own dialect with Qayin's 'Y'Raddu,' where 'kingship' supposedly first 'descended from the heavens' —all to repudiate E'Yahavah's authority! Joining the Alliance is just honey on the bread. 'Mass amnesia,' I call it. Now they want to offer the wormy package to Iyared, who is supposed to bless it like a doddering old fool and pretend it is just a harmless dialogue of reconciliation…"

Muhet'Usalaq interrupted, pointing down at the giant sundial in what used to be the garden. "It is time."

Below the wall, the caravan pushed past the mob, into the portcullis.

The three observers turned from the parapet and made for the nearest turret. Azure domes and granite ziggurats in the lower tiers of the Archon's palace glimmered beneath the pale gold mid-afternoon sky. A monstrous architectural maze, the House of the Holy Cave dominated the City-States of Seti, a piece-meal culmination of over fifteen centuries of building and adding, rebuilding and improving. It nestled on seven walled tiers in the hollow face of a gigantic cliff that overlooked the city of Sa-utar.

Even at his age, Nu still enchanted himself with the idea that somewhere underneath all those halls, fountain pools, gardens, chambers, and courtyards lay a humble cave where the first parents of the human race had started the archetype of all families to come. His enchantment died when he considered how that family had turned out.

Nearby, a bronze statue of Seti the Great in battle with a crested dragon reminded Nu that Sa-utar's caves had originally sheltered his early ancestors against pack-hunting wurms like cockatrice and the enormous gryndel. The name *Sa-utar* itself meant *concealment*. Emzara's warning now put everything into perspective. The connotation of the Holy City's name had shifted over the centuries. It was still a place of concealment, but only in the sense that nobody there was really what they seemed to be.

Muhet'Usalaq, Urugim, and A'Nu-Ahki passed into the reddish-gold orichalcum metal-domed auditorium where the Archon heard foreign envoys. The outer chamber of the rotunda, its walls overhung with shields, banners, and other marks of heraldry, captivated the senses with a decayed grandeur of glory days long past, when the Archons of Seti had ruled more than half the world either directly or through their vassals. A long cobweb stretched from a dusty display alcove to a nearby stone column wrapped in spiraling reliefs that depicted winged sphinxes in red-gold fire.

The current Archon governed a serpentine swath of territory dotted by an atrophied handful of city-states bound only by common religious tradition, the Brotherhood of Dragon-slayers, a regular army, and a small coastal navy of long-obsolete triremes on the innermost of the inland seas.

Incense-thickened air squeezed A'Nu-Ahki's breath like a mood-constricting snake when they entered the Archon's central audience hall. He noticed the icy formality with which the legates and patriarchs of the High Council and priesthood greeted his grandfather. The sons of Q'Enukki had never been popular with the priests, but Archon Iyared — the Seer's father — still held them in high regard. Then it all became clear.

"Pahpi, why is Adiyuri sitting in the Chair of Appointment?" Nu asked, as he watched the fat elder that had just arrived with Bab'Tubila's envoy wiggle into a raised chair below the Archon's platform.

The new quickfire lighting pearls overhead made an oily reflection on the offender's bald, reddish-brown forehead. Although a generation older than Muhet'Usalaq, Adiyuri's cosmetic surgeries, face paint, and beardless triple chin gave him the appearance of an over-fed youth. He must have felt A'Nu-Ahki's gaze, for he glared back at him.

Muhet'Usalaq said, "Let not his sitting there trouble you. He rallied the priests and legates, and got a Declaration of Precedence."

"Based on what?"

"A strained reach—they insist that because Atum-Ra appointed Seti heir after Qayin murdered Heh'Bul, and not Heh'Bul's eldest son, that Iyared should appoint Adiyuri, his surviving eldest, and not me, the firstborn of vanished Q'Enukki. They ignore the fact that Seti was not the next eldest in line-of-succession after Heh'Bul. The choice came by prophecy, not tradition. It is meaningless unless the Archon ratifies it, and that is unlikely."

"You've been named in private?"

"Not yet."

"Why not? The Archon's older than any of his fathers reached."

"Iyared waits. We cannot afford another split in the Upper Family, especially now—not until the last possible minute, anyway."

A hush fell over the hall. A'Nu-Ahki, Urugim, and Muhet'Usalaq quickly found their seats.

A curtain at the back of the Archon's dais opened to admit two acolytes, who helped an ancient man in simple tan linen robes shuffle into a large golden chair at the center. The throne dwarfed its occupant, whose sparsely bearded head bobbed to the rhythmic tremor of advanced age.

Below the chair a herald cried, "All rise for Iyared, Archon Salaamis, son of Archronos Atum-Ra, born when the world was young to be Patriarch of the Children of Man, and Shepherd of the Holy Precincts!"

The entire hall—some thousand or more elders—rose briefly until the enfeebled figure on the dais had fully settled into his seat.

The Herald then announced the envoys. "Presenting the Emissaries from the Council at Ayar Adi'In: the notable Zegus, assistant to the First Zaqen of the Enlightened Fathers at the shrine city of Erdu; and the noble Avarnon-Set, son of the Watcher, Uzaaz'El, Ambassador from the Empire of Lumekkor, and personal minister to its mighty Shepherd, Dumuzi Tubaal-qayin the Fifth, Son of the Dynasty of Steel. Greetings and all hail!"

Nu said, "Shepherd? I thought he was a metalsmith?"

Muhet'Usalaq winced slightly. "The Archon gave him the archaic honorific as a 'thank you' for the quickfire lighting pearls."

"But that term's reserved for priests and acolytes!"

"And sometimes scholars—now shush!"

The envoys stepped forward, where A'Nu-Ahki could get a better look at them. The first dressed as a traditional Khavilak of the affluent merchant-priest class, in a finely spun gold cloak with elaborate onyx and lapis-lazuli ornamentation, and a wedge-shaped nemes headdress.

Bab'Tubila's envoy, Avarnon-Set, stood half a man taller than the tallest man in Iyared's court. The Titan's massive head stretched like contorted havoc against the insides of his long gray hood – part of a robe that flowed around his body like a shadow. Claw-nailed hairy hands protruded from sleeves large enough to conceal twin arsenals.

Nu recoiled when the Giant answered the Herald in a scratchy hiss. The sound itself somehow pricked the mind and made Nu's eyes and ears hurt. The vision of a thorn covered with gnawing insects flashed in his eyes.

As if from far away, the voice of Nu's grandfather whispered, "Plead the A'Nu that an irresistible evil may be resisted today!"

A'Nu-Ahki reached out in his thoughts to the Great God, but the tiny insects on the mind-thorn that was the Titan's voice became an itchy noise inside his head that made it impossible to focus. It only got worse when Nu closed his eyes – he actually saw them in the dark like a writhing mass of ants. He could barely mouth the words, "Be kind to me. Be kind to us... to Iyared. Give us will and sight, power to face... them!"

Slowly, almost imperceptibly, the image of the thorn and its bugs dissolved. Confidence seeped in from unseen cracks. Nu wrenched his eyes away from the towering figure in gray, and focused on the ancient man on the dais. Iyared seemed less feeble than before. A lively gleam sparkled from wizened eyes that offset Avarnon-Set's chill.

The Khavilak priest, Zegus, chanted a reedy monophonic greeting song that praised the Archon with insipid flatteries that gradually segued into his formal address. "...Excellent Archon, Father, and Shepherd of men, despite the disagreements that have divided our rites, we want you to know that we respect your wisdom and authority. Doubtless, our union with Uzaaz'El's Temple Alliance raises many questions. We come today, with the help of your loyal son, Adiyuri the Magnanimous, to explain in Orthodox terms better understood by your court..."

A'Nu-Ahki had expected the Khavilak Envoy to feign sincerity. What stunned him was the amateurish condescension sabotaging the attempt.

Zegus said, "Contrary to rumor, we at Erdu still read Atum-Ra and watch the Star-signs by Seti's interpretive tablets. These codes are as key to us as to you—integral to the governing pact of the Divine M'Ae. I speak of the runes that say: *I will put hatred between the Basilisk and the Woman; and between the Basilisk's seed and the Woman's...*"

Nu's heart raced. Nausea sucked him into a ringing inner void where the seething bugs had eyes. Panic seized his diaphragm just as when the Cockatrice Matriarch had pressed her talons down on him. He gazed over at Avarnon-Set. The Titan also turned and glared straight at him, eyes aglow from the recess of his cowl—from the darkness filled with its army of gnawing bugs. They were identical to the insect eyes.

"You are spared because you are Basilisk's seed. I will collect from you my blood price!"

The words were almost audible. A'Nu-Ahki wanted to bolt from the auditorium, but his limbs went limp. Avarnon-Set's eyes held him fixed, as if ready to lunge from their hole to swallow him in a bug-coated wurm's bite.

Zegus bubbled madly in the background. "...The speaker, of course, is E'Yahavah A'Nu. The key word is *seed*, used ambiguously here as to its plurality or singleness. Everyone knows it is a term for lineage. You, Elder Archon, are the seed of Seti, as I am of Buraki. Yet we would never call ourselves the seed of our mothers!"

The court chuckled. Sounds of humor—something natural and human—somehow enabled A'Nu-Ahki to pull his eyes from Avarnon-Set.

Zegus paused to let them drink in his little quip, and continued, "Our key word leaves room for not only one holy child, but many..."

Here the elders murmured—though not as many as Nu would have guessed or hoped.

The Merchant-priest said, "...For humanity to share the divine restoration of this bloodline, the Seed needs to spread to every family, does it not?" Before the prophetic scholars could object, however, Zegus went on. "It follows then that A'Nu should, through his sons—the Watchers of the stars and planets—let us redeem ourselves by giving our daughters to bear special children with them—children that will advance us into the heavens!"

From among the Archon's own sons, a voice spoke. It seemed to be clumsily reciting a script; "Is this not the promise of restoration that the Seed of a Woman shall crush the Basilisk's headship?"

Zegus flinched, but continued — what else could he do? "Er, yes. That was our conclusion too — only after long consideration — of course. I mean, after all, the Watchers are not male or female in any earthly sense. They artificially write creation codes into the specially prepared host-mothers' eggs to make them conceive. It is not even necessary for them to lie with their wives to do this. They do so only out of kindness — that the daughters of men may know pleasure before the pains of childbirth."

Suspicious murmurs rumbled from tiny pockets throughout the hall. A rising chatter of lurid curiosity over this new information on the dynamics of unnatural conception quickly drowned them out, however.

A'Nu-Ahki marveled, especially on the heels of the obviously staged outburst from the planted voice in the crowd. Such sparse outcry told him that many elders actually wanted the Khavilak to succeed, no matter how pretentious and radical his claims were. That was not all.

Erdu's sages had long read messages into the Star-signs that were abusive to the obvious intent of the Seers' interpretative tables. Now Zegus spoke of how, "Today's readers and listeners — not the tablets of the Seers — created divine truth when the Star-sign Tables spoke to individual hearts." Yet to believe this, Nu must uncritically accept the intent of Zegus, and Erdu's "enlightened sages," that "readers created divine truth" when they read the Seers' tablets, not the text's authors or E'Yahavah El-N'Lil.

Nu had insufficient formal rank as either zaqen or sage to challenge the Khavilak and protocol forbade his elders to do so. It made no difference. Those inside the rotunda would ignore Zegus' logical fallacy anyway, simply because a natural literary understanding of the Seers' tablets was currently unpopular in the priesthood. As a result, many now felt the Star-signs and tablets could mean nearly anything to anybody. This meant that, in the real world, they could no longer mean anything of any substance at all.

Zegus raised his hands, as if to smooth away near-nonexistent waves of discontent. "I sympathize with your misgivings. They are understandable in view of how the titans behave at times. The Holy Children have shown less-than-perfect obedience to Seti's Code. Yet we must understand; they are different, a step up, but not yet an ultimate fulfillment. If it makes you feel better, they haven't heeded the laws of the Qayinim tribes so well either."

Several legates looked at each other, smiled, and then shrugged as if to say, "Well now, I guess we're not the only ones. All the rapes, massacres, and burnings of our sacred scrolls are just one big misunderstanding then."

Zegus stretched out his arms as if to include all of Seti in a big hug. "Since they are from above—some might even say 'semi-divine'—some prerogatives must be given them. How can we judge their motivations? Certainly, we've seen the Great God, E'Yahavah A'Nu, bring tragedy to those who least deserve it, and wealth to men whose foolishness merited poverty—dare we question his divine justice? The questionable acts of the Watchers, and their titans, whom we have hastily called, 'Nae-fillim'—Fallen Ones—are but mysteries of the same quality, just of lesser degree..."

Over half the court nodded. Nu wanted to smack their empty heads.

The Merchant-priest clasped his hands to his chest in what A'Nu-Ahki hoped was a signal that he would finish. "We appeal to you in the name of E'Yahavah A'Nu, join in healing our divided families! Don't be left in the dust while progress rushes on to restore us our place among the stars! We ask you in love; accept us as sons, as we now look to you as fathers."

Zegus sat down, though his soft eyes still gazed up at Iyared.

A'Nu-Ahki saw too many perplexed faces. Yet one face still had purpose. His was the only one that really mattered.

Iyared stood without help from his acolytes. His voice boomed through the rotunda with no quickfire amplification. "I hath watched the world change since the Watchers first descended upon the Mountains of Ardis and mine own son, Q'Enukki, prophesied against them. I am neither surprised nor confused by thy position. Indeed, I long anticipated this, since we predicted that the Watchers would make such claims for their sons."

The Archon's watery eyes gazed down upon Zegus. "Nor didst we hide this, even as far back as five hundred years ago—thou shouldest be old enough to remember, Zegus—and if thou art not, most everybody else in this chamber is. Consequently, I do not think this idea of thine is well thought. Thou sayest the titans are children. I suppose this is so, since few are older than five centuries. Yet my ages of fatherhood hath shown me that violent children often grow to be violent adults. I hath also seen that sons bear the image of their fathers. This holdeth especially so for the Woman's Seed.

"Need I recite the deeds of these titans, who promise peace, yet war not only against men but each other over petty baubles of land and women? Shall I let the sons of Seti judge whether these be works of a holy seed, or of a dragon's brood? Shall I mention the lands stained by innocent blood; taken in what the titan Uggu hath called 'sports of conquest and diplomacy?' What of the vast harem of wives and concubines he had put to the sword when it was discovered that they could bear him no children because he himself, that 'perfect specimen of manhood,' was as sterile as a mule?"

Avarnon-Set clawed the sides of his seat. Zegus whispered something to the Giant that caused him to relax again. Nu wondered what.

The Archon cackled and shook his head. "Childe Zegus, how can I take thee seriously when thou sayest thy sundered clans still respect mine authority? I hath condemned the perverse fertility rites of Uzaaz'El, and the alchemy of Gununi, which thou supportest. Whilst I vieweth the engineering marvels of Tubaal-qayin as gifts, using them to abuse women and infants in thy Temple is an abomination worthy of my deepest scorn.

"Thou callest this 'progress?' Thy mind-robbing sorcery with its potions, and whoredom—with ensuing plagues and madness—spreadeth like gangrene. Political intrigues hath become gamings where thine Alliance absorbeth tribe after tribe. In Assuri, where many of mine own sons once lived, are empty villages left from slaughters instigated by these men of renown who claimeth for themselves the parentage of gods.

"You want us to join thee? Yet thy hands art stained with our blood! Ye Watchers and their spawn hath seduced our daughters, bullied us, and insulted our fathers and Seers. Now thou wishest us to believe they are the fulfillment of our most cherished prophetic hopes?" Iyared's laugh was a creak of ancient tortured wood. "What makes thee think we are that stupid?"

Zegus folded his arms around himself in a motherly hug. "Eldest Father, I cry pardon for my lack of clarity. I beg leave to explain better…"

Iyared cut him off. "Thou art perfectly clear, Childe Zegus. Do not upbraid thyself so. Thou speakest tragically of a divided people. More tragic still is a united people who arrogantly imagine they can redefine their own Creator. As for me, I sense that thou, Zegus, wishest me to bless thy folly, whilst Avarnon-Set is here to dictate terms to me if I do not. Thus it is a waste of my time to pretend we can ever come to an accord."

"But... but your Eminence..." Zegus sputtered.

"This hearing is over," Iyared said. "My constables are ordered to escort these envoys to the West Gate and send them peaceably away."

Avarnon-Set shot up from his seat. "I would speak!" His voice screeched like locusts on the horizon. The misshapen bulges of his head pulsated through his stretched hood like a sack of squashed faces pressed in airless panic against the inside of some huge taut wineskin for trapped souls. Still the Giant refused to show even the common courtesy of revealing his face. Only his huge insect eyes shone out of the cowl's blackness.

The Archon said, "Be brief."

"We came with gifts for your people—marvels greater than the quickfire that lights this hall and makes the night of your city as day. Since we cannot dissuade your resisting progress, I hope your people enjoy isolation."

With that, the constables herded envoys out politely, but with a lack of normal diplomatic protocol. Behind them, shocked and confused elders bewailed the loss of further technical aid, or spoke of imminent war. Adiyuri sat in the Chair of Appointment, face buried in his hands.

Iyared slumped in his chair, and fumbled for his quickfire voice enhancer. "Children, can we have order?" He trailed into wheezing coughs.

Nobody listened.

The Archon took a deep breath, and roared into the box-like device, lapsing from his customary High Archaic dialect. "Shut up, all of you!"

The hall became silent.

"I am convoking an emergency session of the High Council and whatever advisory staff present, as of now. What is the situation in the city?"

Muhet'Usalaq said, "I just came from the Obelisk Garden Wall."

"The Chair recognizeth Muhet'Usalaq."

"My operatives confirm three factions acting together. This intelligence is solid, since my men were embedded in the suspect groups."

Nu sat up. *My grandfather has operatives spying on the enemy?*

"The main group calls itself 'Children of New-world' and is lavishly financed by outside agitators that have ideological influence over all three sects. The other two factions are local and mostly sincere in their belief that El-N'Lil is leading us to Alliance union. The larger engages in non-violent protest. The smaller, 'Aeden's Dawn,' wants to overthrow the Archonate if their demands are unmet. Urugim's men have infiltrated both sects. Even now this 'Aeden's Dawn' is being taken for questioning about today's riots."

Muhet'Usalaq looked down at a small finger-scroll that a page had just handed to him. "Their latest demands are simple: First, they want us to join the Alliance. Secondly, we must open dialogue with Khavilakki, and be willing to broaden our definition of orthodoxy. Thirdly, and perhaps most significantly, they demand that Adiyuri be named officially as Appointed."

The auditorium erupted into angry exchanges that brought on another call for silence from the Archon.

Adiyuri nervously raised his pudgy hand for the floor.

Iyared said, "I recognizeth Adiyuri."

"Rather than pursue this ugly insinuation, I will point out hard facts. The military engineering of the sons of Tubaal-qayin has advanced beyond our comprehension! Based on my firsthand observation, I doubt our city-states could stand against it for even an hour! I honestly ask; has E'Yahavah chosen to defend our point of view? Look at the purges in Assuri! As the Father said, there is not an Orthodox family left in the entire Near South!"

Adiyuri swept his arm toward Muhet'Usalaq and Urugim. "Does not the blood staining the cliffs of Regati shout that we have been facing this the wrong way? Excellent Muhet'Usalaq, your own brother Guidad died there! Is it fair that we willfully invite the same fate onto our children here?"

Muhet'Usalaq drilled Adiyuri with his eyes until the older man flinched. "My brother knew what to expect in Assuri. He believed the prophecies of the Seers, and was willing to die for them. Are you?"

"The prophecies of the Seers, of course—but not the self-fulfilling variety you want to engineer in my vanished brother's name!"

Muhet'Usalaq repeated facts known to all; "Past council decided that Q'Enukki's words hold equal weight with previous

Seers, sealed by Archonic Decree. I witnessed my father's vanishing in a moment of shadow, then the light of the celestial chariot that took him into the heavens. He saw a winnowing of our people before the Obelisk World-ends..."

Adiyuri pounded the dais. "There is a difference between believing in a dire prediction, and trying to make it happen!"

"Make it happen?" Muhet'Usalaq's laughter could eat through stone. "I was not the one who urged we withdraw from Zhri'Nikkor! I did not tell former Archons 'we had no interests in the Far West!' You and your so-called 'Moderates' pulled our forces back to 'fight for Orthodoxy at home!' Would Lumekkor have seized the West Straits, or the Samyaza Cult Assuri, if we had kept up our strategic interests as I wished? If I wanted to engineer our fall, Adiyuri, I would have hired your party to do just as you did!"

Iyared shouted, "Silence, both of you! I am dismissing all but mine advisory staff. This will now be a closed session!"

Nu's heart sank. He wanted to stay and hear the outcome. He turned to Muhet'Usalaq, who hastily scrawled a message on a scrap of papyrus.

"Give this to our courier and have him make his best speed home and deliver it to your father—eyes only. Seal it before you release it."

"What is it?"

"Instructions."

"For what?"

Muhet'Usalaq growled at him, "Just do as you are told!" Then he softened his voice to a whisper, "Nu, you will want to attach a note of your own for your wife and sons to start packing—only necessities, mind you—for a big move. Tell them to be watchful and ready to travel on short notice."

A'Nu-Ahki took the papyrus and left the rotunda. He found it odd that his grandfather had not sealed it. Wax was available in the dais hall.

Once beyond the doors, and the gaze of prying eyes, he sneaked a look at the note, feeling a twinge of guilt as he did so. It read:

> We will be staying. Execute "Leviathan."
> The tides are coming.

Cold sweat dribbled down A'Nu-Ahki's spine as he rolled the tiny papyrus.

Muhet'Usalaq—*His death shall bring it.*

But as Jared died, tears streamed down his face by reason of his great sorrow, for the children of Seth, who had fallen in his days.

—*2 Adam 21:14*
(Circa First Century AD)

3

ARCHONS

Natural mineral springs gurgled up from the netherworld to massage A'Nu-Ahki's body, and bubble his mind free of the day's tensions. He thought; *Emzara must have loved this place as a child!*

It had not taken all five months since the rejected envoys for him to fall in love with his granduncle's forest estate, especially the geyser pond. In that time he had not, to his frustration, come any closer to understanding plan "Leviathan" than when he had first peeked at his grandfather's note to Lumekki. Instead, he had learned that there were many levels of insidedness to being on the inside. He apparently existed only in the outermost ring.

Nu watched; eyes just above the water's surface, as a bright blue scamper the size of a chicken launched itself from a palm frond to capture a dragonfly in mid leap with its forward claws.

The little creature landed, and then tore off across the lawn on ostrichy hind legs, clutching the giant insect.

The lawn was actually a spongy moss that cushioned the forest floor between the pool and the stairs of Urugim's tree mansion. The estate was a padded world for a padded mind taking a brief respite from the many jagged issues beyond. The scamper paused to bite the head off its prey.

Gold-orange afternoon sky light showered down through the leaves in sprinkly fish scales across the platform halls in the forest's middle terrace. Some of the sparkles even penetrated to the tree-trunk ladder bases. A'Nu-Ahki hoped to own a home just like it—if the world lasted that long.

"Having ourselves a posh little soak?" Muhet'Usalaq's voice cut through the shady silence from the stony bank behind A'Nu-Ahki's head.

Nu said, "Just thought I'd cool off a bit." He thrust himself up from the water and waded ashore to his clothes. Shaking off, he flipped back a thick head full of raven black hair, and secretly hoped to catch the Old Man in its spray.

"You are here to work, Nu, not bask in the geyser pool."

"Is there anything I've left undone?"

Muhet'Usalaq crinkled his face into a peppery grimace, as if he could rattle off a list. Instead, he shook his head and changed the subject. "Iyared wants to see us. I do not think he will last much longer."

"Is he going to name you?"

"As if that would solve our problems? I guess we will soon know."

Nu slid into his tunic, kilt, and belt-wrap. He was still fastening himself when Urugim pulled up in a large open coach drawn by two onagers.

The ride to the city took about a half-hour through giant cedar-filled highlands, and from the gates to the Archon's palace, another hour more along avenues choked with crowded outdoor markets and artisan shops. Up the once wealthy side streets, Nu saw many ancient domed mansions dull from having had their plating of orichalcum scraped off to help pay foreign debts. Many of these were dark and empty, boarded, or bricked up to keep out squatters and looters.

The single-room baked-brick domiciles in poorer sections of town, however, exploded with people, piled on top of each other in mountainous tenements like great ant hills of cubes accessed by a jumble of crude wooden ladders. Rowdy laughter and angry shouts echoed from these, while half-naked children played in the narrow by-ways between them.

The three men rode in silence, each deep in their own thoughts. The Archon was to Muhet'Usalaq and Urugim what Muhet'Usalaq was to Nu. Iyared had founded Salaam-Surupag, and had been its original Prime Zaqen. The two elders must have had many childhood memories of him. For A'Nu-Ahki, however, the Archon was a distant icon of authority—a relic as old as half of human history. *I should not have been so quick to leave Emza home.*

The sun set in blazing magentas as the chariot finally entered the palace gates, and wound its way up the zigzagging parkway to the highest tier. Fortress-like cliffs towered over them, lit in wine-colored afterglow—the first ramparts of the forbidding *Kharir Aedenu* – the Mountains of Aeden. Many days' journey across that impenetrable wall hid the Forbidden Orchard—the paradise lost to humanity at history's dawn.

Livery men met the coach as Urugim reined it to a halt before the upper chamber colonnade. The house physicians were there to greet them.

"How is he?" Muhet'Usalaq asked as he dismounted.

The Chief Healer answered, "Weak, but fairly lucid. I do not expect him to live out the night though."

Urugim said, "He has risked much by waiting for the last minute to do this." He slapped the reins into the hands of an unready stable man.

"I tried to tell him so," said the Healer, who was also one of Muhet'Usalaq's most trusted operatives. "But the Archon has always been one to keep his own counsel."

The physicians led them up the colonnade stairs, past a row of pink granite pillars, and into a colossal antechamber constructed of blue-gray kapar stone blocks. Mosaics and tapestries checkered the walls, depicting scenes from the earliest human history.

The far panel began with the creation of Atum-Ra, and the drawing forth of Ish'Hakka from his side—all done with inlaid tiles. Next to it, emerged the Basilisk before his dismemberment—a brilliant raised dragon with scales and a feathered crest made from set jewels of emerald, ruby, and topaz. It stood upright on two hind legs, much as the cockatrice matriarch had, only with a beauty and nobility that no wurm could ever possess today.

Beyond that, another tapestry showed their parent's expulsion from Aeden and the terror of the Fire-Sphinx set to guard the eastern pass with his flaming sword. Last on the wall came a picture of the First Sacrifice, and the giving of the Three Gifts to Atum-Ra and his wife at the Treasure Cave of Paru'Ainu on the Isle of the Dead between the cataracts of Aeden's River.

The opposite panel depicted the murder of Heh'Bul by Qayin, and the falling star Umara, which had smitten the land of Nhod in the east, and made the soil bitter in the region where Qayin was doomed to roam. This wall ended its history with the birth of Seti, who became the Appointed One – the father of A'Nu-Ahki's people, and heir to Atum-Ra's throne.

The physicians led them up a staircase of polished amethyst to a mezzanine that overlooked the great chamber. The Archon's private quarters lay opened at the end of the hall, carved right into the cliff.

Inside, Iyared's divan curtains were drawn open on three sides, with the Archon propped up on pillows at the head of his bed.

Facing the entrance; Adiyuri stood with his eldest son, Kunyari, and Kunyari's eldest, Rakhau. Rakhau's eldest, Tarbet, stood a pace behind, to the left of his father, ceremonially relegated to the background because of his youth. The elder men looked as if they could each be an image of the same man at different stages of middle to senior age – all flabby, and the younger men with painted eyes more effeminate than those of their fathers.

Tarbet did not resemble any of his elders, however, except in his non-traditional smooth-shaved face. Trim and naturally handsome, he seemed considerably younger than Nu, although that might have been from lack of a beard. His cosmetically enlarged eyes fluttered all over the room, as if bored and impatient to leave. Aside from an overly decorated prince's braid, he kept his shiny brown hair close-cropped in a style popular among the great cities of Lumekkor, but not so much in the Orthodox City-States, except among the very young.

Nu had not frittered his time away at Sa-utar nearly so much as Muhet'Usalaq seemed to imagine. He had made several discreet inquiries about the principle players in the power struggle at hand. These yielded much information about his counterpart from Adiyuri's Line, none of it savory. Not Rakhau's original firstborn, Tarbet had inherited the honor only after an uncannily convenient string of accidents and illnesses had killed his four elder brothers.

As one courtier had put it, "It's safer to be Tarbet's goat than his brother—and, like the Qayinim, Tarbet eats the red meat."

Tarbet's father was less interesting—though not to the palace rumor-mongers. Rakhau had remarkable luck with women, despite his being such a bloated grease pouch. Kunyari was the same as Rakhau, except that here the gossips had more to work with—an ancient rivalry to spice things up.

A'Nu-Ahki saw the fiery glare hit Muhet'Usalaq's eyes when Kunyari looked their way. The palace schmoozes had told Nu that the two zaqenhe's ancient blood feud went far beyond politics, though none would ever hint how far. Whatever its cause, it related to events before A'Nu-Ahki was born. The intention seemed united among even the most gossip-prone of the Zaqenar that knowledge of those events should die with the generation that had witnessed them. Court politicos of younger years with quicker tongues were as clueless as Nu was beyond that.

The sunset outside had become wine red.

Behind Adiyuri's line, slicing up the bloody glow from the bay window overlooking the city, seven legal scribes stood to record Iyared's last words, and any oaths taken by the heirs.

Iyared motioned for both Adiyuri and Muhet'Usalaq to step closer. The Archon's face seemed locked in a premature rigor mortis, his head nearly withered to a skull. The once bright fire of his blue eyes had dwindled to ashen gray. Nu almost gagged at the smell of death near the divan.

The Ancient whispered; his emaciated face locked in an age almost a thousand years past, "I sat at the feet of Seti the Great in the height of his glory. Atum-Ra himself was but recently departed and I played as a child in the presence of ancient Khuva, the mother of us all. She told me everything that the records do not tell, though I was but a small boy.

"I hath watched the greatest of empires sicken to senility under my own hands! I am a failure and I hand thee a kingdom that hath failed." Dusty eyes flared first at Adiyuri, and then softened to Muhet'Usalaq. "One of you shalt be Archon, but it is the other who shalt receive the greater gift..."

Adiyuri said, "What greater gift can there be than to follow in your footsteps, my Father?"

"Shut up and do not interrupt me again!" barked the wax-parchment-bone-relic man, sending himself into a fit of phlegmy coughs. It took him a minute to regulate his breathing again. When he did, he seemed to lapse again into his reverie of things long dead.

"She used to shuffle around the palace and mutter under her breath like a sweep woman bitter for the lost beauty of her youth. Now I understand thee, Eldest Mother! Now I understand thee all too well!

"She would say, 'Gone is my joy! Departed is the hope of life like rotted leaves on the forest floor, filled with worms and dragon's dung! The empire thou seest, my boy, is but a flicker of swamp gas before the waiting jaws of a gryndel wurm! Thinkest thee not, my Son, that thou shalt inherit this lofty kingdom! For it is an illusion, the false light of raggedy specters, dancing like sirens in the moldy night—and that only the first of many. When thou approachest them, they melt away into foul hags that claw thee helpless into their dens to consume thy manhood and waste thy years!'

"On she would rant, our great First Mother. On she would mumble from her toothless, drool-spattered mouth of glories we could not grasp—lost love she couldst but barely remember like a dream. That which we calleth life is but a tattered rag compared to what she lost!

"I now know thy bitterness, my Mother! I hath taken a nation and handed down a beggar's shanty! I saw the glory of Seti decay into skin and bones, the meat of worms! I hath hastened to bury thy dead, but neglected to raise thy children! Thy hope is farther off than thou hadst feared—though it remaineth a distant light. Yes, one of you here today shall be Archon over a field of tombs, whilst the distant hope faint yet fair goeth to the other."

The Archon's face softened a little. "To Muhet'Usalaq I grant all authority as Shepherd over the Holy Precincts here, at Paru'Ainu, and in the Treasure Cave. Into his hands, I commend the keeping of the Cosmic Dynasty Stone, and all the original Holy Tablets of the Seers. The crypt of the First Fathers is also his to manage, with the acolytic order. His is the Blessing of our Fathers—the line of the Promised Seed.

"Muhet'Usalaq shall have the right to open and close, to bind and to loose, and to move or let stay any and all relics that pertaineth to our heritage. For this is a twisted and self-serving generation who knowest not these gifts in honor. But in the house of Muhet'Usalaq I have found some who art worthy to carry on these things."

A'Nu-Ahki felt the pit of his stomach drop.

"To Adiyuri I grant the title of *Archon*, with political and military authority, if only he and his sons after him swear to me this blood oath..."

Adiyuri's eyes lost their luster. "Blood oath, my Father?"

"Yes! That thou wilt in no way seek to destroy, molest, conscript, persecute, or hinder the house of Muhet'Usalaq, especially in the execution of their government of the Holy Precincts, and that thou wilt defend those precincts, and the house of Muhet'Usalaq, with military force against all foreign and internal aggressors. Dost thou so swear for you and your line?"

Adiyuri hesitated, his hands raised, furrows etched in his jelly-soft face. "My Father, what you ask is most disturbing. Why do you speak so ill of your children? Why do you wish to divide the heritage of Seti as a carcass for sacrifice? Do not the Precincts belong to all? How can you give the sons of Q'Enukki license to loot our sacred treasures? Do not..."

"Swear it or I give all authority as Archon to Muhet'Usalaq, and thou shalt have nothing!" bellowed the Archon with a force that shocked a couple of the scribes into dropping their quill pens.

For interminable seconds, eyes of bloodshot fire bulged from Iyared's living skull.

Adiyuri said, "Very well, we swear."

Nu's heart sank. He thought he caught a glimmer of Old Grease Slick's recovering eyes, cast in his grandfather's direction. They mocked him, as if to say, *Oh well, so what if you are recognized as a seer and get to play with museum relics. It is I who now hold the real power of Seti!*

"Thou now havest what thou camest for, Adiyuri," Iyared said, voice now remarkably strong, though his body shook violently as if the entire interchange with his son had been a battle of physical blows. "Go from me. I will see thy face no more."

Adiyuri hesitated, tears welling. He appeared to grasp at the air for something to say that would soften his father's loathing. At last, he must have thought better of it. He gathered his robes to leave and motioned for his sons to do likewise.

As Tarbet brushed past A'Nu-Ahki, their eyes met. A smirk of triumph curled across the younger man's lips.

That arrogant fop thinks he's won some great contest! Nu realized. *Maybe he has, and I foolishly never thought of it in those terms. Now he will be Archon someday, and I will not. He will tear down what I would have built up.* The sense of loss wrenched his diaphragm almost as violently as the blow from the lunging cockatrice had a half a year before.

Iyared sighed and closed his eyes for a minute after Adiyuri left, as if to recuperate his waning strength. Muhet'Usalaq had already gestured for Urugim and Nu to leave also, when the Old Man's lids flashed open again. He called in a quiet voice for them to stay.

The scribes unpacked the scrolls and pens they had just stowed.

The Archon's face had softened much, its skull-like quality filled out by the relaxing of those muscles used for the expression of contempt. "I wish to pray over thee and give thee the blessing."

Muhet'Usalaq knelt by the bedside and laid his head across Iyared's lap in traditional form, eyes turned toward the Elder's feet. Iyared set his right hand on his grandson's head, lacing his fingers in Muhet'Usalaq's wiry salt-and-pepper hair. Whether he did this out of intimacy or simply because he could not hold his hand in place without some form of anchorage, A'Nu-Ahki could not tell.

Venerable eyes transformed as if by fond recollections gazed over the kneeler. Iyared croaked out an antiphonal chant, weak by one world's reckoning, powerful by another's. It filled the room somehow, running waters from dust and ashes:

> *E'Yahavah A'Nu the Eluhar, Creator of ten heavens*
> *and one earth,*
> *Smile upon thee, my Son, and upon thy sons*
> *May the Promised Seed be a shoot from thy tree*
> *A tree with strong roots and clean branches, unwithered*
> *and untouched by the locust*
> *E'Yahavah El-N'Lil protect thee from the crushing*
> *behemoth that eateth the branches*
> *And from leviathan that hideth in the roots beneath the*
> *rivers*
> *And from every hunting wurm.*
> *May thou be preserved from the terrors that come*
> *To sweep away this world in flame and flood*
> *May thou stand with thy Redeemer in that final day!*

Muhet'Usalaq tried to stand when the prayer-song ended, but Iyared held his head firm. "I am not finished yet."

He looked to each of them intently, one at a time, as if sizing them up. Finally, he said, "Where is Lumekki?"

Muhet'Usalaq said, "He could not be here. His eldest, A'Nu-Ahki, stands in his place. He sends his fondest regrets for not being able to attend. Forgive me, for it was by my order."

This seemed to satisfy the Archon, and he continued with his final testament. "I did things this way to buy thee time and as much political stability as possible. You will need both to fulfill whatever work E'Yahavah has for thee. Since there will be no deliverance for this people, I have given them what they wanted in their shortsightedness. They are doomed. But thou art my noble and innocent sons. Do not go down from this holy mountain of truth. Look around thee; see how thy children and thy children's children have all gone down, and estranged themselves through their evil desires.

"But I knowest, through a vision of the Eluhar, that he will not leave thee much longer in the region of these holy mountains because the children have violated his order and that of their fathers. Rather, my sons, E'Yahavah El-N'Lil shall take thee to a strange land, and thou shalt never again return to this orchard, and to these sacred mountains, except in thy hearts."

A'Nu-Ahki interpreted the Archon's meaning. *He's talking about World-end. But where shall we go to escape? Is there some place of safety across the Assuri Ocean in the distant south?*

"Therefore, my sons; set thine hearts on thine own selves and keep the charge of E'Yahavah A'Nu with thee. For then the holy mountain of truth shalt be in thy hearts whithersoever thou goest. And when thou goest from these mountains, into a strange land, which thou knowest not, take with thee the sarcophagus of our father, Atum-Ra. Take with it the Three Gifts, namely the gold, the incense, and the myrrh. Let them rest together where the body of our father, Atum-Ra shall lie.

"To him of you that is left when the terror of those times fall, shall the Messenger of E'Yahavah come. When that one goeth out of this land, he shall take with him the body of our father, Atum-Ra, and lay it at the world's navel—the Umphalos at the geographic center-point of Ki; the nexus of all lands—in that very place where deliverance shall be wrought!

"His sons shall measure out and map the world, for it will be greatly changed through upheaval. They shall mark out the center of Ki, and its cardinal edges with suitable megaliths, as did my son for this world. They must ensure that Ki be compassed so the heavenly signs are clear for future generations—that there may be a bridge for them back to the First Time, and to their own roots. They must be prepared for the Great Rebirth and the journey through Under-world by the Gate of the Morning Star."

The soft hypnotic voice of the Archon, as he laid out all of their futures in that manner of speech reserved for seers, and for those lying on the edge of eternity, soothed A'Nu-Ahki. It captivated his mind so that he forgot Iyared's former wrath when interrupted. The question spilled out of his mouth before he even realized he had voiced it aloud:

"Who is he that shall be left?"

Muhet'Usalaq glared up at his grandson with a homicidal expression, and Urugim scowled. However, both remained silent.

Iyared did not seem to mind the inquiry. Rather, he reached out his left hand to A'Nu-Ahki, smiled, and said, "Thou art he who shalt be left—the Comforter from E'Yahavah A'Nu. Let no one doubt that thou art the one! Thou wilt take the remains of our father, Atum-Ra, from the Treasure Cave and place them in the safe place when World-end cometh. Thy son—the one who shall yet come out of thy loins to pass on the Promise—shalt lay the body of Atum-Ra in the Navel of Ki, which is the center-place where liberation shall be wrought upon the children of Man."

Nu stared, transfixed by the Old Man's sad serene eyes, a prisoner of that gnarled-root grip on his wrist. He wanted to escape. He wanted not to escape. *I am the one who shall be left? There is a son who 'shall yet come out of my loins' to pass on the promise? What becomes of my firstborn Oronis or Asamu'El? Are they not faithful?*

Iyared crooned, "This thing I say from the Divine Wind, it frightens thee, yes?"

"I don't think I can live up to such a task. I'm not exactly the best Dragon-slayer material."

"Dragon-slayer material?" The Ancient cackled, as if Nu had made a joke. "Gooooood! Very Gooood. Keep that outlook about thee and thou shalt do fine. As for the rest of you, I charge thee upon the sarcophagus of Atum-Ra; patiently serve E'Yahavah all the days of your lives. Feed thy people the good teaching in honor and innocence, though few will listen, and many who used to obey will turn away.

"As for me, and the elders of my generation, we hath failed in our responsibility and made thy job more difficult. Forgive us! Few of us have understood the necessity, or have been willing to show the humility needed to reach our own sons. Do not look so surprised that I should say this to thee now. Though everywhere men speakest with the same tongue, our lip forms the words differently, and meanings shift with each generation.

"We in the upper tiers have not considered this well enough. We must sound so stiff and foreign to the young. So archaic, mysterious, and out of touch..." His voice trailed off into a flood of tears that ran down his furrowed brown face and soaked into his pillow.

That stream continued to flow long after the Old Man stopped breathing and his hands loosened from Muhet'Usalaq's hair and fell from A'Nu-Ahki's wrist.

Muhet'Usalaq rose from his grandfather's still form, and glanced alternately at Urugim and Nu.

"Things have definitely not gone according to our liking," he said, after the legal scribes had packed up and left. "Even bound by oath not to interfere, there is still much Adiyuri can do to indirectly hinder the Work. As Archon, he has authority to offer his own interpretation of the Holy Words and Sky Signs and to act upon his so-called 'insights' in public policy, and popular religion. He may not openly oppose me, but he can muddy the waters so that people will tire of the Prophecies."

Urugim turned his back, head hung, and paced toward the window to gaze outside. For a moment, Nu feared he might throw himself out onto the court pavement far below. Night absorbed the city in creeping mists that obscured vision as Adiyuri's theology and politics would soon obscure truth.

Nu asked, "What do we do now?"

Muhet'Usalaq nodded over to the Archon's corpse, and shrugged. "We mourn."

Now a river went out of Eden to water the garden, and from there it parted and became four riverheads. The name of the first is Pishon; it is the one which skirts the whole land of Havilah, where there is gold. And the gold of that land is good. Bdellium and the onyx stone are there. The name of the second river is Gihon; it is the one which goes around the whole land of Cush. The name of the third river is Hiddekel; it is the one which goes toward the east of Assyria. The fourth river is the Euphrates.

—*Genesis* 2:10-14 (NKJV)

4
ASHES

The Sacred Road to Paru'Ainu wound past the southern ramparts of the rocky *Kharir Aedenu,* hugging sheer cliffs on a seemingly endless shelf above the Pisunu rapids that roared through the gorge hundreds of cubits below. The funeral procession moved eastward in double file as it neared the end of its fifth day out from Sa-utar. In front rode the new Archon in a sedan coach gilded in silly gold blossoms with silvery leaves. Behind him crawled the drab black hearse carriage carrying his father.

The other mourners were obliged to march on foot out of respect for the departed patriarch, though livery hands led onagers behind them for those prone to heat exhaustion or advancing age.

A'Nu-Ahki itched all over. The incense ash dumped over his head that morning by the priests had mingled with his sweat into a sticky paste that would not let his skin breathe in the already humid air. The rough camel hair mourner's garment made him itch in embarrassing places.

Muhet'Usalaq and Urugim trudged in front of him in like raiment, eyes down to the kapar stone pavement. Urugim periodically stumbled from the heat, but refused to be taken to the onagers. He had not looked well even before they had left the city, but he had boasted how he would rather roast slowly in Underworld than ride like Old Grease Slick. Nu worried for him.

The hypnotic cadence and groaning harmonics of the priestly antiphonal singers mesmerized the marchers into a love-hate trance repetitive enough to filter into background noise. While his body slogged on, Nu's heart, driven by near hallucinogenic levels of heat and dehydration, flew over the southern mountains and forests to Salaam-Surupag. There, Emzara and their twenty-four children and grandchildren prepared for *Leviathan*—whatever that was.

Nu allowed his mind's eye to focus on his wife's dusky face and nubile symmetry—as he had done on their last night together. Bright eyes flashed their invitation, while her cinnamon skin, like curved satin beneath his fingers, set off gold-red streaks in her darker hair like orichalcum fire.

Burgundy sunset had danced off the river that night. Their wharf suite rested high on poles, its bay window visible only from far out on the wide Gihunu, and able to remain open in privacy. The rising moon through the skylight panel lit off her golden eyes with a passion both holy and earthy.

"Are you sure I shouldn't come with you?" she had asked after they were both satisfied.

Nu had almost relented. "Ah, my Sunrise, unfortunately I need you here. Oronis has never managed our estate before, and you know better how I want things done. The medicinal herbs need to be cured just so."

"We can leave directions."

He shook his head. "Then there are the girls. I did a little checking with the younger children. You were right and I was wrong. 'Ranna and 'Nissa have been discreetly disappearing with their betrothed ones. I'm particularly concerned—they avoid me, and get defensive whenever I bring up the subject of their espousal."

She grinned. "Welcome to my life, my lord."

He hung his head. "It's my fault. I've let too many things distract me. I should pay more attention to them, but now with the trip... Anyway, you know better than I do how a young woman thinks. We need to get to the bottom of these little trysts before something bad happens—if it hasn't yet."

"I know. It's just that we may be apart for weeks." She gazed up at him with forest nymph eyes that had renewed their golden hunger.

Nu hated to douse her passion with logic. "Then there's Illysia—one of us has to be there when our first grandchild gives birth. And Arrakan takes his final test for paladin dragon-slayer this week..."

Emzara smirked, and elevated one of her heavy eyelids. "If you're the one making the journey, how is it that I must be everywhere at once?"

He laughed and kissed her again, as she made him a happy prisoner in her embrace.

"I promise when I return we shall spirit ourselves away together to that waterfall ravine in the mountains, where nobody can find us. Though they search as for vanished Q'Enukki, we shall remain in our hideaway."

She gave a teasing laugh as she pressed herself to him. "Then we shall never return!"

Six months had been the longest they had ever been apart. Whatever *Leviathan* was, Nu hoped it would bring them together again soon. He thanked E'Yahavah that Emzara was in her infertile dormant cycle, with no infants to care for. Otherwise, things would have really been hard.

The Sacred Road to Paru'Ainu curved tightly around a spire of granite on the left, winding out over the rapids along an out-thrust precipice. A'Nu-Ahki breathed a sigh of relief when he reached the bend. The rest of the way descended gently into a widening valley of flowery meads and patches of woodland to the western shores of the great River-head Lake that swallowed up most of the vale's lower reaches. Gold and silver waters sparkled in late afternoon sunshine, a narrow sea with mountains hemming in on either side, its opposite shore lost in the mist over the horizon.

Leftward, the sun-baked peaks of the Mountains of Aeden continued off into the haze, impassable along the lake's rocky north shore. On the right, less sheer but just as high, frowned the *Kharir Urkanu* – the Mountains of Terror—that northern march of the dragon-infested highlands, swamps, and jungle called "The Haunted Lands." There, some claimed, lay the stronghold of Dragon-prince, one of the Basilisk's chief vassals. Nu suspected the fortress to be apocryphal, but no one had ever fully explored the region. It festered, a vast wound of feral wasteland, between ancient civilizations.

Cutting through this range, in the Canyons of Terror, the remaining three of the four Rivers of the northern world, besides Pisunu flowed. The latter river tumbled back safely westward toward Sa-utar. Due south, the lake narrowed into the Gihunu, to which Nu gazed, wishing he could pass its gorge of horrors, and all the Haunted Lands between Paru'Ainu and Salaam-Surupag, to see Emzara.

Southeast, beyond a grassland plateau, split off the Hiddekhel River toward Assuri. At the other end of the long lake, just south of where the River of Aeden made its own entrance over a gigantic cataract, the Ufratsi bent away to water the far eastern plains of Ufratsia and Zhri'Nikkor.

Awaiting the funeral party at a small dock-house near the Pisunu's entrance sat a tiny fleet of longboats manned by acolytes entrusted with the upkeep of the Holy Precincts. The last leg of their journey would be across the long lake to the giant waterfall. There the river from the Forbidden Orchard thundered into the mortal world, dividing itself on the Isle of the Dead—a pinnacle of tunneled rock like a natural ziggurat with the First Altar on its peak, and the Treasure Cave with its crypts at its lake level base.

They reached the boathouse at dusk. The cottage-sized shelter had few indoor accommodations, except for the Archon. Instead, the acolytes had erected tents and prepared frugal meals of bitter herbs and unleavened way-bread for the others.

Nu lost no time bathing in the lake to rid himself of the smothering ash grime. As darkness fell, he, Muhet'Usalaq, and Urugim sat by one of the beast fires, sipping bowls of warm amomun lotus tea.

They sat apart from the other clans, except Urugim's household.

Nu watched as his grand-uncle refused all food or comfort from his children, and their children, sending one after another away. Urugim had accepted the amomun from Muhet'Usalaq before settling down with his back against a tree, but that was all. A'Nu-Ahki hoped the medicinal properties in the tea would revive him some.

They sat for a long time, until Urugim rose to relieve himself in one of the outhouses down the hill. Once he moved out of earshot, Nu slid closer to his grandfather.

"I'm worried about him. He looks anemic, and I can't say he's doing himself any good fasting like he is."

Muhet'Usalaq nodded. "He is not himself. I think he is taking the naming of Adiyuri pretty hard, particularly because of what Old Grease Slick said the night Iyared sent off the envoys."

"Which thing was that?"

"It was about Guidad's martyrdom at Regati—that has always been a touchy subject with Uru. He missed dying in the massacre by only a week. His wife's illness required him to return to Sa-utar. I think he holds on to a peculiar guilt because he is still alive. Probably has something to do with him and Guidad being identical twins and all."

Muhet'Usalaq gazed into the fire and sipped his tea. "They say twins of that kind can tell what the other is thinking. It is odd, because when they were children it happened often that one would start a sentence, and the other would finish it, as if the thought had come from one mind using two different mouths to speak. I got rather used to it, but it always made me wonder just how connected those two must have been.

"Even as adults, they worked together like one mind—Urugim behind the scenes, and Guidad out in the forefront, drawing crowds. Urugim is a thinker, while Guidad was a doer. One was never quite at his best without the other. Guidad never would have thought to make the first printing press if Uru had not complained at the inefficiency of copying our father's books by hand. They actually made the thing together."

Nu's grandfather turned from the fire, and faced him. "A big part of Uru died at Regati. When Adiyuri suggested that all our work there had been misguided, I think it wounded my brother deeply."

"I can understand that," Nu said. "But we can't let Grease Slick get to us—especially now!"

"Do you really understand? At your age, I wonder?"

"What do you mean?"

"A man has to feel as though he is fighting a winnable war. It becomes all the more urgent the closer he gets to the end of life. I think Urugim is questioning his very core beliefs, and wondering if anything we do can really make a difference in this generation."

"Can't say I'm not doing that myself."

Muhet'Usalaq pulled his knees up to his chest. "We must not forget our objectives. Our charge is to explain the Prophecies in a clear, reasonable way that offers people a choice. Clear and reasonable..." he snorted. "I wish I had understood that when I was your age!"

Nu felt a dam inside him break. "But even we don't really know what's coming—fire or water, or maybe both—according to the Obelisks. Meanwhile you have this 'Leviathan' thing! I don't know when I'm going to see Emzara again, or even if I'll have a house to go home to..."

"You talk too much. If it settles your heart any, Leviathan is a defensive tactic your father and I worked out against an invasion from the west. With Khavilakki and Lumekkor formally aligned, it seemed likely they would strike to divide Seti at the narrow point over against Akh'Uzan to cut off and then take the southern city-states if I was named as Archon."

"So, it's that bad?"

"My operatives have been watching a military build-up along the Khavilakki border for months now, while an even larger force masses on the north shores of Lake Bauda'Al, to strike at the Isthmus of Hadumar. The pressure is off some with Adiyuri in the chair, but not much. Once word of the new Archon's oath reaches Uggu, Avarnon-Set, and Tubaal-qayin Dumuzi, they may decide to invade anyway—Uzaaz'El is not about to underestimate me, even if only as an ideological threat."

Nu wondered if his grandfather gave himself far too much credit. "Just what does this plan call for?"

Muhet'Usalaq leaned back against the tree and closed his eyes. "Leviathan is designed to speedily evacuate Salaam-Surupag, and get our families into the mountains and defensible ground. From there we can break into groups and filter across the river valley to the east, through to Assuri. Then we can take shipping to the Younger-lands away south—Ae'Ri is still practically uninhabited, and they say the soil there is rich and well watered."

Nu's heart deflated into hardened wineskin. "Assuri is dominated by the giants of Samyaza! What stops them from doing to us what they did to Guidad at Regati? They're even worse than the titans in Lumekkor!"

"You forget that the Samyaza Cult at least arose from a culture defined by Setiim Orthodoxy. Lumekkor's conversion was never more than a convenient political ruse at best. We will be traveling merchants as far as Assuri is concerned — hardly worth a second look, and perhaps even welcomed the way the economy is down there. We have stockpiled your medicinal herbs. Intelligence reports say some of their giants have inherited Short-lifer's Syndrome from their mothers. They probably won't bother us."

A'Nu-Ahki almost laughed. "Salaam-Surupag is a city of over fifty thousand men, women, and children! That's a lot of traveling merchants, don't you think? And there's no herbal formula for Short-lifer's!"

"Must I spell it all out for you and risk being overheard? We have the equipment. We have worked out the timing, and established several routes! We only need the good will of Assuri long enough to pass through. Now that is all you need to know!"

"When will I see Emzara again?"

"Is the poor gangly 'tween having the flutters? Soon, if all goes to plan! Now drop the subject, Urugim is coming back."

Muhet'Usalaq's brother moved at a brisk pace toward the beast fire.

"There is a commotion up on the road!" he called out.

Nu and his grandfather got up, and moved toward where the road emptied out of some tamarisk trees into a meadow before the boathouse. Up in the lower foothills a single phosphorus torch wound its way down the highway from Sa-utar. It signaled with alternating crisscross and circular motions that it was a military courier. Nu, Muhet'Usalaq, and Urugim arrived just as Adiyuri bustled out of the boathouse in his sleeping robe. All four hailed the unicorn rider as he galloped to a halt into camp.

"Lord Archon!" called the courier. "The alarm is sounded! Three armies from Lumekkor and the Seventh Balimar Corps have marched into Seti from the north. They mass with overwhelming force, but have not shed blood, except to defend their own persons. Nor have they left garrisons at any of our cities. Another report comes from the south: A corps of Assurim regulars and Samyaza giants have invaded Salaam-Surupag over the Gihunu River. The few who escaped last saw the city in flames, and its streets covered with thousands of dead — men, women, and children!"

Adiyuri's jowls tightened. "Have you a threat assessment?"

"Intelligence believes the forces out of Lumekkor are moving to engage the Assurim armies before they can invade Khavilakki. Lumekkor somehow knew the Samyazas were coming…"

"Survivors!" Nu shouted. "Were there any survivors at Salaam from the houses of Lumekki or A'Nu-Ahki?"

"I don't know, sir. There were only a handful making their way north by the Akh'Uzan Road. It's now been eight days since the assault."

Adiyuri pulled himself up to his full height, and suddenly seemed less corpulent as he turned to Muhet'Usalaq. "I have to return to Sa-utar. Since you are master over the Holy Precincts, I charge you to continue and bury our father. I promise you, I will do my best to protect you and this place." Then he looked at A'Nu-Ahki. "If I hear any information on survivors from Salaam-Surupag, young man, I will dispatch a rider to you immediately—you have my word!"

A'Nu-Ahki would not normally have put much stock in the new Archon's word, but he now saw qualities in Adiyuri's eyes that he had never expected—concern, compassion, and a genuine intent to keep faith.

"But I have to go with you, my Father!" A'Nu-Ahki pleaded. "I have to see if they're all right!"

Muhet'Usalaq placed an iron grip on Nu's shoulder. "No!" he said, "You have a duty to perform here—a holy charge! I cannot do without you."

A'Nu-Ahki tore himself free, swung around at his grandfather, and nearly punched him. Trembling, he said, "What have you ever really needed me for, Old Man? And what charge is there that cannot wait until I've seen to my family? They came from the south and east! Not the west! The cult of Samyaza! Not Lumekkor! Did Leviathan make provisions for this?"

Muhet'Usalaq spoke softly, "You are bound by your charge to Iyared, and I have always needed you. You are my bridge to the young, and my eyes into the future. Need I remind you that my own wife is also at Salaam-Surupag? I know by the whisper of El-N'Lil that if you leave me now, you will not return. Then all will truly be lost! I beg you, stay with me and pray—you can do no better for Salaam-Surupag or Emzara than this."

A'Nu-Ahki stood before his elders, every muscle a twitching battlefield of personal kherubim and demons fighting for control. The image filled his eyes of Emzara's warm corpse hewed to pieces in the street after having been the object of gang rapes by drunken Assurim soldiers. He also saw Oronis and Arrakan with Lumekki, making a valiant last stand with swords drawn, outnumbered ten to one.

As if somehow present, Nu witnessed his unmarried daughters carted off to Assur'Ayur to serve as prostitute "wives" for Samyaza, his Watcher hordes, and their giants. Lastly, he saw Illysia's unborn child ripped from her womb by the sword; her straining body cleaned like a gasping fish that still struggled for life.

He crumpled to the ground, indifferent to who witnessed him sob in the dust. He knew he must not go with Adiyuri, perhaps by the same breath of El-N'Lil that had spoken through his grandfather. But it was just a feeling—an impression that violated everything his mind and heart screamed for him to do. Yet to his disgust at his own weakness of will, he knew he could not go. He could not risk violating E'Yahavah's trust as revealed to him in the dying words of gnarled-hand, song-voiced, living-skull Iyared.

"Enough!" Nu barked at his grandfather. "I go to the Isle of the Dead as you go! But do not speak to me!"

Before the Zaqen could answer, A'Nu-Ahki stood up, ran, and grabbed his pack, stuffing it with rations of the leftover way-bread and water. Then he raced down the incline to the shore, and yanked a small three-man skiff from its mounts on the side of the boathouse. Once on the beach, he took a set of paddles and launched out into the lake. His strokes dug into the water, sped by the engine of his own fury. The vermilion light of a giant rising half-moon climbed over the horizon in front of him.

He glanced back over his shoulder to see Muhet'Usalaq, who watched him from shore. Tears streamed until the campfire-lit silhouette diminished to a black dot that lost itself in the lake's swirling mists.

The Sphinx is a figure with the head of a woman and the body of a lion! What is this but a never ceasing monitor, telling us to begin with Virgo and to end with Leo! In the Zodiac in the Temple of Esneh, in Egypt, a Sphinx is actually placed between the Signs of Virgo and Leo...

— *The Witness of the Stars*
E.W. Bullinger

5

SPHINX

The Isle of the Dead loomed above A'Nu-Ahki to misty heights, a natural fortress of stone-ghost sentries on outcroppings that guarded balconies, carved-out halls, and stairwells which honeycombed from the lake-level Treasure Cave up to the First Altar that topped the flattened summit of the island's highest pinnacle like a natural ziggurat. This unique rock formation had architecturally suggested the stepped pyramid ziggurat to begin with. That and it was easier to build over older mounds.

The peak overlooked the upper falls of the river from immortal Aeden, which thundered from its canyon on either side, splitting on the island with clutching fingers of white water called the *Palqui*. The cataract roared in ageless torment, etching a place for the fathers of men to make expiation for the living, and to lay the mummified end of each chapter in the human story since their banishment from Aeden. Stone and water seemed to echo those identical last words on each sacred genealogy: *and he died.*

A'Nu-Ahki's solitary vigil during his five-day crossing of the long lake had given him space to reflect. The timeless grandeur of the island made it impossible to revive his rage while beneath its shadow, even if he wanted to. Or perhaps it was the canticles of the acolytes echoing in endless cycles from the lake-level chapel. All must pass through their antechamber to gain the inner caverns, and none could escape their sonorous harmonies.

"E'Yahavah is One, yet Three," chanted one group of acolytes. A second chorus answered, *"The Only Creator, Head of the Divine Council – Father of, yet not like, the created lesser gods who serve at His pleasure..."*

Nu had arrived the previous evening, and expected that the funeral flotilla would appear soon through the lake mists that had just swallowed the setting sun — which was why he had descended to the wharf.

The Acolytes continued: *"E'Yahavah A'Nu – who resides in the heavens, the unknowable infinite, beyond the stars of time, beyond the watery abyss that is above the First Heaven..."*

A hazy lantern light appeared out on the foggy lake.

"E'Yahavah El-N'Lil – the Divine Wind who brooded over and stirred the Abyssu that was beneath the heavens, and who breathed life into Man; who makes known the ways of E'Yahavah A'Nu to the Seers, and who thunders over the heat of the mountain-tops to remind us that His wrath against our rebellion will not wait forever..."

Other dots of light began to flicker into existence on the lake, along with the profiles of the nearer boats.

"And the Messenger of E'Yahavah who appears as a man to make known to us the Divine Love and the Divine M'Ae; who placed the Fire-Sphinx at the Pass of Aeden to protect us, and who guided our first parents to the Treasure Cave, and to The Place of Concealment – Holy Sa-utar..."

A'Nu-Ahki's anger had cooled. It would not revive — even at the approach of his grandfather's boat — for now, at least.

A silent wounded man who could summon no words, good or ill, met Muhet'Usalaq at the dock. Both quietly decided to let things rest at that, and to proceed with the entombment of Iyared in peace.

The shortened ceremonies allowed as many of the acolytes as possible to go home to their families in the beleaguered City-States of Seti. Nu had already told the Keepers of the Holy Precincts what had happened, but gave no instructions—only suggestions for those who might want to return to Sa-utar, or to some other home city.

Muhet'Usalaq commanded a skeleton crew to remain, and prepare to defend their natural fortress if need be; though he said he doubted it would come to that.

Urugim also ordered a few of his grandsons to accompany the acolytes, and to bring word to the rest of his household. He urged them to withdraw from Sa-utar, and march eastward to meet him at the boathouse.

Nu got the impression they would not be staying in Paru'Ainu for long, though he wondered if it might not be safer if they did. A squad of four acolytes was assigned him to unseal the First Crypt, prepare the removal of Atum-Ra's inner sarcophagus, and ready it for travel. Nobody had any idea where they would ultimately go with it, least of all Nu.

After some two weeks of provisioning from the island storehouse for a long journey, A'Nu-Ahki finally broke the silence he had imposed against his grandfather, and asked him what the plan was.

Muhet'Usalaq regarded him cautiously, as if afraid to reopen wounds. "We go to determine the fate of your father, Emzara, and the others. Perhaps some were able to escape to the mountains after all. If so, they will have established sentinels along the upper Gihunu River to watch for us."

"And if not?"

"Then we return here to wait on E'Yahavah."

A'Nu-Ahki nodded his approval. "When do we leave?"

"Dawn tomorrow."

Early morning brought another unexpected setback, however.
An acolyte assigned to guard the Chamber of the Three Gifts—that innermost recess of the Treasure Cave catacombs, just outside the sealed crypts—rushed into the North Palqui Sanctuary,

where Muhet'Usalaq and A'Nu-Ahki reviewed a last-minute inventory of travel supplies.

"Worthy Father," cried the 'tween-ager, waving a papyrus scrap over his head and jostling back and forth on either foot as if about to wet himself.

"What is it, son?"

The lad could barely speak coherently. He rushed forward, and pushed the scrap into the Elder's hand. "I found this before the Treasures!"

Muhet'Usalaq took a moment to read the note. Nu watched his grandfather's normally rich bronze face pale to the color of yellowed parchment. Without a word, he handed the fragment over to A'Nu-Ahki. The hastily scrawled ideographs read:

> *My family,*
> *I suffer doubts about myself and where the Work leads us. I do not say this to discourage you, only to tell you that I must seek answers found in only one place. It is a two-day journey to the Great Sphinx of Seti at Aeden's Pass, and on the living Kherubar beyond. If they permit me to enter and leave, I should be back in five days. If I am not back by then, you must presume me dead and go on without me. If that my fate, then I wish you farewell. Pray for me.*
> *— Urugim*

A'Nu-Ahki demanded of the young acolyte who had brought the note, "Do you keep any onagers, or other riding mounts?"

"We've a stable on the upper island, in the meadow above the falls."

Muhet'Usalaq grabbed his grandson's arm. "You are not thinking of going after him?"

Nu pulled free. "He didn't say if it was a two day journey mounted or on foot, did he?"

The Acolyte said, "Every hundred years, we go to maintain the Great Sphinx. I went only last year—it's two days by onager at a gentle pace."

"I've no intention of riding gentle!"

"But the roads twist against chasms, and are poorly maintained!"

"Do you think you can overtake him?" Muhet'Usalaq said, as if he had suddenly realized that, with Urugim gone, he alone would be the last witness of Q'Enukki.

"Not if we stand here talking about it!"

A wide shelf concealed behind the waterfall rose up through an airy cave to the other side of the North Palqui Cataract from the Isle of the Dead. It opened onto the ancient trail skirting the northwestern lip of the Aeden River's canyon. By this same path, an age ago, Atum-Ra and his wife had fled the Orchard, descending into mortal lands doomed to decay and die.

A'Nu-Ahki kicked his onager to a gallop as soon as he cleared the cave, but soon found that the Acolyte had been right about the terrain. Fallen rocks and twisting switchbacks along the canyon rim forced him to ease back to a more moderate gait.

Urugim's trail was often easy to see. Spacing and lack of dirt spray around the hoof prints indicated a slow pace. The old man had not expected pursuit. Yet he could have as much as an eight to ten hour lead.

A'Nu-Ahki pressed on as quickly as conditions allowed, awestruck by the severe beauty of rushing water, jagged stone, and brightly flowered vegetation that border-dressed a sheer drop to the rapids below. High above, red gryphons sailed on wings of translucent sun-infused skin, their crested heads acting as rudders in the breeze. Whenever one spotted a fish in the foam far below, it would dive on it like a fiery meteor. A'Nu-Ahki kept his eyes peeled for larger more fearsome relatives of these winged dragons, though rarely would that kind attack anything the size of a mounted rider.

He hoped to overtake Urugim by riding all night, assuming from the Elder's leisurely pace that rest stops would probably be visible along the trail. The moon would be past full, but still large, minimizing the danger of falling through some unseen crevasse.

Day wore on, as the trail bent north to arrive at the western shore of a mountain lake. From here, the rapids poured over yet another cataract, down the rocky stairs towards Paru'Ainu. The road now ran at beach level, gentle and straight, which allowed A'Nu-Ahki to increase to a full gallop. Hope returned as he saw by the same close-stepped, spray-less print from Urugim's mount that the elder had not changed his pace.

A'Nu-Ahki had traversed only half the lake's span northward when dusk fell. He galloped long into twilight, slowing to a trot only when darkness became full. By then he had nearly reached the water's northern limit, where another falls out of the upper canyon graced the reservoir with immortal flows destined for dying lands.

Nu worried, as he still saw no sign of Urugim's encampment. Had he missed it? Could it have escaped his notice along so narrow a tract of land as what lay between the lake and the cliff-face looming upward on his left? He dug from his pack a phosphor lamp and shook it to agitate the fine crystals suspended in fluid that made it glow.

To the left of the northern falls, the trail climbed another set of switchbacks to gain the upper reaches. Apparently, Urugim had gone on, heedless of the dangers—both natural, and those beyond nature. If Nu's memory of the ancient maps served, the River of Aeden took a sharp turn west above this cataract. From there, the path supposedly ran near its bank at the bottom of the upper gorge, rising further on until it overlooked the final cascade. Then it wound over a pass into the eastern gate of hidden Aeden.

Guarding that pass, the ancient sentinel of Seti's Sphinx glowered down upon all who dared transgress the Sanctuary beyond. If the man-made warning proved insufficient, the Holy Tablets assured that a living Fire-Sphinx waited over the pass to assure any mortal glimpse of the Forbidden Orchard would be a final one.

The night grew interminable as Nu picked his way up the winding trail on foot, leading his onager because of the many pitfalls and wind-eroded gullies. Whatever time he had gained along the lake he now lost.

Dawn highlighted the eastern crags before he reached the top. Exhausted, he threw himself down next to a streamlet that tumbled down from the heights to join the river. Eating some way bread, he closed his eyes for what he meant to be just a moment of rest.

When he awoke, the sun had already reached its zenith. Nu cursed himself as he brushed the dust off his cloak. He took a long draw from the stream, filled his skin, and remounted.

The upper river trail hugged the bed for a while, smooth and easier riding than further down. By late afternoon, however, the road began to climb sharply. He could hear the bellow of the last great cataract echoing around a bend in the ever-narrowing canyon.

Despite the open rugged grandeur of the terrain, the air started to grow close and difficult to breathe, as if a peculiar haunting drew away the life-giving essence from its domain. Nu sensed something or someone watching him from the rocks above.

The trail hugged a sheer cliff wall, now high above the raging torrent. As Nu rounded the canyon bend, he reined his onager to a stop. The path continued to climb, zigzagging up a near vertical mass of granite to a height far above even the top of the waterfall. Gloating over the apex of the pass was the Great Sphinx of Seti. Her eyes of giant ruby caught the sun's rays with an eerie sparkle that made them seem alive. They sent dreadful warnings to come no closer. The woman's head attached to a cat's body smiled her knowing smile, keeping secrets from the children of men.

A'Nu-Ahki, by heritage, knew some of those secrets, but not enough to stifle the crawling sensation from his groin into the pit of his stomach. He twitched the reigns and continued up to the megalithic feline's massive paws, hope now gone that he could catch his granduncle before the old fool reached Aeden. Nu thought now only of his own chances.

As he climbed, the heat and closeness of air grew more constricting. The brooding monument cast a spell over the entire gorge that stole the breath like a cat in humanity's cradle. It reminded all comers that flesh and blood could no longer abide the immortal lands and live. Even so, one man since Atum-Ra had succeeded, although he had later vanished.

A'Nu-Ahki reminded himself that the stone sentinel was more than a mere warning. It had once served a happier purpose, long ago.

The Sphinx was made of poured kapar stone blocks, reinforced by bronze bars; the cement-like blocks colored green by copper oxides to contrast with the tawny granite of the surrounding rock formations of the pass. Seti, in his final years, and Q'Enukki, in his youth, had planned the project together — one of many megalithic structures all over the world they had initiated during the height of Sa-utar's power.

They had infused each such monument with prophetic, astronomical, and scientific information—the great battle cat with a virgin's head served as far more than a glorified scarecrow. The sun of the vernal equinox rose at midpoint between the constellations of the Virgin and the Battle-lion, which marked the start and end of the heavenly cycle since creation.

Likewise, the Sphinx also marked in its form the beginning and end of the prophetic story told in the Twelve Star-signs of Heaven. It started with the Virgin, who would bring forth the Promised Seed. The hindquarters spoke of the Battle-lion, representing conquest made by the matured Seed, as Lion-king, who would crush the Basilisk's head in the Last Battle. The Sphinx imitated the dawn of vernal equinox by its form, and marked the place in the circle of constellations where the story began and ended. It faced due south, allowing the path of the sun on the equinox to divide its halves.

Nevertheless, the Sphinx still crouched as a warning, because of its location and because the kherubim of Aeden were said by legend to have the form of winged battle-cats with the heads of men. At least that was how Nu's ancestors had imagined them. The Sphinx marked a division—both in the heavens and on earth. On earth, it divided the mortal from the immortal lands—between respect for the ban of E'Yahavah and its transgression—between life and death. It did that even in happier times.

As Nu considered this, a scraping noise in the rocks above drew his eyes upward. A stream of pebbles tumbled down onto the trail. He thought he saw the swipe of a leonine tail disappear among the high boulders.

Mountain cat or Kherub? He shuddered.

Fortunately, his onager did not spook easily, and kept to the trail at a steady pace. By the time Nu reached the last switchback near the top of the pass, the sun had set into a rose-purple orb. The fiery sky silhouetted the massive Sphinx into an overhanging black gargoyle ready to lunge down and pluck him off the last leg of the path in its mouth to devour him in one gulp.

When the road finally turned back again, it lay on the level of the Sphinx's paws, beyond which any traveler would have to go who wished to transgress the Ban of Aeden. The skulls of presumptuous pseudo-seers littered the dry grass before the stone beast-woman, as if she had plucked them from the path like a gryndel wurm and spit out their deluded foul-tasting heads to bake in the mountain sun.

An unearthly wail echoed across the blood-tainted peaks, an undulating sound made by no beast A'Nu-Ahki had ever heard of, and certainly by no man. The eyes of the Great Sphinx still glowed with a peculiar blood-red life in the failing dusk. In the wine-lit shadows between the megalith's house-sized paws, he noticed Urugim's onager cowering against the night terrors. The old man was nowhere to be found.

Nu pulled his own mount into that three-sided shelter, kicking a skull outside, the Sphinx suddenly no longer a predator, but a guardian of his safety and sanity. No force on earth could make him go any further by night.

Under normal conditions, A'Nu-Ahki could never have slept in such a place, but weariness outweighed the abnormality. Soon after he sat with his back against the innermost recess between the statue's extended forelimbs, sleep abducted him from the realm of the living.

Fitful nightmares fell, diving red gryphons, shrieking, incoherent, upon his dream-scape. Blood ran through the streets of Salaam-Surupag in a river flowing from a gruesome spring in Emzara's slit throat.

His father, Lumekki, did battle in the jungle, first against soldiers, then with a gryndel wurm near twice the height of a man.

Lumekki fought, as in his days as Tacticon Captain of Thousands during the Zhri'Nikkor War. He lunged under the snapping gryndel, and rose beneath its jaws to clasp the creature's tiny arm claw. The little appendage was too short to even bring food to the monster's mouth, and found use only during its mating ritual. Here Lumekki remained beyond reach of its teeth. The gryndel suddenly understood its own danger, and thrashed about wildly to throw A'Nu-Ahki's father from his grip on its one weak spot.

Lumekki gritted his teeth, and wrenched the atrophied arm-claw backwards with all his might. The gryndel bellowed, unable to reach this usurper with its dagger teeth or throw him with any contortion.

Lumekki gave a loud battle cry, followed by a sickening snap. He tore his enemy's limb from its socket and then, in a monumental feat of strength, pulled the arm-claw free from the gryndel's thrashing body altogether, skin, muscle and sinew, until one of the creature's major arteries ruptured. Nu then watched his father dive for freedom between the wurm's two ring-mailed legs and roll away from the swiping range of its tail.

The beast staggered about from loss of blood. It bled to death in a few short minutes—or so it seemed in the dream. Lumekki, whose sandals A'Nu-Ahki could never hope to fill, stood again heroic…

Nu opened his eyes.

The strange face that gazed down at him seemed almost human, with deep dark eyes that peered quizzically through Nu's soul, and the long curled beard of an ancient patriarch-king. However, the head was much larger than normal. Nu looked down at where the man's body should have been but instead saw paws—huge cat's paws. Wings unfolded from behind the creature's head with a swoosh, and A'Nu-Ahki screamed.

"Peace, friend," the Kherub said in a voice that softly thundered over the muted roar of the waterfall nearby. Then he disappeared.

A'Nu-Ahki dropped instantly back into a dreamless slumber that refreshed him undisturbed until the sun rose.

So He drove out the man; and He placed cherubim at the east of the garden of Eden, and a flaming sword which turned every way, to guard the way to the tree of life.

— *Genesis* 3:24 (NKJV)

6
ORCHARD

The sky already shined a bright goldish-white when A'Nu-Ahki opened his eyes again. The two onagers stood outside the shelter of the Sphinx's forelimbs, nibbling some grass amid the skulls along the edge of the outer flagstones. A lonely breeze rippled through their meal.

The vision of last night's Kherub filled Nu's thoughts. However, when he examined the layer of dust on the pavement between the graven forelimbs, he saw only his own prints and those of the onagers. Apparently, Urugim had not taken shelter there. None of the skulls littered about were recent.

He pulled himself to his feet and stretched. Ruby Sphinx eyes gazed down on him, almost friendly in the late morning sunlight. The woman's inscrutable smile was worlds away from last night's gargoyle scowl. Nu hoisted his knapsack and stepped from under the shelter of her giant paws.

To his right, the trail continued upward to a rise, then down into what only three sets of human eyes had ever seen and lived to speak about. Had Urugim managed to become the fourth? If not, would A'Nu-Ahki?

He tethered the two onagers for single-file march, and led them on foot up the rise. As he walked, he called out with cautious reverence to the Holy Watchers, "I mean no offense! I wish to steal no fruit! I come only to look for an old man who may have lost his way! I ask you who guard this place to pardon my presumption, if presumption it be, and let me find who I seek. I have no wish to intrude, or to violate the ban!"

As he neared the top of the pass, bluish-white radiance grew upward from the other side, until it became brighter than the Sun. A bone rattling hum filled the air, and an anti-magnetic repulse froze A'Nu-Ahki in his tracks. He would have fallen on his face to escape the piercing glare, but a strange paralysis locked him upright.

Voices whispered all around him, while a fragrant breeze blew down over the pass out of Aeden. The onagers panicked and tugged at their tethers. Nu released them to gallop back toward the shelter of the Sphinx.

A dark form emerged over the road's horizon, a black gash against the backdrop of unstained brilliance. Gradually the crack in the light coalesced into the silhouette of a man who staggered as if drunk to make the top of the rise. Nu, suddenly able to move again, lunged forward to reach him, just as Urugim collapsed into his arms.

A'Nu-Ahki lifted and carried his granduncle down to the shelter of the Sphinx, to lay him in the shade beneath the great lady's chin. As he passed between the statue's giant paws, he turned to look back up at the summit. The light had vanished, with the whispering voices.

Urugim seemed more emaciated than three days without food could have made him. When Nu tried to brush aside the old man's hair to get a look at his eyes, several curls came out in his hand like dried wool. Then A'Nu-Ahki noticed the redness of his uncle's skin, as if he had stood too close to a fire and been burned. Yet it was like no burn he had ever treated, for none of his uncle's body hair appeared singed—it just fell out in clumps.

He rifled his pack for the water bag, and wet the Elder's lips. Then he pulled out his chemist kit, and mixed some fine amomun with opiate powders into a paste. This he forced into Urugim's mouth with his fingers, coating the old man's tongue. The lotus mixture would speed healing, while the opiate would dull the burn pain. Nu wished he had thought to bring aloe, but burns were hardly what he had expected to find—at least not the kind one could live to tell about.

The old man stirred and opened his eyes long enough to smack his lips and swallow his saliva. Then he passed out again.

Nu wanted to be well away from the Sphinx before nightfall. He checked Urugim for other injuries, particularly broken bones or head trauma, which would make transporting him dangerous. Finding none, he hoisted his uncle onto his onager in front of him. Leading the other animal by tether, they began their long trek back to the Isle of the Dead.

A'Nu-Ahki hoped it would not be Urugim's final destination.

Orange late afternoon light filtered through the narrow window of the upper west chamber. The softened thunder of the waterfalls on either side almost lulled A'Nu-Ahki to sleep as he hunched over his chemist's kit, mixing an aloe salve to spread over Urugim's worsening burns.

Muhet'Usalaq hovered over his brother's unconscious form and prayed silently.

The marks on the old man's body made no sense. At first, they had been a mild redness, like a scorch from working too long out in the sun up in higher altitudes. It should have healed easily by now. Instead, it had erupted into blisters and then, by the time they had ridden down to Paru'Ainu, into running lesions. Was this the wound of the Fire-sphinx's Sword of Light? Nu had always imagined instant flame and ashes from such an encounter, but what did any of them really know for sure?

A barking cough startled A'Nu-Ahki. He turned to see Urugim sitting up in his bed. Muhet'Usalaq almost took his brother's hand, but stopped himself, probably for fear of the oozing burns.

Urugim stared about the room and then motioned for water.

"Are you in pain?" Nu asked, once his patient drank.

Urugim said, examining the lesions on his hands, "No. Looks like I should be though?"

"That it does."

Muhet'Usalaq drew himself up to his full height and almost yelled, "Just what in the name of the Holy Watchers did you think you were doing?"

Urugim threw back his head and laughed in a way that made Nu's skin crawl. "Holy Watchers! Brother, do not speak to me of Holy Watchers, for when I am done, you will have had more of them than you need to last you the rest of your life and beyond!"

Muhet'Usalaq softened. "Sorry, Uru. Tell us, why?"

Nu handed his grand uncle some amomun tea.

Urugim seemed to get a bit stronger as he sipped it. "I suppose a lot of things. But the biggest was the dream I had the night I left here."

"What kind of dream?"

Urugim finished his amomun, settled back against the bed's frame, and said, "I left my quarters, and went down to sleep in the Treasure Cave. I had heard the legend that sometimes dreams come to those who are troubled in spirit, and dare to sleep near the Holy Treasures and the bones of our fathers. I figured such dreams would come all the more readily since we had opened the crypts to exhume Atum-Ra.

"I walked into the Chamber of the Three, and with the authority granted us by Iyared, relieved the acolyte vigil there. I told him that I would take his watch. Then I settled down in the doorway to the inner crypts, within sight of Atum-Ra's disinterred sarcophagus, and went to sleep. At least I think I went to sleep only because of what happened next, though it felt as if I stayed awake the whole time. In fact, I do not remember waking up until now. Perhaps some of it was a vision—I do not know for sure.

"I had hardly settled down, when I heard a creaking noise from inside the crypt. Something ancient and disturbing filled the burial chambers. Though I shook at the thought of looking upon it, my head turned to the inner catacombs. Atum-Ra's sarcophagus had opened!

"I heard a shuffle, then approaching footsteps from out of the tomb's blackness. When the shadow reached the light from the Chamber of the Three, I saw a man wrapped in the linens of one mummified, yet his face still bore the flesh of life. He asked me to cut away the grave clothes and said he wished to walk with me. I somehow knew that it was Atum-Ra, so I took out my utility knife and did as he requested."

Nu asked, "What else did he say?"

Urugim stared off into space as he answered. "Much of it I cannot now remember, except he said that one day the way to the Life-tree would be open again to men, and that I should be afraid no longer. We wandered the stairs and halls as he talked. He also spoke of Q'Enukki, and World-end, though he would give no details. He never told me to go to the Orchard, but I noticed as we drew near the upper island stables that I was suddenly alone. It was then that I knew what I must do to find my answers.

"I returned to the Chamber of the Three, and wrote you all a note. Then I climbed back to the stables, chose an onager, and slipped away.

"I remembered the longing of our father to gaze upon the Life-tree, and how E'Yahavah had allowed him to actually dwell near it for three months in holy solitude. I guess I forgot how sick he became afterward. No matter. There really was no big reason for me to fear the Fire Sphinx anymore. Our world is ruined beyond repair! If the Kherubar found my reasoning presumptuous, at least I would die with a vision of unspoiled creation in my eyes—a vision of the way things were meant to be!

"I kept my onager's pace up the canyon trail unhurried, peaceful that soon my bitter heart would have its answers. It all started in Aeden, and I determined that in Aeden it would finish—at least for me, anyway.

"Only when I fell under the frowning gaze of Seti's Sphinx did I begin to doubt my wisdom and sanity. I felt as though she watched me approach in the night with sad pleading eyes. If being up there alone in the dark with all those skulls did not terrify me enough, the mad conviction came over me that the thing was actually alive and would speak!

"Unearthly noises echo in those peaks—ghosts of the tormented dead who called to each other for meager comfort, or who perhaps signaled that another foolhardy meal approached. The skulls whisper at the border of the fallen and the holy—at the battle line of life and death—where I was about to march across naked through unseen volleys of flying darts.

"I shook such thoughts from my mind. Then I laughed aloud—a disquiet alien sound on that pinnacle of solitude. I felt I had disturbed something ancient by my outburst, and realized that I was probably the first human to laugh in that place since before the expulsion of our First Parents. I made not a blasphemous laugh, my Brother, rather a cleansing one. I felt better afterward, and went on past the Sphinx. For all her ability to provoke fear, she made no move to stop me.

"In the half light before dawn, I climbed the rise just past Seti's marker. There I dismounted and allowed my onager to graze free. I did not feel right taking the animal in with me, for it had served its purpose. The creature immediately bolted for the shelter of the Sphinx. I then thought I saw movement in the shadowy rocks around and above me. Whispers called out indistinctly from the darkness. This time it was not just the skulls.

"My legs pushed me forward of their own accord, as I fell into a sinking terror. I did not yet know whether this desire to see the Life-tree came from E'Yahavah to uplift me or from the Basilisk to complete my destruction. War waged all around me! Shadow-voices grew more distinct the higher I went. In the battle for possession of my will, the whisperers opposed each other. Some called for me to turn back; others to march on.

"I crossed the top of the rise, until two rock pinnacles stood like natural gate posts on either side of the path. Barring my way between the stones, stood the fabled Fire-Sphinx bearing the Sword of Light. He shone like a small sun! How can I describe that which no mortals save Atum-Ra and our father have ever lived to tell? That terrible eye-burning brightness! It stung and penetrated not only my eyes but my deepest inward parts! It permeated my flesh so that when I held up my hand to shield my face, I could see my bones right through it! No part of me escaped his scrutiny.

"That sword laid my spirit bare along with my body. I felt as naked as Atum-Ra and Ish'Hakka had on the day they ate of the cursed fruit. The marrow of my bones burned as molten lead within me. My ears buzzed with the Light-sword's high-pitched hum—a fiery, crackling resonance. Yet I also heard in it the rush of great waters, like the crashing of ocean waves. As I listened, the noise seemed to shift and blend. It pounded with the cadence of marching armies, and the wails of men and women in torment, until it all swirled together in a violent whirlpool of sound!

"Then the Fire-Sphinx spoke like quiet thunder; 'Do you transgress the Sanctuary?'

"The voice did not seem angry. Nevertheless, my legs wilted and fell out from beneath me at the realization of what I was doing. I trembled in the dirt, face down, and answered that I did not wish to trespass, but merely to look from a distance upon the Life-tree.

"A pause followed in which I imagined that white-hot blade poised above my head to strike. When this did not happen, I risked lifting my eyes.

"To my joy and surprise, the Guardian had moved off behind one of the stone pinnacles. I had an unobstructed view of Aeden's Orchard!

"The Fire-Sphinx spoke to me again; 'To see the tree from a distance, travel half a day's march more down this path to an overlook from which the Orchard is visible. The Life-tree lies on a small island out on the lake where the River of Aeden begins. Be warned, Son of Man. This place emanates power as all substances once did before the pollution of the Deathing-Curse. Your body will not long stand these forces, for mortal things cannot endure the immortal.

"'Look, and be assured that your Life is real, but do not stray from the path. It is only because your father was granted special immunity that you are able to proceed this far. Now go, for you have until dusk to reach the overlook and return. Any longer, and I cannot tell your fate.'

"I scrambled to the gate posts on all fours and pulled myself up against the rock for a better look at the Orchard in the rising sun. I had expected to see mist and bright lights, a spiritual ether of trees and flowerbeds, perfect but insubstantial. It was not like that at all!

"They were real! More real than anything you could imagine! The trees were greener, the flowers more colorful, the life more vibrant than I could have imagined! Indeed, all that we have known outside or come to consider solid and binding is but a shadow of what lies beyond those stones! How can I even begin to tell you? How can I make you understand the beauty? The beauty and the loss — the terrible loss!

"I took the trail as the Fire-Sphinx had told me, until I reached the overlook. In the distance, I saw the lake and the island, where E'Yahavah's Bright Ones tended the inner orchard as Father Atum-Ra had done before his rebellion. In their midst, standing as a living pillar to hold up the very heavens, was the Life-tree. It reached seemingly even to the height of the mountains I saw in the distance behind it.

"Once I beheld it, I understood the depth of E'Yahavah's wisdom in sending us away. For from it the Orchard drew its vibrancy, and all that ate of its fruit would find everlasting life. Yet to live eternally in our present condition would mean to live forever growing more corrupt, even as the Basilisk and the fell Watchers. The doom of our mortality is the very instrument that allows us still to be redeemable. The fallen Watchers have no such limit! Human evil has an end on Earth. Theirs does not—until the A'Nu Eluhar brings World-end and chains them in the deeps of fire and water!

"My question as to E'Yahavah's distance found its answer in his mercy—he subjected us to this futility for a time so that we need not be forever lost to him, as are the fell Watchers. Though the world ends in violence, provision is made for us. The Life-tree is reserved for that day.

"Yet even as I considered these things, I saw something that caused me great distress, greater than any I have told you until now. I saw a man in the distance stand next to the Life-tree, with his arms raised to heaven. He uttered a command that broke the skies like mountain thunder.

"The ground shook, and the newly risen sun was blotted out! The sky itself opened to reveal a great chariot of fire, greater even than what took our father! It descended over the Life-tree, and lifted it up into itself.

"The Life-tree's Island lay shorn—a bare rock, burnt, and barren in the lake. Only the withered claw of a second tree remained—the skeleton of the one our parents ate from, dead and diseased.

"The great vessel carried away our father's joy into the sun, and I was left alone on that peak, half-ready to throw myself off. I fell to the ground and wailed uncontrollably in utter abandonment. It was one thing to be driven from the Orchard and forbidden access to the source of what little life we still had, but at least I had always believed that there it remained, and would continue until the end of days.

"The end of days! Now A'Nu has taken the Life-tree from the earth, and I knew this to be the last sign! World-end is upon us!

"In my despair, I disregarded the Fire-Sphinx's warning, and continued down the trail. I tried to find solace in a garden valley that still out-shone any outside. Only as the sky faded pink did I realize my danger. I found the trail, and began climbing at sunset. I dared not even stop for rest.

"There I met one of the lesser Kherubim—a strange creature of spirit who appeared to me with the head of a venerable man, the wings of an eagle, and the body of a battle-cat. He told me that one of my own awaited my return at Seti's Sphinx, but that I had overstayed in the Orchard more than what my body could endure. He walked with me, until I met the Fire-Sphinx again, late morning the following day.

"The Bearer of the Light-sword moved out from behind one of the pillar stones after I passed, to block any further view of Aeden's Orchard. The warmth at my back seemed to be that of his sadness, rather than the heat of anger. He spoke no word of rebuke that I did not heed his warning.

"'Go now and fulfill your errand in the little time left to you,' he said, 'for we must remove the Life-tree until the Promised Seed. Then new heavens and a new earth shall be created for it to be transplanted into.'

"I wanted to ask when that would be, but I did not dare—I had already presumed enough on this magnificent being.

"The last thing I recall was the Fire-Sphinx behind me, urging me up the last hill. Then I fell into A'Nu-Ahki's arms and woke up here."

Nu and his grandfather sat in silence for a long time after Urugim's account. The delivery had taken much out of the old adventurer, and he passed into an uneasy sleep.

In the following days, Urugim awoke only a few times more, but it seemed a dementia had overtaken him. His hair and beard continued to fall out in great clumps, and what parts of his skin did not crack with the burn-like lesions grew sallow and pale. The man seemed to age three centuries in a couple days—doubtless, the effect of having overstayed in a place not subject to the same laws of death and decay imposed on the rest of creation.

In one last moment of clarity, five days after his return from Aeden, Urugim awoke and scribbled out his story on a vellum skin, along with instructions to his children that they should follow Muhet'Usalaq as their own patriarch, and receive legal adoption into his clan. He then called for his brother and A'Nu-Ahki.

Urugim croaked, now little more than a living skeleton, "I leave now. I ask you, Muheti, to be a patriarch for my children, and guide them to whatever strange land you go. Bury me here, and make haste, for by now my sons wait on the lake's western shore. Nu, thank you for the risk you took to come for me. What I saw is important for you to remember. May you be blessed above men, and prove a second father to all when the time comes."

Urugim spoke no more after that. A few minutes later, he went on to join his fathers who rested beneath the Treasure Cave.

A'Nu-Ahki and Muhet'Usalaq entombed him in Atum-Ra's place—another man who had been to Aeden, and understood its wonders too late.

The last monster to be destroyed by Beowulf (and from which encounter Beowulf also died in the year AD 583) was a flying reptile which lived on a promontory overlooking the sea at Hronesness on the southern coast of Sweden. Now, the Saxons (and presumably the Danes) knew flying reptiles in general as *lyftfloga* (air-fliers), but this particular species of flying reptile, the specimen from Hronesness, was known to them as a *widfloga*, lit, a wide (or far-ranging) flyer, and the description that they have left us fits that of a giant Pteranodon. Interestingly, the Saxons also described this creature as a *ligdraca*, or fire-dragon, and he is described as fifty feet in length (or perhaps wing-span?) and about 300 years of age. (Great age is a common feature even among today's non-giant reptiles.)

— Bill Cooper
After the Flood

7

GORGE

The long boats glided south across the lake in misty pre-dawn half light. A'Nu-Ahki's paddle gouged the water in furious strokes while he ground his teeth to keep from cursing. The mental solitude and physical exercise only magnified his reflections on Urugim's last struggles.

Perhaps it was best that the Elder had not lived to find out how superficial and apathetic his children had become. Maybe he had known. Nu recalled how Urugim had held himself aloof from his sons during Iyared's funeral march. Few of his descendants had respected him enough to heed his call to leave Sa-utar. That remnant had reported of Adiyuri's promise to restore order. Most of Urugim's clan had elected to stay where they were.

Nu rested his paddle to keep the boat on course. He had no such option for resting his thoughts. *No wonder zaqenim get cranky –*

to have so much experience when nobody listens to you. I'm turning into Pahpi!

Only three sub-clans out of Urugim's twelve had shown up at the dock-house. The boats carried more supplies than they did people. Suddenly Iyared's death-bed prophecy took on grim new meaning.

They would need either to cache much of the stores or make two trips along the steep portage route through the Gihunu River's Canyon of Terror. Nu figured a hoard somewhere on the lake's southwest bank made more sense. From what he had heard, nobody traveled through the Canyons of Terror more than once if they could help it.

By mid-morning, the flotilla reached the entrance to the Gihunu, above the rapids. Serene hoots and honks from a pod of marsh-drakes on the opposite bank serenaded the unpacking of the boats. Two male dragons hopped into the water to establish their territorial limits. Nu was more curious than concerned. Although bipeds like the lethal wurm-kin, draken kinds ate only wild vegetation or the occasional fish they snapped up in great duck-like bills. Dragon-slayers did not even bother much with them; drakes normally kept shy of human habitations.

A cave in the lower foothills discovered by one of the youngsters from Sa-utar served well as a cache. It was not far from the beginning of the portage trail that led down into the canyon. After the noon meal, they began the arduous over-land journey with four men to carry each boat. Women and children were loaded down with as many packs as they could haul.

Twelve longboats snaked through the lower foothills down into the gorge, a marching column of elongated turtles. Fallen rocks littered the path, which skirted steep drops, both making the already exhausting task of portaging boats extremely hazardous. Nevertheless, Nu thought the name "Canyon of Terror" an overstatement. He would have described it as "The Canyon of Back-breaking Loads and Sweaty Grime."

A'Nu-Ahki and his acolytes carried one of the middle boats — the only one to be portaged right-side-up because it had Atum-Ra's inner sarcophagus bolted inside. Nu took the port beam, close to the rim of a vertical drop to the rapids hundreds of cubits below. The women and children marched between the boats with the packs.

The acolytes, apparently unused to working so closely with someone of A'Nu-Ahki's rank, kept silent. Nu tried to lighten the mood by making small talk. Well into a hopefully amusing story, an air-ripping screech above stopped him mid-sentence. Other hopes far more important quickly died.

The shadow swung down from the heights, over the trail, and arced out into the ravine. It tore through the air so quickly that it was impossible to make out its form until a pair of great webbed wings thundered outward, as if from nowhere, to slow the gigantic creature into a glide over the gorge. Another shadow followed; this one with a croaking hiss.

Nu stood transfixed by the lethal symmetry of the odd gargoyles, until one swooped past and carried something out with it from the line of boats ahead. A woman's shriek echoed from the canyon walls.

Then it rained falling shadows, as voices in the wind whispered and squawked like a vulgar ghosts.

The vultch gryphons dove from their roosts above. Dull gray, and hard to spot when perched, nobody knew they were under attack until the woman screamed. Swarms of wings opened all at once over the ravine in a staccato of wind slapping leather. A gryphon had lanced the wife of one of Urugim's sons in the stomach, carrying her over the gorge as it curled its pelican-like neck back over its own body to center the weight.

Nu watched her struggle against her skin-kite tormentor as it floated on the breeze in sickening slow motion. Far larger than the red variety he had seen on the Aeden trail, these air dragons had an adult wing span of some twenty-five cubits—well able to provide enough lift to carry a person. It clamped her body to its long skewer with its lower jaw.

The woman wailed and beat her fists against the bony awl that impaled her, while the dragon circled down toward a rocky perch by the rapids below to make a meal of her.

Nu hardly realized that he had frozen, while everything slowed to a syrupy pace. His eyes met those of the doomed woman, as foamy blood began to replace the shrieks in her mouth. Her twisted face sailed past him almost close enough to touch. Helplessness drove him to his knees against the boat, then belly to the ledge, when he realized the piercing shadows still fell. Everybody else dove for cover beneath the other boats, while Nu's acolytes pressed against their vessel's outer hull on the other side.

Forced to watch over the cliff, where the gryphon circled with its struggling prey, A'Nu-Ahki's prayers turned to mush. The woman's cries became a gurgle as their eyes met again. All he could do for her was to get a quivering mental grip, and silently plead for her end to come swiftly and mercifully.

A battle cry broke through the wing-flapping maelstrom. A spear flew from the trail just ahead. It pierced the dragon's wing and tore the thin membrane like ripped linen. Vultch gryphon and woman plummeted, broken kite paper and sticks, to the rapids below. They separated during the fall, the gryphon striking the stony bank. The woman's head exploded on a rock in the middle of the torrent. Nu watched her body slide away in reddened foam.

The other gryphons landed along the trail to peck and scratch at the overturned boats. Everyone but Nu and his men managed to crawl beneath the upturned vessels in safety.

The crew of Atum-Ra's boat reached inside the gunwales between gryphon lance jabs. They grabbed for their spears, which they then held up to fend off the webbed wings. Nu fumbled for his, only to push it further into the boat. He managed to draw his sword and hack at the talons and bills careening around him. His left hand clutched the boat's port gunwale to keep himself from rolling off into the chasm, while his right swung against the squawking demon heads. He thought he heard them calling his name.

Pain stabbed his left hand.

Nu almost released the gunwale and tumbled off into the gorge. Somehow, he forced himself to hold on. Again the pain struck—a dagger that repeatedly jammed into the tendons below his fingers. This time he clenched his teeth and pulled himself up to face his attacker.

The vultch gryphon perched atop Atum-Ra's coffin, wings flexed wider than the boat's full length, generating a wind sufficient to blow Nu over the cliff. He barely had time to raise his sword before the creature's pointed head shot at him. His blade poorly poised for a good swing, all Nu could do was deflect the end of the bill just enough to prevent it from puncturing his face. The dragon's wing-blast and his own momentum almost sent him tumbling backwards into the ravine. Nu's sword fell to the rapids as he clasped the edge of the boat with both hands.

Head and torso above the gunwale, he had served himself up as a helpless meal to the enraged gryphon, whose neck coiled for a second strike.

The creature's head flew forward.

A'Nu-Ahki closed his eyes rather than watch it pierce his flesh. When seconds passed and nothing happened, he risked another look.

The spear of the young acolyte on the other side had skewered the monster from behind. The beast lay draped; its unfolded wings an unholy burial shroud over the bloody sarcophagus of humanity's first father.

Nu looked around and saw that the rest of the gryphons had landed. They pecked and scratched at the other boats to try to get at the soft flesh curled like snails within. His acolytes, way ahead of him, had already noticed the vulnerability of the distracted dragons. The young men began to spear them one by one. Nu grabbed his own javelin, and began to attack the beasts near the next boat behind his. Soon a tally of some ten dead gryphons lay by the nearest three boats.

Once the remainder of the swarm saw their danger, they took off over the canyon and circled out over the rapids to wait for the humans to move on so that they could feast on their own dead.

The boats began to prop open like cautious clams. A'Nu-Ahki leaned on the gunwale and panted to keep himself from vomiting. From the corner of his eye, he saw a large, dark-skinned man moving toward him from the front of the line. The approaching one stepped carelessly over gryphon carcasses, and kicked several off into the ravine with cursing shouts. Huge bulging eyes smoldered like coals in his face as he drew closer.

Nu managed to stand up again just as the dark man reached the sarcophagus boat.

The man with the burning eyes stood silent for a moment with arms folded, his thick lips curled downward at Nu. Then he spoke. "Tell me something, O fifth level Dragon-slayer, how long were you going to let my brother's wife squirm like a fish on the end of that devil's spike before you picked up the spear laying right next to you and used it?"

The Dark Man's words stunned Nu speechless. He now saw, several boats forward, the man's brother laying belly-down on the path, head over the ledge, shrieking his wife's name with hysterical tears, as her body tumbled out of sight. *Tunnel vision! Why didn't I see him before?*

Perhaps because I'll soon be doing the same over my Emza!

The Dark Man stepped forward and sneered in Nu's face, "I had to let go of my boat to rifle for a weapon! I almost sent the other men into the chasm because of the imbalance, just to get a shot at the thing! What's the matter? Weren't you sure that the monster belonged to Dragon-prince? Or maybe it was just one of the wild dragons still doing whatever it is A'Nu put them out here to do?"

"I..." Nu began.

The man whose brother had lost a wife cut him off. "My name's Henumil, son of Karmis, son of Tarkuni, son of Urugim. I worked with your brothers out of Ayarak fifty years ago, A'Nu-Ahki. They told me that you were a heretic who thought Dragon-slaying was a waste of time. A'Nu's Comforter? You have too much of a reputation for bad fieldwork! But I've heard other stories too — questions about your real lineage that are no longer questions in my mind! You proved them here today!"

"Then why did I kill my share of these gryphons that litter the cliff?" Nu's defense sounded lame even to him.

The Dark Man launched himself at Nu, knocking him backwards into the boat so that he slammed his head on the sarcophagus. The dead gryphon's blood smeared across his face, into his hair and beard, mixing with his own from the split lump growing on his scalp. Henumil's weight pinned Nu down, his huge face but a finger's width from his own.

Henumil said, "I saw the whole damnable thing! You picked up your spear only after that green acolyte 'tween-ager had the presence of mind to do what should have been second nature to you! Don't you dare try to paint yourself the hero!"

A'Nu-Ahki's mouth dropped as he stared up into space. He only distantly saw his acolytes pull Henumil from him.

It had not even occurred to Nu to try to kill the gryphon, and put the woman out of her misery. Not even the memory of her head shattered on the rock could undo Henumil's common-sense conclusion. Nu could have done nothing to save her, but he could have done that much to end things more mercifully for her. It just never came to his mind in the heat of the moment. Why hadn't he thought of it? Why had he crouched there so helpless?

The memory of his cousin Uruk from that crimson afternoon at the boy's academy so long ago came flooding in again, unbidden but stronger than ever — *I couldn't fight! I didn't fight! I tried to fight, but I was too slow! I'm always too slow! Always too late…*

Three nights after they reached the base of the portage trail and took to the river again, the remnant of Q'Enukki made camp on a thinly wooded islet in the center of Gihunu's stream. They hoped to avoid the larger hunting wurms that plagued the banks on either side of the ever-widening canyon floor. Shrieking monsters in the trees, and hidden leviathans beneath the water kept the refugees huddled close by the fires.

Even so, Nu kept to himself. Few, except Muhet'Usalaq and the acolytes assigned to guard the sarcophagus, would speak to him. It seemed that Henumil's opinion was well-respected among Urugim's clans. Even the priestly keepers of the Three Treasures, who had also joined their party from the Isle of the Dead, stayed clear of him.

"You are not to blame, my Elder," said the acolyte who had saved Nu's life by lancing the gryphon on Atum-Ra's coffin. "Too much was happening — they are being unfair to you!"

"Thanks, Nestrigati. You're very kind and generous to your captain. But truth is I should have thought to do what Henumil did. I was closest, with the clearest shot."

"Then we would have had one less spear to take on the other draca."

A'Nu-Ahki would have continued gently arguing the youth's kind logic, but a woman's scream from the center of camp brought both men to their feet and running at the source of the noise.

A 'tween-aged girl about forty years old, from among the children of Urugim, writhed in the dirt near one of the beast fires, panting, shrieking, and beating the air above her as if trying to fight off something invisible.

"Nooooo! Get awaaaay! Not meee!" she wailed, flailing with one hand as she ripped at her own clothes with the other.

A stern voice split the night, as if a warrior of old had stepped from the shadows of legend.

"By E'Yahavah El-N'Lil, as Keeper of the Promise, I order you to leave this girl alone and trouble not the Clan of Seers!"

The girl ceased struggling, her shadow assailant vanquished.

Muhet'Usalaq stood over her, and held out his hand.

She took it, and he lifted her gently to her feet.

A blood-chilling chorus of howls broke from the shadows on both banks of the river, drawing everyone's attention away from the fire.

Muhet'Usalaq clapped his hands to regain their focus. He then hugged the girl into his mantle. "You did nothing but sleep," he told her tenderly.

"I did nothing, my Father," she said, tears running down her face.

The Old Man ran a weathered brown hand through her dark hair. "Have courage, child. I'm sure it was just a nightmare—the stress of traveling through the Haunted Lands. It gets to all of us at times."

"Perhaps," the girl agreed, as she rubbed her neck.

Nevertheless, when her hand came away from her throat, A'Nu-Ahki saw the gigantic suck mark there. Maybe it was just a bruise caused by her rolling over a rock in her nightmare. Even with all the traditions, it seemed a bit melodramatic and nonsensical to suppose that one of the fallen sons of the gods lurked in the Haunted Lands just waiting for unsuspecting maidens to assault—as if they had no better hunting ground.

Nu had lived long and traveled wide enough to know that the situation with the Watchers was more complex than that, that it played out in different ways in different parts of the world, some crude and tribal, others far more sophisticated. They always shifted with the times.

Nu wondered all the same.

For twelve years the Danes had themselves attempted to kill Grendel with conventional weapons... Yet his impenetrable hide had defied them all and Grendel was able to attack the Danes with impunity. Beowulf considered all this and decided that the only way to tackle the monster was to get to grips with him at close quarters. The monster's forelimbs, which the Saxons called eorms (arms) ... were small and comparatively puny. ...Grendel, however, is also described, in line 2079 of the poem, as a *muthbona*, i.e. one who slays with his mouth or jaws, and the speed with which he was able to devour his human prey tells us something of the size of his jaws and teeth (he swallowed the body of one of his victims in large 'gobbets'). Yet, it is the very size of Grendel's jaws which paradoxically would have aided Beowulf in his carefully thought out strategy of going for the forelimbs, because pushing himself hard into the animal's chest between those forelimbs would have placed Beowulf tightly underneath those jaws and would thus have sheltered him from Grendel's terrible teeth.

Bill Cooper
— *After the Flood*

8

WURM

By evening of their fifth day on the river, nobody, least of all Nu, felt any longer that the legends of the Haunted Lands had been overstated. Leviathans in the fetid mists menaced the boats by day; one of which sank suddenly with the loss of all hands when a tremendous set of jaws lunged at it from out of the fog. Nu heard the clamp of teeth into the boat's gunwales, then wood snapping and people screaming, as the creature pulled it sideways into the churning waters and capsized it. The splash and gurgle of large bubbles into an instant heart-pounding silence made him want to scream.

In the evenings, a virtual wall of beast fires fed continually by an army of watchmen surrounded the river bank campsites. More than half the company stayed awake any given night. Few got the rest they needed to maintain strength and alertness for the hazardous days in the boats.

If the fires scared off larger predators, they attracted dragonflies in fanning droves — bugs longer than Nu's arm with prickly spiked legs and veined mica-glass wings that sliced skin — that got tangled in hair whenever they lighted on somebody's head. Crocodiles larger than the boats slowly worked their way in among sinister curling ferns. Spearmen constantly patrolled the river's edge in pairs to drive them off.

None of the men except the sarcophagus squad would work with A'Nu-Ahki. He almost didn't blame them, though it hurt to think that his own brothers had denounced him simply because he had doubted that all dragons were demonically possessed. It was a hard position for him to maintain in the Haunted Lands; especially when he thought he heard mocking evil whispering and squawking amidst the shaggy black trees. If he had such doubts, he kept them silent.

On their seventh day on the river, they began to notice a large predator stalking them on the western bank. It followed by day, hiding itself in the dense foliage except for the rustles made by the passage of its tremendous size. The eastern bank dissolved into marshy bogs extending far in from the stream, hiding still larger leviathans that ventured out onto the river by dusk. These sometimes shifted around the firelight like the shadows of moving mountains during the night.

A gigantic golden eye glowered in at them from beyond the campfire on the eighth, ninth, and tenth nights. Each evening it moved a little closer. By late afternoon of the eleventh day, no one had yet identified the creature, though few doubted it to be anything less than a wyverna or a gryndel — both carnivorous biped wurms of immense size.

Muhet'Usalaq ordered his tiny fleet ashore, as bloody sunset draped the river mist. Soon, one by one, the beast fires crackled to life. Nu was about to brew his squad some amomun tea when a shriek came from the north side of camp, where a fire had yet to go up.

A'Nu-Ahki turned in time to see an enormous gryndel's head disappear backwards into the foliage with the bottom half of a watchman's body hanging from its mouth. The creature's dagger-like front teeth had snapped the man's spine instantly.

Nu gave the alarm. Within seconds, a band of spearmen followed into the green darkness to give chase. He sensed they would not want him along, so he stayed back with the main company to guard the women and children. Nobody knew who the widow was for sure until the hunting party returned an hour later with only the belt of the victim to show for their efforts. They had never even caught sight of the gryndel.

Henumil, who had led the huntsmen, shuffled past A'Nu-Ahki and flashed an accusatory glare in his direction, though he said nothing.

The following afternoon, Muhet'Usalaq ordered the boats ashore two hours before sunset to ensure plenty of time to light enough fires before half-light. Once he secured Atum-Ra's boat, A'Nu-Ahki helped the women unpack the cooking supplies, since none of the men wanted him around.

All the while Muhet'Usalaq kept to himself, unless called upon to settle disputes or make major decisions. He said nothing to alleviate Nu's pariah status. Nu figured the Old Man did not want people viewing him as taking sides. Maybe the Prime Zaqen saw the gorge incident as a fulfillment of all his warnings to A'Nu-Ahki about keeping up his hunting skills. Nu hoped not. Salaam-Surupag was clearly another world. Raised in the Haunted Lands, there would never have been any question in Nu's mind about such priorities, demons in dragons or no demons. Here dragon-slaying was still a common-sense way of life for survival.

Ready for his evening amomun, Nu took it upon himself to start the cooking fire. He scraped off some resinous pine bark with his utility knife and brought it over to a makeshift pit, which was just a slight depression in the earth between a couple rocks. He barely noticed the child playing beneath the low branches of the pine to his left, while he began to hack at some dry kindling with his knife.

A loud snap of dried undergrowth drew Nu's eyes upward. He saw nothing until an earsplitting bellow came from the direction of the pine trees and the playing child. *Not again! Oh please, E'Yahavah, not this time!*

The boy cowered by a tree trunk, sheltered by a meager spread of branches. Towering over him, its maw filled with bristle cones, the furious gryndel tried to shake its teeth free of the sticky splinters.

Nu clenched his utility knife between his teeth, and lunged toward the wurm before he could even think.

The beast, occupied with purging its mouth of the pine twigs, did not notice the puny man that scrambled beneath its shadow.

Just at the height of A'Nu-Ahki's face, the gryndel's tiny arm-claws flailed uselessly. What followed took place in an instant.

Nu clasped the nearest claw, and tried to bend it backward the way his father had done in the dream up on Seti's Sphinx.

The thing would not budge.

Nor could he gain the footing necessary to offer enough leverage to use his full strength. He bet Lumekki could have, though; but as always, he was far from being Lumekki! Then he realized that his father was no taller than he was; that only height could give him that kind of advantage. His moment—and his life—were now up.

Great! Fooled by a dream that paints my father bigger than life!

"Quit whining!" said a silent voice from somewhere beyond the inner reaches of Nu's mind. *"If I had put you in the dream as the dragon-slayer, you would not have taken it seriously! Do what you know to do!"*

The gryndel now knew of his presence—in that one place where its jaws and mighty tail could not reach. Before the dragon could react, Nu clamped his arms around the beast's armlet, pulled his legs up, wrapping them rope-climber style around its other mating-claw, and held on.

The beast began to bird-hop around the camp glade, trying to shake him loose. Neck-jarring pain seared down Nu's spinal cord, as cold scales made gravel-paper against his skin. He bent his right arm around the gryndel's left claw, snaking his forearm in to clasp the monster's twitching limb at its base. *Hop! Thud! Rattle! Jab!* He applied pressure to the armlet's artery with his thumb. *Snap! Buckle!* This freed up Nu's left arm—almost.

A coiling spin almost shook A'Nu-Ahki loose. The wurm, no doubt hoping to smash its tormentor off, rammed him instead into a cushioning tree that allowed him the split second needed to get a better grip.

With Nu's legs now locked like a vice, the gryndel could no longer move its right arm-claw either. By now, A'Nu-Ahki's one-armed snake-hold on the left armlet had cut off its circulation completely, making it easier to free up his own left arm to pull the utility knife from between his teeth. He eyed the soft yellow hide underneath the beast's weakening arm—the one area of its body not covered in scale armor—one of two places where blood steadily engorged itself because of the blocked flow to the armlets.

Nu leaned his right shoulder in toward the gryndel's torso, learning now to ride the thrashing, and take advantage of its increasingly predictable cadence. A blur of faces swept by— Muhet'Usalaq and the Dragon-slayers with spears aloft, as though none of them dared to get close enough to jab.

A'Nu-Ahki drew back his arm and struck.

The spray of hot pressurized blood in his face almost blasted him from his hold, when the knife dove deep into the gryndel's side. A howl broke from the monster's snapping jaws, and it nearly rolled over into a coiling mass on the ground to crush its stinging antagonist. It must have stopped short only because it caught sight of other man-creatures moving in with their terrible needle-sticks. Surely, the gryndel knew by instinct that if they struck at its vitals while it rolled on the ground, it might not have the strength needed to stand up again and face them.

A'Nu-Ahki drew back his knife and struck again.

This time something sinuous gave way, and another gush of blood, darker but less pressurized, surged down the gryndel's side. The ostrich-snake dance steadily slowed. It became harder for Nu to grip the arm-claw because of the lubrication from the creature's life fluid. He felt the wurm's breath growing labored as it stumbled and almost fell on top of him.

He drew back his blade for another plunge. This time he thrust it so far in that some spasm of the gryndel's deep torso musculature sucked it clean from his grasp. The motion must have severed another major artery, perhaps the one that led up into the creature's neck.

The wurm staggered like a drunken man, slippery in its own redness. Nu dropped from his hold and landed between two wobbly three-taloned feet. They supported pillars of iron-bone about to cave in on themselves and him. Remembering the escape route taken by his father in the dream, he scrambled between the legs, and rolled into some ferns as far out of range of the tail as he could reach in one leap.

For a long moment, the gryndel simply stood there, its life flow draining out, as if in disbelief that something as insignificant as a man could take down the matriarch of wurms.

None of the Dragon-slayers dared thrust a spear, as if by doing so a sacred moment in the history of their order would somehow be defiled.

The gryndel wobbled once then staggered sideways toward the spearmen, who leaped away at its approach. It made one last effort to right itself, but it had simply lost too much blood too quickly.

The beast crashed to earth right on top of the fire pit where its slayer had thought to brew tea.

Nobody made a cheer. Nobody made a sound.

Nu crawled from the ferns drenched in blood and caked in dirt. Slowly, in a reverential procession, the Dragon-slayers surrounded him with their spears held aloft in solemn military salute—all but one.

Henumil stood off, a scowl twisting his huge face, while his spear stuck in the ground with a contemptuous wobble.

The circle broke to admit their Zaqen, who walked over to A'Nu-Ahki, and saluted his grandson as a junior salutes a senior. Then he reached down his hand to give Nu a lift up.

"In the history of Seti's Brotherhood, no man, even on an armored tricorn mount, much less armed with only a utility knife, has ever taken down such a gryndel!" Muhet'Usalaq said. "Truly we have had among us the greatest Dragon-slayer of all time, and we have not esteemed him!"

The company of Seti's Brotherhood broke into delirious cheers, and repeated salutes with weapons presented front.

A'Nu-Ahki's conscience howled, *This isn't right!*

He understood their need to vent. Nevertheless, he held up his hands to ward off their adulation. "No! You don't understand!"

The cheering subsided to a confused murmur. A'Nu-Ahki noticed that even Henumil in the shadows perked up to hear what he had to say.

"This thing is of El-N'Lil! You all know me—I'm a lousy hunter! I couldn't spear a behemoth at ten paces..."

The spearmen and Muhet'Usalaq began to object loudly.

Nu saw that things were getting out of hand. Joy should have flooded his senses with vindication. Instead, the cheers of his kinsmen screeched in his ears like a cacophony of locusts while the mist-shrouded earth wheeled sideways into a twisted nightmare. Then he remembered the saged example of their great leader, Iyared. "Shut up all of you! Listen to me and use your heads!"

The company rumbled to a perplexed silence. They were his to command, but he had never wanted to command them. Now that he had their attention, the surreality of the situation snapped him up, as the wurm should have done. Nu stammered out his first few words. "Up on Seti's Sphinx, when I went to meet Father Urugim, I-I had a dream.

"In that vision, I saw my father kill a gryndel in a way similar to what happened just now—he twisted off one of the creature's mating armlets and it ruptured a major artery. I hadn't the strength or leverage to twist anything, but the dream showed me where I might strike to sever a main blood vessel. Think! I saw this in a dream sleeping under the Great Sphinx! E'Yahavah told me what to do! I can't take honor for that kind of work. Look at my past field record! What Henumil says I should have done up in the gorge is true, though not what he says about my lineage…"

A'Nu-Ahki instantly knew that mentioning Henumil was a mistake, but the words were already out. The saluting Dragon-slayers now turned to face the big hunter, and began to murmur against him whom they had believed without question until just a gryndel kill ago.

"The gryndel was only a whelp!" Henumil shouted, as he pushed through the circle formed around A'Nu-Ahki.

Muhet'Usalaq turned on the big hunter, and struck him across the face with the back of his hand, as he would a mouthy child. Henumil raised his fist, but stopped himself before striking back.

Muhet'Usalaq stared Henumil down with heavy-browed eyes that carried the authority of over six centuries and a seer's spirit. "I grant you pardon, only because of the loss your brother suffered up in the gorge. Any novice can see that this wurm was entering its prime. And another thing," he added. "You have been spreading ugly rumors about A'Nu-Ahki's lineage—rumors that should have died centuries ago! I am the one who went to Paru'Ainu and got the story on A'Nu-Ahki straight from the mouth of a holy Kherub. Have you ever seen a Kherub, Henumil?"

"No sire." The hunter grimaced, rubbing his face.

"You would not forget one if you had. But since I am an eyewitness and you are not, I suggest you keep your wagging tongue in its mouth! Maybe you from Sa-utar have not heard? In my court, tale-bearing carries a heavy penalty of restitution—and I am one of the few Zaqenar who is not afraid, at need, to employ the death penalty for treason."

The others began to murmur the word uneasily under their breath.

Their Elder continued, "None of you are unaware of the prophecy spoken about A'Nu-Ahki by Iyared before he died. This man is A'Nu's Comfort! I do not think our highest earthly authority would choose the son of a fallen Watcher to carry the cask of Atum-Ra! I trust this matter is closed."

Henumil looked down and stood at attention, though he spoke through clenched teeth in the Formal Voice; "I ask forgiveness, my Father, and did not intend treason. It was but grief and the heat of the moment."

"Then we shall speak no more of it," commanded the Zaqen, who then turned to the others listening on. "And neither shall any of you!"

They saw the sentinel three days after A'Nu-Ahki killed the gryndel.

The watchman stood atop a large rock, where the river, having run due west for most the day, turned suddenly northward on its alluvial plane and emptied into a wide lake. He called out for them to enter the lake and make directly for its opposite shore, where a thorn-enclosed camp awaited.

It took the rest of the day to paddle across, each moment of which was an eternity for Nu. Would Emzara be there to meet him? He had not recognized the sentinel, and had been afraid to ask him—or had he simply been afraid of the answer?

The nightmare of Emzara's blood gushing in rivers from her throat haunted, but also prepared him for the worst. Since the gryndel dream had come true, there seemed no reason to think that the vision of his wife's corpse would prove any less so.

Since learning of Salaam-Surupag's fall Nu had quietly repeated to himself that he would meet Emza again, if only in the restored Orchard after the end of the world. But the whispered words came each time as crunching ashes on his tongue, which froze like water-cooled lead at seeing the sentry.

Without a body or a witness to a body, there would always be the nagging doubt that maybe she existed somewhere in forced prostitution to some Samyaza giant. Also without knowing, there could always be hope that somehow only the gryndel part of his dream was inspired, and the other a mere accident of stress. After the sarcophagus boat passed the sentinel, Nu cursed his own inability to decide whether to prolong his ordeal with the demon of not knowing, face the demon of knowing, or worse yet to discover the demon that there was no longer any way to know.

Sunset maroons bathed the lake, as beast fires guided the tiny fleet to rest. The acolytes pulled his boat onto the beach, just as Nu saw the heavyset silhouette of his father standing against a backdrop of flames.

Lumekki embraced Muhet'Usalaq first, and exchanged a few hushed words before he turned to his son.

The moment rushed with the blood from Nu's head in that last second of hopeful ignorance. Pain glimmered with the refracted fires in his father's eyes. It told him all he needed to know before Lumekki spoke.

"Emza's dead, isn't she?"

His father looked down. "Yes, son. I take full responsibility."

A'Nu-Ahki had prepared himself for this, but it struck him like a blow to the diaphragm anyway. Then the relief of knowing — ultimately the lesser of his three demons — brought forth tears like a cleansing waterfall out of Aeden. His ordeal had been too long and exhausting for anything other than the brokenness of acceptance to come along and claim him like an orphaned waif on life's battlefield. At least he knew she was gone. There would be no haunting. Healing would come someday, but not today.

When Nu composed himself, he laid a hand on his father's shoulder and said, "You couldn't know the Samyaza Cult was coming. The best intelligence you had told you to expect an assault from the west."

Lumekki shook his head near hard enough to snap his own neck. "So like a fool, when I heard the first alarm horn, I rallied the women and children to the eastern escape routes without confirming the direction of the sighting! My scouts on the west road had not reported in, so I figured they'd been captured or killed in a rapid self-propelled chariot advance..."

"Pahpo, it's not your fault..."

"I thought the direction of that first alarm horn sounded wrong! I could have confirmed it! By the time word reached my headquarters that the invaders were to the east and not west, it was already too late. I had sent them like trusting sheep into the mouth of the dragon!"

"Father, you couldn't have known..."

"It was my job to know! Based on our assumption that Lumekkor and Khavilakki were attacking, I knew it would not take long for them to surround the city with their self-propelled siege engines, and that it would be a race for our people to reach the forest cover. The plan had been for them to march into a deserted city. Instead, the Samyaza giants charged into a melee of unarmed women and children!"

The Tacticon spoke with an accustomed military detail with little attempt to spare Nu's sensibilities. In fact, Lumekki seemed to be trying to provoke his son's anger—perhaps out of self-punishment. Nu understood his father too well to let him succeed. *I will not make that mistake again!*

"How do you know Emzara and the girls were not captured?"

The Old Soldier sighed. Nu had never imagined what defeat could do to a man like Lumekki—the beaten dullness in his eyes, the slouch of his back, and even the smell of distilled liquor on the breath of a man who hardly ever drank wine, much less while in the field.

"I led a force through the northern forest rim southeastward to try and outflank the titans, but found that more of them were crossing the river with a well-guarded supply line. Any attempt to break through would have stalled into a pitched battle where my light infantry would have been outnumbered ten to one by at least two divisions of heavy tricorn, and four of medium unicorn cavalry.

"There were five more infantry divisions of Assurim Regulars coming over the river, not to mention the elite Titan's Guard. I pulled back, and made a sortie closer to the city walls, where they had rounded up some captive women. I hoped at least to free some of them in the confusion.

"We lost over a thousand men in the attempt—more than half of what remained of my army. All of your sons except Arrakan fell there, Nu. We almost broke through, until a company of Titan Elites reinforced the Assurim Regulars who left to guard the captured women.

"It became a rout! I could barely hold my van together for an orderly retreat, and none of my flanking units managed even that much. If the forest cover had been any farther away, none of us would have made it out alive.

"It was during the retreat that I noticed Emzara's body propped against the city walls with an arrow in her throat—at least she died quickly, Nu. At her feet was your mother, also dead, with three of your married daughters—two were Ziraha and Dolerna, but the third had her face half turned, and I wasn't sure if it was Khella or Qaransa. I'm sorry, but we couldn't risk going near enough to the wall to find out, nor to give them a decent burial. The ramparts had fallen, and we were still within bow shot as it was. It was a miracle I even saw them among so many dead."

Nu was strangely detached now from his grief. He listened to his father's account as if the family destroyed in it belonged to a stranger. His healer's training told him distantly that this was merely shock. Yet his mind became disturbingly clear and morbidly fixated on details.

Lumekki continued, "We managed to regroup in the forest after nightfall. From there, we continued to make commando raids for several days afterward on their supply line. But the giants eventually found our main base and wiped out all but about three hundred of my remaining men, who were out on a mission with me at that time. This happened during the night while Arrakan and I—did I tell you, Nu, how bravely he fought?—led a force to try one last time to reach the women.

"For some reason—probably just to provoke us—the giants kept them in pens outside the city like cattle, within sight of the forest edge…" Tears streamed from his eyes, as his voice became a strangled croak. "They would rape them in the open, knowing we watched from the tree line. We could never have hoped to free them if they'd been kept in the city, but that was what they wanted—for us to grow angry enough to try!

"We did try! That night, we smeared ourselves with black mud to blend in with the earth. Swords sheathed, we crawled forward along the decline that parallels the east city wall. We came out to a distance of just fifty paces or so from the nearest pen, where we took out most of the nearest guards silently with our bowmen firing horizontally from the defile. I then gave the hand signal to crawl up and charge in silence.

"We were able to free the fifty or so women kept in the nearest pen before the alarm sounded. Arrakan was just about to take down the guards at the second pen's gate, but he didn't make it. Took an arrow in the stomach, he did—though a couple of his men carried him out of there. We made it back to the forest with minimal losses, militarily speaking, of course, thankful we'd been able to free as many women as we had. Arrakan told me he saw two of his sisters in the other pens—the ones we couldn't get to. I don't know which two. He died before he could say their names.

"When we found our base camp destroyed, we fell back to the 'Leviathan' supply cache we had established many months ago up in the mountains to the north. We picked up a few more stragglers in the woods, including a dozen Girl's Academy maidens led by my mother, who had left by the north forest gate rather than the east quarter because it was closer to the academy. I suppose there may have been other refugees in the woods, but we could not afford to wait around any longer to gather them.

"After we reached the cache, we packed as much of it as we could carry and took the mountain trail north to Akh'Uzan. There I fortified the ruins of the old monastery, and laid an ambush on both sides of the pass into the Gihunu Valley. Then, leaving most of my men at the monastery, I marched east and established this camp to wait for you.

"News of Iyared's death had reached us even before the fall of the city, so we surmised that you would take the most direct route from Paru'Ainu rather than risk capture in occupied Seti. I figured you would try to keep as close to the original plan as was still practical and that it would be our best chance of meeting up again. So here I am, for what it is worth."

A'Nu-Ahki embraced his father. "It's worth everything to me! I see not failure in you. Even while you were nowhere near, you were used by E'Yahavah to save our lives—mine especially." He went on to tell Lumekki of the dream on Seti's Sphinx, and of the slaying of the gryndel. Muhet'Usalaq nodded along, and embellished whatever Nu under-told.

Lumekki placed his arms around both his father and his son. "Come, let us rest around the fires, and drink some tea. Tomorrow we march back to Akh'Uzan for a meeting with some army officers from Sa-utar. There's another bit of dark news I still have to drop on you."

"What now?" Muhet'Usalaq said.

"A rider came into camp yesterday with word that Lumekkor and Khavilakki have halted Samyaza's advance. Sa-utar is joining forces with them to keep Assuri bottled up in the lower Gihunu Valley."

Nu said, "That could be worse."

"There's just one thing," added his father, hesitating again.

Muhet'Usalaq said, "What is the catch?"

Lumekki scowled. "Tubaal-qayin Dumuzi has offered to let Seti keep its autonomy on condition of treaty sealed by a politically arranged marriage. Otherwise, he's got forces already in place to make us his vassal."

"So one of Adiyuri's sons marries a woman of Qayin—they do that all the time in his house anyway," Muhet'Usalaq said.

"The Emperor of Lumekkor wants no man from Adiyuri."

"What are you talking about?"

Lumekki's eyes reflected the blaze from one of the beast fires. "The Dynasty of Steel wants a union with the Seer Clan—and not just with any young buck. They've specified he be a full-aged man of Q'Enukki's direct lineage with the prophetic gift."

This is what the men of the generation of the flood used to do —
each would take to himself two wives, one for procreation and
the other for sexual pleasure. The one for procreation was
almost like a widow, though her husband was still alive; while
the one for sexual pleasure was made by her husband to
swallow a cup of root-drink so that she would not conceive. She
sat in his house painted like a harlot... You can readily see that
it was so, for even Lemech, the best among that generation,
took two wives — Adah, 'apart from (scorned by) him;' and
Tzillah, 'who dwelt in his shadow (was inseparable from
him).'"

—Rabbi Azariah,
in the name of Rabbi Yehudah bar Shimon
A Midrash in the *Jerusalem Talmud*
(circa 400 AD)

9

DYNASTY

The work of Lumekki's refugees to fortify the old mountainside monastery at Akh'Uzan impressed A'Nu-Ahki, not only in the quick repair of the ramparts, but for the care given to the comforts of life inside. These came though the rescued women under the direction of Muhet'Usalaq's wife Edina, whom everyone fondly called "Mamu."

Nu marveled that even a massacre could not change her much. As he passed into the courtyard, he saw the plump pixie of a woman somehow still doing what she always did—pestering some poor minion of her husband's into taking a break to eat whatever happened to be her confection of the day.

"The trowel can wait ten minutes for you to eat some sweet cakes," Mamu said, as she yanked the tool from the lad's hand and threw it away.

"But the Zaqen wants this wall in by tonight!"

"Nonsense, you leave the old tyrant to me. You have been troweling since before dawn—trowel, trowel, trowel—now you need a bite. Now do not make me sit on you and force these cakes down your throat."

A'Nu-Ahki laughed for the first time in weeks. "Better listen to her, son; she's done it to larger men than you."

"Nu!" Mamu thrust the basket of raisin cakes into the mason's hand and ran to her grandson with a charging hug.

"I'm so glad they didn't get you," he whispered into her embrace.

"Oh better they had gotten me a thousand times than your wife and daughters and all those young girls and children who never had a chance to live. Your grandfather has not even stopped to sleep. When did you arrive?"

"Late—after midnight, I think. I see Pahpi's already riding the workers. Say, what's the story on these officers from Sa-utar?"

Mamu shrugged. "Do they ever tell me anything?"

"Since when have they ever had to? You have your ways of wheedling information."

"So! You think your old Mamu is a sneak?"

"In a good way."

"You are right!" She cackled. "Sneaky like a Sphinx! And do not forget it. Those two are from the Archon's Elite Guard—intelligence division, I would guess. They talk nice and polite, as if they want something very badly from us. Watch yourself, Nu. Do not be taken in. Whatever they are up to, it smells of Adiyuri."

"I think I know what they want, and I may already be caught in the fowler's snare." Nu didn't elaborate on his meaning. *What does it matter now? My Sunrise is dark and our children dead or in hopeless captivity! I want to blame Pahpi, but I just don't have the will or the strength for the rage — or anything else. What does E'Yahavah want from me, anyway?*

Mamu said, "They are not even giving you a chance to mourn." The twinkle in her eye told him she knew more than she let on. "May E'Yahavah watch over you and protect you, then. The men are waiting for you in the hearth hall. Keep your words few, lad. Do not volunteer for anything!"

A'Nu-Ahki patted her on the shoulder. He wished he really had the option of taking her advice. He left her and entered the hall where the two officers waited with his clan elders.

A fire snapped in the great hearth that faced A'Nu-Ahki at the other end of the lodge from the newly refurbished doors. On either side, holding open the heavy timber planks, stood two young infantry regulars in dress kilts of bright maroon and gray.

Army stewards served drinks around the long stone table where the two officers and the three remaining clan elders of Q'Enukki reclined—the Prime Zaqen, Lumekki, and Tarkuni the eldest son of Urugim.

In that same room Muhet'Usalaq had parted from his father for the last time many centuries before, only now the roofing smelled of fresh cut pine instead of moldering thatch—the new Archon had sent carpenters to help with the renovation.

The Prime Zaqen motioned his grandson to a cushion at his left hand by the table's head. Lumekki reclined at the right, followed by Tarkuni. The army men sat next to Nu.

At a wave from the senior officer, the sentries closed the doors and turned the dead bolt lock. "I am Arch-Straticon Zendros, of the Uvardenic Clan, a Dragon-slayer of the twelfth order. My associate is Sub-Straticon D'Narri, Clan Axernis, ninth order, for those of you who just arrived this morning. My best wishes to all of you, and special honor to the Dragon-slayer, who single-handedly took down that gryndel." He looked straight at Nu.

"An act of E'Yahavah," A'Nu-Ahki said in a clipped tone that communicated too firmly that he was tired of hearing about it.

The Arch-Straticon's eyes fell, as if bewildered at such a negative attitude from a Dragon-slayer, but he let it drop.

Muhet'Usalaq cleared his throat. "We understand the son of Tubaal-qayin wishes a politically arranged wedding between one of his daughters and a son of the Seer. Seti's autonomy would seem to rest in the balance."

The Arch-Straticon appeared equally unused to such directness. "Not one of his daughters," he said. "Tubaal-qayin the Fifth 'Dumuzi' has no children. He pledges the very sister of his Patriarch—first of the Tubaal-qayin name. She is a virgin—once betrothed, but never married."

Lumekki said, "You want to marry one of our boys off to a hag?"

Tarkuni roared. "Unacceptable!"

The officer laughed. "No, no, you misunderstand. Though Princess Na'Amiha is daughter of L'Mekku by the same wife who bore the first son of the Steel Dynasty, she is from her mother's final cycle—younger than our gryndel killer here. She is the child of L'Mekku's old age. Her mother died birthing her. Tubaal-qayin the First was the son of their youth."

Muhet'Usalaq frowned. "Still, L'Mekku has been dead a long time."

"That is why they request a suitor of full age…"

A'Nu-Ahki said, "Who has the Seer's Gift."

"Correct. The wedding is set for after the first of the year."

Lumekki leaned back into his cushion. "There are less than a handful who qualify and even some of them are questionable. Until recently, all of them were married."

Arch-Straticon Zendros shrugged. "Even in the court of Sa-utar it is a debated issue as to what constitutes a seer's gift."

Muhet'Usalaq said, "Not so here."

"As you wish; I do not pretend to be an expert in such matters."

"Well I am," said the Prime Zaqen. "And the suggestion that a seer of E'Yahavah be married off to some woman of Qayin, who lies before heaven-only-knows-what, is a serious matter indeed!"

"So is our national crisis."

The second military official, D'Narri, nodded at Lumekki. "And your tribal one, seeing as you are not more than a week's march north of the current battle lines here." The man apparently recognized Nu's father as an ex-army hero who could appreciate the tactical situation.

Muhet'Usalaq flipped the back his hand at D'Narri. "The Archon is under oath to defend this place come what may."

Zendros spread his palms up on the table. "An oath he has every intention of honoring—but one which he will not be in power to honor if we are forced into thralldom. At least with Adiyuri in charge of an autonomous Sa-utar you will be free from obligated military service and guaranteed military protection for whatever holy work the Fathers have entrusted to you. Under Lumekkor, you have no such assurances and in all probability can count on the taking of this fortress as a fall-back position for Dumuzi's army. They will send you all packing like beggars without a thought."

Lumekki said, "Not without a fight."

"True enough," agreed Sub-Straticon D'Narri. "You will make them pay dearly for this place, Lumekki. Not only is it defensible, but I know of your war record as First Tacticon at Zhri'Nikkor. For every man you lose, they shall lose ten—even with their superior weapons, most of which they could not bring up the narrow trail from the valley. But for every ten, they have a thousand more! In the end, you will sell yourselves dearly, only to be slaughtered to the last man, woman, and child. I believe you've seen enough of that at Regati and Salaam-Surupag to want more of it here."

A'Nu-Ahki's father hung his head, apparently unable to dislodge the army officer's logic twisting its dagger in his vitals.

A pall of silence settled over the hall.

A'Nu-Ahki gazed sullenly down at the table and saw two wheat kernels probably left from some recent meal—two insignificant mites.

The Silence invaded the room like a pressurized fluid that seemed to expand inside to quell the noises of the outer court. A voice whispered two words from somewhere in the stone crack shadows—a tiny breath of wind from nowhere and everywhere gave Nu its sound—two words in the same voice he recognized as having spoken only two words to him once before, up on the Sphinx, where the Kherub had said, *"Peace, friend."*

It said, *"Two seeds,"*

Nu did not need to look up to know that none of the others had spoken. He knew now what E'Yahavah wanted of him. With his life in shambles and nearly everything that had lent convention to his existence destroyed, he did not hesitate. For a second he almost allowed himself the delusion of feeling noble for what he was about to do. Then he realized the truth and with it came freedom.

He laid his hands, palms up, on the table. "I have walked with E'Yahavah, though not as closely as some. I've had visions on the lap of Seti's Sphinx and seen the face of a Kherub and the light of the Fire-Sphinx's sword. I can predict where things are going from here. I suppose that qualifies me as a seer by most definitions…"

Muhet'Usalaq shouted, "Nu, shut your mouth!"

"Not this time!"

Lumekki's eyes pleaded with him. "Son, she'll take you down! This smells of Avarnon-Set! He's trying to create a gateway for Uzaaz'El right into our very midst!"

Tarkuni hissed, "You will betray the Work!"

"What is left of the Work to betray? I've lost my wife and all my children, with their children! I know what I'm doing and it does not betray the spirit of our labors!"

Tarkuni's eyes burned, unconvinced, but he retreated behind a wall of silence. He no doubt still smarted from the Prime Zaqen's warning to his grandson Henumil about A'Nu-Ahki's office.

Muhet'Usalaq said, "You can find a wife among Seti's children."

"Like I'm looking for a wife here? I'd be a real catch as a beggar in a land of slaves! And how does marrying within Seti further the Seer's Work, anyway? The children of Seti play whore with the Watchers nowadays as easily as Qayin's daughters do! No! There are two major branches of Atum-Ra's race and it was the Seer's original objective to reach them both."

The two elders over Nu bowed their heads in resignation, knowing this was true, but Tarkuni scowled.

A'Nu-Ahki said, "I will marry this Na'Amiha on one condition."

Now Zendros interrupted, "We are hardly in position to make demands of the Dynasty of Steel."

Nu shouted, slamming his cup on the table, "Nevertheless, I make this demand! You don't impress me, Straticon, because I have one thing going that not you, the Archon, nor the Dumuzi can match!"

Zendros narrowed his eyes. "What might that be?"

Nu leaned into the man's face and grinned; he somehow sensed that his own eyes had become dead smoky glass. "I don't care." He said the words softly as an arid breeze from the wastelands of Nhod. "Never forget that, Straticon. I don't care if the World-end of flame consumes you and everyone in Sa-utar now. I don't care if it blasts us as we sit here this second. So you will hear my demand or I will laugh while Lumekkor strips you naked and the bloody Archon with you. Are we clear on that?"

The Straticon's face had turned to ash.

Nu smiled as he cracked his knuckles. "Now then, I will marry this Na'Amiha only if she renounces whatever gods she serves, and swears fealty to E'Yahavah in the heavens alone—not to the Archon, as in the old days—just to E'Yahavah A'Nu."

The two officers exchanged distressed glances.

"It holds no political implications. It is a spiritual matter only—the technocrats of Bab'Tubila will see it as a trifle we are using to save face. They trust to their machines. I hear that even their traffic with Uzaaz'El isn't so much a religious thing. It will be a meaningless word game to them."

"What of the woman?" Muhet'Usalaq said. "Will she also see it as a meaningless word game?"

"She will see what E'Yahavah has given her to see. This thing, like the gryndel, is of the A'Nu Eluhar – a sign of our times."

"And each sign gets darker than the last!" Lumekki growled, as he got up and left the chamber.

Urugim's son followed him. However, Tarkuni turned at the door, and said, "Tell us, O Seer of A'Nu's Comfort, what is the next sign? Shall we be called upon to marry our sons and daughters off to the beasts of the field and then watch them rut in the meadows?"

Pavilions filled the upper valley floor, watched over by the rebuilt monastery-fortress of Akh'Uzan, which sat like an ornament of princely rank on the shoulder of Mount N'Zar – Q'Enukki's ancient place of sacrifice.

Parading infantry and armored cavalry – both the old-fashioned "ceremonial" tricorn quasi-dragons and the sluggish new self-propelled monstrosities being used in the war against Assuri – dazzled the spectators and wedding guests with colored ensigns and mock demonstrations of military might designed for more than mere entertainment. They made a statement: *Sa-utar is autonomous, but only as far as its chain, forged in Bab'Tubila, the City of Metal-smiths, will stretch.*

Three of the principle men in the day's festivities stood by one of the great war machines currently not in use on the parade field.

Tubaal-qayin Dumuzi "The Shepherd" hardly seemed the demigod A'Nu-Ahki had expected. Thin and slightly shorter than most men, with pale skin, light red hair, and a sparse beard that gave him an almost satyr-like quality, he had a squawky voice that grated the nerves if it went on too long. Unfortunately, the young Emperor seemed to love to hear himself talk, especially once Lumekki and A'Nu-Ahki had shown grudging interest in the new military hardware.

"Armor plating an eighth of a standard cubit thick around the belt and a tenth overhead," the Metalsmith-king said, rattling off the dimensions of the strange contraption. It resembled a house-sized, self-propelled ziggurat of steel with a rotating wedge on top.

The wedge housed what Nu recognized as a cannon barrel. In front and back and along the center of the rolling band treads Tubaal-qayin called "millipedes," bristled smaller gun barrels.

"What's that thing on top?" Lumekki said, pointing to the wedge-shaped chunk of metal.

The Emperor answered, "The main cannon."

"I know that! I mean the wedge it's sitting in?"

"Oh. That's a rotating turret. The cannon swivels any direction, and elevates to a seventy degree angle. The *Behemoth* commander need waste no time maneuvering into firing position if he comes under attack. The main gun fires a cylindrical exploding shell with a conical head—smoothed out for less air resistance. We call them 'thunder-darts,' after the thermal air rumbles of the high mountains. The secondary cannons below still fire the old rounded shot—that'll change on the new model though."

"But what makes it run on its own?"

Tubaal-qayin slapped his knee and laughed—a hacking bray from a nasally impaired donkey. "As an old soldier, you're gonna love this! It runs on the same thing armies have always run on— grain spirits!"

"Liquor?"

Tubaal-qayin grinned. "Burns it in a special engine—but any more detail than that is a family trade secret."

A'Nu-Ahki only half listened to the little satyr's explanations. Normally, he would have been almost as fascinated by all the machinery as his father, but today he would meet Na'Amiha for the first time. This consumed him with all sorts of nasty possibilities. *Great E'Yahavah, please don't let her look like a little Tubaal-qayin! I don't think I could deal with losing Emzara only to be forced to marry the Goat Princess!*

Nu said, "Hadn't we better be getting to the banquet tent?"

"Quite right," said the Emperor. "Mustn't keep the bride waiting."

A'Nu-Ahki reluctantly appreciated how Dumuzi the Shepherd had conducted himself thus far; not as an overlord but an equal, when he clearly had it in his power to do otherwise. Lumekki trailed the other two, still thrilled to envy by the military hardware.

A'Nu-Ahki took the opportunity to speak with the Metalsmith-king candidly. "I'm a bit surprised you didn't bring Avarnon-Set. He and Uggu are so big in your court. I'd have thought them high on the invitation list."

Tubaal-qayin shrugged. "The High Aunt—your bride, that is—forbade it. She seemed sure that their presence would offend your clan."

"She was right."

"Why do you dislike titans? I mean, there are some nasty ones, but there are many helpful ones too. We've learned much from their fathers."

The question seemed honest enough. A'Nu-Ahki felt it deserved a straightforward answer. "You're the one who wants a seer of E'Yahavah in your family. Are you prepared to hear what such a seer has to say on that?"

"Well, actually, this was not my idea. Na'Amiha herself brought it up on her own and suggested it to Avarnon-Set, which is strange if you ask me, since she and Avarnon-Set hate each other. Then the two of them together sold me. I can see the benefit of a seer's insight here and there, plus I think the people of Seti will fight on my team more readily if they get to keep their own political leaders and military infrastructure in place."

Nu raised one eyebrow.

Dumuzi continued, "Frankly, though, I think your bride played our good titan for the fool. She convinced him that having you as husband would bring the Seer Clan under his power, for whatever that's worth. But if you knew her like I do, A'Nu-Ahki, you'd realize that's the last thing she'd want. If anything, I bet she's counting on you to influence me into clearing my court of the titans altogether and to stop communing with the Powers—though I have to be fair and tell you, that's not likely."

How does this little blabbermouth trust himself with his own state secrets? Nu wondered. *Or is he just playing me to see how I'll respond?* "Tell me," he said, "why would Na'Amiha want you to reject the titans?"

"Can't figure." The little Goat Emperor shrugged.

Nu began to see this as his defining gesture, a noncommittal twitch of his shoulders, which was either a convincing subterfuge or evidence that Tubaal-qayin Dumuzi really meandered through life clueless.

"Granted, we came up with the engines that drive things like that *Behemoth* back there on our own, but there are other things—things in the Temple laboratories—that it would have taken us centuries to discover without Uzaaz'El' guidance. He never seems to give us anything more than what he thinks we have the social maturity to handle. I wish he would be more forthright with his knowledge — especially now."

Nu said, "Yet, you don't worship his kind as gods like most tribes?"

"Why should we, when he's told us plainly that he isn't? The only reason we still use words like 'priest' and 'the Temple' in connection with him is that they are leftover terms from a more primitive time — before we realized that we were simply dealing with intelligences that have been around a little longer than we have. Someday we'll encounter lesser minds than ourselves — perhaps like the wild men of the East who have Short-lifer's Syndrome — and we'll be to them what Uzaaz'El is to us: Gods at first, and later, as they grow out of social infancy, benevolent elder intellects."

"And where does your 'elder intellect' claim he comes from?"

Tubaal-qayin shrugged again. "He makes no claims at all. It's not as if I see him all that often or get to converse with him the way you and I are speaking right now. Frankly, the more Uzaaz'El keeps to the Temple, the better I like it. The Powers are unsettling to see and even worse to hear. It's much better to let the titans deal with them."

"What then do the titans claim for them?"

"They say that there were intelligences abroad in the universe before the Powers, and before those intelligences, other beings, and so on."

"You mean then that the cosmos had no real beginning?"

Dumuzi twitched his narrow shoulders. "None worth pondering."

"How can a nation of engineers believe that when the mathematics of Q'Enukki — who taught the physics your technology is based on to the first Tubaal-qayin — demonstrates that the spatial heavens and time itself had to have had a beginning point, and thus an ultimate Creator?"

"I didn't say the cosmos had no beginning, only that we don't think it's important, especially since this alleged creator of yours has made himself unknowable. What's of consequence to us is where the world is going."

"I don't think you're going to like a seer's answer to that one either," Nu said half to himself, as they entered the banquet tent.

A'Nu-Ahki's first impression of Na'Amiha was a bittersweet spring of mixed emotions. Thankfully, she was not the goat-lady. Yet even in her royal wedding garb, she came across as comfortably plain at best—thin, her feminine endowments given only in the most meager quantities, with strawberry blond hair, green eyes, and a slightly large, hawkish nose.

Tubaal-qayin's description of her hatred for Avarnon-Set and the Watchers tended to color her favorably in Nu's sight, if believable. He decided that, in time, he could learn to find her physically attractive enough—though a generous imagination would help. Right now, he was concerned with much more important matters—issues that would have been the same whether she had been as rare a beauty as Emzara or had galloped in like the goat princess of his worst fears.

When he reclined across from her at the table, he noticed how her eyes tended to dart about nervously at almost every sudden sound. He suddenly pitied her and was not completely sure why.

Tubaal-qayin Dumuzi, Adiyuri, and Muhet'Usalaq stood at the head of the table with joined hands lifted over their heads. The Emperor of the Dynasty of Steel chanted loudly enough to be heard throughout the large tent, "A'Nu-Ahki, son of Lumekki, son of Muhet'Usalaq, First of the Seer, I give you your bride! Claim her as your own, for she is Na'Amiha, daughter of L'Mekku, the First Emperor, and sister of my father, Tubaal-qayin the Great. Na'Amiha of Lumekkor, I give you to your husband, A'Nu-Ahki of the Seers!"

The entire pavilion cheered. To Nu their faces seemed strained, their noisy laughter like wails, as the merriment in their eyes poorly hid a terror beneath. People he had known all his life suddenly looked like strangers.

Nu turned to his new wife. When his face met Na'Amiha's fully for the first time, he did not see a temptress or a political manipulator; rather, a plain woman who searched his own face for something to hang her hopes on. But what were those hopes? Would they coincide at all with his?

Nu tried to give what those large emerald eyes—her most endearing feature—seemed to want. He smiled at her, hoping to quell her anxiety—whatever it was. She returned his smile then quickly glanced away, as if frightened by something he could not see. He looked around the tent, but noticed nothing threatening.

A'Nu-Ahki began to consider the possibility that Tubaal-qayin's comment about her might be true.

They did not get to talk together until after the banquet. Even then, Tubaal-qayin's chaperons hovered nearby, so they could not speak openly.

Nu felt like a 'tween-ager again. "Awkward, isn't it, talking for the first time like this?"

They stood outside the main tent, watching the sun sink into its magenta glory.

"I feel like a 'tween-ager all over again," she said, her accented voice huskier than he would have imagined or hoped.

"I was just thinking that."

That seemed to relieve some of her tension, but not all. Her eyes still darted furtively about.

"Is something the matter?"

Na'Amiha lowered her voice to a panicked whisper, "We'll talk later—the chaperons!" Then she added in an overly-loud voice for the sake of the listeners, "No, just having wedding jitters, I guess." She made the loudest, most obnoxious laugh Nu had ever heard from a woman.

A woman of Lumekkor unskilled at intrigue?

He tried to smile. "Don't worry on my account. I think you look stunning in your gown." It somehow felt like the worst lie he had ever told.

"Thank you." Na'Amiha smiled, and looked into his eyes. She seemed at that moment to find there something she liked. "I understand you recently lost a wife who was very dear to you, and that this wedding is more or less being forced on you. I'm truly sorry about that. I want you to know that I will try to be as good a wife to you as she was, and that I mean to learn your ways and keep to them as I have sworn."

Nu turned away and bit his tongue. *She thinks to replace Emza!* Then he realized that she had intended no offense, and forced his voice to soften before he opened his mouth. "No woman ... could ever replace Emzara, and I don't want you under the ... ah ... burden of feeling that you must try. But I ... ah ... appreciate the sentiment."

Stilted. Devoid of the passion that he had once known with the woman he now realized he would dream of for whatever remaining centuries he had. Nu suddenly understood that he would have to calculate expressions of kindness for this new wife rather than have them spring spontaneous from his heart—would need to manufacture military hardware gestures of tenderness as metal hammered into shape in the city of Na'Amiha's birth. He wondered how he would ever sleep with her on the following night without feeling that he slept with a strange woman—a political whore.

Great E'Yahavah, must you really preserve the line of Qayin?

The wedding ended at last. Its pavilion packed up; the caravans now made their way like a glutted snake down the valley to more populated lands.

The new couple was alone and unguarded for the first time.

A'Nu-Ahki had erected a tent further up the trail that climbed Mount N'Zar from the fortress, near the base of a small waterfall in a clearing that Q'Enukki had once called "Grove Hollow." The divan smelled of roses, wild flowers, and cinnamon. Hangings spoke of nuptial blessings. Yet he did not feel married to this woman. Neither of them seemed anxious to get on with the consummation. The last of the groom's men and bride's maids, who had helped set up and furnish the tent, had left only minutes before. Again, there seemed to be a layer of ice to break.

A'Nu-Ahki's curiosity would wait no longer. "Can you speak now of what troubles you?"

Moonlight bathed her face in pale golds. In the dimness, he found her almost appealing. The fear that still held her eyes captive brought out his instinct to protect her, and to eroticize that protection. He resisted the urge.

She said, "I need you to understand that I never meant to take advantage of you. When I plotted to escape the Powers, I knew there was only one place I could go. What I did not realize was how my plans would affect you personally."

"Any woman who seeks refuge from the Watchers has my sympathy. But you speak in riddles. How would you know to come here? And how could you convince Avarnon-Set, who suspects the spiritual protection we are under, that it would be to his benefit to allow you to come—especially since you two hate each other?"

"Oh, you know about that." Her eyes lost their luster.

"I really need to understand," he said, trying not to allow his tone to grow sharp. "I have no wish to mention any of this to my elders, but I need to understand it."

She glanced away from him. "I promised Avarnon-Set I would work to keep you all from making trouble in the Empire. I've kept my true feelings to myself for a long time in Lumekkor." She turned back to him with a wild intensity. "Don't worry, that's one promise I have no intention of keeping, so don't think ill of me. I was desperate! I had to get out of there!"

"Why?"

Na'Amiha laughed bitterly. "I'm two-hundred and fifty-two years old! Do you suppose they've never tried to marry me off before? I'm lucky I'm not as well endowed as most women—oh, you can stop pretending you haven't noticed! It's because of them – what you call the 'Watchers,' and what we call 'Powers' – they make you insane if they don't get what they want, and even more so when they do! Most don't find me that attractive, but because of my position, they never stop! They visit you in your dreams! They make things move without touching them! They touch you in the night!"

Nu said, "That must have been terrifying."

"They crowd you in your private chambers, invisible, when you're supposed to be alone, until you feel like you're naked in front of leering sailors all the time! They send Temple messengers asking your compliance! It never stops! I tried to arrange a wedding once, when I was young, to a man of your Archon's clan. I thought I could escape—Sa-utar was much more powerful back then—no offense."

"None taken. What happened?"

"Well, let's just say the match didn't work out."

"It had to have been more than that. At least this fellow would have been human, and you would have been free from the Temple of Ardis."

She gave a loud sour laugh. "Just barely! Do you know Tarbet?"

"Son of Rakhau, Line of Adiyuri—we've met."

"Do you know what he's like?"

"I know he's popular, and that he's a womanizer. I know he cares for nothing but power and prosperity."

"Then let's just leave it at that."

"Fair enough."

"You're probably wondering why I'm not enthralled with the Powers like most women of my clan."

"I was rather hoping you would get around to that."

She scrunched her face, an expression Nu suddenly found cute and girlish. "Where do I start?"

"Try the beginning."

"It's a long story. I'm sure you want to, well…"

"I can wait. I'm more interested in getting to know the woman I make love to before I make love to her."

She looked up at him from her pillow, and her face melted. "I'm so sorry! I didn't think I would find myself with a man as kind-hearted as you."

"We're not all beasts. Tell me your story. Then, if you like, I'll tell you mine. We have all night and many centuries afterward for everything else. Usually we have a long betrothal before we marry around here, but the national crisis and all…"

She smiled at him—this time her face glimmered in the moonlight with a cool radiance that Nu actually found naturally attractive.

"Okay. First, you already know I was the last child born to my father in his old age, and that my mother, Tzuillaeha, died giving birth to me. She had taken the concubine's root most of her life, after bearing Tubaal-qayin the Great when she was still quite young. She placed too much importance on her beauty, and all those centuries on the root weakened her health. I guess I take after my father in appearance—lucky you!" She gave a harsh snort, while her eyes took him backward with her in time.

"My mother paid steep for her illusion of youth. She went off the root in the end because she wanted a child in her old age. By then, pregnancy was too much for her. My father's first wife, Udaha, raised me. She, like me, was the daughter of her parents in their old age—her mother was the last direct offspring of Atum-Ra and Khuva.

"Udaha and L'Mekku had long been estranged, and she too was quite old when I came along. She had a heart for children, and loved me like her own. Though the sons of Tubaal-qayin would have little to do with her, her own children, especially those of her firstborn twins, Iya'Baalu and Iyu'Buuli—you met Sengrist, one of 'Baalu's chieftains, at the wedding—loved her dearly. I spent lots of time with them, especially after L'Mekku died when I was only ten. Udaha, being a direct grandchild of the Archronos, taught me about E'Yahavah, whom I know to be the Creator of all."

Nu cocked his head.

"Yes, that's right!" She giggled. "It must be hard to believe, but there is, after all, one of those pale-skinned, loose women among that wicked people you call 'the Qayinim' who actually follows E'Yahavah. It used to be there were more, but that was before I came along.

"One day, Udaha brought me into the library, where she kept copies of the scrolls of Atum-Ra, Seti, and some from Q'Enukki. She told me the true nature of the Watchers, and said that as long as I called on E'Yahavah, they could not touch me, though they could still frighten and harass.

"As I became a 'tween-ager, I saw with my own eyes how some women—some of them my close friends—died after being in the Temple fertility chambers. The priests and sometimes even the Powers themselves often just abducted girls barely of age—even from highborn families. The high clans tried to hide this from the commoners, but we in the court sometimes witnessed things most people wouldn't be allowed to see.

"Usually it was the priests that did all this, but I saw the Powers a few times in material form, once even in broad daylight—not just in my dreams or when I was only half awake in my chambers—all aglow like sickly gray death. Their black eyes contain bottomless hate when they look at you. It usually happened when I was by the Temple Pyramid, and just managed to peek inside. My friends who went inside saw more.

"Afterward many of these girls fell from strange diseases, some to madness, and others from what looked like beatings. The Temple priests would surgically implant things into their bodies—horrible things that seemed to have no other purpose but to cause pain and horror! I never knew if the surgeries had any reason beyond that. Usually those who died were girls of some depth—women who offered more than just well-rehearsed sex for the priests during rituals where the Powers somehow merged with them. That was how they did it most of the time.

"I think the Powers can only take material form for short times and with great effort. It is not their true nature. Mostly they manipulate open minds with hallucinations and false memories to fake having actual human relationships. They plant images and words in our thoughts to the point where it is hard to know what is and isn't real anymore. At least that's the impression my girl friends gave me. The toll it took on their personalities ruined them. Just the Powers sending messages to me left me unsure of reality. Please don't be shocked if you find I'm not quite sane."

She grinned and giggled with her teeth bared in a way that briefly reminded Nu of a starved wolf-hound. He tried not to shudder.

Na'Amiha continued, "I tried to warn my friends—but even most of my court playmates who had seen the same strange things I had, thought the Powers would enrich their lives. It's what they were told all their lives. The ones who lived through the ordeal of being ceremonially married to them always seemed to be the shallow worthless ones. They actually enjoyed it, or at least pretended to. And they could pretend pretty well. Sad to say, in a way, but they were the majority—so much so that stories of the others, with evidence so elaborately ignored, fell mostly on deaf ears.

"You can bet I called on E'Yahavah fast and hard, especially after I too began having dreams, and getting night messengers from Temple. But Udaha was right. When I called on the Divine Name, none of them could touch me. She was also right about how they could harass and intimidate. The never had me, though. Of that I am certain."

Her eyes sank into hollow circles. "Udaha died when I was thirty-two. Then the intimidation really started, while my will began to wear down. Sometimes I could actually see their dead-man hands in the night, and feel them touch me. They don't just touch the body, but the spirit. It makes you feel sick and helpless all over—like you really have no choice in the end.

"Several times I almost gave up hope when I would wake up to find them gathered around my bed with their big heads glowing down on me like pale gray moons. For a long time it became very hard to believe that I really did have a choice. Sometimes it's still hard. But when I felt their cold caresses, I would scream out for E'Yahavah again, and I guess he would remember me, and make them go away—for a time. The hardest thing I ever did was return to Bab'Tubila after my betrothal to Tarbet failed."

Her eyes narrowed, and her voice became cold steel. "I vowed not to give in! So I made myself like stone, and waited. I kept up with the world situation, and played whatever political games I had to—short of giving myself to the Powers—while I looked for my opportunity. I'm not proud of everything I did in those decades, least of all, in what I finally used as my gambit—when Salaam-Surupag fell, and this tragedy struck you and your clan. I'm so sorry!" Tears rolled down her cheeks and into her pillow, as she stared up at the tent top, as if afraid to look at him.

Nu gazed at her, his mind in the grip of strange epiphanies. He knew this was no act, though he didn't quite know how he knew for sure—she was certainly melodramatic enough to be playing on his sympathies. Maybe there was just something honest in her eyes. Honest and scary.

It is not to save the line of Qayin that E'Yahavah has done this to me. It's her! He just wants to rescue her!

He fought to keep himself from trembling with—was it rage, hope, bitterness, shock, awakening passion, or despair? *No! I can't do this!*

"You must do it. It is the only way," said an internal whisper that A'Nu-Ahki knew Na'Amiha could not hear.

But Emzara! Why my Emza?

"Good people go to Heh'Bul's Fields before their time. Did you imagine an exemption for Emza? You will see each other again."

But it hurts too much! Now this strange woman is in my bed! Her eyes! It's weird! What am I doing? How did I get here?

"I brought you here, and I will bring you through it."

Nu wanted to shout that it was not enough—that it could never be enough! His best friend—his Lady—the too-recent memory of a woman he found so intoxicating in ways that went infinitely deeper than mere physical attraction… The outrage was too much to face alone!

"But you are not alone. You will never be alone."

Then he saw Na'Amiha truly for the first time—vulnerable, frightened, and waiting nobly to suffer his wrath against all her brutal honesty. She shook as he did, if for different reasons.

She could never compete with Emzara, especially by the crass standards of mere sex—which Nu's body ached for more than he had been willing to admit. Yet this plain woman from Bab'Tubila somehow shared Emzara's deeper beauty—or at least something akin to it.

Nu peered into her eyes, and surprised himself that he was no longer angry—not at her, and even more strangely, not at E'Yahavah. *But can I ever really love her?* He wondered. Then it struck him that he was asking the wrong question. *How do I dare not to love her? She has to be highly prized for E'Yahavah to have worked on her behalf this way.*

He began to understand, if only a little. The love he would have for her would be something placed in him from above; tenderness from the heavens that did not originate from his own desire, though he knew desire would eventually come — was already approaching.

As if to prove to himself that he would not recoil from her, Nu gently slipped his arm around her. She suddenly did not seem so strange. He wiped away her tears with his finger.

When he went to kiss her, she stiffened like a corpse.

He drew back, and released her. "I'm sorry. I just want you to know that I accept you — from my heart. You never need fear them again."

"I should apologize to you. I am, after all, your wife."

He brushed her hair back, where it had stuck to the wetness on her face. "No, my mistake. I've been used to the familiarities of marriage a long time. My loss is still recent. I promised to tell you all about myself first."

"So tell me." She sniffed then laughed — not quite so loud this time. "What is it to be a seer?"

Nu told his story, careful not to dwell too much on Emzara and his children. Dancing around them was not easy, and he had to tell her some.

Na'Amiha promised she would bear him other children — not to replace the ones he had lost, but to add new memories of hope. Eventually they fell asleep in each other's arms.

They never did consummate that night.

I, Enoch, was blessing the great Lord and King of peace. And behold the Watchers called me Enoch the scribe. Then the Lord said to me: "Enoch, scribe of righteousness, go tell the Watchers of heaven, who have deserted the lofty sky, and their holy everlasting station, who have been polluted with women. And have done as the sons of men do, by taking to themselves wives, and who have been greatly corrupted on the earth; That on the earth they shall never obtain peace and remission of sin. For they shall not rejoice in their offspring; they shall behold the slaughter of their beloved; shall lament for the destruction of their sons; and shall petition for ever; but shall not obtain mercy and peace."

—*1 Enoch 12:3-7*
Ethiopic Manuscript

10

SAMYAZA

The pilgrims never stopped coming, even after seven decades. Akh'Uzan sat so conveniently near the road to the perpetual carnage of the Southern Front that warriors of every stripe could easily detour a single day to visit the Gryndel Slayer. First they had come out of the Brotherhood of Dragon-slayers from every remaining city-state of Seti, then from the lore masters, but now—and most intolerably persistent—came the titans of Lumekkor.

A'Nu-Ahki had gotten so tired of it that to appease the influx he had printed up a scroll outlining the wurm's weak spot. The acolytes down in the village handed them out for a small printing fee. This seemed to satisfy most comers, except the titans, who considered themselves important enough to warrant personal attention from the "Wurm's Bane" himself.

"Gronka fight! Gronka learn from holy man!" insisted the latest Cyclops, his single eye slightly off center below a beetle-browed, apish forehead. It rolled in its socket, a demented marble window into a house filled with warlord ghosts waging eternal combat with each other. Facial muscles twitched at every shadowy blow. Every so often, it seemed as if a single demonic entity would gain mastery over the others for a moment, and peer out at the twilight world through that bloodshot hole from the Abyss.

The creature's entourage stood at the monastery gate, bathed in the wine-berry sunset. A'Nu-Ahki stood with them outside.

"It's not like there's any special technique," Nu said. Cold sweat crawled like maggots from every pore in his body as he stood alone under the Beast's flaring gaze. "The mating claw is a weak joint. Either cut it or twist it off if you're big enough for the leverage. I'm no martial art master!"

"Gronka is patient. Gronka learns fast and practice hard! Good little holy man show. Gronka bring gryndel tomorrow."

"No gryndel!" Nu snapped, no longer afraid of getting his head torn off. *At least it would put an end to this nonsense!*

The Cyclops tilted his head with an almost childlike whine. "Why?"

"Not a game! That's why! You want to learn so you can call yourself a Seed of Promise! So you beat a stupid dragon to pulp in some arena! What does it prove? Men still die! The war goes on! Evil grows! Goodness withers on the vine! I'm not your master, and I certainly won't be your slave! So take the little scroll and tell all your titan friends not to bother me anymore!"

"Ahhh! Gronka tired of you! He go now! You not so smart! Could be big man! Big power in North Country, if you smart. But you not smart!"

"That's right!" Nu said, "Gronka right! I not smart!"

The Cyclops waved him off with a gesture of disgust, and turned back down the forest trail.

"I thought he would never leave," said the low voice of Na'Amiha from just inside the gate.

"I'm surprised he didn't clobber me!"

"You don't know Cyclopes like I do. The Temple only use them as guards, mostly for ceremonial stuff—either that or as shock troops—not much brains for anything else. The fact that you'd killed a gryndel probably was more than he could handle. He fears your sorcery."

Nu joined her inside the courtyard, pulled the gate shut, and barred it behind him. "That was over seventy years ago! What is wrong with these people! How long can this stupid war go on?"

'Miha said, "Last I talked to Tubaal-qayin, he said everything had stalled again. Since the Samyazas captured some of our *Behemoths* and began to produce their own self-propelled chariots, all we can do is throw men and machines at each other. I think my nephew used the 'stalemate' word again."

"That's not good. But not unexpected either."

"He predicted that the fighting could still go on for decades."

Another bell-ringer outside the gate signaled for admission before they could even start back across the courtyard to the common hall.

"Who is it now?" Nu growled, half expecting Gronka with a gryndel. He turned back while Na'Amiha continued to their loft above the library.

"Please open up!" called a muffled voice from outside.

"Gronka, if that's your spokesman, give it up! I'm not going to teach you how to fight gryndel!"

"It's not Gronka, if he was that Cyclops I passed on the trail a moment ago. I'm a courier from the front. Tubaal-qayin Dumuzi needs to confer with a certain seer named A'Nu-Ahki. It's a matter of urgency!"

A'Nu-Ahki unbarred the gate, and let the messenger in.

The young soldier immediately handed him a sealed scroll.

Nu broke the wax circle and carried the roll into the hearth hall's firelight. The courier followed at a respectful distance.

He read the message silently and then re-rolled it.

"I need to confer with my elders," Nu told the courier. "Wait here and refresh yourself—there's wine, bread, and cheese in that cupboard by the fireplace. I'd serve you, but this is fairly urgent. Please help yourself, and make yourself at home."

The soldier thanked him.

Nu rushed out the door again, across the courtyard, to Lumekki's tower, where he climbed to his father's turret suite. He found the old Tacticon sipping tea by his hearth, as if readying himself for bed. A'Nu-Ahki did not even wait for an answer to his knock before entering the room.

"What's the matter, Son?" Lumekki asked.

"Take a look at this."

Lumekki grabbed the scroll and unraveled it; laying it across a small reading table he kept by his fireside chair.

A'Nu-Ahki's father pursed his lips in disbelief, and then read the communiqué aloud: "Tubaal-qayin V 'Dumuzi,' to the Seers of Akh'Uzan, especially A'Nu-Ahki, my kinsman through marriage; greetings. I send this urgent message because the two eldest sons of Samyaza have signaled from across the front that they wish a truce and a parley with the sons of Q'Enukki. If there is any chance we can achieve a negotiated end to this war, I ask that one of you should come as a delegation to speak to them. I await your answer, and ask you to think of the many lives that could be saved."

"What do you think?"

"Why should the Samyazas talk to us? They went berserk when E'Yahavah rejected Uzaaz'El's plea for clemency through Q'Enukki. Nothing's changed. It's not like we can bend the will of heaven for them."

"Maybe it has nothing to do with that."

"Well, if it's a negotiated peace they want, I hardly think they would call on us to mediate. We have more reason to hate them than anybody! I think it's a trap."

"To what end? Whoever goes will be under armed escort."

"An assassination plot cares nothing for a melee," said the Tacticon with a dismissing wave of his hand.

"So they assassinate one of us—what does that buy them?"

"Nothing. But they're religious fanatics! They don't think rationally about these things. For all we know they might be convinced that any blood shed from Q'Enukki will purchase Aeden's bliss for whoever can pull it off. Remember Regati."

Nu was dubious about his father's reasoning, but did not want to countermand him. "I'm going to notify Pahpi," he said. "Whatever's going on, the only way for us to find out is for one of us to go. I intend to leave in the morning, if the Zaqen permits."

Stench from the unburied dead filled the air long before A'Nu-Ahki came within sight of the battle front hunkered down less than a week's mounted journey south of Akh'Uzan. The fortified arc stretched from the foothills north of enemy-occupied Ayarak, southwestward, all the way to the Central Sea, just east of the Great

Havens. It had effectively kept Samyaza's forces bottled up in the Gihunu Valley, and away from the prizes of Near Kush and Khavilakki, which had been the invader's original objectives.

Nu's military escort broke free of the foliage on top of the rise where Tubaal-qayin's artillery engines rested. A clear view of the ghastly no-man's land between the fortified trenches assailed his eyes with an undiluted taste of the war of attrition that had dragged on now for seven decades.

The pocked landscape of mud and exposed corpses attracted carrion dragons from out of the patches of nearby jungle, along with croaking hordes of web-winged amphipteres and gryphons, which swooped down to snag whatever remained from the dragons. Bones, long ago picked clean, littered the bleak strip where fresher dead lacked, ever churned up by the plowing millipede treads of charging *Behemoth* machines.

The lieutenant who had escorted A'Nu-Ahki most of the way from Akh'Uzan had them all dismount before proceeding down the hill to the command bunker.

"Thunder-pikes and hand-cannons have been used by both sides since early on. You can easily get picked off even at this distance," said the young officer, who doubtless thought that Nu's lack of technological sophistication warranted such explanation.

He shouldered his own weapon when he dismounted, making it more visible to A'Nu-Ahki. It looked much like a short metallic spear, but with a wider butt handle, and a hollowed steel staff below the offset blade tip. The device fired small metal projectiles by means of chemical explosive pellets from a chamber inside the shaft, like a miniature cannon with a breech load.

The Officer smiled as he held the thunder-pike out for A'Nu-Ahki's closer inspection. "The Samyazas sometimes still use spears and swords during their charges, but they've caught up with us pretty well—they always have ranged pikers covering their melees at a distance to conserve whatever modern weapons they've either captured or copied from us."

Nu instantly knew the young officer blustered from the obsolete military paradigm in which the war had started—probably before he was even born. Age and experience told A'Nu-Ahki a different story.

"They must 'conserve' pretty well for the front to have stalled here for over seventy years," Nu said, with a wry arch of his eyebrows that instantly shut the lieutenant up.

The path to the command bunker wound about halfway down the copse behind a combination of well placed rocks and soil berms. The lieutenant ushered A'Nu-Ahki past the guards at the bottom of the trail, and into the close darkness inside.

"Greetings," said a tired familiar voice.

Nu's eyes adjusted to the gloom. "I've come at your request."

Tubaal-qayin Dumuzi stepped into a shaft of light from the half-opened door. "I appreciate your quick response." He looked grimy—not at all like the Emperor of nearly a fifth of the world's entire land mass.

"Do you know what they want?"

Tubaal-qayin shrugged. "I'd hoped you might have an idea. Ivvayi and Ayyaho themselves just arrived, with Isha'Tahar from Assur'Ayur Temple. Something big must be up for Samyaza's First Wife to join her two eldest sons all the way out here. From what I understand, they massacred many of your kinsmen long before Salaam-Surupag, so I don't imagine they're expecting to get any fair hearing from you. Maybe they have something you want, and want to bargain. My hope is that you'll put in a good word, and try to get a feel for any possibility of peace talks."

Nu thought for the first time in years about his unaccounted-for daughters last seen alive in these titan's hands. He could not imagine how they could be of any political worth in a parley with Tubaal-qayin Dumuzi.

"I'll try for peace talks, but I don't have anything to bargain with."

The little Emperor twitched his shoulders in what, to him, must have been a conciliatory gesture. "Sorry. I'm just baffled by this."

And this is a revelation? Nu fumed to himself. "I guess there's only one way to find out what's up. We might as well be done with it. Just how much negotiating leverage are you willing to give me if they want to talk?"

"They can go back to their pre-war borders unmolested. Anything else you need to confer with me."

"Understood."

Tubaal-qayin summoned his chief signalman. "Send up the truce flags. Let them know the delegate has arrived."

Queen Isha'Tahar, First Wife of Samyaza the Watcher, had lost little of her renowned dark beauty over the centuries, though it had taken on a marked severity in middle age. It was no secret that, soon after birthing the twin titans, she began drinking concubine's root to preserve her looks, and prevent the conception of further children. Superstition told how she had ascended into heaven by Samyaza's leave and granted immortality. Nu figured that particular superstition wouldn't last much longer.

Her two sons stood nearly a man's height taller than A'Nu-Ahki. Inhuman exoskeletal armor ridged their faces and creased the skin of their bare arms and chests like bronzed facets on a pair of human armadillos. A ring of sharpened horns encircled their cranial regions, growing right from their flattened skulls and making any form of helm redundant. They waited in no-man's land, bones piled at heavily shod feet like scraps from their latest meal. Stories had them eating whole roasted camels in a single meal, though Nu figured such tales were likely apocryphal.

Their mother sat in a bier on the shoulders of four giant guards of similar appearance, minus the horns.

A'Nu-Ahki, Tubaal-qayin, and the Emperor's titan escorts halted about twenty paces in front of them. Avarnon-Set was part of the Dumuzi's retinue—Nu felt the wolf-headed creature's baleful eyes burn into his back.

Nu found it anticlimactic to see Avarnon-Set's face unveiled for the first time. Old Urugim's description now seemed morbidly over-blown—all Nu saw was a hairy, disfigured parody of a man. At certain angles, the Titan's face appeared to have an ape-like quality and his pointed ears vaguely resembled those of a wolven-hound—if one waxed melodramatic. The creature's eyes were all-black, however—the most formidable thing about him—except maybe for his size.

The old terror that had frozen Nu back in Sa-utar so long ago was gone. For some reason, Old Dog-face just didn't seem that formidable any more. Nu wondered if he had somehow grown or if the Beast had just shrunk.

He put it from his mind.

For a moment, the truce parties faced one another in silence, each trying to read their opponents. Nu could make nothing from the unhuman faces of Samyaza's sons, at first. Yet buried beneath the layered composure of Isha'Tahar squirmed the restless shadow of a fleetingly visible fear.

Samyaza's wife said, "Which of you is the Son of Q'Enukki?"
A'Nu-Ahki stepped forward. "I am."

She gazed down upon him with cool, half shut eyes once used
to ensnare men, and those supposed to be more than men. "Thank
you for coming. You know both my sons and we know the
Emperor of the North and his adviser, Avarnon-Set, so I think we
can dispense with any further pleasantries. We are here because
certain rumors disturb my god-husband—rumors based on
prophecies that originate with the Seer, Q'Enukki, whom Uzaaz'El
once consorted with to curry divine favor."

Tubaal-qayin turned puzzled eyes to A'Nu-Ahki, but said
nothing.

Avarnon-Set did not seem the least bit surprised by her
statement—or if he was, he did not allow it to show. Nu simply
tried to pretend that the former envoy was not there. While fear
had diminished, distraction had not.

"Do not be so surprised," Isha'Tahar said to the Emperor. "Your
Power was once my husband's lieutenant and they were both
answerable to higher Powers than even themselves before they
came to Earth."

"They still are," A'Nu-Ahki added, hoping to rattle both
Avarnon-Set and the Queen's sons just a little. "They still are, and
it terrifies them."

"Perhaps," the Queen said. "Or if it does not, then maybe it
should."

Her response stunned A'Nu-Ahki, but he did not let it show.

Tubaal-qayin demanded, "What is this about?"

"Be assured, good 'Shepherd,' it is not about you," said the
Woman.

Nu asked, "Which prophecies concern Samyaza so?"

She stared past him off into the battlefield, a tear breaking as a
clear acid-crystal jewel from her left eye. "The ones he destroyed at
Regati in his madness. The being named Metatron, who comes
from the presence of E'Yahavah El-N'Lil, bade him to seek out a
son of Q'Enukki who would tell of the coming Edict of Desolation.
This Metatron refused to leave his former estate when Samyaza
came down to redeem us. Yet they were once close.

"Metatron warned my god-husband that the end of the world is
rushing at us from out of the heavens. At the same time, my sons
Ivvayi and Ayyaho—demigods both—also had dreams.

"'Vayi saw a Watcher come down upon a flat stone with a chisel, and inscribe upon it the ideogram of the Divine Name. His brother dreamed of a large beautiful orchard, like that of Aeden, planted with all kinds of trees. In the orchard were Watchers, and in their hands, axes with which they cut down all of the trees but one. When they awoke, my sons told their visions to their father in the Temple, and he informed them of Metatron's warning. We come for an interpretation of this matter, and to see if there is any way of averting this catastrophe."

A'Nu-Ahki said, "I have at least two daughters, captured at Salaam-Surupag. I would have them returned to me."

Tubaal-qayin interrupted them. "You've put this war on hold over a religious superstition?"

The Queen said, "If you were sensitive to the Alter-world, and not so dependent on your machines, you would not accuse us of superstition!"

"I don't see any hesitation on your part in copying my genius and sending out your own machines to fight!"

"Please, let me handle this, Emperor," Nu said, stepping between the two heads of state.

The Metalsmith-king folded his arms and scowled, but nodded for the Seer to continue.

"What are your daughter's names?" asked the Queen. "I will see what can be done."

"Problem is that my son, who saw them alive and captive, died trying to tell us about it. He was never able to say which of my girls he saw alive. Many girls died that day and we could not identify all the dead. They could be any of four names—Uranna, Bethara, Tylurnis, and Zhavra," Nu said. "I should think my help is worth the return of all the female captives of Salaam-Surupag. After all, it's the end of the world we're talking about."

"Many of them have been married and assimilated. It will take time to track them down across all of Assuri."

"I will show my good faith by starting to replace the scrolls you have lost and by summarizing them for you verbally now, if you wish. It is also my hope that we can perhaps start talking peace."

One of the horned sons shouted, "We are not here to parley!"

"Peace, 'Vayi!" hissed his mother like some gryndel pack matriarch. Then to Nu she said, "While it is beyond my stature as a woman to mingle in affairs of war, I can see how this has become a battle of attrition that serves neither of us. I will bring the matter up with my god-husband, but I can promise no answer from him one way or the other."

A'Nu-Ahki said, "Since the end of the world is upon us, does it not make sense that we should turn our hearts to E'Yahavah and to peace?"

Isha'Tahar nodded, and seemed momentarily, for all her authority, to be a creature trapped and in pain. "I would tend to think so. I want nothing more than to escape the divine displeasure that is upon us."

"Since this is so, I will seek the Great God to interpret the dreams of your sons for you here and now. I will return with the books of my Ancestor in three week's time—I need to have my monastery presses run new copies, for nobody has requested any in a long while."

The Queen seemed pleased. "I, in turn, will send for those captive women from Salaam-Surupag who are willing to come—though I cannot promise to find them all. I shall also raise the question of peace—though I will not push my divine husband if he is disagreeable."

"I can ask no more."

The first titan, Ivvayi, stepped forward, and stooped down before the Seer until they met at eye level. "Tell me what my vision is," he commanded in a throaty snarl. Smoldering red eyes glowed with biochemical fire-fly light, while his breath stank of ale and rotten camel flesh.

A'Nu-Ahki no longer feared the demonic strength that reached out to smother him. It seemed that Avarnon-Set was not the only giant to have lost that power over him. Whether from E'Yahavah's gift, or the weird deference the titans all gave him since his reputation as the gryndel killer, or from a little of both, he did not know. He opted to believe a divine gift gave him calm clarity to gaze into this creature's face, and to read what he saw.

Although alien in so many ways, Samyaza's hybrid son seemed trapped by a very human, almost child-like fear. For a moment, it caused Nu to wonder if the Nae-fil actually had the capacity to trust E'Yahavah, and cast himself on the promise of the genuine Seed.

"Your dream shows a heavenly Watcher descending upon a flat stone. He carries a chisel, and writes on the stone the ideogram-glyph of the Divine Name. This is because both Metatron's warning to your father, and your brother's dream about the orchard, are set in stone by E'Yahavah and immovable. A'Nu shall destroy the entire world, except for a tiny remnant. The earth is bloodstained. Your father, with the other Watchers that fell with him, perverted life's natural order, while men eagerly follow them."

The Giant stood and balled his fists. "I could crush you!"

A'Nu-Ahki fixed his eyes upon those of the Creature, and answered, "You can do nothing to me unless my Master gives your master permission to let you—and that's not likely to happen. Besides, haven't you already tried to stamp out these words at Regati and Salaam-Surupag? Did not such madness bring Metatron down to you, and make this journey necessary?"

The second son of Samyaza stepped in front of his brother, and knelt down on one knee before the Seer to meet A'Nu-Ahki's eyes. "Please, what of my dream? I had no part in how I came to be on this earth and I for one can regret many things I have done here. Are you saying there is no hope at all for us, no matter what we choose?"

The question struck Nu at the very foundation of all he believed about the Nae-fillim. Had he not feared the integrity of his own lineage for many decades in nearly the same way? Hesitation clutched his tongue.

"Please." Ayyaho's eyes softened. "I really need to know."

Nu's answer spilled out in half-coagulated lumps, taking on more fluency only as he went on; "You … are born … as man, from the womb … of woman. Blood flows through you and a heart beats. You think, you dream, and can make choices to do good or evil. Yet forces drive you toward evils that you enjoy too much to resist seriously—so far. There is something else in you that is not of man—a darkness that moves you and holds you. Those that conceived and raised you did much to desecrate and contort the Image of E'Yahavah in you, but they cannot destroy it. So yes, there is hope for you."

Ayyaho's eyes did not flame with rage as Nu had expected. "How do you know the Image is not destroyed?"

Nu answered softly, "Because you still share in the Great Curse—that you are doomed to someday return to dust. Thus it is possible also for you to share Man's hope—but, I'm sorry to say, only with great difficulty."

"Man's hope?"

"Yes. The hope based on the genuine Seed of Promise, which you must publicly renounce all claims to being. In addition, you must make sacrifice for and turn away from your sorceries, sexual deviations, and war atrocities. If you call upon E'Yahavah, and humble yourself before him to be instructed in his ways, and love him with a true heart, you can find not only hope but security."

The Creature nodded as if truly considering it. "Hope and security."

Nu continued, "Your dream's meaning is plain. The orchard is the world. The trees are all the families of humankind. World-end comes as the Holy Watchers with their axes to chop down all the trees of the orchard but one. The father of Q'Enukki, Iyared of Sautar, prophesied over me that I would be the last tree—my house would be the remnant to survive.

"If you would have security, then you must put down all you have in Samyaza, and take up what E'Yahavah offers you in me, and follow. I am the prophesied Comforter from E'Yahavah A'Nu—only a shadow of the Seed to come, true. But I am the only shadow given to this world. In the end only one tree will stand. That is the interpretation of your vision."

The second son of Samyaza trembled, then shot to his feet. His eyes narrowed to blackened slits, as humiliation and contempt exploded with the acid saliva foam from his mouth.

"Do you expect us to dishonor our father, who is great and powerful, to become mewling acolytes of a pompous little self-styled seer from an insignificant land that is squashed like an insect between two empires! If you had only said to put away my past atrocities, and to spend the rest of my days walking the earth to do good I would have done so gladly! Had you even said to make peace with the north, I would have tried in good faith! But you are as arrogant as your fathers at Regati! You want to control us—to bring us under your heel with the sword of mere words!"

A'Nu-Ahki grieved. Something that had been ever so briefly alive in Ayyaho's eyes was now quite dead.

He turned to their mother. "And what say you, Queen Isha'Tahar? What will you do with E'Yahavah's only hope?"

The wife of Samyaza seemed to have aged many decades. Her eyes grew dull, as her face paled from its former reddish brown to the color of yellowed bone. Nu even saw wrinkles he was sure had not been there before.

"Take me away from this place of death," she said to her bearers.

A'Nu-Ahki asked, "Shall I bring the scrolls at the appointed time?"

"What good would it do?" she said, as her chair turned from him. "No one will believe, and it will only cause further division."

"What about the captives?"

She ignored him.

He turned to face Tubaal-qayin Dumuzi helplessly.

The Emperor said, "Next time I call for your help, leave your little valley cult at home! Lives are at stake here! Or are you blind to the bones you're standing on?" He turned and trudged off for his command bunker.

A'Nu-Ahki followed him at a discreet distance.

For a moment, his eyes met those of Avarnon-Set. Though the wolf-headed titan had kept silent through the whole exchange, Nu saw a glinting fang peek through tangled hair and crusted drool in a triumphant smirk.

A new artillery barrage erupted from the Assurim cannons that hour.

Behold, I thought then within my heart that conception was (due) to the Watchers and the Holy Ones ... and to the Giants... and my heart was troubled within me because of this child. Then I, Lamech, approached Bathenosh [my] wife in haste and said to her, '... by the Most High, the Great Lord, the King of all the worlds and Ruler of the Sons of Heaven, until you tell me all things truthfully, if...'

Then Bathenosh my wife spoke to me with much heat [and] ... said, 'O my brother, O my lord, remember my pleasure ... lying together and my soul within its body. [And I tell you] all things truthfully.'

My heart was then greatly troubled within me, and when Bathenosh my wife saw that my countenance had changed... Then she mastered her anger and spoke to me saying, 'O my lord, O my [brother, remember] my pleasure! I swear to you by the Holy Great One, the King of [the heavens] ... that this seed is yours and that [this] conception is from you. This fruit was planted by you ... and by no stranger or Watcher or Son of Heaven.... [Why] is your countenance thus changed and dismayed, and why is your spirit thus distressed? ...'

Then I, Lamech, ran to Methuselah my father, and [I told] him all these things.

— "Lamech Fragment" of the *Genesis Apocryphon*
The Complete Dead Sea Scrolls in English
Translated by Geza Vermes

11

INTENTS OF THE HEART

T he window light behind Nu's wife danced off her hair like fire. She said, "I'm sorry things didn't go so well. I'm sure you did your best."

Na'Amiha's sunny disposition somehow seemed overdone. Nu thought he caught a sideways gleam in her eye—one that suggested she was actually happy about the backfire of his diplomacy mission.

They hadn't spoken much when he slipped into bed late last night, upon his return from the front—only enough for him to convey that the war was still on, and the Dumuzi was not pleased with him.

A'Nu-Ahki turned away from her, and looked out the window at the sunny courtyard of Q'Enukki's Retreat. His breakfast was getting cold.

He had gotten over any real suspicion of his wife early on—most of it during their protracted conversation on their wedding night, so long on talk and short on lovemaking. *No, that's not fair! We'd both thought that best!* His conscience corrected him inside as it so often did these days.

Every so often over the years 'Miha had said off-beat things that would yank the chain of Nu's "Dragon Paranoid," but it had always turned out to be a mere clash of dialect semantics—never a real conflict in her loyalties. They would always laugh about it afterward. And the discords were rare—very rare—hardly more than a handful over seven decades.

Her eyes could barely contain their elation just now.

Nu said, "There was no chance. It was never about the war."

"What did that woman want, then?" She said the words *that woman* with an almost over-the-top cattiness.

How did she know about Isha'Tahar being there? I never mentioned it to her and all I knew before I left was that the Samyazas wanted a parley — nothing about Isha'Tahar herself being their delegate.

A'Nu-Ahki jerked his eyes back onto his wife. He thought he caught 'Miha's face shifting in mid-stream. Her elbows were on the common hall's stone table, chin in cupped hands. She immediately sat back, away from him, out of reach.

The best intelligence operative is the one that nobody notices. The best way to hide something you don't want people to notice is right out in the open. His Dragon Paranoid was in rare form this morning.

Just stop it! His accustomed view of his wife, thankfully, would not go down without a fight. *She's proven her character more than enough over seventy years! Any problems she's had were over things she couldn't help — things that are getting better now! You're thinking like Tarkuni or Henumil!*

Usually this was the point when he would begin to feel good about himself for his rising above all the callow suspicions. *You know, like the ones your father used to have about your mother...*

Not this time. It still didn't explain how she knew about Isha'Tahar.

Nu stopped short of yelling out for his own thoughts to shut up.

"You looked like you were about to say something, dear. What was it? Can I get you more tea?" 'Miha was already half out of her cushion.

"No. No. I'm good. Relax, enjoy your food."

"You haven't eaten hardly a thing, Nu. I'd have guessed you'd be hungry after your long journey. The cakes aren't overdone are they? I can never seem to get them right..."

He hated it when she berated herself. He'd always assumed it was a nervous habit, but now she almost seemed to be fishing for a compliment. *That or it's just a method she's used to manipulate me over the years...*

"'Miha, the cakes are fine. I just have a lot on my mind."

She relaxed back into her seat. "Why don't you tell me about it? I always find that if I can just tell someone what's bothering me, that it makes me feel better. I'm glad I can always talk to you."

"It has nothing to do with how I feel, 'Miha..." which wasn't entirely true, "it has to do with a complex situation and how it will unfold."

"I'm sorry. I didn't mean to upset you." She said it almost as if he was getting ready to walk out the door on her, slam it, and never look back.

"I'm not upset with you, Green-eyed Lady." He smiled for her.

That was how things so often seemed to never-quite-end with her—her green eyes screaming their panic lest she make one simple misstep—like the eyes of their wedding guests seventy years ago, whose laughter and good cheer had masked some brooding terror underneath.

It's not like I've paved the road of our life together with eggshells!

"You know, you could always tell me if you were upset," she said.

Which actually meant that he couldn't.

At least things are better in the bedchamber these days, Nu thought, feeling guilty that he even had to go there just to find a positive feeling for his wife. He gazed into her eyes in a way that she would certainly, and quite mechanically, misread if he didn't stop it. The bedchamber had been such a nightmare for so long! *But it's better now—isn't it?*

He'd been sure for a long time that most of it had stemmed from all she'd gone through in Lumekkor. *Who wouldn't have such problems after that?*

'Miha had allowed him to mourn for many years before trying to claim from him the full duties of a husband. Yet her claim was valid, and Nu had never refused her awkward advances—even those early ones that had always ended so badly.

He recalled a particular time—some ten years into their marriage—not long after he had first told her that he'd put the worst of his grieving for Emza behind him. *If only that could even have a chance at being true!*

'Miha had called him up to their bedchamber in the middle of the afternoon—fortunately while Lumekki, Muhet'Usalaq, and Mamu had been away on an inspection tour of Paru'Ainu.

He had entered the room expecting her to ask him for some silver for market, or something. Instead, she was stretched out on top of the divan, stiff as a dagger (her feet being the pointy end), dressed in this ridiculous red silk and gold-laced bag that bunched-out over her near-non-existent breasts and clenched thighs in matted fabric knots. It turned out this had been her idea of what a Far Kush harem girl outfit might look like. What made it so hard was that she had apparently put so much work into the monstrosity.

If that had not been weird enough, she had spent hours painting her face up so thickly that she resembled a depressed Khavilak theater clown. How a woman, raised in the hub of a society where harem girls and theater clowns were so common, could have had such a poor handle on the basic cosmetic differences between the two was beyond him. But there she was.

Nu had successfully kept himself from laughing at their chamber door, only to realize that she also looked like a frightened, affection-starved little girl playing some truly horrible game of dress-up. The very fact that he even made this connection appalled him further, putting up yet another iron barrier against his libido—a barrier he then feared for a few seconds might actually break for all of the wrongest of reasons. This had sent him into absolute, exponentially intensifying horror.

"I'm ready," she had said in what she must have imagined was a sultry voice. It was several octaves too low and came out all man-husky.

Nu had wanted to run screaming from the room. *"I'm not!"*

Instead, he had gotten onto the couch with her and tried his best.

Both fortunately and unfortunately for him, it was 'Miha who had made the whole thing impossible in the end. She simply could not make the "dagger blade" be scissors, much less soft pliable ones. Which was fortunate for Nu only because of his inability to muster even a trace of desire; thus, she could not blame him for slacking off on the job. It was unfortunate in that it meant 'Miha would torment both herself and him with what she would call her "failure as a wife" for many decades to come.

Either way, much shrieking and bawling had followed, which he had managed to console only on the most superficial level by the time the others returned home. *Can you say, "Hidden dragons in the endless green?"*

Eventually 'Miha had waited for Nu to become more ready to move on her. That had gone a little better. Since none of the villagers would befriend her and Mamu never seemed able to fully relate to Na'Amiha all that well, Nu had taken upon himself the bizarre functions of both husband and *best girl friend* — or whatever women these days called those female chums they did up their hair and faces with. He found it mildly disturbing when he actually began to enjoy experimenting with her red-tinged gold hair and cosmetics. The up-side was that touching her in this manner had slowly gotten her used to his touch in other, more husband-wife-like ways.

Nu had also gotten to make her up in ways that he at least found somewhat attractive. It had been a difficult field to plow, but things had improved to where the bedchamber was no longer a chamber of horrors — most of the time. He was thankful, but also profoundly sad. He had hoped for more. He had wanted something supernatural to happen between them, in view of what E'Yahavah intended for 'Miha. But no elevating power from heaven ever came — just raw endurance, incrementally less disturbing mental images from both in and outside the bedchamber, and emotional weariness.

At best these days, 'Miha was able to relax somewhat. She insisted she wanted him, but it was almost like being with a dead woman. For Nu, whatever seemingly one-sided passion they shared happened by him closing his eyes and pretending she was Emzara. He always felt beaten-up guilty for it afterward, but it marshaled his enthusiasm for the work at hand. The problem was, 'Miha didn't talk like Emza, didn't move like Emza — didn't move at all — she felt nothing like Emza in his embrace.

Of course she doesn't, old boy! That's because she's not Emza. She's Na'Amiha.

Nu wanted to believe that he cherished their growing friendship, even if the natural attraction of man for woman was forced. He performed his duties to her with a smile and would never quit. But they were mere duties all too often, no matter how much he tried to put her first.

He gazed across the breakfast table at her and was relieved when Muhet'Usalaq bellowed for him to "get his under-kilt" into the library.

"Shut the doors and sit down!" The Prime Zaqen of Akh'Uzan sat at an oversized reading table, pounding a small rolled-up scroll like a dagger into the surface.

A'Nu-Ahki slid the library doors shut and sat down on one of the other reading consoles. "I guess you want my report."

Muhet'Usalaq glared at him. "Considering it is already past mid-morning, that would be nice!"

"I was going to write it up for you."

The end of the little scroll crumpled and split. "How thoughtful of you. You can still write it up—in fact, I insist! But first I want you to recap the high points—that is, if you really think there are any."

Nu told him everything that had happened once he had arrived at the front—even his conversation with the army lieutenant who had tried to give him a remedial explanation of thunder-pike tactics.

Muhet'Usalaq softened considerably after hearing about the dreams of Samyaza's sons. "Tough corner, that. Are you absolutely certain El-N'Lil breathed your interpretations?"

"I wasn't just making it up off the top of my head—of course I was sure! What would you have had me say?"

The Old Man looked down at his crushed scroll. "I suppose that diplomacy and prophecy rarely mix well. The Dumuzi sent a letter for me along with your escort. It basically says that the next time he asks for our help, I should send Lumekki."

"If E'Yahavah breathed the words, would my father's answer to the Samyazas have been significantly different?"

"No, I suppose not. Go on get out of here. Take your wife for a walk up to Grove Hollow or something. You can write up your report tomorrow."

⊕

Nu stepped out to the courtyard after handing in his report to Muhet'Usalaq the following afternoon.

From the corner of his eye, he saw Na'Amiha slip through the small castle's outer gate without opening it more than a crack. She had a tiny cloth-wrapped package tucked under her arm.

Nu rushed to the gate after it closed.

Usually 'Miha made a big production whenever she left Q'Enukki's Retreat—especially if she was headed for the village. She always wanted Nu, Lumekki, or at least one of the household servants to know where she would be. In the early years, the Tacticon had even sent a soldier or two with her from his rotating platoon of the reserve Seer Clan Regiment that he kept at the fortress. Things rarely went well for her down in the village.

Tarkuni and Henumil had seen to that long ago.

Nu poked his head outside the gate and saw her trot down the cliff base section of trail toward town. Waiting for her to vanish into the foliage farther down, he stepped outside to follow.

'Miha kept up a brisk pace on the winding forest path, as if she didn't want to be gone from Q'Enukki's Retreat long enough to be missed. Nu had to run in several places to keep up.

Once, at a bend in the trail around a rocky cave-filled outcropping, he slid to a halt just in time to avoid running into her.

'Miha turned at the sound. "Who's there?"

Nu pressed himself against a large rock on his left. He watched her through a crack between the narrow bolder and the cliff-face, as she back-tracked several steps. A cloud passed in front of the sun. He glanced up, certain that a vultch-gryphon had meandered over the mountains from the Haunted Lands somehow to snatch him up. Heart pounding, Nu froze his diaphragm and aching lungs, lest his wife hear him panting from his run.

"Is anybody there?" 'Miha stopped back-tracking and looked around.

Nu saw tiny pin-lights swirl around his face, as everything else started to go black from lack of air. Still he held his breath.

'Miha turned again and continued down toward the village.

Nu waited for her to vanish into the green before he exhaled, and loudly caught his breath. *Why is she afraid of being seen?*

He didn't want to know; now he had to.

Once his breath evened out, he stepped back out onto the path and continued his pursuit—this time at a fast walk.

The foothill forest opened into a meadow just before the small un-walled town. Akh'Uzan Village stood on the same open space where the wedding tents had seventy years before.

When Nu reached the edge of the trees, 'Miha entered town. Instead of following the last part of the trail through the open field, he moved toward the hamlet, skirting along the tree line. This gave him an elevation advantage sufficient to see over the low roofs of the nearest set of shops. The trading post was the largest of these, but 'Miha walked past it to disappear under the awning of the tackle smithy.

A'Nu-Ahki broke into a run. He came to a halt on the small rise behind the tackle smith's shop and ducked behind a tree overlooking the back end of the row of little baked-brick buildings. He squatted to try to see into the shop. His footing almost slipped and sent him tumbling down the hill from the shock of what happened next.

Na'Amiha and the shop's owner stepped out the back door—where presumably they could remain unseen—and had a rather long, apparently quite friendly conversation. At least it seemed long to Nu.

She handed the Tackle Smith the package and then they talked some more. She even laughed a little, albeit nervously.

I should think so. Town always makes you almost as uneasy as the bedchamber used to – if that's possible! Not quite so jumpy now, are you?

Nobody in Akh'Uzan Village would so much as talk to 'Miha, much less laugh with her. As Tarkuni had made clear before Nu had married her, she was *Qayinim*—unclean, uncouth, pale, and bloodless—a despised spawn of the Murderer. Where Tarkuni went, the villagers usually followed.

Who was this tackler?

Nu had seen him around, but could not recall his name because the fellow had been one of Urugim's descendents who had come to Akh'Uzan later, after the wedding. They would need to meet behind the shop because if the villagers ever saw him talking to 'Miha in a friendly way, the Tackle Smith would have been shunned as she was—possibly even worse.

A'Nu-Ahki put his fist to the soil between his knees to steady his squat as he watched them between two fern clumps. *What's next? Are they lovers? Is her whole tragic trauma princess thing an act?*

'Miha might be a little over three hundred years old, but she's a young three hundred without any marks from child-bearing. Maybe this guy likes flat-chested women who can almost believably paint themselves up as little girls playing dress-up!

Nu fell against the tree and slid to the ground, weak and sick.

The Tackle Smith smiled, and reached out to touch 'Miha's arm. She pulled away—almost playfully, it seemed.

Nu felt all dark and sticky inside, as his wife talked a moment more.

I wonder what she's telling him? She doesn't seem put out at all!

Whatever it was, she kept it short. They vanished back into the shop. Nu counted the seconds until he saw her emerge from under the awning on the building's front side—not too many seconds later, thankfully. She looked around as if to make sure nobody was watching and then made a fast walk to the meadow trail. He waited until she entered the trees before slowly rising to return behind her to the monastery-fortress of his ancestor.

Nu thought, *Great E'Yahavah, what am I going to do?*

He made no effort to keep up with her. She had only one possible destination once on the trail. Instead, he shuffled along at a moping pace—would have meandered had the forest and rocks not defined the path—terrified at what awaited him at home, and of what he would now have to do.

It's my duty to report this. There isn't a range of possibilities here.

She's your wife, Nu, chosen for you by the Divine Name.

A'Nu-Ahki was unsure if he was mentally arguing with himself, or if E'Yahavah spoke softly to him, or which words came from where even if the latter. It was not at all clear like the dream interpretations of Samyaza's sons had been. Things hid in his inner murkiness—dark things, even dead things.

It doesn't matter! I still care about her. I can't let this happen!

He passed the caves on his right; the same place he had stopped to keep from overtaking 'Miha in his pursuit. Evil eyes seemed to watch him from amid the bat guano piles. But when he looked inside, no one was there.

You have no choice! Your duty to the Work binds you.

It was my duty to Q'Enukki's Work that got me into this marriage!

Yes. And maybe your duty to the Work will free you from it as well.

Maybe I don't want to be free of her!

Nu reached the steep part of the trail that skirted the ledge below the rock-facing on which Q'Enukki's Retreat stood to his right. A shrill amphiptere called, glide-circling over some dead thing far off above the woods with several vultures. The treetops over the lower foothills were an endless lumpy carpet off a steep drop on his left. For a split second, he considered throwing himself over the side. He imagined himself impaled like a discarded doll on some sharp up-ended branch, pecked at by the flying carrion eaters. *They're already singing for me.*

Don't be absurd! Be free of her! She's a burden too great to bear!

Nu saw 'Miha, all painted up like a theater clown, in her tacky little-girl dress-up harem princess outfit, impaled on that same tree. The web-winged razor-toothed amphiptere gorged itself on her middle, while the buzzards pecked out her wide-open unseeing eyes.

Which is it? You or her?

It's a question of duty both ways! What do you want from me?

Silence.

Not even the amphiptere and vultures screeched.

Nu approached the fortress gate as if it was a dragon's cave because he knew what was inside. *At least we have no children. There's always that.*

He did not remember making any choice. He simply passed inside, climbed the wall stairs, and walked along the parapet toward his father's corner turret apartment. He paused outside, but in the end, entered because he saw no viable alternative that could work in the long-run.

He found his father dusting one of his little wooden models—a third-generation *Behemoth* war engine.

"Pahpo, I need to talk."

"Sure, Nu. How can I help?"

A'Nu-Ahki wasn't sure how to start. "Ever see something you never wanted to see in someone you love?"

Lumekki laughed. "Please, are you kidding? Aren't you the kid who once would have beaten me to within a hair's breadth of my life if you had only been big enough at the time? I'm the master of suspicion, remember?"

Nu smiled. "Yeah. I was a little hot-head back then, wasn't I?"

"No. That time you had a right to be."

"No I didn't. Not really. I wasn't there to see what you saw."

Lumekki said, "I should have seen what was right in front of me."

"I've learned that making sense of what you see right in front of you isn't always so simple, even when you ask for Divine help. I was wrong then. Maybe you were too, but that's for you to judge. I only know that things aren't as simple as that petulant self-righteous boy once imagined."

"Just what have you've seen, Son?"

"I'm seeing and hearing stuff from 'Miha that's starting to scare me—stuff I never went looking for."

His father motioned him into a couch and sat down next to him. "What kind of stuff? I don't exactly have the best battle record on marriage, so if it's personal... Well, I'm just saying up front."

"No, it's nothing like that—well, not entirely, anyway. It is possible Clan business, though. That frightens me."

"What do you mean?" Lumekki's warm eyes suddenly cooled.

"She's been doing odd things lately. I watched her slip out the gate and followed her down to town. She met up with that fellow who owns the tackle shop—a distant member of Urugim's clan—I forget his name. They both stepped out the back—I watched from the forest edge. She handed him a wrapped package. It looked like it could have been a bundle of letter-sized scrolls. Not only that but yesterday, over breakfast, she let something slip that she couldn't have possibly known."

"Which was?"

Nu's stomach was in knots. 'Miha was a handful, but he didn't want her hurt. "She was trying to console me over what happened at the front. She mentioned Isha'Tahar by name. I hadn't told her anything about who the Samyazas had sent to meet me..."

Lumekki let out a long puff of air. "Son, before you go any further can I give you some fatherly advice?"

"Pahpo, she was happy that my mission failed—she could barely contain herself! She tried, but she couldn't..."

"Nu, don't be an idiot! Of course, she was happy! She's your wife! She was terrified every second you were at the front. Nothing that keeps you from ever needing to go to an active war front again can exactly make her unhappy! Think hard before you embarrass yourself the way I did with your mother—may E'Yahavah comfort her! My dreams are still haunted by her cries of 'remember my pleasure with you when we lay together...'"

Way too much detail, Pahp!

"Even decades after I begged her forgiveness, and she gave it, things were never quite the same—no matter how much either of us tried."

"Pahp, I'm not repeating your mistake, I'm looking for a way not to!"

"Nu, 'Miha and I had tea before you got up that morning. I told her about Tubaal-qayin's dispatch, which had mentioned all about Isha'Tahar."

"You told her?"

Lumekki made his crooked little smirk. "Yes, Son. Everything Pahpi reads, I read too—remember? I even read to her from it."

"Was that wise?"

The Old Tacticon looked at him sideways and then playfully smacked the back of his son's head. "Seer it out! On second thought, never mind, I suppose I should have told you before..."

Nu smoothed his ruffled hair back down. "Told me what?"

"'Miha informed me just a few weeks after you two were married that one of the incoming sons of Urugim settling the village at the time was actually an agent of Lumekkor. She then explained to me about Avarnon-Set's intentions for her in your marriage. I thanked her for her candor and asked her not to say anything to anyone else—even you."

"Why? Can't I be trusted anymore?"

Lumekki's brow arched. "Remember that little principle called 'need to know?' I told her to send information to this operative occasionally—misinformation coming from me. Nu, 'Miha volunteered to let me use her to feed bad intelligence to Old Dog-face. I sent her with that package today because I want Lumekkor to think we reprimanded and demoted you over how things went at the front. It frees up both you and the Seer Clan from any real repercussions they might otherwise send our way. It's also an important tool I use to influence Avarnon-Set's thinking."

"Am I being demoted?"

Lumekki laughed, slapping his son's back this time. "Don't be such an oversensitive woman, boy! You're starting to scare me now! 'Miha's one of my heroes and so are you."

That night, for the first time, Nu did not need to take his wife's desire for him as an article of faith. She responded—not like Emza because she wasn't Emza. She was 'Miha.

Afterward, A'Nu-Ahki basked in the joy of her inner healing; certain it meant that the wounds of her past were finally mending and that she would freely experience the kind of love from him that E'Yahavah had intended.

It would not take long for him to discover however, that things with 'Miha were not that simple.

Both sides spent a mountain of slain in contest for a scabrous ridge.

—S.L.A. Marshall
World War I

12

FIREFALL

A' Nu-Ahki watched the carnage from a hill.

Fanatical Samyaza Cult shock troops, driven by the plate-skinned spawn of their god, fought the cruel, calculating techno-savants of Tubaal-qayin in pitched battle. The Samyazas stormed the trenches, only to be mowed down by the spitting crank cannons of the northern titans. These man-things, some with horns and malformed pseudo-bestial heads, fighting beside huge six-fingered warriors, and ape-like cyclopean nightmares clawed though the frenzy in terrible vanguards that clashed in the fetid jungle mists. Thousands of "lesser" men swarmed after them into the melee; cannon, auto-pike, and sword fodder, endless fuel for a relentless wartime inferno that had burned now for over a hundred years.

The giants roared, and their men obeyed. Fiery *Behemoth* war engines churned both into the bloody mud, crushing them under abortive advances that stalled uselessly upon the mounds of broken bodies. Endless streams of young men formed behind the battle lines to take their turn at the slaughter. Seers and sages ranted their prophecies and ideologies like fire in their ears. The inferno spread to their hearts and engulfed them, until it glowed impenetrable from their eyes.

Titans fanned the flames with speeches of the war's glory. Then the boys went off to the trenches where they discovered the awful truth. By then it was too late. The sons of the gods took ownership of them, and proved to be the violent terrors that had haunted humanity's primal nightmares since their expulsion from Aeden, and who's "sons" would continue to haunt them long after their physical form faded to man's mythic race memory.

A'Nu-Ahki saw. A'Nu-Ahki knew. He was the conduit. Yet he was powerless to help the young men. He knew they did not want his help. Their fiery eyes glared up at him in accusation, as they marched by below him.

He understood their rage.

While their entire generation fed itself to the slaughter, the Valley of Seers in Akh'Uzan prospered. Its men, exempt from military service, were able to grow fat and wealthy selling food and lumber to the hungry war machine of Lumekkor. A'Nu-Ahki had bought this unholy exemption through his politically-arranged marriage. Instead of a haven for the spiritual Work of Q'Enukki, it had become a pocket of greedy self-righteous indolence. Thus, the young men hated him, and he could not blame them.

Weary of watching a battle he could do nothing about, Nu turned to gaze off into the green distance on the other side of the hill. The place was higher than it should have been—more exposed than any summit had a right to be in such times. He felt the eyes in the sky beat down upon him, as a roaring wave mounted in the west.

Below, on the other side, Akh'Uzan Valley sprawled as an agricultural empire that fueled the great slaughter. Farmers had staked claims in the meadows. Foresters harvested the hillside resin giants. Urugim's children, who had wanted no part of their father and Muhet'Usalaq at Paru'Ainu, had since emigrated from Sa-utar in hordes to avoid conscription. Impostors by the score faked their family tokens to join in the riches of the exemption—like the village tackle smith. Hungrily they set up house to divide the spoils.

The consuming wave out of the west struck the valley, but it was not water. Fluid filth consumed Akh'Uzan in its sticky sickly-sweet crash and undertow. Nothing held it back. Following it, a swarm of biting insects came, drawn by the rotten stench. Nobody could see it or smell it but Nu.

Something huge and dark snatched his senses; everything he saw, heard, and felt then warped violently toward it. Yet when the shadow passed, the scene was unchanged. The filthy wave drew out, leaving the landscape coated in its ooze, with clouds of flies swarming down.

A sting bit into the back of A'Nu-Ahki's neck. He slapped at the insect, but instead pulled away a great blood-sucking leech. He stared at the dying creature in his hand, all awash in his own redness. It writhed, turned over, and came up changed. Nu screamed, threw the thing down, and ground it under his foot. It had grown a human head, with his face on it.

"Whore lover!" The accusation came from the valley below.

"Wraith-faced tramp!" said another ungrateful mouth. "Does she make it worth the price of your soul every night with her whorish skills?"

All of Akh'Uzan gathered below to heap insults on Nu and his wife.

Tarkuni stepped up, shouting something about their children procreating like beasts in the field. His grandson Henumil joined him, eyes blazing holy hatred for the "Great Betrayal." A'Nu-Ahki recoiled, and almost turned back to the awful battle on the other side of the hill.

A single moderate voice sounded among the valley dwellers. "They are being unfair to you, my Captain. Too much was happening!" It came from Nestrigati the Acolyte, though the others drowned him out. Nu watched his former assistant shrug his shoulders, and bow out of the growing mob.

"We have our refuge!" Henumil balled his fists. "Why do you defile it with that woman? Divorce her!"

"We could go back to the way it was before if not for you!" Tarkuni added, "To the days when such things were not done!"

"No!" A'Nu-Ahki said, fed up with their stupidity. "Morons! Your own prosperity grew on the fact that I married her! You can't go back! We can never go back! Don't any of you understand? It can never be how it was before! Not now! Not ever! All we can do is turn from where we are now, and let E'Yahavah do something new. This is all coming to an end!"

He woke up with the crowing of the pre-dawn cock. Icy sweat ran down his face. Nevertheless, his dreams revealed nothing he had not already seen or heard in waking life.

Cool air blew in from the window, and ruffled Na'Amiha's fine straw hair next to him. He rolled out of the divan to pull on his clothes.

When he went down to the cooking hearth, he found that his father had already boiled water for the morning tea. He poured himself a bowl, and walked across the courtyard to climb the parapet walkway. A'Nu-Ahki and his father greeted the dawn as always, taking in the cool air high up on the battlements that curved around Lumekki's tower chamber.

The valley lay shrouded in pre-dawn mists while sunrise vermilions over Mount N'Zar gathered. Steam from their lotus tea curled the crisp air as they faced south, vapor sprites defying the great bloodletting that stretched across the land deceptively hidden just a few days march below the horizon.

"You got in late last night," Nu said at last. "What's the news?"

The old Tacticon grunted. "Same story—a futile attrition strategy. No movement, no change, just bigger cannons, and casualty counts. You'd think the commanders would learn after more than a century that they can't hope to bleed each other dry. E'Yahavah made the earth's resources too rich for that. I told Dumuzi, for instance, that they couldn't possibly wear each other down simply because the breeding life of a single married couple can last over five hundred years—that's not even factoring in polygamy!"

Nu's eyes narrowed. "The sons of Uzaaz'El and Samyaza are like three-hundred-cubit-tall giants eating the world's resources. Then when that isn't enough, they gobble up generations of men for dessert! You'd think the maths were simple enough for these supposedly semi-divine geniuses!"

Lumekki said, "Fortunately the giants aren't really so huge— except in peoples' minds, and in the stupid marching songs of their troops!"

Nu peered down into the mists, and felt their chill tendrils seeping over the land like clammy fingers. They smothered the morning's hope before the sun could fully rise. "With the Samyazas using the same industrial prefabrication techniques as

Bab'Tubila, things can keep going like this indefinitely, can't they? Both sides have the resources."

His father laid a hand on his shoulder. "Not indefinitely, Son. But for a long while yet—Assuri may have the method down, but it can't build Meldur up to Bab'Tubila's production capacity quickly enough to keep up forever. Not unless something radical happens to change the balance of power. That's one thing we have going for us."

"Listen to us! We're talking like this is really our war."

Lumekki said, "It may not be our war, but it affects our ability to do the work Iyared entrusted to us."

Nu gazed off into space. "Just what work would that be exactly?"

Silence.

The eyes of both men locked onto something that moved over the hills on the southern horizon.

"What's that?" Nu said; pointing at what he had first taken to be low-laying clouds forming over the forest mists.

"I don't know. But they're not clouds."

Minutes passed, as things focused. A'Nu-Ahki had long ago thought he was incapable of shock from anything more this war had. He was wrong.

Arcs of blood-red fire creased the eastward sides of the floating behemoths—for so they appeared to be; fleets of great elongated eggs, each with four stubby appendages on their undersides, two in front, and two aft. They approached with confident ease as they bludgeoned through the lifting dawn clouds, first in silence, then with a rattling drone, as they got closer.

The sun rose to color what appeared to be great airships in golds, reds, and blues—the colors of Samyaza's standard. Fiery serpentine seraf Watchers and gold leonine Kherubim with bows of lightning drawn in anger stretched across the rounded fronts of the approaching sky-boats. They swarmed over the valley in groups of four, in diamond flight formations. Nu noticed that their tails had crossed vertical and horizontal fins, with cords that pulled rudders left or right, up or down. The four pods on each ship all held some form of rotary fan engine—the source of the rattling drone noise.

Nu asked, "What keeps them up?"

"Lighter-than-air gas!" Lumekki said over the growing hum. "They must have found a fast, controllable way of extracting the lighter-than-air gas in huge quantity—probably by passing quickfire through water! But according to our chemists it's dangerously explosive!"

"Explosive or no, it looks like they've broken the stalemate."

As the fleets approached the farmland and villages, huge bay doors opened in the bottom of each craft.

"This isn't good," A'Nu-Ahki whispered, as one of the floating colossi veered their way.

"I should have never retired the platoon up here! Quick, help me get that cannon the Emperor gave you as a wedding gift out of the wall shed!"

"It can't be angled up high enough!"

"We might be able to rig something—all we'll need is one hit if that thing's filled with the lighter-than-air gas. It'll go up like a small sun!"

Giant grenades resembling flower pods at the monastery's distance began to drop from the slits underneath the airships as they over-flew the villages and farmlands. A hundred or so tumbled from each vessel, screaming demons making playful somersaults toward helpless targets below. They struck with a crackling staccato that outdid Nu's imagination of the fiery World-end. Green Akh'Uzan became a maelstrom of flame and swirling black smoke within minutes.

The airship that had detached to attack the monastery rattled nearer.

A'Nu-Ahki helped his father drag out the cannon and position it between wall buttresses. They placed a couple of kapar stone blocks beneath the forward wheels to increase elevation angle, and locked the carriage brakes. Lumekki returned to the wall shed, and re-emerged with a bag of powder packets in one arm, and two old-fashioned round shot.

"We've only got twenty rounds in there. Keep feeding them to me," he said to Nu. "The good news is that one hit is all we'll need."

"You already said that. What's the bad news?"

Lumekki shrugged. "It usually takes more than twenty rounds to bracket a moving target that's higher than you are."

The flying machine slowed, and seemed to be trying to gain altitude. Nu wondered if maybe its pilots saw a danger of being unable to escape the blast radius of their own bombs against the monastery's higher elevation.

Nu peeked over the parapet again as his father jostled the cannon to what he must have figured the best angle and azimuth for their first shot.

The nearest village of Akh'Uzan, by the tackle smithy and markets, had become a cauldron of flame. Smoke from the ruins threw sparking tendrils out into the surrounding meadows and woodlands in hundreds of panicky flame-spiders. Fields burned out of control, while farm workers ran like ants to flee the spreading inferno. A few houses escaped damage—usually the most secluded ones. However, if the fires continued to burn, these too would be in danger.

A'Nu-Ahki looked up again at the approaching airship.

On closer inspection, the flying machine did not seem to be very sturdy. Its skin appeared to be nothing more than a varnished cloth stretched over a light frame, probably made of reeds or wood, which buckled in the mountain breeze. It began to look as if the ship itself might be growing more difficult to handle the closer it flew into Mount N'Zar's thermal currents.

"How soon before it's in range?"

"Another minute or so," Lumekki said, as he squatted down and squinted at the cannon's aiming combs. He seemed to be making some hard calculations, so Nu left him alone after that.

The turret door swung open. Na'Amiha rushed out, followed by Muhet'Usalaq, and Mamu.

Nu's grandmother, on seeing the airships and the fires in the valley, buried her face in her husband's arms and began to shriek.

Na'Amiha ran to Nu as if he could actually protect her.

"What are they?" she shouted, as she grabbed his hand, and pulled his arm over her shoulder like a shawl. Her nails bit into his wrist.

Nu let her sink into the crook of his arm, and replied, "Samyazas have broken the stalemate by teaching men to fly!"

Na'Amiha said, "Surprised it hasn't happened before now." She let up on his wrist some. "Unless the Assurim dreamed them up on their own; some of Lumekkor's machines have nothing to do with Uzaaz'El."

"Yeah, but Assuri has always been backwards in such things. They tend to copy rather than invent."

Lumekki said, "I think it's in range!"

A'Nu-Ahki looked back at the airship. It now clearly showed signs of trouble in the wind currents. As it rose, a gust from the west at a higher thermal layer pushed it steadily toward Mount N'Zar. The rudders cocked hard dorsal and hard-a-port to steer it away from the treacherous rocks that overlooked the monastery. Peaks spiked away southward before bending east toward the Haunted Lands Pass. Even the vessel's fan-engines rotated now to add extra thrust against the breeze to escape them.

The higher the air-leviathan went, the stronger the wind became, until all its power worked just to maintain station-keeping. To do that, the ship came about to a lengthwise profile, parallel to the south rampart that held the gun—a target aspect larger than Lumekki could have hoped.

The cannon fired.

The barrel recoiled in its carriage slide, as the shot screeched away. It reached the top of its arc, level with the airship, but fell short.

"Up elevation angle by two degrees and more powder!" the Tacticon said to himself. He then rushed to the shed, and returned with a wooden slat, which he tried to wedge under the cannon.

Nu broke away from Na'Amiha to lift the carriage, careful not to sear his hands on the hot barrel.

The floating monstrosity angled closer, despite its inability to pull forward and away from the mountain.

Lumekki adjusted the gun's position, and roughed out a new firing solution. The airship continued to wrestle the thermal currents.

Nu figured the wind must be unnaturally strong to hold back four huge engines. He smiled, while 'Miha pushed her way back under his arm.

The wind's strength did not behave unnaturally as much as it did providentially. He quietly gave thanks, and squeezed his wife's shoulder.

Lumekki unleashed another round.

This shot tagged one of the ship's forward fan blades to shatter the engine pod without striking the upper bladder that held the lighter-than-air gas. The force absorbed by even this grazing impact sent the vehicle into a wobble that revealed the tiny pilot's cabin on its underside, between its forward engine-mounts, for the first time. It took almost a minute for the pilots to stabilize their craft, during which time Lumekki fired a third volley that missed several cubits right of target.

The airship could ill afford the power lost from its missing fan. It began falter in its battle with the wind, and drift now toward the rocky crags.

Lumekki fired two more missed shots before the air currents pushed the airship too far left, beyond the azimuth allowed by the rampart's fighting port. They watched the craft struggle for another fifteen minutes, first as it tried to drop out of the thermal layer, then by tacking southward. Neither move did more than prolong the inevitable.

A'Nu-Ahki's father had not overstated the effect of an impact on a flying machine held aloft by the lighter-than-air gas. It bounced lightly into the cliff face and teetered back out about forty cubits before collapsing into a roll of flame that consumed its fragile infrastructure like melting cobwebs. Staccato explosions shot from the tumbling fireball as its bomb load cooked-off and blew part of the mountainside down on top of the wreckage, which extinguished the fires as quickly as they had erupted.

The rest of Samyaza's air fleet had by this time heaved to, and retreated over the southern hills.

When Nu gazed over the devastation of Akh'Uzan, he was glad the cannon had not directly hit the airship as planned. The ensuing fire would have enveloped the wooded hills around his fortress home.

He caught his breath, and tightened his hold on 'Miha before his muscles started to quake uncontrollably. She melted into his embrace with a satisfied sigh, seemingly unaware he was simply clutching her so he wouldn't collapse into a post-stress panic attack like those he had often experienced after the kind of hunt back at Salaam-Surupag when men had died under his command. Emzara had intuitively understood the shaking. Na'Amiha just seemed content to huddle with him in destruction's aftermath—as if he had actually done something to protect her.

Nu's illusion of the war's distance was forever shattered. He decided to let his wife keep whatever illusions she had about his embrace. All the rules had just changed.

Although El-N'Lil, the Divine Wind of E'Yahavah, had blown protection across A'Nu-Ahki's family fortress, uneasiness remained, along with barely concealed tremors and silent thanksgivings.

He knew that the fire from the sky would soon be back.

A'Nu-Ahki set up the Akh'Uzan field hospital tent outside the ruins of the nearest village, under a canopy of gigantic redwood trees, to keep it camouflaged from the air.

Three times a week the flying death returned. The airships did not always strike the same targets, but they kept the region in continual turmoil.

The Valley of Seers had grown wealthy for over a century as the breadbasket of Tubaal-qayin Dumuzi's southeastern front. By its largess, the Dynasty of Steel had been able to keep Samyaza bottled in the lower Gihunu Valley, away from Khavilakki and the Near Kush headlands. Now payback from the enemy had arrived in full.

Twice more, air units had detached from their main fleet to attack the monastery fortress, each time using more ships. Both times, the Divine Wind, El-N'Lil, returned to send the fragile bombers into N'Zar's jagged teeth, one on top of another. Lumekki no longer even felt the need to man his cannon, as the enemy soon gave up on attacking Q'Enukki's Retreat.

Not so the farms and villages.

Over two hundred people had died in the fire storms so far, and almost twice as many lay with severe burns or lost limbs across the field hospital's dirt floor—more than half of them children. A'Nu-Ahki learned not to eat in the morning because the stench of charred flesh would only bring his breakfast back up on him.

Mamu and Na'Amiha had taken to scouring the meadows for wild aloe plants because they had to harvest Nu's entire medicinal crop in a single week to treat all the burn victims. Bathing vats lined one side of the enclosure to contain the worst cases. Amomun lotus water, steeped, then cooled to lukewarm, continually had to be poured in and drained to regulate body temperatures and keep the victims hydrated. Most people burned this badly did not live long anyway.

Nu's greatest fear was not that the airships would discover their infirmary and destroy it, but that his opiate pain powders would run out, and that the groans and weeping would turn instead into shrieks while he debrided the dead tissue from the burns.

Mountain birds sang madly over the dead and dying. Nu paused to rinse his bloody hands and stretch. The sudden urge to dash from the tent and never return wore itself down to his grabbing a seat on a barrel by the flaps to catch a little of the deceptively sweet outside air.

A woman about half Nu's age with half her face burned away lay on a blanket nearby, repeatedly counting her fingers aloud to herself. He recognized the other half of her face as belonging to one of the women rescued from the pens at Salaam-Surupag a hundred years ago.

"One, two, three, four, five..." she switched hands, "...six, seven, eight, nine, ten... not enough—there's never enough! One, two, three..."

"Make her shut up!" A priest demanded of Nu.

The local Keeper of the Altar lay on a linen sheet next to the counting woman. He glared up at A'Nu-Ahki as if he had power over the woman to make her speak or be still.

"One, two, three, four..."

"Make her be silent!" said the Priest, who no longer had any legs. "How can anybody offer a proper prayer with her constant noise? It's disrespectful to the Divine Name!"

Nu slid down off his seat, and squatted next to the woman so he could look into her eyes and get her attention.

"Why do you keep counting your fingers?" He said to her softly.

Her glazed eyes met his, and seemed to peer right through him. "I don't have enough fingers. I try to make sure they're all there, but I'm missing too many."

A'Nu-Ahki gently clasped both of her hands in his. "Look, you have five fingers on each hand—just like me."

She jerked her head back and forth, and shouted, "No! You don't understand! I'm trying to keep track! At Salaam-Surupag, I had sixteen children, and I couldn't keep them together in the rush! I tried to count their heads as we moved beyond the gates. Then the armies attacked! I saw twelve of them killed, and the others... who knows? They were my first fertile cycle. Yesterday fire rained down from heaven, and the eight children from my new cycle all burned! I'm trying to count heads, but I don't have enough fingers. I never have enough, and their screaming never stops!"

She laughed like one of the mad song birds outside.

"I'm sorry."

She looked up at him, suddenly more lucid. "They say you have the seer's gift, though my husband calls you a heretic for 'marrying that whore of Qayin,' as he puts it. Me, I'm not so quick to judge.

But tell me, why does E'Yahavah hate me? I'm a reasonable woman—I understand that bad things happen in life. After Salaam-Surupag, I didn't even blame him or curse heaven as many did. But twice? If you're a seer, surely you have insight?"

A'Nu-Ahki stared at her, wanting to avert his eyes to avoid the question, and the wretchedness. Instead, he locked them onto hers. *I owe her that much, since any possible answer must seem trite and empty.*

"E'Yahavah does not hate you."

She laughed, blowing half-clotted blood from her nose. "Where does he hide then? Where's his power and protection for the Seer Clan?"

"I lost my family, too, at Salaam-Surupag. There's no magic shield for us against mortality and suffering—no special power to sidestep pain."

She relaxed her head back into the rolled clothes she used for a pillow. "Then what good is trusting him if there's no power? He's just another broken hope that doesn't work in the real world. What good is it?"

A'Nu-Ahki hated that he knew what to say to her. He hated even more that his conscience wouldn't allow him to not say it, and that he had to say it to himself as much as to her. "It isn't about what works, but about what's true. I find it unsatisfying too sometimes, but there it is."

"What good is truth if it doesn't work?"

"A lie works fine in the short-run to evade painful realities, but the truth eventually catches up. Denying truth doesn't work in the end. Living under the authority of a real Creator who has the right and power to give and take life in the real world—like anything else in reality—has a down side. Even so, it has unending advantages over believing in something we create in our own imaginations simply to comfort ourselves."

"What advantages?" The indignation in her eyes burned.

"Only a God who is really there can help. Our comfort fantasies—even when couched in Seti's religion—have only our own affections behind them. They seem to work if life does not demand too much of us. But they were not enough to help me through the loss of my first wife and family—though I used the very prayers of the Seer himself, when I prayed at all."

He mopped the sweat from the unburned side of her brow with a towel. "Truth is I was mostly too tired even for that. But the Great

Maker responded to me anyway. Call on him. I'll not inflict any further litanies on you. They tend to sound too much like mockeries when we're inside the cauldron. I've found that E'Yahavah understands this too."

"Is your litany any less a mockery?" She swiped his hand away.

"Perhaps not, but my words aren't meant to mock you. You asked me and so I've answered. I say that if you trust him, E'Yahavah will see you through this. Beyond that, I know little."

"Then you don't even know that much! If this is how he shows his love; who will there be to help us when he shows us his hate?"

"I don't pretend to have the answers. My first wife and my children were my entire world. Even so, I know he has not abandoned us."

"Leave me alone. I have too many dead babies to count. One... Two... Three..."

A'Nu-Ahki rose to leave her in peace.

"Make that woman shut up!" the Priest demanded again.

Nu dropped to his knees again and stuck his finger right in the fellow's face. "You shut up and let her count, or I'll let you miss a few doses of opium powder, and see how well you like the feel of things! Get it?"

"So it's true," the Priest said. "You really are a heretic. Only a heretic speaks so to a priest of the Altar."

But he gave A'Nu-Ahki no further trouble.

The new light cannons pointed skyward like angry needles in the sunlight. They surrounded the small military compound at the crossroads village in the mouth of the Akh'Uzan Valley. Wreckage from four Samyaza airships still burned in the outlying fields.

The Titan straticon snarled, "It's a waste to station so many sky cannons this far back. Samyaza gains ground beneath his air fleet!" His huge misshapen head reminded A'Nu-Ahki of a lumpy up-ended pear.

Lumekki said to Tubaal-qayin Dumuzi, "Lord, you cannot allow the continued disruption of your supply line."

The Titan scowled down at Nu's father.

Tubaal-qayin did not. He nudged his signalman. "How soon?"

"We should see them any moment, Lord, if the last oracle dispatch is accurate on their departure time."

The Emperor scanned the northwest horizon over the grasslands, and then turned again to the small knot of officers and local elders he had called to meet him. Nu had accompanied his father down from Q'Enukki's Retreat more out of curiosity than anything else.

Since Dumuzi gave each village a mobile sky cannon unit, the "Samyaza Gas Bags" had begun to take as good as they gave out. New casualties at the hospital tents began to decline after months of carnage.

Tubaal-qayin said, "Gentlemen, the issue is now moot."

A'Nu-Ahki heard a buzz out of the north, like a giant swarm of angry wasps. He gazed over the meadows to where the Dumuzi watched.

What looked like a cloud of locusts began to take shape over the horizon. As the objects drew nearer, Nu saw that they did in fact resemble giant insects, though they flew a straight course toward the military camp. When they arrived, the small flying machines began to circle overhead, where Nu got a better look at them.

They had no gas bladders, but a wide sandwich of fixed wings attached perpendicular to twin cylindrical bodies that housed large rotary engines. Between the two engine nacelles, at the wing layers' center of gravity, Nu could see the pilot cabin and its sky cannon mount. The invert pentagram of Uzaaz'El emblazoned the underside of each wing.

One by one, the strange flying machines began to dip down like birds to light upon the open fields outside the army camp.

"I call them *aerodrones*," Tubaal-qayin said to his dumbstruck guests. "Faster and more maneuverable than Samyaza's lighter-than-air ships, they shall soon cover a huge counter-offensive in the south that will outflank Assuri's drive on Kushtahar and the Great Havens."

Lumekki said, "They look like mating dragon flies."

"We've actually been working on them for a few years—even before Samyaza unleashed his air fleet," said the Emperor. "The trick was to develop a grain-spirit-fueled engine light enough to provide the thrust needed to cause moving air to lift under the wings."

Nu said, "More help from Uzaaz'El?"

"Not much. The power plants are air cooled, which got rid of the water weight of a conventional coolant system. In fact, I actually ordered them built and flown south against Uzaaz'El's wishes."

"Why would he not wish you to use them?"

The Emperor laughed, which seemed to rankle his titan straticon. "He wanted us to explore an air route over the *Kharir Aedenu* – fat chance! Every time we sent a drone up into those peaks, it never returned. I decided to quit wasting prototypes, and mass-produce a combat model. I hear my glowing friend was furious, but he'll get over it."

Nu was glad to hear there were still some limits the Watchers and their minions could not violate.

"How far can they fly before refueling?" Lumekki asked.

Tubaal-qayin shook his head. "No statistics, gentlemen. The foray into the Mountains of Aeden was to search out advance bases – the drones would not have made it all the way through to Assuri and back. Likewise they can't cross your Haunted Lands to Samyaza's industrial centers."

Nu asked, "Will these machines enable you to win the war quickly?"

The Emperor shrugged. "Eventually – unless Samyaza produces drones of his own. There's no magic answer here, but I'm hopeful."

Nu disliked the lack of assurance in Tubaal-qayin's tone. It haunted his ride back up to Q'Enukki's Retreat the following day and well beyond.

The Dumuzi's words proved more prophetic than any Divine whisper A'Nu-Ahki had heard in a long while.

The better aircraft tipped the scales of war over to Lumekkor for a time. Tubaal-qayin Dumuzi soon retook the ground lost to Samyaza during Assuri's air superiority, and even make good his counter-offensive. It did not take long, however, for several of Lumekkor's craft to crash inside enemy territory. Within a year, the Assurim copied the technology just as they had everything else.

The fighting stalled again at a pitched line just a few days journey southeast of the old fortresses. By the end of the second year into the Age of Flight, it was almost as if nothing had changed – except that casualty counts were higher, and life behind the lines for soldiers on rest leave had lost its recuperative quality due to the persistent threat of air attack.

The constantly improving aerodrones of Lumekkor ensured that few Samyaza raids ever reached as far north as Akh'Uzan again. Soon the countryside was dotted with landing fields, until rarely a day went by that Nu did not see or hear at least one of the machines buzz overhead.

Again, the years of distant warfare stretched on, while Nu and his wife settled back into their dull routine. It became hard for him not to wonder if the Divine Name had simply forgotten them. The world changed quickly outside, while life in Akh'Uzan seemed frozen in its timeless cycle of watching and waiting. Nu could not help but ask, *waiting for what?*

He didn't know that he was asking the wrong question.

In 1938, Dr. Wilhelm Konig, an Austrian archaeologist rummaging through the basement of the museum, made a find that was to drastically alter all our concepts of "ancient knowledge." A 6-inch-high pot of bright yellow clay dating back *two millennia* contained a cylinder of sheet-copper 5 inches by 1.5 inches. The edge of the copper cylinder was soldered with a 60-40 lead-tin alloy comparable to today's solder. The bottom of the cylinder was capped with a crimped-in copper disk and sealed with bitumen or asphalt. Another insulating layer of asphalt sealed the top and also held in place an iron rod suspended into the center of the copper cylinder. The rod showed evidence of having been corroded with an acidic agent. With a background in mechanics, Dr. Konig recognized this configuration was not a chance arrangement—the clay pot was nothing less than an ancient electric battery.

However, Dr. Konig also found copper vases plated with silver in the Baghdad Museum, excavated from Sumerian sites in southern Iraq, dating back to at least 2500 BCE. When the vases were lightly tapped, a blue patina or film separated from the surface, which is characteristic of silver electroplated onto copper base. It would appear then that the Parthians *inherited* their batteries from one of the earliest known civilizations.

—Lumir G. Janku
The Modern Past: Batteries of Babylon

13

FIREDRAKE

The summons had roused A'Nu-Ahki from the tedium of hovering anxiety and dwindling hope. The regular clop-clop of the onager-drawn carriage reminded him of his own existence—how he simply did what as expected of him year after year, like a bridled beast, just tolerating life. He tried not to let it show around 'Miha. When she noticed the distance in his eyes, she tended to blame herself. But this wasn't her fault.

Lumekki sat next to him, while Muhet'Usalaq snored on the seat across from them.

The Old Soldier raised his tufted brows. "What's wrong, Son?"

Nu became aware that his father had been watching him for some time. He wasn't sure how, or even if he wanted to answer.

"Just looking for some sort of sign or direction—been looking far too long," he finally said, after his father would not turn away.

"Ahh, the Big Divine Silence—I know it well. At least you're still looking."

Nu chuckled without much mirth. "Guess I'm too much a son of the Seer Clan to ever stop doing that entirely."

"But you've slowed it down a bit. It's good you go forward, even if slowly. E'Yahavah doesn't reveal everything clearly. Often, you just have to ask for wisdom, trust that it's been given, and then take your best shot. "

"I feel the energy of my youth shriveling up. Is it me or have all the villages of Akh'Uzan tripled in size since I last came down this road?"

"A common malady once you settle into your four-hundreds. Gray patches in the beard, a less forgiving back..."

Nu cut him off. "That's not what I mean."

"Na'Amiha's worried about you."

A'Nu-Ahki stared out the window. "You know, I've been married to her now for almost as long as I was to Emza—can you believe that? I listen to her bubble along about her days—a husband's supposed to listen—I say the right things at the right time. But the truth is... by Aeden, we've done nothing here! And the time—it just slides by faster and faster while this infernal war goes on and we lose what little vitality remains..."

If the summons had roused A'Nu-Ahki, it only left Na'Amiha with a worry-creased forehead. She'd opted to stay home, which was just fine with her husband. He would never deliberately hurt her feelings, but he needed a break from her—could he tell his father that?

"I know she didn't want you to come," Lumekki said. "She's afraid because she loves you. Whenever her nephew calls, I see it in her face..."

"I know. But I really needed to get away." *She's been insatiable lately. It's either feast or famine with her! Only now, I'm the one who can't perform! Never saw that coming...*

"All couples need a break from each other now and then."

"I never needed one from Emza."

Lumekki frowned. "You and Emza were young. You're not..."

"No, of course not!"

"I didn't really think so."

"No worries Pahpo, you saved our marriage a long time ago. It's just that lately I feel like I've lost the ability to hold up my end of things. It's like she needs something from me that I just don't have — and I've no idea what that is or how to get it. Am I just not affectionate enough?"

It's more than just the bedchamber, Nu wanted to add, but didn't. *Her clingy hunger is as spiritual as it is emotional and physical. No number of walks to Grove Hollow, no amount of quiet evening conversation, no deluge of affection is ever enough! I can't even go to the water closet without her fearfully asking me where I'm going and when I'll be back!*

Lumekki shrugged. "I can't help you there, Son. You seem attentive. Sometimes, you just have to do what you have to do when it's time to do it. She's a good woman — better than I ever expected from her background — much better than you would have done locally, I'm ashamed to admit."

"I know."

"The Zaqen and I were not too happy about the sudden journey either, but I guess a day's ride to Farguti Crossroads is little more than an inconvenience really. And it's time you show your face around the Dumuzi again, whether he likes it or not. Besides, you needed to get away."

Nu felt the carriage turn through the gates of their destination.

The once-tiny hamlet at the mouth of the Valley of Akh'Uzan had expanded much even in the few years since Nu had last seen it. Over a century of soldiers and war matériel passing through it to the Southern Front had enriched the house of Farguti son of Urugim far beyond the wildest dreams of avarice. Nu found that ironic, since Farguti had been one of Urugim's many younger sons that had refused his father's call to Paru'Ainu, and had only relocated later to Akh'Uzan because of the military service exemption provided by the acceptance of Muhet'Usalaq's fosterage.

The Prime Zaqen — who woke up as the coach bumped to a halt — had found Farguti's fortune far more than just ironic. Earlier, on the road down from Q'Enukki's Retreat, he had grumbled that it was a personal insult to have the conference at this man's gigantic and overdone new home.

Nu found Tubaal-qayin Dumuzi's presence at the gate unsurprising — though usually one of such high rank would have left the greetings to professional courtiers. The Metalsmith-king's titan bodyguards, who tried unsuccessfully to blend into the floral background scenery, surrounded the place like gigantic bronze sculptures done by an artist with extremely poor taste. *The*

"Shepherd" wants something again. Nu saw that the Dumuzi had that 'please help the pathetic satyr' look in his sunken eyes.

Despite A'Nu-Ahki's negotiation debacle with Isha'Tahar a few decades ago, the Emperor of Lumekkor had continued to rely on Lumekki as an informal advisor. Military thinking was timeless in some ways. Aside from the wisdom of Nu's father, who tried to keep his tactical theory up to date for the latest battlefield technology, Tubaal-qayin also knew where his army's bread, ore, and lumber came from.

"Welcome, and thank you for coming." Tubaal-qayin extended a hand to each of them in turn. "I leased this wing of your kinsman's house for our meeting because I did not want to inconvenience you too much. Please come inside and refresh yourselves."

"Thank you, Your Highness," Lumekki said, once it became clear that Muhet'Usalaq was going to play things tough, sour, and silent.

Nu realized immediately that his father would do most of the talking, while the Prime Zaqen observed. He also knew that his grandfather was not just being difficult. Rather, it was for the purpose of plausible deniability—if it seemed that Lumekki got into trouble in his representation of Seer Clan policy, Muhet'Usalaq could always claim that his son had misspoken.

Nu also understood with a shudder his own place in this relationship. He was supposed to be the "expert" adviser—and indeed his expertise ranged to a variety of things. If both Lumekki and Muhet'Usalaq found themselves buried by their own words, A'Nu-Ahki existed mainly to take the political fall for having misadvised them. The approaching doors to the mansion began to feel like the jaws of some huge animal.

Inside Farguti's gigantic ante-chamber lay a banquet table. The travelers from Q'Enukki's Retreat stacked themselves each a moderate plate, but limited their drink intake to a goblet of sweet new wine apiece. Nu made sure to take only a single sip for courtesy's sake, and to leave the rest stand.

After everybody had eaten, Tubaal-qayin signaled the conference to begin by ordering the servants out, and the big doors shut. The whole time, his cordial smile never met his eyes, which seemed to sink further into his skull as he spoke. Nu figured that a century and a half of trench warfare would do that to a man—usually worse. This one didn't seem smart enough to change a foreign policy that was bleeding his empire dry, however. Maybe he was too oblivious to notice the uselessness of his strategy, and too unimaginative to think outside that paradigm.

Kings had been so foolish before, but not usually for so long. Then again, maybe by now his titan generals were the ones really in control. Nu had heard distant rumblings to that effect.

Tubaal-qayin said, "I've called the Seer Clan because what we've recently discovered affects them as much as it does our general war effort."

Nu didn't know whether to be frightened or excited. Either way, the Emperor's opening words ensured that he would be attentive.

"First, let me assure the Seer Clan that I fully intend to respect the terms of Iyared's Oath for the Archonic Line. My logistics status is greatly enhanced by that agreement, and I will not threaten so important a treaty."

A'Nu-Ahki felt a momentary relief—until he heard the rest of what Dumuzi "the Shepherd" had to say.

"Several weeks ago, one of our patrols east of Salaam-Surupag shot down a courier aerodrone carrying the latest code machine from Samyaza's high command. Though the courier died, the pilot survived the crash. We flew him, and the machine, out from a secret drone field we have up in the mountains nearby. We placed into the wreck a smashed model of an earlier decoder and arranged for the crash site to appear far more destructive than it had actually been. We also replaced the pilot with a body flown in from another drone crash before we simulated a fuel fire in the wreckage.

"When we interrogated the pilot, we found that his mother had been a woman captured at the sacking of Salaam-Surupag. The young man was most cooperative, and volunteered all sorts of information about enemy drone engineering and movements, little of which turned out remarkable. He also informed us that his mother, and indeed many of the captured women from Salaam-Surupag, were still alive and settled at Samyaza's chief Temple-run industrial city of Iglat-Meldur."

Lumekki asked, "Can you verify his story?"

The Dumuzi's Master Assassin, who also served as an intelligence adviser, said, "To some degree, yes. We've had information for two decades that many of the women from Salaam-Surupag were settled in Meldur..."

"Why didn't you tell us?" Nu said. Visions of his lost daughters flooded his heart like angry ghosts for the first time in many years.

"We didn't think you had a need to know..." the Master Assassin tried to explain.

"Need to know!"

Reactions and counter-reactions across the table began to fly out of control. Tubaal-qayin raised his arm for silence, and somehow regained command of the proceedings. He suddenly seemed far more in touch with things than Nu had ever given him credit for being.

"It can be argued fairly that this information could have been shared with the Seer Clan," said the Emperor. "But would this intelligence have been actionable for you? We would have risked the compromise of several important intelligence sources simply to provide you with information that might have been nice for you to know, but impossible for you to respond to."

Lumekki nodded, apparently able to see Tubaal-qayin's position. Nu also saw, but felt less sanguine about it than his father seemed.

Muhet'Usalaq spoke for the first time. "So why tell us now?"

Tubaal-qayin folded his hands on the table in front of him. "We have here an opportunity to establish an intelligence network inside Samyaza's chief industrial city. The pilot confirmed our suspicion that many of the wounded Assurim veterans of the Salaam-Surupag Invasion have since settled at Meldur, and taken work in its Temple factories. Many of your women have been kept as concubines by these men, and by the disabled titans that led them, to compensate for their injuries."

The room seemed to turn purple for Nu, as he pictured his twin daughters 'Ranna and 'Nissa struggling against the obscene pawing of...

Lumekki said, "So what do you want from us?"

The Emperor looked down at his folded hands. "None of the women from Salaam-Surupag have any reason to trust my operatives. I understand your people actually suspected that I would be the invader of your city and that the Samyazas took you quite by surprise..."

"You want one of us to go there," Nu concluded aloud.

"To sum it up, yes. But I will not force you against Iyared's Oath."

"Though not to rescue our people," Nu said.

Tubaal-qayin nodded. "No. We need them to stay put for now."

"Then why should we do it?"

"There will be a treaty of repatriation when the war ends. Assuri will owe huge reparations not only to us, but to your people as well. I will insist that repatriation be a part of that."

"You assume Lumekkor can break a stalemate that's lasted a century and a half." Lumekki said. "Yet your own strategy of attrition has set up this self-sustaining slaughter!" By now, it seemed a useless litany even to Nu.

"Only if all things continue unchanged," said Tubaal-qayin.

"What is going to change?" Nu asked, staring into "the Shepherd's" eyes to see if so much as a twitch there would reveal a lie in his response.

"I can't talk about that. But things are changing. When the time is right, a properly placed network of operatives could hamstring Samyaza's industrial capacity long enough for us to exploit a major offensive along several fronts. There are also other factions involved. That's all I can say."

No twitch, no lies; at least none for the moment.

Tubaal-qayin Dumuzi added, "What if the mother of this pilot knows the fate of your daughters, A'Nu-Ahki?"

"What do you care about my daughters?"

"Frankly, my war plans don't even consider them. But I'm not a heartless monster, as some of your local religious propaganda paints me."

"Our press prints only the books of Q'Enukki, and that piece of nonsense about how I killed the gryndel," Nu replied.

"Then another press operates in Akh'Uzan in your Zaqen's name."

A'Nu-Ahki exchanged glances with his two sires.

Muhet'Usalaq spoke again. "Thank you for bringing this to my attention. Be assured that I have not authorized such a thing. It will stop."

"That is good to know," said the Dumuzi. "I didn't really think you had. The scrolls say some pretty rancid things about the Royal Aunt, and your grandson here too—something about the 'heresy of a false Comforter' —whatever that means."

Nu looked at both his father and grandfather. Muhet'Usalaq nodded to him ever so slightly.

"I'll go to Meldur," A'Nu-Ahki said. "How do I get there?"

Nu's sudden confidence wilted when Tubaal-qayin told him.

The *Firedrake* multi-terrain light armored chariot had an extended fuel range enhanced by additional tanks attached to its outer covering. These sat beneath a façade of flexible plates and ringlets that camouflaged the vehicle as a large spike-tail dragon to passing aerodrones. Not that there were many of those around. Neither Lumekkor nor Assuri had aircraft with fuel ranges to sortie across the Haunted Lands of Southern Aeden and back. Intelligence had the Southern Watcher's fleet of obsolete "Samyaza Gas Bag" airships patrolling the mountains on Assuri's western border, however.

Except for the heat and constant weaving through dense foliage, the amphibious millipede-tracked vehicle made travel through the Haunted Lands almost comfortable. Not enough to take away the shadow that hung over the place, but enough so Nu could leave much of the vigilance to others, and sleep most of the way. Dragons still ruled here, if only over the heart.

The *Firedrake* carried enough firepower to kill a large gryndel at close range—as Nu had seen it do with its hidden aft tail cannon. The ease with which it had done so gave him little comfort. For one, the gun was only for ground targets; it could not be elevated against their real threat—airships. Only the aero-cannon under the spike-tail decoy could take on those; but if it came to that, it meant that their insertion mission was already a failure. Secondly, the tail cannon's use on the gryndel only heightened Nu's sense that he traveled with men doomed by a suicidally blind over-confidence.

The monster had stalked them since the river—a gryndel matriarch as large as any Nu had ever seen. The driver had intentionally slowed to let their stalker catch up. Had it lunged just right, the huge wurm could have torn much of the *Firedrake's* facade off in its teeth—including the rear gun-port and false tail— cannon and all.

The Guild mechanic had cackled like an idiot when he fired into the gryndel's howling mouth. The Dragon Queen's massive head and throat—which had filled Nu's childhood nightmares and adult hunting patrols with such terror—rippled and bulged for a rolling half-second before it exploded like a wet, meaty joke. Its legs, body, and tail walked on for several discombobulated steps, unaware that the head was gone. Then it fell over, just a ludicrous load of collapsing slop to feed smaller carrion wurms.

Nu had no love of gryndels. What disturbed him was how these men made everything seem like a twisted joke. He had no patience with the shallow traditionalism that had eroded the Dragon-slayer Order—at least as it had degenerated in Akh'Uzan under the watch of such as Tarkuni and Henumil—from a noble line of paladin sages to a glorified jousting club that resented anything or anyone that encouraged depth of thought, ethics, or humility. Yet Nu's present traveling companions had lost even that veneer.

He sensed that these Guild men and Dumuzi's "Assassins" would find it equally comical to mutilate something that was as much a symbol of good as the Dragon had been of evil. It made no difference to them, either in form or substance. They just liked to blow up anything big and alive that would do a raggedy death-dance for them as it went down or flew apart.

Relative safety and lack of desire for such companionship was not why A'Nu-Ahki found it easy to sleep so much of the way, however.

The *Firedrake* had started out about a week ago from a temporary fueling depot not far from the Gihunu River campsite where Nu had met his father after his previous trek through the Haunted Lands a century and a half ago. Tubaal-qayin's Guild had been testing a new kind of armored chariot there that ran on distilled oil from the resinous *glakka* tree. Nu discovered at the fueling station that Lumekkor was slowly building its capability to traverse the wide dragon-infested Gihunu River valley with tracked vehicles; someday hoping to strike Samyaza's naturally protected heartland.

The *Firedrake* still ran on grain spirits however, which burned too quickly, with too little released energy for such ambitious operations—at least according to the Guild mechanic Nu had briefly befriended at the camp. There A'Nu-Ahki had learned that Guild mages and mechanics were so proud of their machines that he could easily get them to talk about them.

They even called them by feminine pet names, like women in their own shared metallic harem. *Squat, hard, and ugly girls with the tempers of gryndel matriarchs,* Nu thought. *One day such careless bragging will be their undoing.* His written debrief to the Prime Zaqen would be an epic at least, worth all the trouble in itself.

Two vehicles had set out; one loaded with extra grain spirit fuel to extend the range of the other, which carried A'Nu-Ahki and a team of two Guild drivers, a mechanic, and six Imperial Assassins. They parted company with tanker *Firedrake* two days before, to await their return. They had killed the gryndel matriarch the following day. Except for briefings and necessary interaction, Nu kept to the very back of the vehicle, tucked under the tail cannon, between the water and food stores.

He tried to collate his observations for his future report, but found his mind wandering instead. He thought of the captive women in Assuri, so long destitute even of his regular prayers, and melted with shame.

What will I say to them after all these decades? He wondered, as the diffused green light slipped in through the firing slits from the thinning forest highlands outside. *Will they understand what happened? How will I even be able to look them in the eye and tell them that I must leave them in bondage still for years longer? Maybe I am just a false Comforter.*

Nu's eyes closed again as the images came unbidden. The darkness only made them clearer—girls being raped and abused, then left to care for multitudes of bastard children in fortressed bordellos. Filth, squalor, and misery—how many bastards could they have born in one hundred and fifty years? If his daughters drew the resting half of their fertility cycle first, as their mother had, the number might not be as many. On the other hand, maybe some of the soldiers had been decent enough to take them as wives or concubines. Tubaal-qayin had said as much.

They had looked so much like Emza—especially 'Ranna and 'Nissa! Is that why I try not to think of them anymore? Is that why my prayers for them turn to soggy pulp in my mouth?

"*You have not given up on me. More to the point, I have not given up on you,*" said that long absent Voice that was not just an inner voice.

"No," Nu whispered to himself, "But except for the Firefall, I've lived in comfortable insignificance, and grown weary even of the one thing I could still do for them. What does that make me? Certainly not a Comforter from A'Nu—or anyone else for that matter."

Inner silence.

"I thought as much."

Nu fluffed his pack, turned on his side, and went back to sleep.

Sub-Altern Inguska of the Assurim Demigod Corps tugged on the sleeve of the pilot next to him in the flying ship's wheel house. He had to shout to make himself heard over the droning engines. "I thought I saw something down there. Swing about!"

The pilot spun the wheel and slowly brought the lighter-than-air monstrosity into a circular flight pattern. They were far enough west of the mountain range not to worry about inversion turbulence.

Inguska lifted the telescope to his eye again to try to re-establish contact with what he thought he had seen. Something large moved through the high brush—probably just a behemoth—though they usually stayed down in the swamps at that time of year. Whatever it was, carved a swath through the greenery that seemed just a tad too straight for an oversized snake-necked, battering-ram-tailed cow looking to sample the highland flora.

"There!" Inguska pointed down to the left. The creature crossed through a break in the foliage.

The pilot laughed. "It's just a stray spike-tail."

"Its movement doesn't seem right," said the sub-altern, who adjusted his spy-glass to squeeze more magnification from its lenses. "The tail doesn't swing from side to side."

"So?"

Inguska said, "I grew up on the Northern March, near the eaves of Wyverna Wood! I saw many spike-tails and even killed me a few that stomped my father's sugar cane. When they run, their tails sway to the rhythm of their hind legs. That one is moving like a wyverna is chasing it, but its tail just drags. I can't see the legs so well in the undergrowth."

The pilot swung the airship around one more time. "Maybe a wyverna *is* chasing it and already got a bite in at the meaty part. It could be wounded so the tail doesn't swing."

"I don't see a wyverna."

"I think the boredom of border watch is getting to you. You want to be where the giants are."

Inguska wanted to shout about the divinity in his bloodline. Instead, he pointed out to the starboard aerial cannon mount on the outside deck that surrounded the pilot's shack. "Let me take a shot at it to make sure!"

The pilot, who was a full Altern in command of the craft, shook his head. "Not today, 'Guska. We have to make it back through the pass before the dusk winds with enough fuel to reach the Southern Fortress. We'll come back tomorrow and see if we can pick it up again. I'll even let you fire the light cannon at it for practice — though it's just a dragon."

Inguska scowled as the great airship heaved about on a south-easterly heading for the mountains.

The *Firedrake* stopped in a small gorge up in the foothills of the mountain range that divided the Haunted Lands from Western Assuri. A few hundred cubits higher was a seldom-used pass. The armored carrier could take them no farther and still have enough fuel to return to the waiting tanker deep in the lowland jungle behind them.

The drivers had followed a well-worn behemoth migration trail up to the heights. The gigantic long-necked herbivores came up from the swamps once a year to the more sparsely wooded foothills to calve and nurture their young on highland shrubbery, where fewer large predators roamed.

They had spotted a "Samyaza gas bag" yesterday that circled them a couple times at high altitude before moving on. The Guild mechanic had squeezed into the quadruple mount, rotating anti-drone cannon array on the *Firedrake's* roof, just in case they had to jettison their camouflage plates and open fire. Fortunately, the airship had moved on.

Even so, the Imperial Assassins took no chances. The first thing they did when the vehicle slid to a stop was jump out and pop up a green and brown net awning over the *Firedrake* to help hide it from the patrolling airships. One of them also ran back to the nearest stand of trees, grabbed a fallen branch, and started to brush away the last of their tread marks.

Nu emerged from the cramped vehicle just as the assassins finished tying down the last of the camouflage net. His ears still rang with the drone of the *Firedrake's* engines, so he rubbed them to make it stop.

He realized something was wrong when the hum grew louder.

Sub-Altern Inguska shouted for the second day in a row, "There!"

"What? I don't see anything," said the pilot.

"Take her down to about a hundred cubits. I'll show you!"

The pilot shook his head, but he threw the latches to bleed off some lighter-than-air gas and decrease their altitude. The dials for the pressurized tanks showed almost three-quarters full, so it would not hurt to indulge his excitable young partner. It might even break the monotony of sentry patrol.

"Look at the furrow now!" Inguska handed the pilot his glass.

"Yeah, I see what you mean," the pilot said, after several seconds of sweeping the ground with the telescope.

"That is definitely the print of a millipede tread chariot."

The pilot's head snapped up as he handed the telescope back to the sub-altern. "Get on the oracle to the gods. Let's see where this leads."

"Get down!"

One of the assassins tackled A'Nu-Ahki and pushed him into a swath of brush next to the shrouded *Firedrake*.

Another crawled back into the vehicle in case he had to blow the "dragon-hide charges" that would jettison the spike-tail camouflage to open a firing field for the anti-drone weapons.

The airship emerged from behind the last stand of trees down slope, flying lower even than those that had tried to attack Q'Enukki's Retreat during the Firefall Raids. It rose like a fiery moon, so near that Nu could make out two men in its gondola—one inside the wheelhouse and another on a narrow railed platform surrounding the cabin. The one on the platform used a spy-glass. Fortunately, the sun was getting low on the western horizon, which made the shadows in the small canyon long and distorted.

"I had just enough time to sweep our tracks back to the trees," reported one of the assassins to his leader. "They might not see us here."

The Lead Assassin, who crouched right behind A'Nu-Ahki, cursed. "They might've seen our tread marks where we crossed that open meadow! I knew we should've stopped to sweep them once we made the bush again."

"Would've exposed us for too long," said the Junior Assassin.

"If they saw tracks, they're following our bush furrow right to us!"

A'Nu-Ahki said, "Maybe not."

Both assassins turned and glared at him.

Nu explained. "When Samyaza first came out with the gas bags they tried several times to attack my ancestor's monastery. They never could pull it off because the inversion updrafts near the mountains gave them too much trouble. Maybe they're just following this game trail up through the pass to get back to their base on the other side before sunset, when the winds shift."

The Junior Assassin said, "He might be right."

The airship pulled past the trees and over-flew the rocky meadow between the wood and the *Firedrake*, until it hovered above the camouflage canopy. A'Nu-Ahki watched up through the netting as something small and round dropped from the airship's gondola and plummeted straight at him.

Rock hounds collecting geodes in the Cosa Mountains of California discovered what appeared to be an electrical device of vast antiquity [inside one of the geodes].... Even more surprising perhaps is the discovery of an object located on a ship that was sunk in the Aegean Sea before the time of Christ. It appeared to be some kind of mechanical computing device.... The object discovered on this ship sunk before Christ's time was a fairly sophisticated analog computer.... At first, one might be tempted to think that these and other "out-of-place" artifacts are just a few oddities. However, many such artifacts are known and are documented in various sources.... Instead they attest to a high and technologically advanced civilization in the distant past.

— Donald E. Chittick
The Puzzle of Ancient Man:
Advanced Technology in Past Civilizations?

14
NETWORK

The lacquered canvas hull of the airship shone through with the red light of the lowering sun, casting a bloody glow over the vessel's wheelhouse.

"The track furrow disappeared back before those trees!" Sub-Altern Inguska barked over the engine hum. "I can't find it on this side."

"We need to get over the mountains before the sunset inversions get too bad," the pilot called back to him.

"We can't lose them now! It will take weeks to get a decent ground search going this far out!"

"We can't risk the pass after sunset! They won't get far at night. Do you think you can find this place again tomorrow if I drop a marker?"

The sub-altern glanced around to try to memorize landmarks. The problem was that at this low altitude, near the pass, everything looked alike — an endless labyrinth of gullies stuffed with highland greenery in a miasma of stretched shadows. Only the mountain peaks were useful terrain features, and this close to the ground even some of those were difficult to spot over the nearby lower ridges.

Inguska said, "I think I can find it again if we leave a trail of them up to the pass."

"We have only five. I can maybe drop them at two thousand cubit intervals."

"It'll have to do."

Splakk! Nu was sure the tumbling sphere should have landed on his face. Instead, it exploded on the other side of the bush he hid under, just outside the *Firedrake's* canopy net. He had expected to die quickly in an envelope of flame. He could not understand why he felt wet and sticky instead.

Then he opened his eyes and watched the airship rise above the canyon walls and struggle up toward the pass. Only after the floating colossus disappeared behind a rocky crag did A'Nu-Ahki try to find out why he was wet. He ran his hands over his midsection and discovered spatters of bright orange paste. When he got up from under the bush, he found himself inside the radius of a gigantic paint splat.

"Cover that mess with dirt and leaves; dress it up good," the Lead Assassin commanded one of his men. He then jerked his thumb at A'Nu-Ahki. "You, Jek, go wash that stuff off — there's a streamlet about a hundred cubits off that a-way." He pointed beyond the *Firedrake*.

For some reason, the Leader had taken to calling him "Jek" during the long journey. A'Nu-Ahki had no idea why.

When he returned from his makeshift bath, A'Nu-Ahki found the assassins setting up their backpacks. One of them pointed Nu to his load. A dry tunic lay folded on top of it. It was the assassins' way of saying "speed it up" nicely. They said few things nicely.

The Lead Assassin lifted his pack down from the *Firedrake* and barked to A'Nu-Ahki in that thick Kushtim brogue Nu was really starting to hate, "Sun's almost down. Be ready to move, Jek! We be hoofin' over the pass. The big floaters'll be bobbing all around this place after sun-up. They'll prob'ly have a higher watch to cover the pass. I told the Guildies to move camp into the trees after we leave. We'll hide before dawn and sleep during the day until after the patrols go home for the evening."

"What'll we do once we're on the other side?"

"Our contact be a rubber planter. His house is not too far from the foothills at the other end of the pass. Now, hoist that pack, Jek."

"My name is A'Nu-Ahki!"

"Good'nuff, Jek." The Assassin patted Nu's shoulder as he would a small child's and went off to jabber with the Guild mechanic and the drivers. The latter would remain camped with the vehicle until the others returned or else three months passed — whichever came first.

Nu watched as the Assassin Leader helped the Guildsmen unload from the *Firedrake's* concealed roof a strange crystalline pyramid with a metal rod jutting from its apex. It took all four men to lift, and they handled it carefully, as if the object was either important, fragile or both. They hid it in a small wooded gully about a thousand cubits north, completely out of site from the game trail. It was the fourth such device Nu had seen them dispose of at stops along the way.

When they returned, the four joked together like old friends. The Lead Assassin laughed as he finished instructing the mechanic and drivers in something Nu could not make out except for the end: *"Don't be drinkin' no spirit juice, Guildies! Old King 'Baul-qayin put nasty dirties in the fire juice! Make you puke yourselves inside-out!"*

"You assassins go assassinate somebody, or whatever it is you do!" the Guild mechanic said, who was a pale-skinned man from the Far North. "We know what's in the fuel spirits better'n you do!"

The Lead Assassin sauntered back over to A'Nu-Ahki and his men, and hoisted his pack as he passed. "Come 'long, Jek. We gotta get over these mountains by second night fall."

"What's that thing you hid in the bushes?" Nu asked, as he tightened his straps. He hadn't cared enough before to inquire about the other three.

"Oracle translator."

The words were gibberish to A'Nu-Ahki. Normally an oracle was a person that spoke for the gods, not a crystalline pyramid. "What's it do?"

The Assassin smiled with tolerant superiority. "It takes vibrations in the spirit realm, charms them, and grows them up so they can cross the Gihunu Valley. That way, our oracle priests can hear the spirits that carry the voices of our operatives through the oracles from Assuri."

Nu was not sure he wanted to know anything further. His father had mentioned that Tubaal-qayin's Guild had machines that could project sound over great distances. What that had to do with using "spirits" to carry voices was not something Nu understood. He sensed that he would get little useful information from the Assassin on the subject anyway.

All the assassins were of either Kushtim descent or refugees from the fallen Orthodox Setiim City-State of Ayarak—red-tan men who could easily affect a West Coastal Assurim accent. The speech of Salaam-Surupag was closer to the classical dialect of Sa-utar, though Nu's complexion also blended well enough, if he didn't talk too much. There was only one person he was required to speak to anyway and she was still a long way off.

The pass proved an easier hike than it looked. The trail at the head of the gorge climbed up onto a series of switchbacks over a relatively smooth grass and brush-covered hump wedged diagonally between two larger mountains. Nu's spirits raised some as he walked off the torpor from the long jungle ride. Behind him, two of the assassins carefully brushed their tracks clean with small branches to erase evidence of their passage.

Near midnight, they came upon another giant paint splat dropped on the trail like a turd from some huge gryphon. It glowed faintly in the dark.

"Must be a phosphorus mix," Nu said, as he stooped to examine it.

The Lead Assassin said, "Let's get some dirt over it."

They took a half hour to scoop and smooth some course sand and gravel over the orange glow-slime, though the rocky terrain made it harder to get good cover soil. The assassins then took another ten minutes to make sure the clean-up job would look natural from the air—a hard thing to be absolutely sure of in the dark.

They made good distance, almost to the top of the pass, before the pre-dawn light creased the eastern horizon atop the highest ridges. The assassins found a box canyon with some overhanging shelf rock on either side, where they turned in to hole up for the day. By the time Nu heard the rattling hum of a Samyaza gas bag struggle over the pass, the hikers were already reclined in the shadow of a large outcropping and almost asleep.

It did not bode well for his slumber to hear a second, third, and fourth airship rattle by in line after the first.

The sun-infused lacquered sail cloth of the lead airship turned Sub-Altern Inguska's world into solid gold. They had the squadron commander aboard. If all went well today, a promotion for the young Demigod officer might well result. All he had to do was stay sharp and pick up the trail as he had done yesterday.

"There's the last marker we dropped as we went over the pass," Inguska said, pointing to an orange spot on the rocky ridge below.

"Adjusting course to two-nine-seven degrees; decreasing altitude by four hundred cubits," the pilot responded, as he glanced at some notes he had made the evening before.

Their commander stood out on the observation platform silently with Inguska and let the two Demigods do their job.

"I see the next one!"

"New course, three-one-four; leveling off."

They flew for several more minutes over a series of smaller ridges.

Inguska frantically swept the rills and gullies for signs of their next marker. "We should be over it by now, but I don't see anything!"

The pilot said, "Maybe it landed in a shaded crevasse. I'll lose some more altitude."

Inguska tried not to let his growing apprehension show. He had divine blood in him, after all—on his father's side—the Demigods accepted nothing less. Anxiety was a beggarly earthbound trait.

The Commander simply watched him with impassive eyes.

Inguska shouted, "It's been too long. Make the next course change!"

"Coming to two-eight-two, decreasing altitude by another hundred cubits," said the pilot.

For another fifteen minutes, they flew on with no sign of any further marker spots.

Inguska tried to fight down his growing panic. "I don't understand; the markers should be here!"

"Maybe some of the bladders didn't break," the pilot said. "It's been known to happen."

"No! I saw every one of them burst! Somebody cleaned them away!"

Finally the Squadron Commander spoke. "Don't feel too bad, Sub-Altern. You've done well. I'll order the other airships to fan out from here. It was probably just a long-range recon team looking for an easy route into our heartland. They'll see it's impossible and turn back. Either way, I'll be able to make my case to Command that we strengthen the mountain passes."

While that took some pressure off Inguska, he was still troubled. "My Lord, what if they're spies? They'll creep over the pass, hire on at some rubber plantation for a year or so, and then migrate south to Assur'Ayur or Meldur with the season. Then they'll disappear!"

The Commander nodded. "An astute observation, Sub-Altern. I'll notify the local sovereign and have him increase security. In the mean time, I'll double the air patrols in this vicinity."

The other side of the range looked almost identical to the misty low land jungle of the Gihunu Valley in the sunset reds, except that the chimney smoke of hidden arboreal platform homes curled up from several points on the horizon. The forests on this side of the mountains were cultivated with rubber, sugar cane, and timber, the plantationers of which had such a superstitious dread of the Haunted Lands that most probably did not even know that the pass used by Tubaal-qayin's insertion team even existed.

Not so the increased aerial patrols.

While the airships were easy to avoid for the assassin team crossing the mountains, Nu grew increasingly concerned for the *Firedrake* camp.

"That's my only ride out of here when this is over!" A'Nu-Ahki said to the Lead Assassin while they trekked down the last of the foothills toward the deeper shadow of the woodland eaves.

"Keep it low, Jek. The Guildies know how to hide and stay put. For the gas baggers it'll be like trying to find a little green flag on a dark pole in the Great Dragonwood of the west."

"So you're not concerned at all?"

The Lead Assassin turned and stopped, so that Nu bumped right into his chest in the dark. "Listen Jek, I done this pass ten times since the war started. The first four were without *Firedrakes*. Half the men that came with me back then ended up as wurm bait! Don't tell me how to do my job! Yeah, our odds got worse when the gas bags increased their patrols. They got worse—not impossible. They can't know where we're going and who we're gonna meet. So keep yer head and don't turn into an old woman on me!"

Nu took a diplomatic step backward, glad the night concealed the humiliation in his eyes. He kept silent the rest of the way down.

After about an hour, they came to a little-used road that wound up into the foothills farther to the north. There the assassins halted.

Nu said, "Is this the place?"

The Lead Assassin pulled a small mechanical time piece from his belt and looked up at the stars. "He'll be along soon."

About five minutes later, they heard the clop and rattle of an onager-drawn cart ambling up the hill from the south. The other assassins pulled A'Nu-Ahki into the brush while their leader remained at the roadside. The cart crested the gentle slope just as the moon began to rise. Nu had just enough light to make out the onager as it drew to a stop.

A basso voice came from the cart, "Wandering the hills under the stars is tonic to the soul like the wine of the gods, is it not, my friend?"

"I prefer the moonlit ocean," answered the Lead Assassin.

The others stepped out into the open, and drew Nu along with them.

The fellow on the cart lit a small lantern that hung on a post behind the driver's seat. He jumped down to greet the Lead Assassin with a cordial bow. Nu had never seen a fatter man that could still stand up and mount a drawn cart.

"Call me Telemnuk, gentlemen. Pile you into my cart, and dine with me tonight at my manor. I've just hired some cargo teamsters, and they look hungry from their long journeys."

None of the assassins said anything as they climbed into the cart, which Nu found uncivil in the face of such courtesy.

"Thank you. My name is A'Nu-Ahki," Nu said as he passed the driver and pulled himself in behind the others.

The ride along the woodland trail to Telemnuk's home took less than an hour. A'Nu-Ahki saw the window lights through the thickening trees long before the cart pulled up to the mansion's ladder-base. The stairway spiraled up the trunk of a giant cedar to the first platform of a veritable palace, larger even than Urugim's old tree-home outside Sa-utar.

Telemnuk called to his servants as he passed through the main entrance to the house's first level. "I have met the cargo masters I said would arrive tonight!"

Within a large triangular dining hall braced between the trunks of three equal-sized conifers lay a semi-circular banquet table that partly surrounded a huge central hearth. Their host invited them to eat, and had his servants pour out large goblets of a pungent red wine.

The assassins mostly ate in silence, so A'Nu-Ahki found himself doing most of the talking when Telemnuk attempted to make casual conversation around the table. Tubaal-qayin Dumuzi had made it clear what Nu could and could not discuss, and so had the Lead Assassin during the long ride through the jungle and up on the pass. Their host never ventured into forbidden territory, and Nu found himself rather enjoying his company.

The only time the assassins interacted much with their contact was when Telemnuk dismissed his servants and briefed them on the following day's activities.

"I have a shipment of raw rubber for processing at our plant about a day's ride east of here. With the proceeds, you must purchase a load of earthenware at the junction town two days more down the Forest Road—you can't miss it. You will carry the shipment of earthenware south from there to Meldur, to a market place at the address on this slip of papyrus."

Telemnuk handed the tiny cargo manifest scroll over to the Lead Assassin, who secreted it inside his cloak.

Nu asked, "How will I make contact with the woman?"

"That has been arranged by the merchant at that address. He will have you deliver some wares to her husband's house. Then it is up to you."

"What can you tell us about the increased air patrols near the pass?" asked the Lead Assassin.

Telemnuk lowered his eyes. "Honestly, I feared for you when I saw four of them fly toward the mountain from my upper terrace flat these past two days. We're halfway between the North and South Sky-Lords' fortresses here. Airships from both bases reach us. My sources have heard rumors for months now that the Demigods grow concerned about the passes into the Haunted Lands. The increased patrols may be a coincidence."

"I think not," the Assassin Chief said. "They may have seen through our vehicle's camouflage or spied tread marks on a low pass over the highland meadows. Our Guild crew can keep things hidden well enough, but I'm concerned about ground patrols — they'll have more than enough time to bring them in before I can get our guest back over the pass."

"Our guest may be a welcomed foreman," the Rubber Planter said.

Nu said, "Hold on, gentlemen; I came as a personal favor to the Emperor! I have other responsibilities! I *will* get back to that *Firedrake* on time, with or without your help."

"Easy, Jek. That's still the plan."

Telemnuk seemed distressed that he had upset his guest. "I was only speaking of a worst-case alternative, my friend. Please do not be offended."

Nu suddenly realized that his host was offering to put himself at great personal risk in the event that something bad happened to the *Firedrake*. "I am grateful, not offended, Telemnuk. Your home is as fine as any I've ever seen, and I'm sure we would get along well together."

The corpulent plantation owner nodded. "My home has seen happier days and I can't say I wouldn't be glad for the company. Still, I understand your fear. I will keep my eyes open while you are away south."

Soon after the business was concluded, all the assassins except the leader excused themselves and were ushered by servants to a higher platform where they could sleep. The Lead Assassin poured himself another goblet of wine, and retreated to a cushion in one of the hall's triangle points where he sat and drank quietly. His eyes never left A'Nu-Ahki, who was not tired and had remained behind with their host. Nu suspected that the ranking assassin wanted to insure that "Jek" did not let the wine loosen his tongue too much. Telemnuk also seemed eager for another goblet of wine, but even more for conversation. Nu sensed a loneliness in the man—a naturally social and jovial fellow surrounded by people he could never fully trust enough to open his soul to. There were no signs of a family in the house.

"Do you mind if I ask you a personal question?" Nu also accepted some more wine from his host. He looked around to make sure none of the servants had returned.

Telemnuk shrugged. "I am but a scroll unfurled."

"Why are you helping us?"

The fleshy rubber planter's eyes sank for a moment. "You mean, why have I betrayed my gods?"

"I don't believe Samyaza and his Watchers are gods. Certainly their sons are not."

"No, I suppose not—especially the sons." Telemnuk's face darkened as his hand gripped the cup so tightly that it looked like it might burst in his clenched fist.

"What happened?"

Telemnuk looked up, his eyes pleading with A'Nu-Ahki. "It is not something I often speak of, though I find myself strangely drawn to speak of it to you. Do you always engender such instant trust from people?"

Nu chuckled, "Not always."

"Perhaps it is that we share something in common. I know by your speech that you come from Salaam-Surupag. I understand the nature of your mission far more deeply than would normally be wise for a man in my position. You had daughters taken, didn't you?"

At these words, the Lead Assassin perked up from his wine, and decided that it was already time to pour another. When he drew closer, his flared eyes warned Nu to speak carefully.

"Yes, I had daughters taken."

"As I thought." Telemnuk sighed. "A man is connected to his daughters in ways that are both holy and wonderful. Mine was a dark beauty with eyes of lapis lazuli and laughter like the forest brooks. Her singing once echoed through these halls like a melody from the Ninth Heaven. I so miss that sound. There is no peace for me without it." He looked down quickly to hide the flood of tears in his eyes.

"Samyaza?"

"Na, one of the lesser ones. They make forays from Assur'Ayur to gather new wives—though I use the word *wife* in its loosest sense. It is more like abduction than marriage. We saw the shining halo above the tree that supported my Lyria's suite for only a moment. I rushed up to her room and found her taken from her bed. She was barely a lass of thirty summers. A month later, I received an official courier who informed me that my daughter had been 'honored' by being chosen as a wife for one of the gods—they never said which one. They never do, unless it's one of Samyaza's High Seven. A dowry of a thousand gold skels came with the notification. I heard nothing more for over three years."

"But you did hear from her again."

Tears broke from his eyes. "Oh yes. She appeared again in her suite after three years, in the same way they took her. With her were two sons—both Cyclopes, with their single eyes offset on the left side their malformed faces! I would have thought them at least ten years old, but neither was weaned.

"My Lyria's spirit was broken. The twin ogres demanded and got every bit of her attention. They devoured her joy and strength like ravening wurms! Never again did she sing since her return. Though she remained with me nearly two more years, it so changed and destroyed her that I hardly knew her. Her eyes had lost their luster, and she could barely eat, though those two monsters nursed her dry and refused weaning!

"I would hear her weep in the night and wish for something I could do to console her. It got so that she would hardly leave her room. She would only speak to me at her door, as if to protect me from… them! The servants feared even to go near her stairs.

"Those sons of that god who is not a god often made a horrendous racket. They would quarrel and throw things about, until they reduced my daughter's suite to a filthy den! The Temple couriers that came by periodically to check on her warned me that it was best to leave them be. The messengers always came laden with more gold, and left with invocations of blessing on my household that sounded blasphemous to my ears. Each time, they reminded us of how women in the cities competed for such status in great beauty contests and ritual arena sport.

"Then one day, I heard horrible growling from her suite, muffled by the door at the top of the stairwell. The sound sucked my strength away, as I climbed the steps to check on my girl who was no longer my girl at all. It took my last remaining courage to open that door."

Telemnuk buried his face in his hands. "You must think me weak, A'Nu-Ahki. How could I have let this thing go on in my very house? I would not blame you if you had no respect for me! I have none for myself any more. I was afraid—not just of what I would find behind that door! Afraid—all along, and in every way! I'm still afraid. Things happen to men who resist the gods of Assur'Ayur—terrible things that I will not describe."

A'Nu-Ahki rose, and rested his hand on the man's shoulder. "I think no ill of you. We live in a world where the evil has grown beyond any of us. I fear none of us would pass such a test completely—if any would pass at all. What happened to your daughter?"

Telemnuk reached up and clutched Nu's arm, as if for support. "She lay dead on the floor, her wrists slashed by her own hand. I could understand her despair! But those filthy cyclopean sons of that god—they hunched over her and tore into her flesh like carrion wurms! Right here in this house—their blood-smeared faces looked up at me indifferently and then buried themselves back in their feast on their own mother's corpse! And I stood there, unable to think, unable to move, unable even to scream in the madness that still chases me in my nightmares!"

Nu clasped the poor wretch's shoulder, his mouth as paralyzed as Telemnuk's body had been at his daughter's door. Now the same madness had spotted him also and turned to the chase. All during the Rubber Farmer's horrendous tale, Nu had seen the identical faces of Uranna and Tylurnis in the place of Lyria's in his mind. His legs felt like rubber and the room seemed to spin.

Telemnuk reached for more wine, and recovered some of his composure. "The sacred disk came once more, even as I stood over my little girl's body. The glowing ones somehow entered the suite, and took their filthy brood with them into the sky—I suppose back to Assur'Ayur.

"Once more a Temple courier arrived with gold, and thanked me for my patriotism and my sacrifice to the gods. I used that gold to finance this network of subversives against Samyaza—men like I am who had daughters or wives—men who dared again to feel a little like men, although it meant a burden of shame too heavy to bear! The rest is as you see it."

The gilded ceilings of the greeting hall inside the Northern Demigod Military City in Satyurati sparkled down on the speakers, amplifying the shafts of quickfire light like golden sunbeams that promised warmth, but gave only a cold metallic sheen.

Inguska stood at attention with his squadron commander before their Divisional Titan. It was the first time he had ever been so close to such a high level of divinity, not to mention that the fellow stood over a cubit taller than did even his commander.

"I'm afraid even a company-sized detachment is out of the question," answered the Titan. "We need every man for the next offensive."

Inguska's chest tightened at the denied request for ground patrols.

"I understand, Lord," said the Commander. "May we increase the ordnance our sentry ships carry? We need something that will pierce armor."

The Titan grinned. "Of course, Zhaka. I'll increase your allotment by as much as you need. The gods are well pleased with the good work you both do. I will also notify Internal Security at all the Temple cities to step up their watch. Our young winged basilisk here speaks with prophetic wisdom when he says that something may be up."

"One other thing, My Lord…"

The Titan leaned in to hear Inguska's squadron commander more clearly. He nodded eagerly when the Demigod officer finished. "You have my approval for this too."

Pillars of fire and smoke dominated the sky-line of Iglat-Meldur, belching sacred obelisks lined atop blast furnaces and wood-burning quickfire dynamos that, for all their exquisite Temple architecture, only fouled the city with soot. To the west of a bustling seaport, pyramids hoary with age stood in decayed grandeur, no longer useful for their traditional purpose of star-gazing because of the continual brownish haze.

According to Telemnuk, the Temple had long ago converted the old observatories to service the arcane activities of the gods more directly. Doubtless charting the heavens no longer seemed so critical centuries after the "divine ones" had descended to earth. Whatever activities these gods engaged in was a topic on which the average Assurim dared not speculate—or so Nu surmised during the long journey down the North Forest Road.

The city gates sloped downhill from the gentle rise where the woodland ended. A'Nu-Ahki crawled into the back of the wagon amid the cargo, lest he should accidentally speak and arouse suspicion. The two Imperial Assassins from Ayarak drove, since their speech patterns were naturally closest to the Assurim. Behind them, next to where Nu had moved back from, the Lead Assassin leaned out from the cargo cover and continued to scope out the city. The other three members of the team had separated from the wagon back in the forest, to enter the city on foot by other gates.

Nu practically held his breath as the ten-onager team slowed before the gate. He saw only slightly past the Lead Assassin, just enough to pick out the heavily manned guard stations in the walls on either side of the road.

One of the guards called to the wagon, "Hail to Lord Samyaza, mouthpiece of the God of Heaven and mediator of his law on earth!"

"In the name of Ar'Murras, patron god of munitions, and of this day and hour, we greet you," the driver responded in a perfect timberland twang from Telemnuk's region.

Nu immediately knew something was wrong when he heard the clatter of other armed guards approaching the wagon from either side.

"Step you all down," commanded a new voice.

The Lead Assassin motioned for Nu to come forward and dismount.

"You're a mute," he whispered, as Nu struggled past him. They both dropped down from the wagon together.

The guards opened the back cover and searched through the cargo.

The man who had commanded them to dismount wore a red cape and priestly nemes headdress modeled after the Setiim style.

He lined the assassins up, all of whom looked down to their feet to emulate the expected Assurim fear of offending a representative of the gods.

Nu did likewise.

One of the priestly guards searched them, one at a time. Fortunately, Nu's trembling seemed entirely appropriate to the situation when the sentry patted him down. None of them carried weapons in any event. The Lead Assassin had told Nu earlier that concealed weaponry was more of a liability than an asset for this kind of work. That was easy for an assassin trained in dozens of ways to kill with his bare hands to say.

The red-caped Priest-commander asked, "Who is overseer?"

The Lead Assassin stepped forward. "I am, Sacred Mediator."

"Your name?"

"Loxal of Satyurati, Lord."

The Priest-Captain positioned himself directly in front of "Loxal" and tapped the side of his face with a small wicker baton. "And do they not recite the holy days and their patrons in Satyurati?"

"Forgive our venial blasphemy, Sacred Mediator. We have traveled many days, and I am sure the driver simply lost track of what day it is."

"Then you shall atone for your servant by reciting the correct patron god for *this* day, pay a half-skel of silver, and it shall be enough."

"Gladly, to make our hearts pure and bring blessing to our journeys again," answered the Lead Assassin. "In the name of Rasu'El, patron god of medicines, and of this day and hour, we greet you."

Nu's heart pounded in his throat. The Sentry Priest remained silent.

The guards that searched through the cargo finished, and informed their leader that it was just a normal shipment of earthenware pots.

"Your cargo manifest and destination?" the Priest demanded.

Nu heard the Lead Assassin reach slowly into his cloak to produce the tiny scroll that Telemnuk had given him.

"And your penalty fine?"

The Lead Assassin lifted his outer cloak, and produced his money cord. Nu heard him unfasten it and slip off a half-skel-sized ingot of silver.

"Be you blessed of Samyaza, and may you find the joy of walking in the light of his holy patrons. Go in peace."

Nu did not breathe again until he was back aboard the wagon and they had passed beneath the city arch. "Why a priest on guard duty?" he whispered to the Lead Assassin.

"Unlike Lumekkor, they have no Guild, Jek. These people make nothing of themselves—only their Watchers, titans, and high priests have the know-how. The workers just follow orders and do the repetitive no-brain jobs in the foundries and assembly plants. This be a Temple-run city because it be their main industrial center."

Yeah, and the only reason it isn't the same in Lumekkor is because the first Tubaal-qayin already had his foundry and had learned his physics under Q'Enukki before the Watchers came down, Nu didn't say aloud.

A'Nu-Ahki was now certain of one thing; his sires had grossly miscalculated their "Plan Leviathan" escape route in many more ways than one. The superstitious children of Assuri would have never permitted the Seer Clan passage to the ocean. Not with everything regimented right down to which "god" to invoke in common greetings on any given day.

A wild desperation spawned by fear of the Lumekkor Alliance must have driven Muhet'Usalaq and Lumekki during the last days of Salaam-Surupag. They had seemed so sure of themselves, despite what they had known of the situation in Assuri since the Regati Slaughter. Although Nu's fathers had an intense hatred for Samyaza, they had underestimated the Watcher's ability to condition the masses on a grand scale. On top of that, they had missed his falling-out with Uzaaz'El entirely. Their lack of up-to-date intelligence had also been a function of the down-sizing of Sautar's defense budget, which had begun long before Iyared was Archon.

Nu did not know whether to weep for the shortsighted sins of his father's fathers or to scream.

The morning had been a tedious exercise of wandering about the city. Actually, Nu simply followed the drill his assassin tutors had conditioned into him during the long caravan ride. They had to assume that Samyaza's agents had followed their wagon from the gates yesterday and take countermeasures. The assassins had tagged three city dwellers possibly shadowing them after they entered Meldur.

Their local merchant contact had a network of watchmen stationed throughout the city, monitoring Nu as he passed them. They checked any followers or repeat followers. The last such sentry had finally scratched his head, giving the "all clear" signal. It was time to do the job. Nu picked up a small pushcart full of pottery placed out for him at a nearby market shanty and began to roll it toward his destination.

The house of the woman A'Nu-Ahki was to contact lay on a narrow side street close to the foundries. A dark, cramped structure, it almost seemed that its builder had squeezed it in like an afterthought between two larger homes equally as depressing. The city's black grit smudged the masonry and a slender wooden door that opened almost onto the street. The merchant at the address Telemnuk had given them had mentioned that the woman's husband worked as a foundry overseer, and would be away most of the day.

Nu set his cart of clay pottery against the wall and knocked. He called inside, "I have delivery of special wares to the lady of the house." He had practiced saying those words in the accent of Meldur all last night.

The door creaked open to reveal a slight dark woman whom Nu instantly recognized as one of Emzara's friends, though he could not recall her name after a century and a half. His heart jumped, while the woman's eyes grew wide and her mouth dropped. A tiny squeak escaped her throat like a startled mouse.

"You've come for us," she almost shouted. "The Comforter sent by the vast A'Nu of E'Yahavah has come to us in our captivity!"

Nu put a finger to his lips to hush her. Her outburst collapsed on him like lead bludgeons of horror and shame that pummeled any composure he had mustered, leaving him dazed and listless. Of all the things for her to remember! Of all the expectations to fill! It dawned on him how his face must have burned in her mind the whole time since the Sack of Salaam-Surupag—or even before. It never seemed that anyone had taken his being the Comforter from A'Nu so seriously in those days. It now felt more like a curse than a prophecy. Maybe it always had.

"Can I come inside?"

"Of course, my Lord. Let me help you with your cart."

After she shut the door behind them, she fell to her knees before him and wept.

Nu's head swirled while his stomach flip-flopped. "Please, my Lady, I am sorry, but this is not what you think…"

Her eyes glowed manic with fervency. "You must have braved the Haunted Lands to lead us from captivity! For by no other route could you have come with the war!"

"Please stand up. You should not bow to me…"

"I knew you would come! Even when the others doubted! I knew you would come and fulfill all the prophecies of Comfort for us!" She buried her face in the carpet as her sobs became inconsolable. "We are not worthy of you! All of us—all of us are defiled and many have lost faith!"

The house shrank in on Nu, airless panic inside a coffin. What could he tell her? How could he tell her? She began to cling to his feet until he almost fell over backwards. He wanted to scrape her off his legs like flaming tar, but how could he?

"My Lady, please! I'm the failure! I can't even remember your name, though you and my wife were like sisters! Forgive me!"

She continued to sob into the carpet and clutch at his legs. It was useless. She seemed not to even hear him.

"The Seer Clan has returned to Akh'Uzan," he told her, hoping to turn her attention to better news. "Some of the women were rescued or escaped on their own. Our clan is growing again."

"Biriya," she said.

"What's that?"

"My name is Biriya."

He remembered. She was daughter of one of Muhet'Usalaq's younger sons—he could not recall which.

Her hands relaxed from his calves and her weeping abated.

"Can we sit and talk awhile? I'm sure we both have many questions for each other."

Biriya slid back onto her knees and slowly stood. "Of course; I am a poor hostess. I have not even brought you water, much less wine to wash out the dust of your long journey."

"Water will be fine."

When she returned, Nu saw that she had also taken time to compose herself. "We can sit in the greeting chamber. There is still more than an hour before my children return from Temple indoctrination and many more hours before my husband comes home from the foundry."

She guided him to the next room, onto a large floor cushion. She took a smaller one opposite him.

"I must confess to you, Lady Biriya, I cannot at this time deliver you from your captivity. I wish I could."

"But you will take us back?"

Nu's swallow of water felt like acid. "Of course you will be taken back, but not until the war is won."

"The war!" She spat. "It has already claimed my oldest son!"

"Your son lives. He told us how to contact you."

Her eyes lit up. "Though he is son of a foreign man, at least he is son of a man—or mostly a man. My husband's great-grandfather was a giant. Even so, I love the boy, for he was always good to his mother. Not all of us have been so fortunate."

"You will see him again, but it may be some time yet."

Her gray eyes tightened to little beads of steel. "What can we do to serve the Archon?"

"Are you still in contact with any of the others?"

"I speak with many of the captured women at market. Some even live in this street, though I fear not all can be trusted. A few have adjusted to their new lives a little too well, if you take my meaning. You are in danger here."

"I know." Nu's eyes fell. "Are any of mine and Emza's daughters among the others? If so, even if they cannot be trusted, please tell me?"

Biriya shook her head and wiped her eyes again. "I saw 'Ranna and 'Nissa during the long march, but we were separated. While they settled many women here, others were marched on to Assur'Ayur. Your girls were in that group. I'm afraid I don't know what's become of them. I wish I could give you such good tidings as you have given me today. I'm sorry."

"At least they were alive and well enough to travel," Nu said. "By E'Yahavah's will they probably still live in some other city."

"By E'Yahavah's will," agreed the Woman. "Now how may we serve our true lords?"

Her face did not flinch at all when Nu told her.

The evening forest shadows grew as the wagon turned onto the last stretch of road to its owner's arboreal mansion. Only the

Lead Assassin had accompanied A'Nu-Ahki on the long haul back to Telemnuk's plantation. The five others remained behind at Meldur to establish the network and develop their contacts among the women. The Leader would run rubber shipments and information between there and the plantation, where a hidden 'oracle' would convey the take back to Tubaal-qayin.

The outfitting of most Assurim military units happened at the southern foundry city, where the women would see them come and go while they learned from the assassins how to identify the soldiers by unit insignia. Their husbands also talked at night about work in the weapon factories…

The journey back had been quiet. Nu had learned long ago that his companion was no talker. A tall dark man with long dark secrets, the Lead Assassin seemed beyond the need for human companionship.

"I don't even know your right name," Nu said aloud, half to himself.

"Loxal," said the Assassin.

Nu turned toward his companion's shaded profile. He had not expected an answer. "That's the name you gave to the priest-sentry at Meldur. Are you also from Satyurati?"

"Kushtahar. It's never a good idea to lie more than you must, Jek. Every time you lie, you have to remember your story. Pretty soon your life is made up of too many stories to keep straight."

"Are you speaking from experience?"

Loxal burst into throaty laughter. "You've been a pain in the backside of my kilt, Jek, but I'm glad to have known you!"

"Why is it you call me 'Jek'? Do you always arbitrarily rename people after your own liking?"

The Assassin just chuckled some more, as he yanked the onager team into the yard beneath Telemnuk's home.

Nu smiled. "Keep your mysteries, then."

"Good'nuff, Jek."

Telemnuk met them at the spiral stair around his great cedar. "I trust everything went well?"

"Aye," Loxal said. "And here?"

"I fear the Demigods lie in wait for you on the pass."

"More gas bags?"

"Many more, I'm afraid—even at night, which is most unusual. They wait for the mountain inversions to settle long after sunset and then bathe the approaches with swords of quickfire light.

Come upstairs and let me help you wash the dust from your mouths, and tell you more. I fear a harder journey still awaits you."

A'Nu-Ahki asked, "Could they have found the *Firedrake*?"

They entered the triangular sitting hall, and took cushions around a bottle of Telemnuk's red wine.

"My sources at the Military City in Satyurati have heard nothing about any captured or destroyed armored chariots," the Rubber Planter answered. "But they could be hushing it up."

Loxal tossed back his wine in one long gulp. "I guess we find out starting tomorrow night."

We beheld in the sky what appeared to us to be a mass of scarlet cloud resembling the fierce flames of a blazing fire. From that mass many blazing missiles flashed, and tremendous roars, like the noise of a thousand drums beaten at once. And from it fell many weapons winged with gold and thousands of thunderbolts, with loud explosions, and many hundreds of fiery wheels. Loud became the uproar of falling horses, slain by these missiles, and of mighty elephants struck by the explosions... Those terrible Rakshasas had the shape of large mounds stationed in the sky.

— *The Mahabharata*

15

SKY-LORDS

Nu did not like the plan.

"If you're going to stay on with Telemnuk, why risk yourself nurse-maiding me back to the *Firedrake*?"

"It's my job, Jek. King 'Baul-qayin T'muzi told me personal-like not to let anything happen to you. Though you be a good learner, you're not trained to think like we do. The Guildies won't be in the same place."

Nu and Loxal left the road from Telemnuk's house at sunset to exploit the inversion winds when the airships would have trouble navigating over the mountains. They were well into the upper foothills by midnight.

That was when they heard it.

The rumbling engine hum came suddenly from behind a rocky hillock off to their left. Nu froze when a shaft of white light shot through the night mists like a lance. The mountainside a few hundred cubits ahead exploded with a brilliance that made his eyes hurt.

"Don't look at it, Jek! It'll ruin your night vision."

"What do we do?"

Loxal crouched behind some brush. "Sit here for a bit. It's just a random sweep, probably for navigating the pass more than anything."

"Why not just fly high over?"

"Oh they be searching the pass alright, make no mistake. Still, it's a stab in the dark for them. No coincidence—they spotted the *Firedrake* or our treads on our way in. Worst case, they've destroyed it, landed and captured one of the Guildies. Guildies'll sing if they're caught and tortured. The Demigods could be expecting us."

"Should we turn back?"

Loxal snorted. "What happened to 'that's my only ride back' Jek? We don't know nothing. Until we do, we stick to plan."

Nu pointed to the receding lights in the sky as they slipped behind the mountains. "It's going up through the pass."

"Let's get going."

"I can't see a thing!"

"Told'ya not to look at it! I'll uncover the phosphor lamp for a couple seconds. Memorize the path ahead of you. The moon'll be up over the mountain soon."

Several more times they had to duck for cover while airships carved the night into ribbons with javelins of light. By dawn's twilight, they made the tiny crevasse where they had camped before. But something was wrong.

"Jek, did you see the floaters come back through the pass after their last sweep?"

"No. I didn't hear them high up either."

Loxal said, "They took a fragment from our scroll."

"What do you mean?"

"Fuel. They must've tanked extra to extend their range."

"Or their duration aloft."

Loxal grimaced as he pulled a dead thorn bush in front of their rocky sleeping place. "Kinda makes you wonder what else they're carrying extra."

Inguska's promotion to full altern felt heavy on his new shoulder-boards, especially with the commanding titan of Second Sky-Lords riding in his gondola.

Although two additional grenadiers to operate the light cannons don't hurt none, the new airship commander thought. *Not to mention the other extras.*

The *Vimana*-class lighter-than-air ship's gondola could support eight men aloft for three days when the aft bomb bay was loaded with an extra fuel tank. That could get an airship across the Haunted Lands to Akh'Uzan, but not back. The *Vimana* could not easily defend against the faster, more maneuverable aerodrone, however; thus, it had fallen in status from premier air-to-ground attack platform to behind-the-lines border patrol.

That did not mean it could not still function admirably in its original mission on a leveled playing field. And Inguska was sure that whatever they were playing cat-and-mouse with down below was about to discover that the field had been more than leveled.

For weeks, the patrol ships of Second Sky-Lords had made quickfire-light-etched plates of every square cubit of the region around the pass. Last night, more tracks had shown up on examination of the plate images, with subtle changes in the ground cover patterns from the day before—not the kind caused by a passing behemoth, either. A millipede tread vehicle and at least two men were definitely down there, shifting position and camouflage, thus changing the details of the landscape ever so slightly. The operation spawned by Inguska's attention to detail was about to pay off.

"How soon until we are over the target area?" the Commanding Titan asked. He was an imposing hulk with a pair of short horns that broke from the front of his skull like sharp bony tumors that had cut their way out through his mottled skin from the inside.

Inguska said, "We've been crisscrossing it for a half hour, my Lord. We only wait for the sun."

Four high-intensity quickfire pearls cowled by concave mirrors blasted from the airship's cardinal bearings beneath the gondola's outer mezzanine. The grenadiers manned these, scanning the ground below with penetrating shafts of white light.

The Titan asked, "Where are you from, Altern?"

"Northern Province, beyond the Two Rivers and along the eaves of Wyverna Wood, Lord."

"Wild territory, that. Your hunter's instinct has served you well."

"You honor me too much, Holiness."

"Not too much." The Horned One sniffed. "How far back in your lineage to divinity?"

To any but a titan, Inguska would have proudly answered. Before the Horned One however, he felt dwarfed. "My father's father is Ingdra, who led the Vanguard Giants at the invasion of Salaam-Surupag. He was a son of the gods who took seven women for himself there. My father was born to his first concubine, so I am third generation removed."

"A respectable bloodline; you can make Arch-Tacticon with such a pedigree."

But no higher, Inguska's thoughts added. The levels of divinity were as immutable under Samyaza as the mountain range. Third generation was more than enough to get him into the Demigods, but not enough to get him to flag rank. He did not even look any different from a common earth-born man. At least his father carried the stigmata of six fingers on one hand.

The airship swung around again for another leg in its figure-8 search pattern. The other *Vimanas* farther out circled like the legendary celestial chariots of his all-too-distant divine forebears.

Inguska handed the con over to his co-pilot, and stepped out onto the mezzanine to take the night air. The hum of his vessel's four rotary engines almost lulled him into a trance, until one of the grenadiers on the lighting pearls shouted.

"Ground contact, bearing three-five-null, off the port bow!"

The second night of A'Nu-Ahki and Loxal's hike over the pass went uneventfully until just a couple hours before dawn.

They rounded a rocky outcropping where the trail began its last set of switchbacks down to where they had left the *Firedrake*. The early morning sky was suddenly alive with probing shafts of light that cut through the thin highland mists like fiery razors. Nu counted six Samyaza gas bags circling over the immediate vicinity where he and the assassins had left their vehicle almost three months before.

Loxal said, "We better move quick. We'll be badly exposed on the switchbacks."

"Can we just cut straight down?"

"Too steep in the dark, Jek. You'll twist your ankle or tumble down hard to a lasting stop. Follow me and jog; don't run or you'll go too fast to swing around the hairpins. If the lights hit us, dive to your belly. Maybe the ground mist'll hide us a little. Keep thirty paces behind me; we don't want to bunch too close and make a single target. Now, count to ten and go!"

Loxal began what otherwise would have been a leisurely trot down the hill side, with Nu a fair distance behind. There was just enough moonlight to see the trail in front of them.

They made it all the way to the first switchback before one of the airships veered close enough to the slope to start carving it up with its lights. Two shafts of white energy began to weave across the zigzag path with both vertical and horizontal cross-hatchings. One caught Loxal about half-way down the third switchback. Nu heard a distant shout from up on the airship's deck as the light began to follow the Assassin.

Braaak-ak-ak! The night exploded with a stream of fire from the airship's port sky cannon.

Nu dropped behind a small ridge of stone and looked ahead into the roving light to where Loxal should have been. The ship's cannon opened up with a continuous spray of glowing shot that traced up and down the trail for what seemed like an hour, but could only have been about twenty seconds. Exploding impacts walked past him, then back down the trail again while he flattened himself against the meager shelter of the tiny outcropping. The lights wobbled as if trying to zero in on Loxal's initial movement.

Nu slid forward on his belly to see if he could find his companion. The creeping ground mist both obscured his vision and protected him some from the lights.

By the time he got to where he thought he had last seen Loxal, the airship was forced to come about to avoid the mountain. The cannon crew had to switch off to the lights on the opposite side of the mezzanine and reacquire their target. Meanwhile Nu frantically scraped around in the dirt for some sign of the Assassin. His hand landed in something wet.

The airship was about halfway through its turn, moving away from the slope. The lights danced back and forth more erratically.

Nu hissed, "Loxal!"

238 | K. G. P O W D E R L Y J R .

"Down here," came a faint reply.

A'Nu-Ahki poked his head over the steep slope at the edge of the trail. Directly below, the next leg of the path widened out to include a narrow stand of thorny shrubs about twenty cubits down.

"Roll down the slope into the brush before they finish their turn!" Loxal's voice cracked as if he was in pain.

Nu tumbled over the side and slid into a cushion of thorns. He clenched his teeth to keep from crying out.

The airship completed its turn, and began to interrogate the trail again with its lights from further out.

"Where are you?" Nu whispered, too terrified to move despite the giant thorns sticking into every part of his backside.

"Over here," said a weak voice behind the bush Nu had landed on.

The search light swept the trail just beyond the thorny row. Nu caught a glimpse of Loxal, laid out on his side with both hands clutching his leg. He also saw that the prickly hedge covered them both.

Nu scrambled from his thorny nest on his hands and knees and slid over to his companion, who seemed to be more in the shelter of the bushes than inside one. That was when he felt more warm wetness.

"You're injured," Nu said, as he patted around Loxal's thigh.

One of the cannon rounds had torn through the Assassin's leg above the knee. Nu's medicinal training took over. He slid out of his pack and sliced one of the straps off with his utility knife to make a tourniquet. Then he grabbed an extra tunic from inside the flap and used it as a compress, securing it with a second strap.

The Assassin groaned. "They'll have opium powders on the *Firedrake*. I'm okay."

"You've lost quite a bit of blood. Try to stay awake."

"No dragons in this den, Jek. I gutta get you home."

"I think our roles have just reversed."

Another sword of light swept along the trail outside the brush.

"There wouldn't be so many ships if they'd found the *Firedrake*," Loxal said. "They'll have to pull back from the mountains before the dawn winds. The canyon below is too narrow for them to navigate during the inversion shift. We'll hole up here until then."

"I can carry you the rest of the way."

"Prob'ly won't be necessary, Jek, but I 'preciate the offer."

"You said the Guildsmen will have moved. How will we find them?"

"They'll find us."

"How will they know we're here?"

Loxal rifled through the pack he had stuffed behind his head and pulled out a tiny crystal pyramid. It reminded Nu of a smaller version of the devices he had watched the Guildsmen unload. "I left this with Telemnuk when we went south."

"What is it?"

"A magic talisman."

"Don't patronize me, Loxal. I really hate it when you people do that!"

"No, that's what we really call it. The crystal sings out across the spirit realm to the oracle aboard the *Firedrake*. The Guildies already know we're nearby. They'll be watching for us."

"Can you speak to them through it?"

"No. It just sings to the oracle."

Nu checked Loxal's compress. The bleeding had slowed with the tourniquet.

"How long till dawn?"

Loxal squinted up through the brambles. "Less'n an hour. We'll have the mountain shadows and the valley mists in our favor. We may just get out of this yet."

Inguska was incensed. "Cease fire! You'll only waste your steel!" The Grenadier released his weapon. "I think I got him, sir."

"Then where is he?"

The Titan of Second Sky-Lords leaned out into the night and followed one of the spot lights with his eyes. "He could have fallen down the slope and landed in that foliage down there. Even if he survived, he's not going anywhere. Can we lower some men?"

This was where Inguska really hated the fact that Titans did not need to work their way up through the lower officer ranks, and be intimately acquainted with the men and machines under their command.

"There's no time, my Lord. Soon we must pull away from the mountains. Our engines don't have enough power to safely fight the inversion winds. We'll be out of weapons range at least, possibly out of spy glass range too. Anybody on that slope will be in the mountain's shadow."

"How far was the ground contact from the suspected hiding place of the enemy vehicle?"

"At least two thousand cubits, Lord. We will have to pull out even beyond that, I'm afraid."

The Horned One scowled. "Will we still see it if it tries to move?"

"We should, Lord. An all-terrain chariot is much larger than a man."

"Then we shall be prudent, my young Demigod, and pull back from the mountains with all eyes facing east."

With the sun's glare rising over the peaks at us. Inguska kept the thought to himself.

N u listened as the engine noises faded to the west.
He made Loxal drink the rest of his water and chew a dried fig.

"Ready to move?"

"Yeah, just help me up and let me lean on you."

After two tries, the Assassin slumped down again and moaned.

Nu said, "Looks like you'll have to take me up on my offer."

"Guess so, Jek."

A'Nu-Ahki squatted down, draped his companion over his wide shoulders, and then lifted with his legs. They left the packs, except for Loxal's singing crystal.

As Nu stumbled from the thorn row, he saw six airships recede into the distance over the Gihunu low lands. The sun was already hitting them, which made them appear like gold and scarlet clouds of molten metal over the shadow-draped meadows and distant forest.

The trail got steeper after the final switchback. A'Nu-Ahki slid down most of the last leg into the narrow ravine where the *Firedrake* had left them. He lurched along the tiny streamlet toward the clump of trees where Loxal had told the Guild crew to hide the vehicle. Just as he entered the small wood, two men appeared on either side of him, and lifted Loxal from his shoulders.

"You both took your sweet time!" one of the drivers said. He looked grimy, wild-eyed, and unkempt.

"We saw one of the ships attack the trail," said the mechanic. "Not entirely without effect, it looks like."

They slipped under the camouflage canopy. The *Firedrake* sat in a small space under the trees at the opposite edge of the wood. Nu helped them lay Loxal near one of the side hatches.

"Get him some opium powders. He's in shock," A'Nu-Ahki said.

"So, what do you think, you're in charge now 'cause you were that big gryndel killer when you was young?" The mechanic laughed. "I think that sacred dragon-slaying stuff is just a load of manure!"

"So do I; I'm a healer. I need to clean his wound and replace the compress or he'll get infected."

"We gotta blow the dragon shell and fight our way outa here before they call in more gas bags!"

"Why can't we hole up until night? Let me bind him properly first."

"Bind him fast," said the mechanic. "I think they've spotted us and they're just waiting for the morning updrafts to lift so they can blast us out of here with rockets. They hung practically right over our heads all night and they ain't never done that before—not so close anyway."

One of the drivers said, "We can't drive through this kind of terrain at night anyway. We'd need light and our head lanterns would draw them like moths now that they're risking night patrols. Our only chance is to make an armed break-out. We're in slightly better shape as a moving target."

The other driver tossed over the apothecary kit. Inside were clean bandages, grain spirits, and syringed vials of opium solution with additional powders. Nu worked quickly.

The mechanic said, "I spent the whole night oiling the feed and swivel gears on the sky cannon mount."

Nu tightened Loxal's new bandage and adjusted the tourniquet. "Can you shoot down that many gas bags with one cannon array?"

"Sure. The question is, will we survive their first rocket barrage long enough to do it?"

The drivers stowed the canopy and mounted the drake.

"I'll help you get him aboard," offered the mechanic. "I'd say we have a half hour's space before they pull back in toward the mountains. But they'll see us long before that."

Inguska would not have been so sure. He chafed at the sunrise delay. The fiery gold on top of the mountains obscured the shadows of the foothill ravines on the west slopes. Even so, they trained all telescopes aftward at the clump of woods in the mouth of the small canyon where they were sure the intruders hid. At this distance, it looked like a darker spot in a rocky landscape of identical darker spots on a field almost as dark.

"I think I've got some movement near the tree patch!" called one of the grenadiers.

Inguska checked his wind direction flag and decided that the air could go either way, too rapidly to predict. He yelled, "Ready all rocket-clines and aerial cannons port and starboard!"

The Titan of Second Sky-Lords said, "How soon can we engage?"

"It's too soon to sweep in so close. Maybe fifteen minutes at the earliest." Then he ordered the pilot, "Stand by to come about on my signal and oracle the contact to the other ships."

The *Firedrake* emerged from the trees in a weaving downhill dash. Nu jostled in the back with Loxal, who seemed to be coming back to himself on the painkiller.

The mechanic asked the drivers, "Should I blow the cover charges yet?"

The second driver hunched over a periscope that reached up through the false spike-tail plates.

Loxal barked, "No!"

Even the driver turned to look at the Assassin's outburst.

"No," Loxal said in a quieter voice. "Let them be overconfident and draw in closer. Their clines can only aim rockets by crude line of sight. If they see we have an anti-drone mount, they'll launch their missiles from farther out, maybe beyond our weapon range.

They'll get mostly misses, but all they need to do to cripple us is take out one of our treads."

"He's right," said the driver, who had turned back to his narrow recessed view-port. "They can expend their rockets, leave one ship high up to shadow us, and go home to reload. They can also oracle for more ships."

Loxal's tactical analysis took a lot out of him. He flopped back onto a cushion of packs and groaned. Nu felt his forehead for fever and worried for the clamminess of the Assassin's skin.

Loxal grinned. "Wanna know why I call you Jek?"

"Only if you want to tell me."

A weak chuckle, "A Jek is like a round cartouche in a square slot,—no, that's not really it, either. In Kushtahar, Jeks don't fit because they're too good for the places they have to fit into. Centuries ago, our fathers called the faction that supported the Archon 'Jeks' because most of our people wanted to be independent from Sa-utar in those days. So instead, they followed Lumekkor. Yet the sons of Kush lived much better as the Archon's vassals than they do as 'Baul-qayin's. Everybody old enough to remember knows it, but nobody wants to admit it."

"So you're saying it's a compliment?"

Loxal grunted at a bump in the path that slammed a pack into his bad leg. "It depends on the inflection of my voice."

"You always seem to say it the same way."

"I guess you have to be from Kush to notice the difference."

Nu shook his head and laughed. "Well, thank you for clearing that up. Do you know any good scrolls on the unique voice inflections of the Kush dialect?"

Loxal smiled. "Only a Jek would ask that." His eyes closed.

Nu took his pulse and found his respiration normal for sleep.

"How close are they?" he asked.

The second driver twisted with his periscope a full three-hundred and sixty degrees around. "They're moving toward us. Make ready to blow the cover charges."

The mechanic clasped the charge controller. "Cover charges are armed and ready."

"Hold steady. They're almost close enough."

"Watch their rocket-clines. Are they rotating?"

"Launcher clines are moving! Blow the charges!"

The mechanic mashed down on the contact. Nu felt the whole vehicle shudder as the dragon-assembly plates and their framework blasted away from the *Firedrake* in pieces. Light flooded through the firing slits.

The second driver scrambled from his periscope up into the circular mount chair of the aerial cannons in the vehicle's roof. The mechanic took his place at the periscope.

"Target bearing at three-null-two, range; two thousand cubits," said the mechanic.

Nu heard the quickfire winch slew the circular cannon mount to face the first target.

Fum-fum-fum! The first volley flew up at the approaching airship.

Nu scrambled to one of the right-side firing slits to try to see the results. The white glare of the exploding airship flickered against the trees, rocks, and grass that sped by.

"New target at two-five-four, range—two thousand twenty," called the periscope watcher.

Another longer burst of rapid fire issued from the quad mounts.

Nu flung himself over to the left side, careful not to kick Loxal. This time he saw the airship erupt into a small sun and then tumble in on itself as it plowed toward the ground off to his south. But behind it was a third ship with flares smoking from the underside of its gondola. The rockets leaped from their rails, slanted down in the Firedrake's general direction.

"Steer right!" the mechanic ordered.

Nu's face pressed into the firing slit as the vehicle lurched hard the other direction. The rocket array slashed into the ground like flaming claws, so close to the drake that Nu felt the sting of debris hit his cheek as fire and flying earth enveloped his field of vision. The shock wave came a second later, tossing him on top of Loxal.

More chatter broke from the quad cannon until the third airship exploded.

"Rockets from two ships; steer hard left!"

Nu huddled down with Loxal as two barrages crisscrossed over their heads and slammed into ground the *Firedrake* had just cleared.

Again, the anti-drone mount spat burning steel and again one of the airships crashed and burned.

The smoke-filled sky slid through and around Inguska's gondola.

"Pull up! Pull up into the smoke!" he yelled to the pilot, who was already frantically flipping the valves to flood the airship's auxiliary bladders with gas.

The port aerial cannon chattered to answer its ground-based counterpart, until the cumbersome air leviathan lurched around and up on an escape course.

"What happened?" shrieked the Commanding Titan of the Second Sky-Lords.

Inguska took the con from his pilot and kept the airship behind the smoking pyres of its less fortunate sisters. He steered an escape vector designed to get them out of range of the enemy's anti-drone cannons as fast as possible while using the smoke as a screen.

"My Lord, the target shed its disguise. It unmasked an anti-drone mount! I'm taking us out of range to resume the attack from higher up. I recommend we call in more ships."

The Titan took that task on himself, while the pilot continued to adjust the bladder valves.

A minute later, they emerged from the southward drift of smoke well beyond enemy cannon range. One other airship to the northeast had also escaped destruction. It too kept its distance from the ground target.

The Horned One looked up from the oracle set. "We'll have reinforcements in a little over six hours. Until then, we shadow them."

Nu listened to the grinding noise from the left tread assembly and tried to pretend it wasn't serious. The worried crease on the mechanic's face told him it was no time for make-believe, so instead he started to pray again.

The second driver, who still manned the aerial cannon, said, "If it's a shot bearing, we're in for it."

The mechanic replied, "Sounds more like a partially thrown tread. How soon before the game trail hits some real forest?"

The driver at the steering console answered, "It's mostly rocky meadow until early tomorrow. If we stop to fix it, we become a stationary target. Even at high altitude the gas bags'll be able to compute an easy firing solution."

"Can you see any trees at all?"

"None worth the effort."

Nu checked Loxal's forehead again. It was getting hot. The Assassin emitted a low groan.

"I'm giving him another dose of opiate."

Nobody seemed to care, so Nu expended another of the syringe ampules into his patient's good thigh.

The noise from the tread remained steady, but grew no worse. The two airships kept their distance, but the Guildsman in the swivel cannon seat kept reporting on their positions. They hovered just out of weapons range and showed no sign of going away.

Nu handed out some dried fruit and everybody ate something.

Loxal shuddered and shouted. "Oracle!"

A'Nu-Ahki bathed his forehead with a damp cloth. "What is it, Loxal?"

"Get on the oracle and — and relay message to base... translators are up. Warn them Telemnuk's route is compromised, but don't say his name..."

Nu said, "I don't understand,"

"Say that Route-line Cattle-king is compromised..."

"I think he's delirious."

"No," said the mechanic. "Cattle-king must be your contact's code name. I'll spool up the oracle."

"Does this mean the women are in danger?"

Loxal grunted, "No, just Telemnuk's station. He'll get word on today's check-in to destroy his oracle. He should be okay too after that."

"Then we did this for nothing! The information from Meldur can't get through!"

"It'll get through, Jek. Cheer up. We have back-up routes."

"I see more gas bags pouring through the pass," said the cannon operator. "I count four. They're still quite a ways off, but that'll change."

I nguska could also see the four new airships approaching out of the east. "Recommend we circle at our ceiling altitude and saturate them with rockets. It'll mean moving in closer, but I think we'll still be outside their cannonry range."

"You think?" demanded the Horned One.

"Lord, they have a new kind of chariot. It's impossible to be absolutely certain. If they hit one of us, the rest can move out farther before the target can take another shot."

"Very well; signal the others."

"They're circling around us at the very edge of our weapons envelope," said the guildsman on the cannon.

The mechanic was on the periscope. "Range is between six thousand and sixty-five hundred cubits. Their clines are angling down... Rockets launched! Rockets inbound! Fire! Fire! Fire!"

The quadruple mount began to chatter in a continual stream. The earth shook like thousands of drum beats from an angry god. The driver twisted and turned, slowed and sped up to try to avoid the shrieking missiles, tossing Nu around the aft compartment.

Whump! Whump! Whump! Three rockets slammed in on either side and to the rear. The grinding tread rattled and screeched, but somehow did not break.

The aerial cannon rotated with a steady barrage. "I see one airship spiraling and on fire, two more are burning but holding their attack course!"

Another round of missiles plowed into the earth just in front of the vehicle. The *Firedrake* dropped into the fiery crater and then bounced up over the other side. Nu felt the heat on his back as flames roared in through the firing slits. The bad tread shrieked louder and rapped continually after the chassis crashed down outside the crater wall. The driver poured on speed.

Again, the sky cannons pounded from the roof.

Two more explosions rocked the sky.

The mechanic reported from the periscope; "Direct hit and one of the burning gas bags just blew up!"

"That leaves three and one of them's burning," the Guildsman on the sky cannon added. He loosed more shot where two of the remaining ships had foolishly clustered together on almost the same attack vector.

"There they go!" whooped the mechanic after two more concussions slammed in from overhead.

The gunner shouted, "Where's the last one? I can't see it!"

The mechanic swept the periscope three-hundred and sixty degrees around and used the tilt-angle up in all directions. "I don't see it either."

Inguska's ship dove into the smoke when the last two *Vimanas* blew up. The contours of the highlands allowed him to dip down into a shallow ravine that roughly paralleled the game trail toward the lowlands.

"It seems you've underestimated their weapon's range," said the Titan of the now much-diminished Second Sky-Lords.

"I have failed, my Lords," cried the Altern with just the right plaintive whine that he knew was expected. His mind was really on the terrain that swept by so close below.

The pilot, who had worked the gas valves during the dive, reached over for the oracle set. "Should I call for more reinforcements, Lord?"

"No," said the Horned One. "We'll do this the old fashioned way. Better to get prisoners we can interrogate, anyhow." He walked around to where Inguska could see him. "How well do you know the land here?"

The Altern swerved to keep the gondola from striking a clump of trees. "They're using a behemoth migratory trail down to the low land jungles. It must go all the way to the river."

The Titan smiled. "Can you get ahead of them and set us down where the trees thicken and the trail narrows?"

Inguska saw redemption dawn like the sun. "I know just the spot."

The mechanic switched off the oracle and took off the ear piece. "Here's the new plan," he said to the others. "The tanker drake is moving forward to meet us—has been since our report this morning. A third vehicle will cross the river with extra fuel to get us all in. If our tread breaks, we're to wait. Loxal's talisman will lead them to us — or at least notify when they're close. They want us to stay off the oracle unless it's life or death."

The driver said, "Looks like Command is in tune with the gods for a change."

"I'm still worried about that missing gas bag," said the guildsman on the sky cannons.

"Relax. You must've got it or else it would have called in more ships. They had plenty of time today for a third strike."

The *Firedrake's* tread had screeched and rapped all through the afternoon since the last attack, until they had found a complex of small forested knots to hide among for the night.

The mechanic reached toward the hatch. "I'd better use the time to repair the tread. We need the canopy spread, so I can use a phosphor lamp."

Nu checked Loxal's dressing and found him asleep from his most recent opiate infusion. Then he wiggled out the hatch just as the two Guild drivers finished erecting the camouflage web. The mechanic was already on the ground examining the tread. Nu squatted next to him and watched.

"Fortunately we didn't stop with the broken part down," the mechanic explained, as he clasped two detached tread rings and pointed to where only a single remaining ring had held the millipede together. Two other segments were broken completely off.

Nu asked, "Can you fix it?"

"I can roughly secure the two detached segments, but I can't replace the missing two. It'll still be pretty noisy, but it may hold long enough for us to close the distance with the approaching tanker."

That was as good a bit of news as A'Nu-Ahki had heard all day — good enough that he slept most of the remaining night.

They started up again before sun-up. The mechanic wanted to make heavy tree cover as soon as possible. By mid-morning, clumps of jungle got larger and more frequent. The guildsman on the aerial weapon continually scanned the skies but saw no further sign of airships.

Just after noon, Nu sighted a pack of wyverna feeding on a spike-tail carcass — a sign that the rain-forest drew near. Minutes later, the jungle rapidly closed in, with only sporadic clearings every few minutes.

Nu crouched forward to the periscope to ask the mechanic for a quick look through the device.

That was when the world flipped upside-down and collapsed in a fiery tangle of blood and steel.

From down the trail, Inguska watched the explosion under the *Firedrake* with immense satisfaction. A nice hidden package of solid rocket propellant lit off by a single shot from his hand-cannon had done the trick.

The Titan clapped him on the shoulder and stepped out from the concealing foliage. "Sometimes the older, simpler ways are best."

Inguska heartily agreed as he followed his leader, with his hand-cannon leveled at the partly crushed and overturned vehicle.

They had left the *Vimana* to hover over the last big clearing, several thousand cubits deeper into the jungle—well behind the wall of trees from their approaching quarry.

As Inguska drew near the smoldering wreck, he saw that the driver was surely dead—the recessed window showed a half-decapitated body. Likewise, the weapon operator could not have survived beneath the weight of the twisted hulk. Nevertheless, one side of the vehicle had not collapsed completely. From there the Altern was sure he heard movement inside.

Nu did not know what had happened; only that a folded sandwich of blood and wreckage had crushed Loxal from his waist up. Had A'Nu-Ahki not crawled forward at the last second, he would have suffered the same fate. The coughing mechanic squirmed underneath him.

Nu rolled off him and, almost without thinking, reached toward what remained of Loxal. Inside the dead Assassin's kilt pouch was the singing talisman. Nu pulled it out and placed it inside his own belt.

The mechanic, seeing what Nu had done, said, "Swallow it."

"What?"

The bruised and bloodied guildsman pulled himself up to a low sitting position around the wrecked periscope. "It'll come out harmless in yer stools. Otherwise they'll take it and toss it."

Somebody rapped on the hatch from outside.

Nu popped the talisman in his mouth and willed himself to swallow.

The mechanic kicked open the hatch and showed his empty hands to the man who looked in at them.

"Get out!" commanded a dark-faced fellow who brandished an ugly looking hand-cannon in their faces.

Nu and the mechanic wiggled their way out of the wreckage and stood unsteadily before their captor.

That was when A'Nu-Ahki noticed the horned giant looming farther off. He loosely resembled the sons of Samyaza, but slightly smaller, with fewer horns and less hide armor. The man with the hand-cannon shoved them forward to meet this creature.

The Titan peered first at the mechanic then Nu. "What were you doing on our borders?"

Both remained silent.

"Fair enough," the creature smirked. "I haven't enjoyed skinning a man alive since Salaam-Surupag. Let's get them back to the ship, Inguska."

The man with the hand-cannon nudged them forward and walked them further down the trail into the jungle. Nu tried not to let his mind fix on images of friends and relatives flayed alive. He was too shocked to focus on anything good or bad anyway.

The noises of the rain-forest seemed to mock the prisoners as they walked in front of Inguska and the Titan. Nu almost yearned for the simple days when only cockatrice and gryndel haunted the jungles of his life. After stumbling on for what seemed like hours, they reached a clearing where an airship's engines rattled close above the trees. A rope ladder hung over the small swath of grass, and dragged on the ground. Nu stepped from the trees into the airship's shadow.

Inguska said, "You two, up the ladder first."

The mechanic started up the swaying rungs, followed by A'Nu-Ahki, whose arms burned with each pull on the ropes. Nu looked down, and saw the Demigod Altern pointing his hand-cannon up at him while the Horned Giant stood farther off.

Some birds flew from the trees at the other side of the clearing. Nu looked up to see his next hand-hold while his heart sank at the enormous silhouette of the floating leviathan's belly. More birds screeched into the air at a sudden movement caught only in the corner of his eye.

The great airship exploded into a fireball sixty cubits above.

Everything after that seemed to move by in blazing slow motion. The mechanic dropped past Nu and landed on Inguska, knocking the hand-cannon into the weeds. The burning airship began to rise and heel over.

Nu released the ladder, and tumbled over the mechanic into a thorn bush that could have been a down cushion, as numb as he felt. The hand-cannon lay in the grass, halfway between him and the stunned Titan.

A'Nu-Ahki fought a swimming head and the screech in his ears. He scrambled for the weapon, just as the Giant regained his wits and saw him.

The burning airship howled over him, as Nu threw himself at the hand-cannon. A secondary explosion above the trees crackled through the air. It slammed both man and giant to the ground like flies in its concussion. The Titan held his hands to his ears and screamed, while Nu's head spun.

A'Nu-Ahki pushed himself to his feet again on the swaying earth. *Where's the weapon? I've got to find that weapon!*

The Giant was also up, still holding his head.

There – at the Horned One's feet!

A'Nu-Ahki bowled himself into the boots of the Commander of Second Sky-Lords, knocking the Giant over again. He snatched the weapon from the dirt then rolled on top the fallen Titan, where he brought the hand-cannon up to the creature's stunned face.

A tanker drake rumbled through the trees at the other end of the clearing, and rolled to a stop almost on top of A'Nu-Ahki.

In seconds, two Guild fusiliers had weapons trained on the Giant's head while another helped the mechanic subdue Inguska.

Nu didn't even hear the final crash of the flaming airship a few hundred cubits off in the trees. He busily crouched over on his knees, shaking, and vomited his guts out with the talisman.

Now this Seth, when he was brought up, and came to those years in which he could discern what was good, became a virtuous man; and as he was himself of an excellent character, so did he leave children behind him who imitated his virtues... They also were the inventors of that peculiar sort of wisdom which is concerned with the heavenly bodies, and their order. And that their inventions might not be lost before they were sufficiently known, upon Adam's prediction that the world was to be destroyed at one time by the force of fire, and at another time by the violence and quantity of water, they made two pillars; the one of brick, the other of stone: they inscribed their discoveries on them both...

— Flavius Josephus
Antiquities of the Jews, 2:3
(*circa* 95 AD)

16

STAR-SIGNS

The comet blazed across the evening sky, visible even before the last light of day faded over the horizon. It signaled the end to many, for it had emerged out of the constellation of the Dragon Breaker and moved steadily into the head of the Great Leviathan that stretched over the southern sky.

A'Nu-Ahki muttered, "Unfortunately, it's not the end people think."

He stood atop a new ziggurat observatory that overlooked the Akh'Uzan monastery from next to the huge quarry where masons had cut the stones for both. Nu's father sat with him on the circular track stone of the pyramid's giant telescope to gaze at the brilliant cosmic interloper. The telescope assembly had arrived from Sa-utar the previous year.

Lumekki seemed in a talkative mood. "The priests say it's a sign the Century War is ending. It's about time, since it has actually dragged on for two. I guess nobody wants to remember it as the 'Two Century War.' That just doesn't have the same ring..."

Almost five more decades! Nu lamented. *Have the women in Meldur given up by now? I would have!*

Rather than bring his father down, he said, "So what are the priests ranting about this time?"

"Nothing original; they paint Uggu of Lumekkor as the Dragon Breaker, and the Samyaza giants as the Southern Sea Monster. The movement indicates Assuri's fall, which became certain after the armored breakthrough in the Battle of the Haunted Lands three years ago. Assuri's inner fortifications are collapsing. Meldur will fall any time, according to the courier in the village. After that, Assur'Ayur is naked. Then you can count the days."

A'Nu-Ahki spirits lifted some. "Now *that's* prophetic insight! Anyone with half a year's military training could have predicted that outcome, especially once Far Kush and Y'Raddu aligned with Lumekkor and the Iya'Baalim nomads invaded Assuri through the mountain passes from Nhod. With a multi-front war closing in on Samyaza, and the Kush Straits opened up to Dumuzi's modern fleet, it was only a matter of time. The priests! Next they'll want credit for their insight when the armistice is signed."

"No doubt." Lumekki's laughter never touched his eyes. "Near Kush gets its blood money at our expense—Salaam-Surupag and Ayarak for services rendered by a willing vassal."

"There's still the repatriation. We've already seen over a hundred of our women returned. I notice each liberated city oracles-in lists of captured women to us first thing. Tubaal-qayin must have really lit a fire under their beds to make them so eager to appease us. I wouldn't fret too much about Salaam-Surupag— it's nothing but ruins anyway." Nu sighed as he squinted through the eyepiece of the great tube. The telescope mechanism hunched like a gigantic cannon over half of the ziggurat's flattened apex.

Lumekki said, "I wish I could be so philosophical. This war has changed the face of the world so much in such a short time that it will take another two centuries just to sift the rubble."

"It must be hard for you, having watched from the army while Iyared's father frittered away our strategic holdings. The sons of Samyaza were right about one thing—E'Yahavah has withdrawn most of his protection from Seti and left us a mere buffer state between powers that used to be our vassals. However they reshape the world, it won't last long in its new form."

"You put that so well," Nu's father mumbled with a sour grimace, as if Nu were trying to rub his nose in a decline that chronologically happened to coincide with his own lifetime of service.

Nu tried not to sound so serious. He lifted his face from the eyepiece and winked at him. "I'm supposed to be a seer, remember?"

"Yeah, well, it's always easier to analyze the past than to predict the future. Which reminds me, when are you and Pahpi leaving for the peak? We need to seek E'Yahavah for an interpretation of this comet. I'm surprised nobody's been up to inquire by now."

"Why come to us when the priests will say exactly what you want for a price? And aren't you coming too? I'm not the only seer around here."

"No, I don't feel up to it—the heat, that is. Pahpi gets a strange thrill from all the self-affliction and you need to melt off a few skels of fat. I think I will just wait it out down here in happy ignorance, if you all don't mind."

A'Nu-Ahki snorted. "Oh great, you mean you're making me go up there alone with him!"

"A little suffering makes the heart tough."

"Then why is that only Pahpi is such hardened steel?"

They both laughed.

"Day is done," Lumekki said, once levity subsided to wistful sighs.

"Yeah, I'd better get down and see how 'Miha did in town. Market days are still tough on her. I keep offering to go with her, but... you know."

"By Under-world, it's been two hundred years! After all she did for them during the firestorms, are they really still that petty?"

Nu said, "More so, though they may not be as vocal about it since Pahpi closed down that rogue printing press."

They took the ziggurat stairs down to the back courtyard.

"Well, give her my love," said the Old Soldier.

They entered the back gate. Lumekki turned for his chamber overlooking the ramparts. A'Nu-Ahki climbed the cut-log stairs to the loft apartment he and his wife shared over the library.

As he opened the door, the sound of suddenly stifled weeping met him from the darkened interior.

"'Miha?"

"Uh, hi Nu." She sniffed, trying to mask that she'd been crying.

"What happened?"

He popped a spark pellet into the oil lantern by the door, and illuminated the interior. Her eyes were red and wet.

"I thought it was over." She slumped back onto their bed. "I really imagined that after all this time I had gained some measure... I mean, nobody has said much to me for years. But I guess things don't work that way around here."

"What'd they say this time?"

"Tarkuni's widow caught me at the market and 'warned me by the prophetic spirit' that the reason we have no children is because our marriage is cursed and that I'm barren! Why do they still hate me?"

"Wish I knew. Old prejudices die hard, I guess. Maybe we represent something they fear deep inside."

Sitting down by her on the divan, he cradled her in his arms.

"They're not the people I thought they would be back in Bab'Tubila. I mean, I expected you all to be stern, but not so mean-spirited!"

"They're not the same people I once thought either," he said, stroking her hair. "I'm sorry that peace still eludes you."

"No it doesn't. Not as long as I have you. Until I met you, I never dreamed a man's touch could do anything but make me recoil!"

He kissed her forehead, shamed that for him the feelings always paled when compared to memories of another. Still, he was glad she said it. It meant he was doing his job. That was no small thing these days. Most men — even in the Seer Clan — didn't.

He had been married to Emza two hundred years and now another two hundred to Na'Amiha. He understood that the relationship was supposed to mature over time — consciously walked himself through the same internal speeches almost daily. He accepted that passion faded as it properly grew into something better — compassion. The alchemy of attraction was *supposed* to change over the decades. Yet here that alchemy had been artificial from the start. *The truth is, you gave yourself credit for deeper maturity and love than you actually possessed, and now you feel cheated!*

He blocked that little revelation from his mind and changed the subject. "I'm still a bit of a slob though, aren't I?"

"True." She laughed through her tears. "But I can train a slob, given another century or so." Then her pale face sank again, as she changed the subject back. "Nu, what if I really am sterile? I'm getting up there in years. Maybe you should take another wife or a concubine."

"You're just having a long rest cycle. We hardly were together enough during the first few decades for you to conceive. By the time we became accustomed to each other your rest cycle had come—that's all it is."

"For two hundred years? First, I'm frigid, now I'm sterile! I'm not getting any younger! Maybe another wife is needed."

He wanted to shout, *I heard you the first time!* Instead, he held his tongue—like always. Her "panicky voice" was always worst whenever she discussed children. It was getting much harder these days to say the right thing *always*.

He said, "Double rest cycles are common. Besides, you got over the first obstacle and then some." He smiled in a way that he hoped she would find endearing. "The second will take care of itself in E'Yahavah's time. Iyared's prophecy is specific and the Seer Clan does not practice polygamy."

She screeched, "Why not? Everybody else does it—even at Sautar! What good is being a stickler about this?"

Nu answered her quietly, "It was not so in the beginning."

She turned her face from him. "You'd know. You're the seer!"

"Speaking of that, will you be alright while I'm gone?" As badly as he wanted a subject change, Nu immediately regretted saying this. He just did not realize how petty it sounded until the words were already out.

Her shoulders slouched again. "Oh—that's right, soon you leave up the mountain. It seems like you jump at opportunities to leave these days!"

"It's not like I'm eager to be alone up there with Pahpi!"

She gave a resigned laugh—as mirthless as Lumekki's had been. "You two wouldn't know what to do without each other."

"I know what I'd do!"

"What?"

The words came to his lips with desperation of their own, his true source of which he hoped she would never know: "Sleep in more and let you tell me what a good husband I am anyway?"

He felt her mood shift so suddenly it moved the very air in the room. She turned to him again, the life in her green eyes rekindled. Her lips puckered with vampish glee—an overdone expression Nu found even remotely attractive only through much effort.

"Of course," she added, "I'd be 'sleeping in' with you, and you'd be getting more rest if you'd gotten up and gone to work for the Old Man!"

And that, too, was how things always seemed to never quite end with Na'Amiha.

N u was strapping the wood bundles for the burnt offering to the pack-beast when word came in.

Lumekki ran to him from the monastery gates, out of breath. "I just came from the drone field oracle! It's happened! Meldur fell three days ago! Samyaza has surrendered on Lumekkor's terms to prevent a siege and further naval bombardment of Assur'Ayur."

Nu grabbed his father's shoulders and almost shook him. "Is there any word on the women?"

"Name lists are in for both Meldur and Assur'Ayur."

"And?"

Lumekki's eyes lost some of their eagerness. "There was a lot of covert warfare inside Meldur, sabotage, and assassin's work. The enemy compromised your network before the end. Many of our women there were implicated and executed before the city fell…"

Nu demanded, "Biriya?"

"I checked. Her name was not on the list of survivors."

"What about Assur'Ayur?"

"Uranna and Tylurnis are listed with ten others as missing and presumed dead. Conflicting accounts place them at a special school for palace concubines, location unknown. The Dumuzi is looking into it. He thinks there's something odd about it…"

Nu shoved the last armload of wood he had just laid on the pack-beast to the ground. The animal snorted uneasily, and snapped its beak. "This prophecy you spoke over me in my cradle is a bloody curse! You and Pahpi should never have shut down that rogue press! What comfort am I? Each test, I somehow fail! You said that I would 'Comfort you all concerning the elements E'Yahavah has cursed!' What does that even mean?"

The outburst hit his father like a fist. Lumekki's eyes dropped to the ground—a look Nu had seen once before, long ago.

A'Nu-Ahki wanted to die. "Pahpo, I'm sorry! I shouldn't have said that! I didn't mean…"

Lumekki shrugged. "It's alright, Son. You think of those women far away and grieve that you could not save them. But *I'm* the one who sent them out *that* gate. I'm the one who really failed them. It's not your job to clean up after my messes."

Nu shriveled up inside as his father's old wound ripped wide open and bled anew all over them both.

The burnt offering torched up the satiny night like flickering light on jagged stones; dancing serpents from an Under-world phantasm. Fatty brown smoke billowed into absorbing darkness, fragrant incense in the megalithic natural temple that crowned Mount N'Zar. Residual heat from the day's sun made the air balmy, causing A'Nu-Ahki and Muhet'Usalaq to pant. They knelt coated in sweat and cinders with dark bloodstains on their bared chests and arms; flaked remnants of a life spilled out.

The old Zaqen seemed deep in prayer, erect on his kneecaps before the crude altar. Nu wobbled in roughly the same position, and wondered guiltily how long this ordeal would last, or if he would pass out first. He half hoped for the latter. Nobody could drag out a sacrifice like Muhet'Usalaq.

The barren mountaintop gave new meaning to fasting and self-affliction. With the sacrificial ram nearly consumed, the acrid smell of burnt flesh and hair caked its bitter resin in A'Nu-Ahki's nostrils. Any sense of ritual cleansing had long ago crumbled away into an angry endurance test between generations.

The flames began to die. Nu rose from his aching knees to gaze at the sky. He wondered what Q'Enukki had ever seen in this place. *Is there something I'm missing? Or is Pahpi just imitating some nostalgic memory of his father?*

Heat, dehydration, and exhaustion had long ago diverted them from the question that had brought them to the summit to begin with. Nu moved away from the altar, and reclined on a nearby flat rock. *If all this is to weaken my fleshly appetites, then consider them about to drop!*

Silence.

Nu flipped over onto his stomach. *How can I be a seer – much less the Comforter from A'Nu – if I can't even handle fasting and meditation? What good is all this if we just see heat phantoms up here?*

He turned onto his back again and looked to heaven for an answer.

The silent stars flickered. If they smiled down on him, it was with the tight-lipped smirk of the Sphinx on Aeden's Pass.

The cooling of the night sky caused a gentle breeze to filter up from the more temperate ravines below. Above him, the wandering planets slowly followed their courses in the First Heaven. They were in a rare alignment that made them all visible. Dim Qayin flew outermost—offset beyond the circle of his father—alienated. Usually only observable by telescope, Nu knew where and how hard to look for its barely visible pin prick. Glare from the majestic giants almost made it impossible.

The brighter largest planets—Atum-Ra Archronos; Primeval Father, with his golden ring of kingship; and Mother Khuva, ever great with the children of the world—approached to kiss each other and double their already formidable light. Closer in swam blue Tiamatu, the Leviathan of Chaos, purveyor of disorder, and symbol of evil for the sons of Seti. For those civilizations descended from Qayin, however, Tiamatu had become the star of hidden wisdom in new pantheons dedicated to the fallen Watchers.

Nearer still to Earth, red L'Mekku—warrior planet, and Tiamatu's pawn—taunted kings toward madness and bloodshed. Low on the opposite horizon, closest of all, with its days rotating in reverse to the spin of the rest of the rebel cosmos, golden Seti flickered—the evening and morning star. Last and smallest, Lilitua danced as the Lost Daughter returned.

Brighter than all of them, low on the southern horizon, the blue-violet comet covered half the sky as a white-hot blade to excise and cauterize the Earth's putrefying gangrene.

Nu rolled onto his side and glanced back at the altar. Muhet'Usalaq lay face down, hands outstretched, by now probably asleep. The sacrificial fire had died to embers. Patriarchal respect or no, Nu had had enough. He got up from the slab, and went to wake him.

Muhet'Usalaq instantly shot up erect and shouted, "Great E'Yahavah, I am old and white of hair! The end of all things approaches quickly and we do not know what you want us to do!"

Nu jumped back and almost screamed at him, certain the old die-hard had simply awakened to the sound of his steps. Shamed by his own irritability, A'Nu-Ahki remembered why they had come up there, indeed, why they had come to Akh'Uzan in the first place, and what they desperately needed to move forward.

He knelt down by his grandfather and cried out, "The sons of Seti have shut their eyes against the Obelisks of Fire and Water! The Seer Clan forsakes love and truth for fanaticism about ritual, prophetic speculation, and bloodline! Merciful E'Yahavah, forgive us! I know we haven't walked as closely to you as we could have, but please guide us anyway, as you once spoke plainly to Q'Enukki. Do this for your own honor's sake, if nothing else. You've given us the treasury of Paru'Ainu to prepare for the last days, but how can we plan wisely if we do not know precisely what to plan for?"

The breeze gusted slightly.

Nu crumpled, face to the dust, under the weighty commitment he had just affirmed. It terrified him that he still felt so fed up and close to quitting. He feared that if something did not happen that night, he would go down from N'Zar, down from Akh'Uzan, leave, and never come back. He didn't want to feel this way, but he did, and he no longer had the willpower to fight it off anymore. If something did not change, this was it.

Muhet'Usalaq's intonation rang like that of some annoying old mystic from a theatrical satire, "We need to wait."

"Here?"

The Old Man ignored him and returned to his silent prayer.

Nu resumed his stargazing, silently calling out to his Maker.

Because the comet was low to the south, most of the constellations stood out fairly well, their cosmic drama displayed in seasonal signs for the children of Atum-Ra. The brighter stars had one or two pinkish-orange, violet, or gold halos that sometimes represented heads, eyes, or other main attributes of central characters in the heavenly stories. Mostly, the key to interpreting the signs depended more on the names of the stars themselves than on the patterns they formed.

The Virgin, still far off at that time of year, held her sheaf — the Woman's Seed who would deliver creation from the Curse of death and decay. Her minor constellation, The Desired One, depicted her after the holy child's birth, as a mother with her son on her lap.

Nu whispered low enough that Muhet'Usalaq could not hear him, "Please restore my desire, E'Yahavah. I have nothing left…"

Losing prominence on the ecliptic, the Ram constellation spoke of sacrifices by which corrupt humanity may approach

E'Yahavah's holiness through the blood of innocent animal substitutes to pay for their sin...

A'Nu-Ahki amended himself. "I have nothing but the Ram..."

He saw the Dragon Breaker, which pictured the Promised Seed as the ultimate monster-slayer. The Comet had come from this constellation to crush the head of the southern Sea Leviathan—but not of the Basilisk constellation, as must ultimately happen before final restoration could come.

A'Nu-Ahki spoke to Muhet'Usalaq, "Have you considered how the comet crushes Leviathan's head, but not the Basilisk?"

"So? The two are just different aspects of the same thing."

"They are both rebels, yes, but are they necessarily one and the same completely? I don't think so."

"Leviathan is the Basilisk's vassal technically."

"I think we need to be technical," Nu said. "The comet's path clearly suggests World-end, but not the immediate crushing of the Basilisk's headship. The fact that Leviathan is a sea monster might indicate the first World-end will be the destruction of water spoken of by Seti's Obelisks. I figure the World-end of fire would require a sign dominant in the Fire River constellation. Yet part of the Fire River overlaps the forward fins of Leviathan, near its head, which could mean that both World-ends will be almost contemporaneous and work in conjunction with each other."

"That is not the traditional understanding."

A'Nu-Ahki was just glad to get the Old Man talking. "Maybe each World-end will carry within itself a little of the other—the water having with it some of the fire and the fire being accompanied by disturbances at sea."

He knew his speculation stemmed not from any direct revelation, merely from his own knowledge of the Star Sign Tablets. Yet it made sense and was consistent with what those tablets revealed. Nor did Nu demand that it be anything more than a speculation; he just wanted to engage the Old Man.

Muhet'Usalaq remained silent.

Nu said, "Seti's revelations explaining the signs of heaven from the *Cosmic Dynasty Stele of Aeden* provide us the basis of a code. The stele told how the stars made during the fourth day of creation would be *'for signs and for seasons.'* Tracking seasons was just a matter of observation. Signs required a symbol key from the One who had set them there. Seeking that key was Seti's life work, which he passed on to Q'Enukki to give us the basis for our theology and cosmology. Both seers centered their focus on the Woman's Seed and the Two World-ends. I've suggested nothing that violates any of that."

Muhet'Usalaq glared up at him side-ways. "The art of interpreting cosmic changes in the signs, such as the appearance of comets, supernovae, or new wandering stars, demands an objective and honest heart and a thorough knowledge of the heavenly cycle and its revealed meanings. Even with your insights—if insights they are—we are no farther along in our quest for understanding than before: Destruction of some sort approaches the Earth because of growing evil. It will fall when I die. Does the comet indicate the nearness of my death? If so, *near* in terms of what measure—a century, decades, years, months, weeks—hopefully not days?"

"I still read it as a World-end of water," Nu said, hoping to draw his grandfather to a conclusion—even a contrary one.

"Perhaps, though older sages thought the fire purge came first."

"The sages are often wrong, especially nowadays."

"My father often leaned toward fire first, as did Seti in his original opinion on the interpretation of Atum-Ra's prophecy. Atum said the word *fire* before he mentioned water."

Nu replied, "But he also admitted that he wasn't sure, and added that his statement was not necessarily meant to be taken chronologically."

The Elder intoned in the formalistic half-chant that A'Nu-Ahki found so affected and irritating, "In any case, we shall have to seek further."

"With respect, Pahpi, I think we can do that just as well on a lower slope. We're hot and dehydrated up here, and just as apt to hallucinate as to see anything meaningful."

Muhet'Usalaq shook. "How can you even suggest such a thing at a time like this? This is the culmination of my whole life! The final hour! Now you have gone and broken the moment! Do you not understand my father took us up here to…"

"Burn away the chaff of our fleshly appetites, I know," Nu finished. "Mine are sufficiently toasted. Let's go to a lower slope."

The Old Man's eyes fell, imploding stars unable to sustain their own emotional weight. The heat must have gotten to him, for tears started to run down his face and there seemed to be an unusual air of bewilderment about him that Nu had never seen before.

"Every decade you get more and more self-willed!" There was an almost drunken slur to his words. "And now you mock our very heritage! Yet, I cannot believe you would do that! What is the matter with you?"

"I'm tired of your manipulative little endurance test," Nu answered softly but firmly. "This isn't about us! It's time you understood that I'm not another Q'Enukki. I don't have his energy or vision, I hate the heat, and I find it impossible to focus on E'Yahavah or anything else up here. Sacrifices are one thing, but we can seek answers more effectively in a lower ravine where the elevation's heat won't warp our minds. This is too important! I'm sorry if it doesn't live up to your ideal."

The Ancient shook his head in cataclysmic sobs; eyes draining around his inner collapse to unearth emotional artifacts long buried in layers of willful sediment. "I am the one who has left you the wrong impression..." His speech rambled like that of a man half-asleep. "The last promise! The last bloody promise I made to him, and I have broken it with the most important person in the world! I could not even do that one simple thing right! I never could do the most important things right!"

Nu was terrified at the sound of his own self-doubt erupting from the man who had always been a mountain of confidence. "What do you mean?"

"Q'Enukki—my father! He made me promise! And I have broken it! The last promise! The most important one! 'Do not put heavy burdens on the children,' he said—yet that is all I have ever done to you! Truth is, my father was very different from me—insightful and spontaneous, while I am rigid and brittle! I can only imitate! Yet my imitations somehow always turn into mockeries! He taught me much, but could not give me the imagination to apply his wisdom to a swiftly changing world. His wisdom is sound, but my application, inept... It has confused you, has it not?"

Nu stood over the Old Man; dumbstruck by the devastating honesty his own frankness had unleashed.

Muhet'Usalaq crumbled to a drunken slouch on the hot stone. "The only picture you have of Q'Enukki has been painted by the fire of his writings, and by me! But I have given you a distorted image; I see that now."

"No! You taught me well!" Nu tried frantically to put back the bricks of his ancestor's crumbling wall of dignity—bricks that fell too fast for him to catch and replace, and would never again stand as the edifice he had always comfortably known. "I just can't live up to that ideal!"

Muhet'Usalaq shook his head, as the torrid ego shredder of N'Zar's blasted peak ripped away his tormented personal façade. "It is not a matter of living up to anything! Q'Enukki was a man, with weaknesses just like any other! He simply walked with E'Yahavah, and trusted the Sacrifice Ram to cover his shortcomings."

"It's not that simple! What about his power and goodness—I can't even come close to that and I'm still supposed to be this 'Comforter from the A'Nu' my father prophesied of! How? What does it even mean, Comforter? It could mean almost anything!"

Muhet'Usalaq glanced up at him. "Not just anything. It is true, Q'Enukki's walk brought a strength and goodness to him, but that was effect—not cause. You also have it placed in you to awaken a generation—or at least to preserve a remnant."

"What remnant? Even most the Seer Clan thinks I'm a heretic now! What comfort have I been to them? What comfort have I been to anyone?"

The Old Man hung his head. "A lifetime of mistakes has tracked me down and beaten me into this dust. You comfort me from that! I never could inspire a generation the way my father and brothers had!"

Nu had trouble imagining Urugim inspiring anybody—except perhaps at the very end. He had only known his grandfather's other brothers as distant childhood uncles. Most had died as martyrs in obscure parts of the world before he reached adulthood.

"What makes you think I can do what you could not?"

A swath of gray twine hair fell in front of the Ancient's watering eyes. "You are more like my father than any man alive when you simply behave naturally. Yet you seek to emulate his legend by imitating me. All through your childhood I would try to change you and then belittle you when your efforts to change only produced my own kind of pretension!"

"What are you talking about?"

Muhet'Usalaq turned his head up at him with quivering eyes that stared right through him. "You were reflecting me, not my father! And I never liked what I saw in that mirror!" He seemed about to collapse into a child-like breakdown. *They never let me be a Dragon-slayer, you know — not a real one! I had to stay home with the women — Mooma and Auntie were too afraid to bring on the end of the world!*" His dam broke to unleash the cries of a little boy trapped too long in the prison of a name and forced to live out his dreams through the dwindling accomplishments of his children.

"Let's go to a lower slope," Nu said, offering his grandfather a hand.

Muhet'Usalaq took it and replied dully, "I know of this little ravine with a waterfall and a pool. We cannot see the whole sky, though."

"It's okay. We've both seen enough for one night."

And the LORD said, "My Spirit shall not strive with man forever, for he is indeed flesh; yet his days shall be one hundred and twenty years."

—*Genesis* 6:3 (NKJV)

17

APOCALYPSE

Nightmares hunted Nu in his slumber, disrupting the peace and comfort of the waterfall crevasse's cool spongy moss. He had gone to sleep dwelling on the conversations with his father before climbing N'Zar with Muhet'Usalaq.

A'Nu-Ahki found himself at the controls of a type of aerodrone he had often seen overflying the monastery — like three glass-domed cylinders connected by a double layer of gigantic wings with dual tail rudders. He rode in the bubble at the front of the center cylinder, which sat forward of the other two. His hands caressed strange instruments as if they were Emzara's body, fingers reaching here and there across a patch-quilt of glowing knobs, levers, and dials — moving without his control — to keep the giant monstrosity aloft. The insect hum of the machine's four wing-mounted engines made him feel like an intruder in a hive of horrendous wasps.

"Approaching target," said the cold voice of somebody in the glass-metal cabin behind him.

Nu's hand danced across the controls again, performing some unknown adjustment, while his other gripped a mechanical column that must have steered the drone. Outside the window, the land below seemed distant and hazy, unreal somehow.

"Target acquired. Commencing drop," said the voice from behind, as if he were simply switching on a quickfire pearl.

Everything shook and rattled as racks full of bombs tumbled out through open slits in the drone's three underbellies. Shrill whistles followed each projectile down and away into the hazy unreality below. Nu could see the detonations flash across the countryside, but by then he was so far away that he could not even hear the explosions.

A thrill like too much wine pulsed through his body. He heard himself shout to the others inside the machine, "Men we are no longer, but gods! We now wield the thunder of the gods and fly as only the divine ones fly—in chariots of crystal, iron, and flame!"

He closed his eyes.

When they opened again, he was not on the aerodrone but in the citadel of a great wood-burning ironclad. He gazed out across the ocean to a narrow ribbon of land on the horizon. Utterly strange and fantastic, this vessel bore no resemblance to the oar-banked biremes and triremes of little more than two centuries ago. The top-heavy armored leviathan carried huge cannons able to spit giant thunder-darts the distance of a day's journey on mount. Nu watched as these pounded a coastal city and squared off against another wood-burning fortress-ship in the distance. The shoreline erupted in a wall of flames so far off that he could not even smell the smoke.

It was easy; pull a lever and wipe out thousands. The operators of these machines never saw their enemy—never heard the screams of the multitudes of men, women, and children they slaughtered. Nu could sit there, push the meaningless buttons, turn the mysterious knobs all day, and never feel anything. It was even fun in a perverse kind of way.

He closed his eyes again.

This time when they opened, A'Nu-Ahki found himself surrounded by a city in flames. Whistling missiles fell all around him, sending great plumes of wreckage and dirt into the sky like fiery mushrooms. Seared air slammed into his chest with the force of a smith's hammer, and knocked him to his knees. Buildings toppled while men screamed and ran through the shattered streets, bodies on fire. Women huddled in terrified balls of futile protection around their children; all of them crushed to death by the falling buildings or scythed down by flying bits of rock and metal.

The flaming World-end staccato pounded the city and Nu's body like multiplied flame hammers from every direction until only cratered ruins, smoking mounds, and fly-covered corpses remained in the midst of a sudden eerie stillness. The madness worked through A'Nu-Ahki, throttled his insides, while he jerked and twitched. He turned and ran from the holocaust. But the faces of the dead and wounded, burned and shattered, red, black, and gray, followed him through the halls of sleep—the endless damned, condemned to a black-hot prison by humanity's lust to each become an autonomous god. They fell into heaps of bodies, mountains of rotting fertilizer in endless fields.

Nu's pace through the rotting piles slowed as the fires began to fade and go out. Presently, brick masons came along to survey the grisly hills in the holocaust's aftermath. They gathered the skulls, and placed them into a pile with a sign next to it that bore the ideogram for *War* painted in bold red.

Beyond the heap of skulls, they made a second, larger bone pile that seemed like a natural hill from where Nu stood. Time—maybe decades or centuries—somehow passed. A commotion broke out on the second skull heap's far side; raucous laughter of men and women squealing in pleasure, cut off periodically by screams of terror and torment.

Nu circled the skull pile with the sign of *War* on it, and approached the second mound. It was also made largely of skulls, except that most of these bones were far older, grayer in hue, as if they had been accumulating much longer than the *War* pile. The people on the opposite side did not hear his approach, even as he stumbled over crunching stray bones and rounded the heap to see what they were doing.

The spectacle stopped him dead.

Streams of humanity—mostly young women and children— came from over the horizon, led along in chains either by titans or wealthy, prominent men. Many of the prisoners seemed unaware of their captivity, as if under a spell. As they drew nearer to Nu, flocks of tiny multi-colored birds became visible like sparkling jewels over the forced march, singing sweetly to the prisoners as they flitted overhead.

As Nu listened, the bird-song transformed into an evil squawk of foul words and repetitious lies; "This is living. There is no love or life outside of the queue, only death in the void..."

The stumbling women and children laughed and drank with their captors along the way, although the titans and men of power paused frequently to rape and brutalize them. Only when the prisoners neared the mountainous bone pile did their true condition seem to come home to them. There, the colorful birds with their repetitive songs turned black and circled away to sing for others farther back in the line. Their purpose seemed to be to keep the marchers from seeing the bone pile or hearing the screams.

Once free of the birdsong, some prisoners tried to dash away from the skull mountain, until their chains snapped them back. When they reached the ancient mound, their captors would draw swords and hack the heads from the prisoners, and toss them onto the skull pile. They rolled the bodies into a pit of refuse using the forced labor of the next set of abductees.

And the birds sang madly on.

A'Nu-Ahki turned to face the business side of the great heap. He saw that it too bore an ideogram sign that read, *Crime Without Punishment.* The *Crime* pile had more than twice the skulls of the *War* mound.

The surveyors and masons in charge of stacking the skulls from both heaps began to distribute them across the gigantic single landmass called Earth. In all the great cities, people began to use the skulls as bricks to build.

The dream carried Nu through Sa-utar and Bab'Tubila, then to lands beyond—all undergoing vast post-war reconstruction using skull bricks. Assuri had finally fallen before the multi-tribal alliance purchased by Tubaal-qayin Dumuzi's industrial supremacy.

Nu saw cheering, riot, and pageantry, as a new prosperity dawned. Temple brothels at Erdu and Ayar Adi'In gorged themselves to vomiting excess. The Temples fed the poor and diverted them with entertainment, while the rich divided the spoils in secret as always.

A'Nu-Ahki was unsure exactly when the heavenly Watcher joined him, only that it happened before the onset of the real terror.

The Watcher seemed to be a man of luminous animated glass, clear as crystal waters made alive by El-N'Lil, the Divine Breath. His eyes held the fires of judgment cupped in ampules of mercy. When he saw that Nu had noticed his presence, he said, "I am sent to show you what is."

Nu took his hand as a small child would. It felt strangely cool and comforting—like the mists of the waterfall grotto where he somehow knew he still slept. The Watcher led him across a wide plain to a magnificent tower build of kapar stone and fine wood, but also partially of the skulls from the two piles. The castle had an odd hexagonal base, which divided into six turrets, each reaching into the clouds.

Nu said, "What is this place?"

"The house of Atum-Ra," answered the glass-fluid man.

They walked inside though the main gate. Children danced and played in a fountained garden courtyard. All seemed peaceful in the keep—a wedding in one corner, a market place in another. Atop the north tower flared an altar with a sacrifice. Artisans plied crafts. Singers sang songs. Soldiers paraded in peacetime drill. It seemed an idyllic place.

The Watcher held his hands over Nu's eyes, and then removed them. "Look again," he said.

Nu panned around the same courtyard, now translucent and full of pallid light and creeping shadows. Skeletons filled the cornerstones and walls, screaming silent screams. Most were dead children and infants, sealed alive into the stones or behind the bricks, bone-bags twisted in the terror of final suffocation. He looked down to avert his eyes, but found the pavement equally translucent, revealing labyrinthine tunnels of pale light and even deeper living shadows near the tower's foundation and metal staples. When he saw the Monster, a wave of nausea gurgled up from the pit—as if his stomach and the lower catacombs were one.

The gigantic hydra writhed, an obscene iridescent-pus-yellow trunk supporting multiple bore-worm heads that burrowed upward through the walls, into the main tower, and from there dividing through to the six turrets. The wormholes undermined the entire fortress, while the Monster's many heads poked out into the open in numerous places. Each ended as a thick umbilical cord worming into the bodies of several people, all wearing masks.

A'Nu-Ahki panted to keep from retching. "What is this creature?"

The Watcher did not answer, but said, "Follow me."

He led Nu up a squared-off spiral stairwell inside the central tower. While they climbed, Nu could see inside the walls, where not two cubits away snaked one of the bore-worm's oily necks. A rank odor seeped from cracks between the stones.

At the top chamber, they entered a hall surrounded by multicolored windows that bent the light outside into millions of geometric forms that danced in kaleidoscopic profusion across the interior. The airy loft had the hot cinnamon odor of dry-dust mummified corpses.

Inside the chamber, the worm-head curled up from the floor to bury itself inside a man who appeared to be a teaching sage of some sort. He wore a mask with the ideogram letter for *Knowledge* carved into its forehead. Children filled his room, all eagerly listening to what he had to say. He spoke of beauty, peace, prosperity, and enlightenment. Nu even heard him mention the Divine Name once or twice in passing.

After awhile however, it seemed that the Sage only repeated the same words in different ways, demeaning their significance, and distorting their definitions. The longer Nu listened the more apparent it became to him that the masked teacher merely told the children *what* to think, instead of imparting to them the skills of *how* to reason.

Again, the Watcher took Nu's hand, pulling him across a causeway that connected to the ring of outer towers, specifically the one with the altar on it. One of the Hydra's worm-necks snaked through the walls of this outer spire also, to emerge and penetrate a priest that stood before the flaming sacrifice.

The ideogram for *Men Calling on the Divine Name* shone in fiery gold across the front of the holy man's wedge-shaped nemes headdress-mask. Another flock of children knelt before him with terrified eyes locked on his feet. A statue of the Basilisk serpent coiled around the altar's base.

The Priest chanted, "E'Yahavah speaks only to the Watchers. The Watchers speak only to me. Men are not worthy to walk with E'Yahavah. You cannot understand the words of the Fathers without me, for they are mystery words, which often do not really mean what they appear to say."

"Come," said the glass Watcher, who pulled A'Nu-Ahki away from the sacrifice and guided him down the stairs of the Altar Tower with its worm-neck writhing inside the wall. Nu wondered what would happen if he slipped his utility knife between the blocks to sever the twisted thing.

This time they descended past the courtyard, into dungeons in the tower's lower parts, deep in the bowels of the earth where dim red light refracted upward from burning rivers of magma. Here the crawling shadows were darkest. Nu trembled as they approached the lowest chamber, nearest the body of the bloated Hydra in the foundations. The stench of maggot-ridden carcasses filled the air, like leavings from some great hunting wurm.

Crowded around the deepest portal, a throng of pale children peered in at the warm sticky darkness. Nu recognized them as the same group that had played and danced when he had first entered the fortress.

The Watcher nudged him through the tiny mob to the open door.

Inside the cell, on a lavish bed lit by dragon-headed wall sconces on either side that vomited lava into sloping sluiceways, snaked another worm-head—this one buried in the body of a Temple prostitute with face painted so thickly that Nu had doubts as to her true gender. She beckoned two callers who stood on either side of her divan, silhouetted by the molten streamlets from the two sconce mouths.

The first bore the crown of Tubaal-qayin Dumuzi, the little goat Shepherd-Emperor of Lumekkor. The second wore the red robes of Ayar Adi'In's alchemist priesthood in apostate Khavilakki.

The pale children watched from the door with wide prurient eyes. Some giggled their innocence away with monkey laughter, while others cried in confusion, shame, and fright.

Nu pried his eyes from the lurid spectacle and turned to usher the youngsters away as fast as he could. His muscles became cold honey—too slow—always too slow. By the time he had fully turned, the children already imitated what they saw in the chamber amongst themselves. Nu tried to shut the door, but it would not budge.

Small sores and bruises began to form on the children through their awkward, disease-filled play.

Nu cried to the Watcher, "Make them stop!"

"I cannot."

"Then tell me what this means!"

The messenger put a luminous hand on A'Nu-Ahki's shoulder and pulled him away from the door and the mimicking rot-children.

"This is the heart of Atum-Ra's house, where the Basilisk seduces the mighty among men and gives power to those who sink into his bed of religious, economic, and political intrigue. It all starts in the heart. The children see a distorted vision of what they think is life and grow dissatisfied with the reality of their own lot—even the princes and priests."

Nu said under his breath, "Especially the princes and priests."

"Especially them," the Watcher agreed. "They are made greedy for the delights of the whore—delights that not even her lovers truly experience. They are always enticed, but never satisfied."

"And what is the significance of her two lovers?"

"They bring the illusion of life to the Basilisk's manipulation in front of the children. The technocratic Guild of Tubaal-qayin does so by using their Divinely-given gifts to invent great engineering works of metal and quickfire, which they ungratefully set up as proof to the masses that men have unlocked the secrets of Divinity to overcome the hardship of working the soil that E'Yahavah has cursed. Yet their escape is a delusion. Even in the Guild's most powerful art, the frustration of the Great Curse only changes form to multiply in new and unexpected ways.

"The second lover wears the red robes of the priesthood of Ardis and Ayar Adi'In. Guided by dark Watchers, they study the creation codes of life, altering information processed in the tiniest structures of the body. They want to engineer a counterfeit Seed of Promise. Instead, the priestly research corrupts the integrity of all flesh, accelerating breakdown in the replication language used inside all life in ways not even the Watchers can predict."

Nu's guide lifted his hand to heaven. In a flash of light, they stood before the Great Temple at Ayar Adi'In—a massive granite complex that continually hummed with mysterious engines and flickered in exotic quickfire ghost-light. Only instead of standing on the terraced flower-garden hill of Adi'In, this version of the temple pressed down on a bloody mountain of the dead and dying carcasses of millions of squirming, malformed babies, each experimented upon, harvested for tissue, and left to die.

The Watcher blinked and another flash of light returned them to the tower courtyard of Atum-Ra's fortress-house, which now seemed dilapidated, and stank of decay.

"Who exactly are the pale children?" Nu asked, saving this question for last because he feared its answer most. For he already knew the truth.

The Messenger said nothing. He merely spread his arms toward the people in the courtyard, as if to indicate that all, at one time or another, had lurked at the door of the Whore's chamber.

Nu saw the same wedding again that he had seen when they had first entered the tower gates. He followed the couple through their life together. Before long, the man berated his wife when she failed to give him the impossible pleasures that his spying on the Whore's divan had conditioned him to expect. Then the woman wept when her husband no longer praised her with the lofty words of the Great Sage in the upper hall of colored lights that smelled like the mummified dead.

However, Nu heard her whispers in the night—how she too yearned for her own version of the lower chamber—where she could be in control of herself and her man, through the exquisite mastery with which the Whore dominated her lovers by promises of pleasure and pain.

The home of this married couple existed inside one of the kapar blocks of the six-sided fortress. Inside each block lived men and their wives—with lots of children—more each year. These youngsters saw anger, and grew up angry. They knew self-involved parents, and became self-involved. Left to themselves, they drifted with their own affections like falling meteors—not human affections as created in the beginning, but contorted by the grip of the all-encompassing Curse—children born into a continuum they had not caused, but which they could still partly shape and which would wholly shape them unless they fought against its pull.

Bored, under-supervised, they explored the lower chambers seeking excitement and a place to belong. Once they saw the lava-lit dungeon secrets however, nothing could ever seem quite as exciting as the Whore did.

Thus, the cycle repeated, each time weakening the stones of the individual home-bricks a little more. Nu saw the stone house of his married couple crumble with a loud pop. Two more blocks caved in on its space. The odd-shaped skulls from the two great piles, used as bricks in various places to rebuild, added to this unstable distribution of stress. The collapse of their home crushed and bruised the children, while the man and woman went their separate ways from the rubble, dragging their sons and daughters apart from each other with them.

The surrounding house-bricks groaned under the growing maldistribution of pressure. Several more collapsed. Meanwhile, the sores and wounds began to fester, which the children received from the collapse of their homes or from playing in the lower chambers near the Whore. The tower's wise men placed tiny linen bandages over their unwashed ulcers.

By now, the exponential increase of broken stones became so disruptive that they threatened make the entire fortress implode. Towers wobbled, while the outer walls buckled in swaying pandemonium. A corrosive filth foamed up from the lower chambers, rotting the foundations with acid stench.

When people could deny the obvious instability no longer, the children, the wise men, and the parents climbed in panic to the Sage in his hall of lights. He reeked of mummy dust. They asked him to teach them how they might save the tower.

The Sage replied, "Only the woman at the foundations can give you the answers you seek." He carefully refrained from calling her a whore.

Nu watched the tower people race down the spiraling steps to the lower chamber, wading through the filth as it ate at their clothes and skin. The Whore and her two lovers waited with open arms, as if miraculously untouched by all the rottenness, all too happy to help.

"The tower crumbles because it has too many stones," the Whore said. "Give me your children. I will teach them how to control the process so the structure does not fall." She then gave a detailed lesson on the building's architecture that left everyone convinced she was a master builder.

The parents gave up their children and went to the markets to work or to stone homes to amuse themselves while they waited.

The Whore shrieked, "The dance shall liberate your spirits!" while she put whips into the hands of the youngsters and told them to dance as they had always danced in the courtyard. She supplied a symphony of pipers, lyre players, drummers, and singers that began to play a form of music Nu had never heard before. Loud and cacophonous, yet powerful and moving, the instruments wailed in twisted cycles of sound.

At first, the children seemed confused and unwilling to move with it. As time passed, the harmonics intoxicated their senses until its drumbeat slowly captured their hearts and bodies. As they started to jump to the chaotic new tune, the Whore began to suggest different steps to them.

Most of the children followed her directions, though many found her suggestions revolting—obscene contortions of orgiastic rhythmic mayhem. The most willing dancers caught on and used their whips against those slower to comply.

Soon, the play-dancing became a convulsion of leaping shrieking bodies, flogging each other to faster undulations, boys against girls, women against men. The whip-dancers enjoyed tormenting the opposite gender and even gave themselves over to punishment at the hands of other floggers. Growing numbers of dancers avoided the opposite sex, as if fearful of the rejection they could devise so well, or of other pains less obvious but more devastating. Yet the thrill rapidly wore off even for those who enjoyed it. Despair and exhaustion eventually set in for everyone alike, though some were better at faking a smile than others.

Some men turned to other men, and women to other women in their gyrations, drawn increasingly to their own gender until nothing else satisfied. Impulse and chaos ruled, choking out conscience and self-evident human design. Putting the wounds and decay for the design, these couples made desperate attempts to find love and acceptance from the Dance, but confused what they sought with the manipulative fire of the Whore's chamber. A few even paired off to leave the festivities and find shelter amid shards of the broken building blocks. Tired from the competition and pain, they tried to recapture some of the security of a stable brick-home. Yet all they had were broken pieces and dust.

The tired couples built shanties from the debris and tried to pretend that what they had found was better than what they had lost through the Dance. Many could not keep up the illusion, however. Nu watched as these climbed the swaying towers and jumped off. Most of the others gave up and went back to the Dance. They tried to convince themselves that maybe they would do better with their next dance partners.

The tempo grew as the dancers murdered, raped, and stole from each other to get what they now believed was their due. Some dragged away the smallest children in the secrecy of night, casting the finger of blame at E'Yahavah for the out-of-control desires that raged within them to dominate the Dance. Nu saw the whole process — how the drives and compulsions had arisen from the mind-bending poison of their untreated wounds and from the lies that the children had been conditioned to believe about themselves by the Whore. She told them they had no real choice against the Dance.

Even now, the healers and priests who helped the Whore to supervise the dance left the dancer's ulcers to fester beneath linen patches and caked cosmetics.

"What can be done?" They all shrugged. "Has not E'Yahavah created you with these desires?" They told the dancers. "These wounds are simply a part of life. Drink some wine and opium. Do you see any that can truly avoid the dance? How can such a common thing be unnatural?"

When all this failed to keep the fortress stable and only made its collapse imminent, the Basilisk himself appeared again as a messenger of light from the upper chamber to reveal his ultimate answer.

The Basilisk Sage called down from the center tower's balcony, "You can create new realities for yourselves; there are no absolute rules for how to do this!"

Nobody seemed to notice that the claim that "there are no absolute rules" was itself the most tyrannical of absolute rules. As far as Nu had seen, it forced everyone to pay the self-destructive price of denying reality for madness. As civilization collapsed around them, the city dwellers merely looked bewildered.

The Watcher said to Nu, "Come with me to the heaven of heavens."

Immediately they stood before a throne of blazing light so bright, that it rippled the very space around it and blasted things away from itself like a wind. A'Nu-Ahki recognized it from a description in Q'Enukki's Fifth Scroll in the split second before he averted his eyes from the throne's brilliance. Winged Kherubar crouched on either side of the dais; leonine bodies of white-hot flame poised like sentries with heads bowed in respect. Colors of a new primary kind, which no human eyes had ever seen before, arced around the throne like ribbons of sunlight in a bright mist. Thunder rumbled overhead, as dark clouds overshadowed the chair like an awning.

The light itself howled in Nu's ears until he shook violently. He shielded his eyes from the flash-vision and would have fallen to the crystalline floor in a stupor had not the Watcher held him upright and told him to observe.

A'Nu-Ahki knew that the will of the One on the throne held together the very particles and energies of the universe. Even in that piercing glare, the power must have been shaded down so as not to consume lesser creatures. None could approach closer than the cloud awning, nor look directly upon the seated form. Nu felt his presence more than saw him, though he could observe the base of the throne in quick blinding glances if he tried hard.

Burned and seeing spots, Nu's eyes followed the floor away from the dais to a large group of three-toed feet nearby. He slowly peered up and found they belonged to an assembly of coldly luminous man-like beings with immense, hairless heads and black almond-shaped eyes. They stood before the throne at a discreet distance, as if they desired an audience with the One who sat there, but feared to come too close.

The tallest and brightest of this multitude stepped forward; although their brilliance seemed a dirty gray compared to the light blazing from between the Sphinx-like Kherubar. Their faces were not human and seemed ill equipped to convey human emotion. Yet they felt emotions at least akin to those of humanity and Nu found that he could somehow read them through what otherwise would have been almost nondescript features.

The first gray creature leaped forward to bow before the throne in an overdone gesture of obeisance. Soft tendrils grew from his head like a small living crown, whipping in the blast of the Light. His white-less eyes blinked with black heat, as the fire of a once grand purpose burned over his face like a poorly hung mask. Zeal radiated from his every gesture, projecting words, images, and emotions into Nu's mind in a disturbing montage of violent color.

The second gray creature had no tendrils on his head. A restlessly calculating super-intelligence glowered from his eyes, cold and heartless as the Abyss. A fading vapor of good intentions hung around him also like the dead phosphor-glow of his skin or the sickly-sweet aroma of succulent fruit gone rotten. Nu sensed this person had an agenda so all-important and all-consuming to him that he had sacrificed things one should never sacrifice. For all the power hanging like a glimmering shroud around the second creature, the image that stuck in Nu's mind was that of a stubborn angry goat.

This scene also sprang from the Fifth Scroll of Q'Enukki: The two gray man-creatures who stepped forward to address the throne were Samyaza and Uzaaz'El. Their cabal of Watchers petitioned E'Yahavah for permission to go to Earth.

Samyaza thought-projected an impassioned plea though his mouth never moved; *"Please, O great, resplendent, and Holy One"* — his words had a hungry whine in them — *"allow us to redeem the sons of men! For no woman's seed has been born to them and we have heard nothing in all the heavens about when or how this should happen. Could it not be that you have ordained for us, your created sons, to achieve it? Let us go and you shall see how we will hallow you!"*

The One on the throne regarded the assembly with the deliberation of a judge rather than a father. His voice came low and penetrated through the crystal floor up into Nu's body; felt in his bones rather than heard. "My Spirit will not always struggle with men because they are also of flesh. Yet you wish to mingle yourselves with them? The day you set foot on Earth, you will be enticed by the daughters of men, to take them to yourselves according to strange attractions for which neither you nor they are designed. Your rationalizations are elaborate, but I see you."

The second Watcher, Uzaaz'El, spoke with calculated restraint, using his narrow mouth. "Master, it is by our joining with Atum's daughters that the effect of death in humanity shall, in slow stages, be overcome. Our teaching shall correct their moral character and civilize them."

The One on the throne spoke. "Do you really believe your own words, Uzaaz'El? If the situation were that simple, I would have told you. Did you not listen to the overtures of Shining One before I cast him down?"

"It is true I once listened to what the one who is now fallen said—to test it, as did many of us. Unlike many, we did not follow him. It is from him that we wish to win back the sons of man for you."

Thunder rumbled from the throne, as the penetrating light reached out to reveal what lay within the gathered throng. "He spoke of the thrill to be had in possessing the bodies of those in the lower realms, did he not? Did he not complain that men multiplied while your numbers remained constant? Did he not hint that by multiplication men would usurp your place? Is it not your desire to co-mingle and multiply your kind—and not only to multiply but also simply to experience the sensations—to control?

"You cannot even embrace a woman under most conditions, except through the arms of a human host! Keeping material form for more than a few minutes at a time is too draining for you without direct contact with a gateway-symbiont, and they are few.

"Even if the daughters of men could actually bear you true hybrid offspring, it would require tampering with the creation codes in ways that would do far greater damage, rather than heal that which already exists! Do you imagine that you know more than I, who designed both humankind and yours? Is the life I gave you so devoid of richness, or have you just made yourselves blind to it? Even if what you propose were possible, how could you win back the sons of man when you would take women from them and produce only your own sons instead?"

Uzaaz'El shuddered as the probing light pierced his body. "Shining One said that man would usurp us, but we are not threatened by his bent logic. You could help us and bless us with your knowledge so that we would not make mistakes." Yet A'Nu-Ahki saw the Watcher's huge eyes blink and heard the briefest quiver in his voice. "We can do this to your glory and are ready to prove ourselves."

Caustic laughter echoed from the throne. "What need have I of your proof? I know that the day you set foot on Earth, the Basilisk's web will fully ensnared you. Quit this pretense while you still can. You have not Shining One's subtlety and you certainly cannot work this out no matter what information I give you. When you go to Earth, your seduction will be complete. It already is, in fact, for you clearly do not believe me anymore."

Samyaza said, "We will consider your words, Master. Yet we shall prove ourselves strong for you! The women are but a means to the end of human redemption. We will not be seduced!"

The throne darkened, but the Voice upon it remained serene. "Go then, since you have it in your hearts to do nothing else. Your desire for women is not a desire I created in you, but one you have taken out of order to yourselves and nurtured. Slowly it grew and slowly it has dominated you. You will be further ensnared by it, for you are not meant for them."

"We will fight ensnarement!" Uzaaz'El said; yet as one who tried to convince himself rather than one who asserted truth with confidence. "Give us this chance to show you!"

The Light on the throne turned from them.

The Watcher released Nu's hand, dropping him screaming through the heavens swiftly back to Earth. He landed amid the ruined dragon shrines dotting the Ardis Range like empty eye sockets gaping from hollow stone skulls, where long ago Amazon witch-priestesses first sacrificed kidnapped children to bloodthirsty gods of flame and madness. There, the mountains in western Lumekkor brooded under a black sky filled with smoke and strange darting lights. Heat lightening shot through the air with distant thunder rumbles, as spectral voices uttered dark unspeakable oaths that whispered down from sun-cracked peaks.

A crack of thunder commanded A'Nu-Ahki to look up.

The brightest of the darting lights fell like a dying meteor into the Mountains of Ardis with a wail of rage and despair. Another light followed, almost as bright, and then others of lesser magnitude. Nu realized that these were the sons of God, leaving their exalted estate to obey the pull of their new dark master, whom they pretended even to themselves not to serve.

A coiling constellation of poison pin-prick stars, the Basilisk writhed about the globe, hiding his face from the falling Watchers. Nevertheless, he had a remnant of discreet followers waiting for them amid the nameless cave-shrines when they arrived—power mad and power broken men and women ready to be molded to whatever "divine purpose" the sons of heaven might dream up in their new found futility.

Nu watched as the Watchers walked among the scattered tribes of men and spoke to them, working in various ways as messengers of light to teach them how to make weapons, medicines, and new alloys—things humanity was already discovering on its own. They drew on faint tribal memories of the Promised Seed to twist them for their own purposes. For many of the Fallen Ones still believed that they fulfilled, rather than perverted, the prophecies and Star Signs.

Their haunted voices came to A'Nu-Ahki, as they communicated over great distances to one another to plot their options. Soon an argument broke out, then another, and another. The issues always sounded complex and serious—whether to trust human beings with the knowledge of living creation codes and the power of elementary particles, or to keep them in ignorance through making them dependent on sorcery and mysticism. Yet the emotions of the sons of God were those of proud children swaggering for dominance in a playground of human souls.

The Watchers soon realized humanity would eventually discover these things without them—just not as quickly and not under their control. Panic seized the Watchers—a creeping fear of having no place of their own any longer. If humanity could eventually reach the stars without them, what need had men for intermediary gods? Could human beings even redeem themselves? The sons of God now feared for the first time to call on the Divine Name. Had they not left their place against his counsel? Thus, they worked under their own names or under whatever titles men gave to them.

Nu listened as some admitted their ensnarement. These left Samyaza and Uzaaz'El to join the Basilisk openly, although most of the rebels still protested of how they could turn things back to E'Yahavah in the end and find satisfaction in the process. These, led by Uzaaz'El, approached Q'Enukki the Seer to ask him to petition E'Yahavah on their behalf.

The Seer reluctantly complied with the intercession, but refused to join them. Nu watched his ancestor climb the Mountains of Ardis to read their petition to the Divine Wind, El-N'Lil, on the desolate peaks where the Watchers had first made their ill-spoken oaths.

A'Nu-Ahki had often read the prophecy Q'Enukki had received in response to that petition:

> *"Hear this, Uzaaz'El, and the other Watchers that you and Samyaza have mustered; judgment has been passed on you. Your request will not be granted. From this time on, you will never ascend into the heavens. For on the Earth I bind you for as long as the world endures. But before the end, you shall witness the destruction of your beloved 'sons.' You shall not possess them, for they will fall before you by the sword and by the convulsions at the world's end. Neither shall you plead for them or for yourselves. You will weep and beg in silent prisons of hot stone until the day of the end."*

Desperate and deluded, the Fallen Stars fled from Q'Enukki. They told themselves the Seer beguiled himself under a clever device of the Basilisk—he was only a man, after all. The remaining

Watchers resolved still to prove themselves worthy by somehow accomplishing the redemption of humanity; for if they must be bound to Earth, they at least wanted to make it a fit and pleasant place for themselves.

Yet they could not agree on how to proceed. Some established differing codes of law among the tribes they had adopted. Others revealed hidden knowledge, while still others performed various wonders to keep the sons of men in awe of them, but in total ignorance. Nu noticed that all the deeds of the Watchers had one thing in common—they worked to make humanity dependent on them instead of upon their Creator.

The super-human bickering went on for centuries. As Nu listened further, he overheard how the Century War, unbeknown to those fighting it, had actually arisen as a showdown between Samyaza and Uzaaz'El over whether the quest for a deathless seed should continue by means of sorcery and mysticism or through material technology. Though loudest of the otherworld arguments, it was by no means the only one.

Many lesser Watchers gambled on both sides, or in the ruckus, played more remote games of their own among the distant clans and colonies. They each hoped to gain greater power after the two chief rivals had depleted themselves. It seemed that every family on earth welcomed their aid and knowledge except one—and now even that last holdout buckled under their relentless solicitations.

A'Nu-Ahki saw the new Archon at Sa-utar; Kunyari son of Adiyuri mechanically taught the children of Seti the lessons of the Seers. However, these children had also seen the Basilisk-Whore and his two lovers in the lower chamber, for Nu recognized them. They listened to the Archon speak, but Nu could hear them discuss things among themselves afterward.

"Will the old windbag ever change his tune?" said one young man. "When will he figure out that we can make our own truths?"

A smirking girl scratched her sores until they popped open, and answered, "What I don't understand is how he can possibly expect us to take him seriously. The world has changed and everybody knows it."

"He kind of looks like a big grease-toad, doesn't he?" said another. "Eventually, we're just gonna need to crush his kind."

They all laughed.

When Archon Kunyari saw that he had lost prestige, he tried to accommodate his listeners until he sounded like both the Sage in the hall of colored lights, and the Priest on the serpent-polluted altar. He stood with a hand raised to halt the Watchers at the gates of Sa-utar, while his other hand gestured for them to enter the city secretly through the catacombs.

The children saw this and smiled knowing smiles that said, "Yeah, but we're still gonna have to crush you; nothing personal."

With the delusion now complete, a stifling apathy settled like a poisoned evening fog over the city streets.

Nu approached one of the children and pleaded; "Don't you want to know the truth and be healed of your infected wounds?"

The youth looked back at him with dull opiated eyes and shrugged, just as the mists swallowed him alive. "What wounds?" he said. "The only answer is that there are no answers—only opinions—and the questions were all meaningless from the beginning."

Nu woke up to hear weeping, only to discover it was his own. He looked up from his mossy bed.

His grandfather sat dangling his legs in the warm waterfall pool.

The Old Man grunted and tossed a pebble into the water. "Had a vision, did you?"

Nu simply nodded.

"At times I think the reason we fast when we come up here is so we will not vomit when we actually get the answers we seek."

"All I have are more questions."

Silence fell for long minutes like a blanket of heavy wool.

Nu jumped when a gust of wind ripped through the tiny ravine, followed by an ominous rapid darkening of the sky. Heat lightening flickered in ghost-flashes from the turbid air above the small gorge. For a moment, he feared that the sacred Mount N'Zar had become another Mount Ardis and that the rebel Watchers now came to claim it too—along with Nu and his patriarch.

He shielded his eyes from the stinging dust and pulled his grandfather with him under the shelter of an overhanging rock.

That was when the air itself changed.

A tangible presence inhabited the blast, more powerful than anything A'Nu-Ahki had ever experienced in a simple disruption of inverted air layers. Something big and alive lurked nearby that brooded overhead — pervasive and impenetrable. He looked up instinctively, expecting to see pale Watchers looking down on him, clinging to the rock walls like giant spiders, but saw no sign of any other life. Then he realized that the air itself was alive.

The wind shifted until it blew perpendicular to the small canyon, making the waterfall hollow into a shelter. Nu and Muhet'Usalaq rose from beneath the overhang, rubbing their popping ears at the pressure change.

Outside, a tormented howl screeched through the narrow gullies, as if the forces of nature themselves acted as lungs and vocal chords, wailing for lost creation. Trees whipped against rock, while choppy wind blasts slammed into the outer slopes to form airy, but distinct, consonant sounds that merged perfectly with vowels piped through the many stone crack vortices around the ravine.

Then the earth too came to life.

Nu felt the words in his feet as they vibrated throughout every portion of his body — just as the voice at the Divine throne had. The sensation undid his muscles like a loose garment until he fell to the shuddering ground. Every bone rattled with a sound that moaned from the wind outside, yet resonated from within him in the deepest reaches of his soul.

"M-m-m-my-y-y-y spirit will not struggle with man foreverrrr because he is also made of flesh. Hhhhis remaining days arrrre one hundred and twenty yearrrrs-s-s-s."

Thunder rumbled across the crevasse. Nu and his grandfather scrambled on their hands and knees back beneath their ledge.

The Apparition squeezed in to fill the gorge like pressurized-fluid rage. Nu's soft internal organs quivered to the words like waves in jelly. The two seers could only lie there and tremble as they stared outward like living dead men trapped in sealed-tomb claustrophobia.

"I-i- have seen how the corruption of mankind is multiplied on the earth; that every imagination of Man's heart is only evil continually-y."

The scathing denouncement kicked Nu in the stomach.

Despite all his knowledge, despite his terror, as if in a sudden moment of solidarity with the human race, he wanted to object — to point out all the good things people still sometimes did. Yet the piercing light he had watched penetrate Uzaaz'El and Samyaza now lanced through him. It picked open his heart like a locked vault, spilling its damning contents in a splayed heap. What were those good things he thought he had seen but mostly a network of self-protection, arrogance, and pretense? Even his genuine motives at best had worm-holes in them and easily fell to pride.

A'Nu-Ahki the son of Lumekki did not fully know what festered inside the people of Bab'Tubila or Assuri, much less in the thoughts of Watcher-bred titans and giants. But he knew what lived inside his own imagination. He struggled daily with the darkness there. He understood defeat by it extremely well. He knew how selfish and egotistical his own motives often were, even behind many of his most noble and arguably selfless deeds.

But it was worse even than that.

It was not that he never honestly wanted to do anything good except for his own benefit; if that were it, things would be easy! People would be mere vermin. Their extermination would simply be the cleaning up of an infestation, not a tragedy. There was more to it than that. The heartbreak was that some people truly wanted to be good. It was that no matter what good Nu did, something in his own nature—something even in Nature itself—always managed to twist even his best intentions into something dark and diseased, given enough time.

He watched himself drink in the intoxicating praises of plain Na'Amiha, while in the redness of his fantasies he still pretended her to be the perfectly endowed Emzara in the darkened bedchamber. Yet he wanted to be able to respond as naturally and whole-heartedly to 'Miha as he had to Emza. He simply couldn't do it no matter how hard he tried and no matter how much he prayed for strength. So he lived a lie and tried not to hurt her.

Not only that.

The truth bubbled to the surface like swamp gas. He did not just yearn after Emzara, long dead. Any and every woman he might have had freedom to court, had the need of the day not demanded what it had, opened their bedchambers to his mind's eye sometimes. Their images invited him in, as their real persons never would have. Most were younger than his grandchildren would have been, had they lived. He hated such thoughts, but such interwoven impulses hopelessly meshed with his attempts to satisfy 'Miha.

Not only them.

He had visited the fortressed camps of Tubaal-qayin Dumuzi often enough to observe how the armies spent their rest rotations.

Pleasure-women flitted from soldier to soldier like butterflies, no shame, no pretense, and no pressure. Nu had seen them laugh and dance in their tight see-through silks—unavoidably displayed to any camp visitor. He was glad that he had only observed, never participated, and that such observation happened unavoidably, only when legitimate business brought him to the fortresses.

Such images had a way of sticking however, in ways that no man can simply will himself to forget. How often had he desired the momentary release from responsibility such women offered? Having resisted them outwardly, how often had he closed his eyes in his own impotency and willed his wife in the darkness of his mind to take the shape of a dusky pleasure-girl with no inhibitions? How often had he even told himself it was all so he could satisfy his wife anyway?

'Miha wanted nothing more than to be attractive to him. Her attempts at it were still clumsy, insipid, and sometimes even tiresome. Yet in his mind, Nu had magnanimously granted her wish—kind of. He had encouraged her to come out of her fear-frozen shell with all the gentleness and patience of any woman's dream-husband. Yet he often followed through in love-making by pretending she was someone else—truth be told.

Truth – the God-awful truth!

Nu wanted it to be different; wanted to be the man she thought he was from the inside out. 'Miha bathed in the thought that she was the center of his eye, when in truth she was faceless, formless, and forlorn, the wearer of other women's imaginary appeals when the lights went out.

In the throttling trauma of the Voice, and the Light's piercing blade, Nu could only tremble, while his failure as a husband shook to the surface like dead fish in an earthquake-churned lake.

And it was deeper and worse even than that.

The images of last night's vision cavorted around in his head. The pale children wandered into the depths to escape from self-involved fathers and mothers, only to find themselves trapped in the treadmill dance that would unravel their lives until it killed them all in the end.

A'Nu-Ahki was both one of the pale children and a self-involved father. Had he not also reduced timeless absolute spiritual principles into mere sandcastle virtues in front of his children, swept away by the tide? His daughters had languished their final years in captivity somewhere in Assuri and it had often been years between the times he had pleaded for their release with simpering and mealy-mouthed platitudes before this very Divine Wind. At last, he saw himself, another Iyared in the making, or worse yet, another Adiyuri—doubly responsible for having known more at a younger age.

His entire life rattled with shortcuts inside a gleaming façade behind which foamed the rottenness of the castle from his vision. The wormhole-connected private quagmires of self-deception, self-protection, and spiritual pride erupted with the filth of the dungeon at the tower's foundations. Nu began to console himself that at least he was not the only one—that he was far from the worst. He almost added, *better than most*, until he saw what lay inside the enormous blind spot of that outlook.

If one man was an inner vacuum, what happened if every man and woman was the same or even worse? A massive black hole imploded in the heavens, pulling untold billions into the screaming heat of outer darkness. Nothing Nu could say or do would lessen the Apparition's monstrously true indictment.

The storm intensified as its cyclone shifted from a mournful wail to a crescendo of rage. *"I-i-i-i will destroy mankind whom I created from off the surface of the Earth! Not only man, but beasts and crawling things, and the birds of the sky, for it grieves me that I ever made them-m-m."*

The weather trailed off into choppy gusts like convulsive sobs.

Nu rose slowly from below the shelf.

It's all true! Who can have the courage to see it all for what it really is without hiding his face from the howling emptiness of his own heart? What man has power to change on such a scale? How can I even begin to comfort anyone from the reality of the roaring world-wide void? I can't even comfort myself! I can try to do the right thing, but Nature wears my attempts down and twists them into something horrible! And if I let go for just one weary second, Evil erupts in me with consequences that expand to others, who pass them on, exponentially consuming still others!

Nu wanted somehow to reach out and comfort this tremendous, sorrow-filled father. *I'm the Comforter from A'Nu, after all!* He laughed hysterically and nearly choked on his own stomach acid.

It was impossible. *I'm an impossible fool with an impossible job!* Such a concentration of sorrow, anger, and loss would drive anyone who tried to share it insane. *That must be where I am right now—at the Mountain of Madness! E'Yahavah A'Nu doesn't need my support! Self-sufficiency infuses anyone who can speak worlds into existence!*

Nu understood in utter despair how no amount of sorrow on his part could even make up for that portion of infinite grief he himself had caused. This realization left him empty and helpless, with the true motive for his sympathy staring him like a betraying friend right back in his face:

I do not want to be destroyed with the Earth.

With every pretense stripped away, Nu shrieked into the wind, "I'm only a man of rotting flesh! Though my heart has been like Qayin's, I have offered the blood of innocent sacrifice, like Heh'Bul, in my place! I want to be different, but I don't know how—not at the depth you require!"

The wind and thunder subsided. A clear airy voice answered through the shrubs, cracks, and hollows all around. *"The blood of innocence has been accepted for your guilty blood."*

Nu clutched these words to his chest. "Please, tell me how to walk with you like Q'Enukki did! I find no strength—not even from the prophecies you have given me!"

"You have found my favor. It is sufficient."

"But what do you want from me?" Nu's tears rolled from his face into the soft moss. "I don't know what to do! I never have!"

"Plant a seven hundred-by-seven hundred row orchard of straight resinous saplings in the woodlands leading up to the Haunted Lands Pass and let them grow. Wait on me daily for further instructions."

Nu dropped into the dust, dazed, and exhausted.

Muhet'Usalaq lay unconscious, having fainted during the revelation of the Divine Wind.

Perhaps this is good, Nu thought. *No man should have to hear exactly how many years he has left to live.* Then he realized that the Old Man would soon have to discover that information from him anyway.

Darkness broke rapidly to reveal a wine colored sunset. The dazzling sword-shaped comet carved across the heavens in blue celestial warning.

A'Nu-Ahki still did not know exactly what approached to destroy the Earth. But, at least he now knew when it would arrive.

They had a hundred and twenty years left to prepare.

EPILOGUE

Q' Enukki had left Earth in the sky chariot only about an hour ago. At least he thought it was an hour. *Could it have been a day?*

Samuille, the faintly glowing celestial being who commanded the living chariot, had kept him occupied with their long conversation so that he was no longer sure. Time itself seemed to have lost its coherence. Stars slowly shifted their positions in the ebony deep outside the crystal view port, lazy fireflies in the endless night.

Q'Enukki tried to shake his momentary disorientation. *Had it really been only a moment?*

Samuille seemed to be saying something about the fundamental curvatures of the heavens. He used terms Q'Enukki himself had designed to describe subtle and highly technical aspects of celestial mechanics, though in ways that went far beyond the Seer's theory. The serene voice of the holy Watcher confirmed many guesses Q'Enukki had made back on Earth. Yet the Seer needed to know if he had just heard his guide correctly.

"Are you saying the mathematical relationship between time and planetary attraction is not just something I've dreamed up to explain away certain problems?" Q'Enukki asked.

"Yes," said the Watcher. "It is one of the foundations of the cosmos; intimately linked to how the heavens have been stretched out by E'Yahavah and to the speed of light. Light is the constant on which much else rides—a model of the Divine Name. Thus time itself, and all things temporal, must bend to give way when that limit of the created medium is pressed."

"And the waters above the heaven?"

"Look outside the viewport. Tell me what you see."

The star chariot had apparently slowed, for they had pulled abreast of the icy head of a giant comet. It had approached so rapidly that Q'Enukki had not even noticed until they were right on top of it.

"Am I mistaken, or is the comet's solid part made up mostly of frozen water?"

Samuille nodded. "Correct again, though also of frozen airs. On the first day of creation, E'Yahavah had the substance of all the cosmos contained in one great water sphere, which you know from the *Cosmic Dynasty Stele* as the *Abyssu*.

"This watery mass lay deep within the event-horizon of what we call a black vortex. The immense attraction of such an enormous globe of water caused the elementary particles of its own super-compressed interior to be ripped apart and reformed into the heavier elements from which the Earth and all the solid materials of the cosmos were soon to be made. Everything at first was without form inside the deep—void and chaotic with energies building to be unleashed on command.

"When the Eluhar commanded, *'Light be!'* he reversed the heavenly constant—the elastic tension value of space—transforming the black vortex that contained the Abyssu into a white fountain. A fountain is the opposite of a vortex; having an attraction-well that pulls what is inside outward rather than drawing what is outside in. The attraction force has the same mathematical relationship to time in either case. The closer an object is to the attraction well, the slower time—and all natural processes—moves for that object relative to other objects and events happening further away.

"After this conversion, the event-horizon of the fountain began to shrink inward toward the Abyssu, while diffuse vapors started to move through it. On day two, Earth Time Reference, the horizon shrank close enough to the surface of the waters for its attraction to counteract the Abyssu's own. The outward pull of the white fountain increased, as it absorbed space and primitive particles, while that of the Abyssu remained constant.

"E'Yahavah created the First Heaven we now travel in when the two conflicting attractions ripped the outer layers of the water sphere away from its core—creating a space between the waters above and the waters below. The outer waters expanded in a bubble, away toward the shrinking event-horizon and soon passed beyond it.

"The massive attraction of the fountain's horizon had its time-bending effect described in your formulas. Beyond the event horizon, natural events ran many billions of times faster than inside, where the forming Earth remained. The liberated residues—the gases, solids, and energies from the dividing of the Abyssu—soon followed outward through the horizon, as indeed the heavens themselves stretched forth in all directions. Those expanding heavens are the very space in which the stars now reside. For as you have guessed, space itself is a created *thing* vast beyond human comprehension, but not mere emptiness. Time as you know it is merely a property of the substance of space.

"The leftover clumps of gases, solids, and waters passed into the outer realm in great whirlpool storms where the bending of time occurred. This happened because the great size of these masses made it impossible for them to pass through the event-horizon instantaneously. Tremendous stresses acted on the matter streams across the violently different rates at which time passed in the outer, versus inner, regions. The spirals concentrated the matter into massive cores that often became black vortices once freed of the event horizon on the outer side.

"These spiral matter clouds were raw material for what the people of Time's End will call 'galaxies' of stars. Masses of water, and other vapors within them, often froze into bodies like this comet.

"By the end of two days, Earth Time, the equivalent of several billion years had passed outside the white fountain's horizon. My people and some of the other Orders that serve in the heavens, were created and grew ancient because, to the extent that we operated in your space-time cosmos, we did so outside the event-horizon—where the time rate and all natural processes by comparison, was so greatly accelerated.

"Many aeons we waited in wonder for the mystery to be unveiled of what lay within the fountain—your finished world! Oh, we understood the physics of laying its foundations well enough, but not its full purpose. For us it was to be the culmination of all E'Yahavah's handiwork. We did not know he had something further in mind.

"The white fountain shrank until the innermost of the larger matter clumps passed beyond in a great swirling stream to form the Milky Way—that river of stars that is your own galaxy. The Milky Way spiral then had a greater attraction-well than what remained of the white fountain itself—on its outside. The fountain expanded space from itself, moving relative to the core of the Milky Way outward into one of its arms.

"Before the fountain ceased, the last remaining matter—including the waters below the heavens, from which your world was being formed—fell into orbit around the galactic core at the optimal distance, between your galaxy's spirals, to support life. If not for that position between the spirals, you would never have been able to observe most of the heavens. I, of course, describe to you how it appeared to us. From the Earth, the expansion of the heavens simply slowed to their current rate, with your planet's galaxy effectively near the core of the cosmos, albeit not exactly so.

"The last bit of leftover matter was used to form your sun and its other planets. Before vanishing, the fountain remnant took up an orbit around the new sun at E'Yahavah's precise distance and speed so essential for life, with little more left inside it than your world and her forming moon.

"From the time elapsed on Earth, all was completed by the end of the fourth day, when the fountain shrank to nonexistence. The Earth and her moon were the last things to pass beyond the horizon into this current space. Your Sun's system has since orbited slightly away from the central universal axis, as will your galaxy in time."

Q'Enukki summarized the resolution of his own question. "And that is how light from distant stars had time to reach the Earth even though the time it took was far greater than the age of the cosmos itself, when measured from my planet?"

The Watcher nodded. "As time is measured from Earth's surface, yes. While the first four days of creation week passed on your planet, aeons passed simultaneously in the voids beyond the fountain. This is the time-bending effect of a *singularity* – the engine E'Yahavah used to stretch out the heavens at his word.

"So far, you are the only man who understands that *eternity* is not infinite linear time. Time itself is an attribute of space, velocity, and mass – as I said before, a *thing* created by E'Yahavah. It flows, with all natural processes, at different rates in different localities, depending on the attraction-force of whatever mass is in the vicinity. Usually the differences in time-passage rate across the cosmos are not wide; except near event-horizons of black vortices, or as it was in creation week with the white fountain. The other heavens you visited before exist in dimensions beyond those you can normally perceive.

"We in the heavens have greater access to a domain beyond time. We must therefore use much imagination and caution when we communicate with you. Our language concepts reflect our environments.

"Our Master exists in the dimension beyond all others, which includes the sum of them all – the heaven of heavens. From it, he sees the end from the beginning and can intervene at any point, even as you can look down upon a two dimensional scroll unfurled to insert your quill upon any portion of the plane from the all-seeing height of your third dimension. Do you know why I have shown you this comet?"

Q'Enukki said, "It wasn't about the primordial waters?"

Samuille's black white-less eyes took on the gravity of the Abyssu. "No. When we left your world, we increased our speed to near the velocity of light. Time back on Earth has moved more rapidly than for us in this chariot – just as time moved more rapidly beyond the white fountain than for the Earth when it was still inside during the early days of Creation Week.

"When we left Earth's solar system, we deliberately knocked this chunk of primordial ice from its course. It has now fallen into the attraction-well of the sun. It will orbit once, taking one hundred and fifteen years – Earth Time – to do so. We have looped back into the solar system to check its progress, with a few other things that are not for you to know."

"Why will it orbit only once?"

"Because this comet is *Sword of the Breaker*; destined to divide the Leviathan, Tiamatu—that fifth inner planet which the Basilisk has taught the sons of Earth to worship. In a sense, the shards of Tiamatu's cleaving shall destroy the old Earth and be used to create the new."

APPENDIX

ABOUT THE LANGUAGE USAGE AND COSMOLOGY OF THE SEER CLAN AND THE CITY-STATES OF SETI

Any expert will notice that the peoples of the first four books of this novel series seldom behave in ancient Near-Eastern ways. This is because the story assumes that the peoples of the ancient Near East operated from a memory of pre-Deluge patriarch lists without much knowledge of the advanced civilization that existed before the First World-end, when those patriarchs lived. We today often anglicize peoples, names, and events of the Bible and other ancient literature in the same way without knowing it.

Historians, theologians, and mythographers will notice a fusion of theological names in the worldview of A'Nu-Ahki's people that some might understandably find a little disturbing. The implications of Genesis 10 and 11 demanded this approach. If all humanity is of one blood, there is a branching point, historically speaking. It is not my intention to suggest that the polytheistic gods of Sumer and Akkad are at all the same being as the Judeo-Christian Yahweh. I am a student of history who understands the mechanics of revisionist history and how it affects worldviews.

My novels operate on the hypothesis that the polytheistic mythology of Sumer, Akkad, and to some extent Egypt, is a form of revisionist history that altered the character of how subsequent generations viewed their past and its theology. Marxist, Fascist, and Postmodernist historic revisionists do not erase the names of the past and replace them with entirely new terminology and characters; their contemporaries would immediately reject such an approach. Rather, revisionism redefines the characters and terminology of whatever is the traditional history, ideology, or theology system of their times according to its own agenda.

Only in later generations do openly foreign names and grosser departures enter the system. In *The Windows of Heaven* series, the progression follows this pattern. Hence, Sumero-Akkadian polytheistic god names like *Anu*, *Enlil*, and *Ea* are, in the story, redefined terms, distorted in character from whatever concept of history and theology came over on the boat with the historic Noah, which I have tried to portray with respect. I believe we get an undiluted flavor of that original character only in Genesis, for reasons that will become clear in my next novels and their appendices.

In this series, the paganesque names hypothetically stem from before the historical and theological revisionism erased knowledge of the Creator God *E'Yahavah* (understood as a tri-unity of *E'Yahavah A'Nu*, *E'Yahavah El-N'Lil*, and the Messenger of *E'Yahavah*) in the story. The triune Divinity appears as a simpler version of the Christian Trinity in the story, which does no violence to the idea that God truthfully revealed Himself to an earlier people who spoke another language and had a different worldview. The Deity has a biblical character, though the names are cosmetically somewhat Sumerian and Akkadian and may seem foreign to modern Christians. The purpose was not to distance the story from its Genesis roots, but to simulate those roots in a forgotten world with a language predating even the earliest Semitic language (Akkadian), much less the later Hebrew with which we are familiar. The feel of the story is like a reverse-engineering of the layers of Sumero-Akkadian polytheistic revisionism back to a people and worldview who knew their Maker, or who, at least, were not so far removed from their own origins that they had lost historic memory of them.

Given the vast unknowns of such a world to us, the novels have many fanciful elements. It seemed the best way to reintroduce the story to the 21st century as an epic.

Of course, the level of technology my novels attribute to the pre-Diluvians is purely fictional. They were not cave men, but they need not have had flight, electricity, and other more exotic technologies I have given some of them for this story. We thoughtlessly make the error today of imagining "advancement" only in technological terms, completely forgetting our own history; that it was usually the most technologically advanced civilizations that were both capable and guilty of the most savage atrocities. The idea that a civilization "must be enlightened if it has a high level of technical achievement" is an 18th through 21st century myth that any serious look at 20th century history should cure us of.

That myth is dying in the self-evident outworking of history in our own generation. Sophistication of thought and ethics comes through the medium of reasoning with ideas expressed in words, if it comes at all.

I have tried to present English usage equivalents for this society according to the age of the speakers, since I assume that the dialects of the single language spoken in the World-that-Was differed not only according to geography, but also across many layers of contemporaneous generations. For example, the ancient Archon Iyared speaks an almost semi-Shakespearean English, while older but not quite so ancient characters like Muhet'Usalaq talk in a kind of erudite British 19th century style with no contractions. This tries to give readers a feel for High and Low *Archaic*.

A'Nu-Ahki, on the other hand, uses a conservative "mid-twentieth century" American English with plenty of contractions, while the younger generations in the following books of this series will use more invented slang and less "proper English." Contrary to evolutionary expectations, observed historical languages usually move from the complex and refined to the simple and coarse. I have tried to reflect this in the way my characters speak across the generations, while preserving good dialogue in the story.

In developing the names and terminology of the characters, I combined words and concepts from many ancient civilizations, using mostly Semitic, Sumerian, and Egyptian roots for theological terms, while most animal names are a blend of Anglo-Saxon and old Celtic forms. Indo-European languages like Sanskrit, Greek, and Latin, and even some Meso-American also influenced names and terms, though not always consistently. There are themes from prehistory that are very consistent.

Early man's fascination with the heavens and the nearly global fixation on culturally similar zodiac stellar chart systems, show a strong mytho-historic signature of something significant that happened in humanity's infancy that turned man's eyes skyward.

In A'Nu-Ahki's culture, the relationship of cosmology to theology is far closer than in ours. *This is not astrology.* That would be a later corruption of this hypothetical system. A'Nu-Ahki's cosmology includes a fictional divinely-inspired message system that one could learn to interpret according to hermeneutical principles. The stars did not control or influence people's lives in it, nor were they objects of worship. This system stems from Josephus' mention in his *Antiquities of the Jews* (written circa 95 AD) that the sons of Seth *"were the inventors of that peculiar sort of wisdom which is concerned with the heavenly bodies, and their order."*

To shape an advanced cosmology in the story, I used the work of Physicist D. Russell Humphreys, whose "White Hole Cosmology" helped enable me to take ancient creation accounts, particularly Genesis, seriously. Humphreys theorizes that God expanded the universe out of a quantum singularity during creation, which involved the rapid stretching of space and severe gravitationally induced time dilation at the singularity's event horizon.

Space and time are created things in this model, not mere emptiness and duration. Humphreys' theory explains a wide range of observed physical phenomena like microwave background radiation, red-shifts of light from distant stellar objects, more-or-less equal distribution of galactic clusters observed in every direction, discreetly measurable quantized red-shifting of distant galactic clusters at distance-related intervals, starlight travel time, and many other cosmological issues.

I briefly tried to give the reader a glimpse of cosmic creation using theories developed by Dr. Humphreys and Dr. John Hartnett in the epilogue, and probably got many of the details wrong. I attempted to translate a highly technical concept into a sequence observable through the eyes of Q'Enukki in non-technical language and likely failed. We fiction writers often have to fudge a little to keep the pace of the story moving.

My use of the term *Abyssu* for the Genesis *abyss* or *waters* connects our word *abyss* back to its Sumero-Akkadian root *absu* by literary design.

For those who want to learn more about this exciting new (or perhaps very old) look at the heavens, I urge you to read Dr. Humphreys' book *Starlight and Time*, from Master Books.

GLOSSARY OF PEOPLE AND TERMS

The definitions are in relation to the story—some are fictional, others connect with either real biblical history or ancient mythology, and will be identified so as needed.

A'Nu-Ahki – Seer-Prince of Salaam-Surupag and later Akh'Uzan; the biblical Noah.

A'Nu – The person of the Creator God E'Yahavah residing in the Heavens; which describes God in his most vast, beyond human ability-to-know sense. The contraction *A'Nu* loosely translates as *heaven,* and so the name of *A'Nu-Ahki* (in the story) means *Heaven-sent Comfort.* The biblical name *Noah* means simply *rest* or *comfort.* My attempt to fictionally counter-revise Sumerian theo-historic revisionism (their "sky-god" was called Anu or An) may prove incorrect— though it is not unreasonable, as scholars with far more qualification than I have suggested it as a hypothesis. Nor is it an attempt at mix paganism with Judeo-Christian theology, since the Sumerian version of Anu appears as revisionism, and my story clearly defines its own terms on this matter. Since I view Genesis as history, and the implications of Babel are that we all come from common stock, it is not unreasonable to expect the earliest Sumerian priests to have revised the meaning of earlier names to misuse them in their polytheistic mythology. History is full of such examples. Ugaritic Canaanite inscriptions depicted the dignified *El Elyon* of Melchizedec and Abraham 500 years after Abraham in less-than-flattering terms. The Canaanite tablets still presented *El Elyon* as the in-name-only head of their pantheon even in redefined form, nevertheless. In no way do my novels imply that the Sumerian Anu and the Hebrew YHWH are the same divinity. Rather they suggest that maybe the polytheistic Sumerians (or perhaps their immediate predecessors) corrupted earlier names and terms from an entirely different Noahic theological tradition. It would have been easier than trying to use divinity names that people found foreign.

Abyssu – The original massive water sphere from which all other elements and compounds were formed through gravity compaction-induced nucleosynthesis on creation days 1 and 2. The etymology of the English word traces back through Greek (*abusso*) to the Sumero-Akkadian word *Absu*. In Sumero-Akkadian myth, the *absu* was the subterranean fresh water abyss that housed their earth god Enki. The Sumero-Akkadians personified *Absu* as the consort of the ocean-water abyss monster goddess *Tiamat*.

aerodrone – A fixed-wing aircraft that functions by the same aerodynamic principles as modern airplanes. At first fueled by alcohol burning air-cooled internal combustion engines, later models used a more efficient turpentine-like distillate of an extinct conifer.

amomun – A tea lotus with medicinal properties.

amphiptere – A non-crested winged dragon that fed on carrion. Fossils of this creature are called *Dimorphodon* today.

Archronos – The unique title of the Divinely-created first man and Archon. Later corrupted to Chronos, an early Greek god (father of Zeus) who devoured his children, and was overthrown along with the titans.

Assuri and *Assurim* – The pre-Flood Assyria mentioned in Genesis 2, and the people who lived there. The similarity with the post-Flood Assyria is only in name.

Atum-Ra – The biblical Adam, which devolved much later into an early version of the Egyptian creator/sun god Ra, who was the eldest of the gods that ruled during the idyllic "First Time" of Egyptian myth. Although connecting Adam with Atum-Ra is a fictional device, the ancient god-kings of most pagan mythologies have too many commonalities to be coincidental and may be faded deified memories of our much longer-lived early fathers.

Basilisk, the – The oldest and chief of the heavenly rebels of the First Insurrection; the biblical serpent of Eden.

behemoth – The superlative form of *behema* – the biggest and most magnificent of all grazing animals. The description of this creature in Job 40:15-24 resembles most a sauropod dinosaur. (Hippos, elephants, and all other large modern herbivores do not have large "cedar-like" tails but little dinky things—see the Bible passage.)

cockatrice – A chameleon pack-hunting wurm, the fossils of which are today classified in the *Velociraptor*, *Utahraptor*, and *Deinonychus* family.

Comforter from A'Nu, the – A semi-messianic prophetic figure predicted to arise among the Seer Clan that would comfort the faithful concerning the depredations of the Curse and preserve them through World-end. We find a glimmer of this preserved in Genesis 5:28-29, where the biblical Lemech of Seth's line prophesies over his son Noah.

Cosmic Dynasty Stele – The account of creation given by E'Yahavah in written form to the first created man and woman, a version of which survives today as a redaction by Moses in Genesis 1 and part of chapter 2.

creation codes – Genetic codes expressed on the DNA molecule.

Desired One, the – A minor constellation under Virgo that depicts a woman with her small son.

Divine Name – Describes the proper name of the Creator God.

Divine Wind – A spiritual persona of the Creator God that uses natural phenomena to reveal the Divine presence, and which breathes life into prophecy. Called El-N'Lil, or God-as-Air, this name distorted later into the Sumerian storm god Enlil. In this story, it is an early and incomplete understanding of what Christians would later call the Holy Spirit.

Dragon Breaker, the – The constellation today called *Perseus*.

Dragon, the – The constellation of Draco. Synonym for the Basilisk, Dragon-Prince, and Leviathan as spiritual agents of evil.

Dragon-prince – In Setiim theology, one of the chief vassals of the Basilisk. Because early man, at first, struggled for survival against large and pack-hunting wurms, their mythology and theology came to use this form of dragon as one of its chief archetypes for evil, along with the serpent.

E'Yahavah – The proper name of the Creator God (in the story), which was lost but restored in history as the Tetragrammaton *YHWH* during the Mosaic revelation of God to the Hebrews. In this novel series, E'Yahavah has three aspects: E'Yahavah A'Nu—the vast "God of the Heavens and Eternity," E'Yahavah El-N'Lil—the "Divine Wind" of prophecy that uses natural forces to express himself, and "The Messenger of E'Yahavah" who comes in a human form to interact with men when he sees fit. Together they preside over a council of created lesser gods who are beings analogous to the highest level of angels. A'Nu-Ahki's clan and Seti in general do not view this council in a polytheistic sense or in a henotheistic one where a lesser god could actually unseat E'Yahavah's preeminence. (That was a later Sumerian corruption.) Evidence in the Old Testament (Psalm 82, Job 1-2, for example) demonstrates that the early Hebrews had a "divine council" concept in their theology that did not violate the Creator's unique Deity as a monotheistic God, nor the later Trinitarian revelations of Christianity.

Eluhar – The masculine *high majestic* plural (a fictional extinct language form) used with a singular verb to describe generically the Creator God, usually as a judge. It is linguistically related to the Hebrew *elohim* (which also uses a singular verb form), which is the generic term for God.

El-N'Lil – See *Divine Wind*, and E'Yahavah.

Fire River, the – The stream of stars today called *Eridanus*. It is associated with the Greek mythical figure Phaethon, who tried to drive Apollo's sun chariot and was burned.

firedrake – A river dragon with a crested head that contained two glands that manufactured hydroquinone and hydrogen peroxide, which combined in the creature's saliva with an inhibiting agent. When spit at a predator (the *firedrake* was largely herbivorous) the mixture exploded on contact with oxygen and produced a brief flash of intense heat. A similar mechanism exists in today's bombardier beetle. Fossil remains of this creature are today called *Parasaurolophus*.

Fire-sphinx, the – The bearer of the flaming sword that guards the east gate of *Aeden*. See Genesis 3:24.

First Heaven, the and the *Ten Heavens* – The ancient Hebrews believed that there were many heavens, 10 by some accounts, 7 in others. The First Heaven was that which held the stars and planets (the atmospheric sky is just the "face of the first heaven" in this view). The other 9 heavens were inhabited by various angelic majesties on up to the "heaven of heavens" where God alone had access. This view, though not taught directly in Scripture, is reflected in ancient Hebrew literature such as the Enoch manuscripts, originally believed to be written circa 200 to 150 BC. An allusion to the 3rd Heaven is made in one of the New Testament Corinthian letters, and the view of 10 heavens was a part of Jewish tradition well into the Middle Ages. In certain parts of the story, like the advanced physics of Q'Enukki, the 10 heavens are used analogously to the modern physics theory of 10 dimensions. Although this association is interesting, it should not be taken too seriously. Further study in both physics and in ancient manuscripts must be done by qualified people before we can call it a real theory.

First Time, the – Iyared's reference to the age between creation and the coming World-end; later synonymous to the *World-that-Was*. Many historic ancient civilizations saw the history of earth as having previous ages that each ended in a world-destroying cataclysm. The Egyptians looked back to the *zep tepi* or "First Time" as the idyllic age in which their gods ruled. Another version referred to the gods as having come from *Etelante*, which has interesting etymological relationship to the Greek *Atlantis*. The elaborate Egyptian funeral rites were designed to guide the dying pharaoh along the river of Under-world to the stars as they were aligned in this mythic First Time. This is but a dim memory of the paradise lost before the cataclysm.

Gihunu – The biblical pre-Flood river Gihon of Genesis 2.

gryndel – One of the largest of the carnivorous *wurm-kin*, fossils of which are today called *Tyrannosaurus Rex* or by the name of other large therapod dinosaurs like *Allosaurus* in other locations.

gryphon – A flying dragon known for its talons and sharp bill. Fossils of this creature fall into the *Pteranodon* family.

Heh'Bul – The biblical Abel.

Hiddekhel – The biblical pre-Flood river Hiddekel of Genesis 2, which was associated with the post-Flood river Tigris. It is possible that the post-Flood river was named in early times after the pre-Flood one, though the earth was so radically changed in the cataclysm that it has no geographic correlation.

High Archaic – The dialect of the uppermost tiers of the Seti clans, that is, the oldest generations among them. Because humans back then lived to such great ages, the most profound modifying factor of language was age, not distance, as it is today. Imagine if Shakespeare were alive today, or Chaucer—how much would they have resisted the innovations and corruptions of speech made by younger men like H.G. Wells or John Grisham. Imagine also how much more forcefully the young would want to express their own ideas, and the alienation that would have existed between the young and old.

Hunt, the – The idyllic warfare of Good and Evil described in the mythic terms of a dragon hunt. This was overly stylized by A'Nu-Ahki's culture, where too much emphasis was placed on the physical hunting of *wurms* (a dwindling menace), and not enough on the deeper spiritual problems the mythology really spoke of.

Ish'Hakka and **Khuva** – *Ish'Hakka* is the fictional root word for the real Hebrew word for woman, *isha*. At first, the proper name of the created woman, until her husband changed it to *Khuva*—the fictional root word for the Semitic *Chevah*, the real root for *uva, ova, ava, ave, ovary*, which all linguistically relate to motherhood and to the name of the biblical Eve.

Iya'Baalu and **Iyu'Buuli** – The biblical Jabal and Jubal, sons of the Lemech from Cain's line in Genesis 4.

Iyared – The biblical Jared of Genesis 5.

kapar – A watertight cement made from distilled pine bitumens, pumice and other fine ground stones set with natron; also developed as an artificial rock and pavement by the ancients. It is transliterated into the "gopher" of the gopher-wood ark mentioned in Genesis 6, and used by the Sumerians, where it was signified by the cuneiform letters for *KPR*. The kapar process (in the story) was used in conjunction with conventional wood-hardening methods by the technology of this novel. Hence, "gopher-wood" is not a type of tree but a specially processed and hardened wood. This is also the Semitic root of the Hebrew *kippur*, as in Yom Kippur, the Day of Atonement. The word came to mean *covering* as in a covering over sin.

Khavilakki – The pre-Flood biblical land of Havilah from Genesis 2. It was known for its gold, lapis lazuli and onyx. Not to be confused with the post-Flood Havilah or *Haweilan* in what is now Saudi Arabia.

Kherub, Kherubim, and **Kherubar** – A representation of biblical Cherubim; originally visualized by the ancient Assyrians as winged lions with man-like heads, and later by the Hebrews as messengers of Yahweh.

Kush – The land mentioned in Genesis 2 through and around which the river Gihon flowed. Not to be confused with the post-Flood Cush, who became the father of the Ethiopians, Nubians, and others.

L'Mekku – The Lemech of Cain's line in Genesis 4 – not to be confused with Lemech the father of Noah.

Leviathan – The constellation *Cetus,* and one of the Basilisk's chief vassals; also any large flesh-eating marine reptile of the *Plesiosaur* or *Mosasaur* variety. Some had long necks; others (like the *Mosasaur*) were more fish-like or crocodilian in shape.

Ley of the Brothers Lost – The epic of Qayin's murder of Heh'Bul (in the story), a version of which survives in a Mosaic redaction as the part of Genesis 4 that tells the story of Cain and Abel.

Lilitua, the Lost Daughter – The planet we call Mercury, named for the wife of Qayin, who founded the great eastern and northern civilizations of the pre-Deluge world. She is remembered in Hebrew tradition, albeit with much distortion, as Lilith, the wife who rejected Adam and was doomed to wander. I have instead made her the eldest daughter of Adam and Eve, the wife of Cain in this story, which makes more sense. Lilitua also relates to the Lilu demons of Sumero-Akkadian myth.

Lumekki – The biblical Lemech of Seth's line. The father of A'Nu-Ahki.

Muhet'Usalaq – The biblical Methuselah.

nae-fillim – Common plural of Nae-fil, fictional root word of the real Hebrew *nephil* and *nephilim*. It means *fallen one,* and is closely associated with the Greek *gigantes*, which means *earth-born* or *giant*.

nemes headdress – The wedge-shaped cloth headdress worn by Egyptian priests and noblemen, or in this case, a distant forerunner of that style.

Nhod – The desolate region where Qayin was doomed to wander. A falling star blasted the area and poisoned the soil there (see the apocryphal Book of Jasher). The pre-Flood biblical land of Nod (see Genesis 4).

Orchard of Aeden – The biblical Garden of Eden.

orichalcum – An expensive red-tinted gold alloy, though not as red as copper. In Plato's *Criteus* and *Timaeus*, the smiths of Atlantis forged *orichalcum*.

Pisunu – The pre-Flood River Pishon of Genesis 2.

Prime Zaqen – The chief patriarchal elder of a city-state in Seti.

Promised Seed or *Woman's Seed, the* – The messianic deliverer promised at the dawn of time. Often viewed in A'Nu-Ahki's culture (and later) as the greatest of monster slayers, who would suffer a poisoned wound but vanquish his serpentine or dragon foe in the end. The pure version of that promise is preserved in Genesis 3:15. Many ancient civilizations had corrupted versions of it, which reflected in their mythologies and views of the constellations. The deeper spiritual dimension of this figure was often lost upon the people of A'Nu-Ahki's generation. The ultimate fulfillment of this prophetic archetype comes in the death, resurrection, and Second Coming of Jesus Christ.

Q'Enukki – The Great Seer and ancestor of A'Nu-Ahki. A representation of the biblical Enoch of Seth's line, who was "translated" and taken alive to be with God. (See Genesis 5 and Hebrews 11.)

Q'Unukku – The biblical Enoch son of Cain, builder of an early city. Not to be confused with the Enoch of Seth's line or the Great Seer of this story.

Qayin – The biblical Cain, who murdered Abel.

quickening – A transformation of mortal human flesh to immortality with a body that operates under different physical laws than those that bind the cursed creation as it now exists.

quickfire – What we today would call electricity.

Ram, the – What is today called the constellation of *Aries*.

Rest Day – A traditional 7th day of rest, reflecting what God did after the creation. Unlike the later Sabbath of Moses, Rest Day was voluntary.

Seraf and *Serafim* – A lower order of heavenly being associated with the winged fire-serpent and the fallen Watcher Samyaza. Biblically, a *seraph* or *seraphim*, which is a form of angelic being with a fiery aspect.

Seti – The biblical Seth, son of Adam.

Shining One – The title held by the Basilisk before his fall; the biblical Lucifer who became the Serpent or Satan.

skel - A weight measure etymologically related to the later Hebrew *shekel*.

sons of God, the - An Old Testament term for angels; *bene elohim*. In *The Windows of Heaven* it is another term for the fallen Watchers of the Second Insurrection led by Samyaza and Uzaaz'El—The Shamhazai and Azazel of ancient extra-biblical Hebrew legend. This term also shows up in a modified form as *sons of the gods*, though this version of the name speaks more of the hybrid offspring of the *bene elohim* of Genesis. Lumekki, who uses the "sons of the gods" version in speaking of the Watchers, was probably doing so because he had picked up the habit from a non-Setiim source during the foreign wars he fought. Because *elohim* (God) is in the plural form it can be translated either way. Strictly speaking however, the sons of God are not the same as the giants or *nephilim* they spawned.

Southern Sea Leviathan, the - The constellation we call *Cetus*.

Star Signs, the - The constellations of the zodiac and in this novel series, their original divinely inspired interpretations. The interpretations were later so grossly corrupted and confused that the zodiac became a form of idolatry.

Straticon - A military rank at which strategic level decisions are made. Loosely similar to a modern general or field marshal.

swamp drake - A wild marshland dragon, fossil remains of which are identified as *Hadrosaurs*.

Sword of the Breaker - The comet of A'Nu-Ahki, observed to approach from out of the Dragon Breaker constellation, which we call *Perseus*.

Tacticon - An army officer in charge of tactical level decisions, loosely analogous to a colonel.

Work, the - The formal name of the commission Q'Enukki gave to his sons to print their father's scrolls, and to warn the world of the coming World-end judgments, and of the hope of the Comforter of A'Nu and the Promised Seed.

Tiamatu - Root of the Sumero-Babylonian water monster *Tiamat*, out of whose divided carcass *Marduk* supposedly created the present world after slaying the beast. In this story, *Tiamatu* is also the former fifth planet, the remains of which make up many of the asteroid fields and the asteroid belt between Mars and Jupiter. While this theory is not popular any longer among many astronomers who hold to the various accretion theories of planetary development, accretion theories themselves have serious difficulties with the laws of physics, and have not yielded good scientific predictions about the nature of planetary bodies. The 5th Planet is only one of many Catastrophist theories, and not a necessary agent for Dr. John Baumgardner's Runaway Subduction model of the Flood, which looks at other causal possibilities.

titan – A term for the hybrid offspring of the Watchers and human women before the cataclysm. The term arises out of Greek mythology, where it was a class of god or giant that preceded the pantheon led by Zeus and Hera. Of course, even within Greek mythology there are contradictory versions of who Zeus is, and who the titans are. The Greeks also had a deluge in their legends in which Deucalion and his wife Pyrhha escaped in a large wooden box. The titans lived before that deluge. The word *satan* (which the Hebrews originally saw as a group of spiritual enemies rather than one single entity) is linguistically related to *titan*: *titan* – *thaitan* – *shaitan* – *satan*.

Tubaal-qayin – The biblical Tubal-Cain, father of the metallurgy of bronze and iron; first of five kings by that name.

'tween-ager – A pre-flood adolescent. Because of the difference in life-spans the story has youngsters hit puberty at around ages 25 to 35 and a biological adolescence that lasts to age 55 or 60.

Udaha and *Tzuillaeha* – The biblical Adah and Zillah, wives of the Cain line's Lemech of Genesis 4.

Ufratsi – The pre-Flood River Euphrates of Genesis 2, which probably had no geographic correlation with the post-Flood river of that name.

Na'Amiha – A'Nu-Ahki's second wife. The biblical Naamah, sister of Tubal-Cain from Genesis 4.

Under-world – The place of the dead. Analogous to the Hebrew *sheol* or the Greek *hades* and *tartarus*.

unicorn and *tricorn* – Considered quasi-dragons, and thus able to be domesticated, these creatures were used as heavy pack beasts and armored cavalry mounts; though many also remained in the wild. Their fossils are classified as ceratopsian dinosaurs, the unicorn being *Monoclonius,* and the tricorn being *Triceratops*. The word *unicorn* is really of much more recent Roman origin (as is the word *dragon*, which is from the Saxon *draugl*). I used it in the story as a bit of poetic license.

Virgin, the - The constellation *Virgo*, which represents the woman who would bring forth the Promised Seed to deliver humanity from the Curse.

vultch gryphon - A large carnivorous gryphon whose fossil remains are identified as *Quetzalcoatlus*.

Watchers - An order of what Jews and Christians would call angels. In terms of fallen angels, a synonym for the sons of God that rebelled before the Noahic Flood and married human women to produce corrupt offspring called *giants* or *titans*. These creatures are distinct from the original angelic rebels, though only in that they fell a little bit later (according to the Enoch Manuscripts) and were guilty of taking human women as their wives in some sense. The Bible gives us no chronology of exactly when the angels fell or if they all fell at the same time or not. I do not claim that the Enoch accounts (which are not considered canonical Scripture by either Jews or Christians) are necessarily accurate records. They seem to suggest that the pre-Flood world was a time of flux for those we would call angels. Some distortions in the texts seem pretty serious, though there is also some interesting history and legend there. Because of the apparent silence of the Bible on the exact chronology of angelic rebellion, I have gone with some of the more detailed "Enoch" version of these events inasmuch as they don't contradict what the Scriptures do say on the subject.

world-end - A term for two world-destroying cataclysms predicted, according to Josephus (95 AD), by Adam. It is the anglicized fictional root word for the Hebrew *mabbul*, which is a unique term used only for the global Noahic Flood in Scripture. Other normal floods of the Jordan and Nile that are mentioned in the Old Testament are a different Hebrew word. According to Josephus, Adam predicted that the world would be destroyed twice, once by water and another time through fire.

wurm - Used in this story as a broad term for carnivorous dragons whose fossils are today categorized as the various

316 | K . G . P O W D E R L Y J R .

therapod dinosaurs from gigantic *Tyrannosaurus Rex* to relatively small *Velociraptor*. The word itself is ancient Anglo-Saxon in origin. I chose to name pre-Flood fauna using Saxon terms because they are so descriptive yet simple.

wyverna – A form of horned or crested wurm, the larger of which are classified today as *Gorgosaurus* and the smaller as *Dilophosaurus*. Also derived from an early Saxon taxonomic term for a type of dragon, though fictionally, the reverse is, of necessity, presented in the story.

Y'Raddu – The biblical Irad of Cain's line in Genesis 4, also the nation founded by this individual.

Younger-speech – The dialects spoken by the younger generations less than 300 years old or so.

Zaqen and *Zaqenar* – The root term for the Hebrew *zaken*, which means *elder*. In this story, a *zaqen* is an elder with governmental authority in a clan. If one is of princely lineage, like A'Nu-Ahki, one becomes a "first tier" *zaqen* at the age of 350. At 400 one becomes a "second tier" *zaqen* and gains an additional tier of rank after that for every century they live. A 900-year-old man graduates to the seventh tier, though by that time whatever rank or achievement they have attained in their work has more meaning in terms of real authority. Nevertheless, seventh tier Zaqenar are given much symbolic respect—so much that the masculine plural of the three uppermost tiers use a majestic *ar* rather than common *im* ending. The majestic plural became extinct (in the story) after the Deluge, when languages needed to be greatly simplified after events that will be covered in book 5 of this series.

ALSO BY K.G. POWDERLY JR.

- **The Paladin's Odyssey** – Book 2 of *The Windows of Heaven*
- **A Broken Paradise** – Book 3 of *The Windows of Heaven*
- **The Tides of Nemesis** – Book 4 of *The Windows of Heaven*
- **Gate of the Gods** – Book 5 of *The Windows of Heaven* (Coming soon)
- **One Faith – Many Transitions: World-views in Church History** (Non-fiction)

Made in the USA
Charleston, SC
24 May 2012